A WAR OF HEARTS AND FATE

N. E. HENDERSON

Line Editor: Charisse Hankins
Developmental Editor: Victoria Ellis
Proofreader: Beth Hale
2nd round Proofreader: Shelley Charlton
Cover Artist: Fay Lane
Interior Formatter: Nancy Henderson

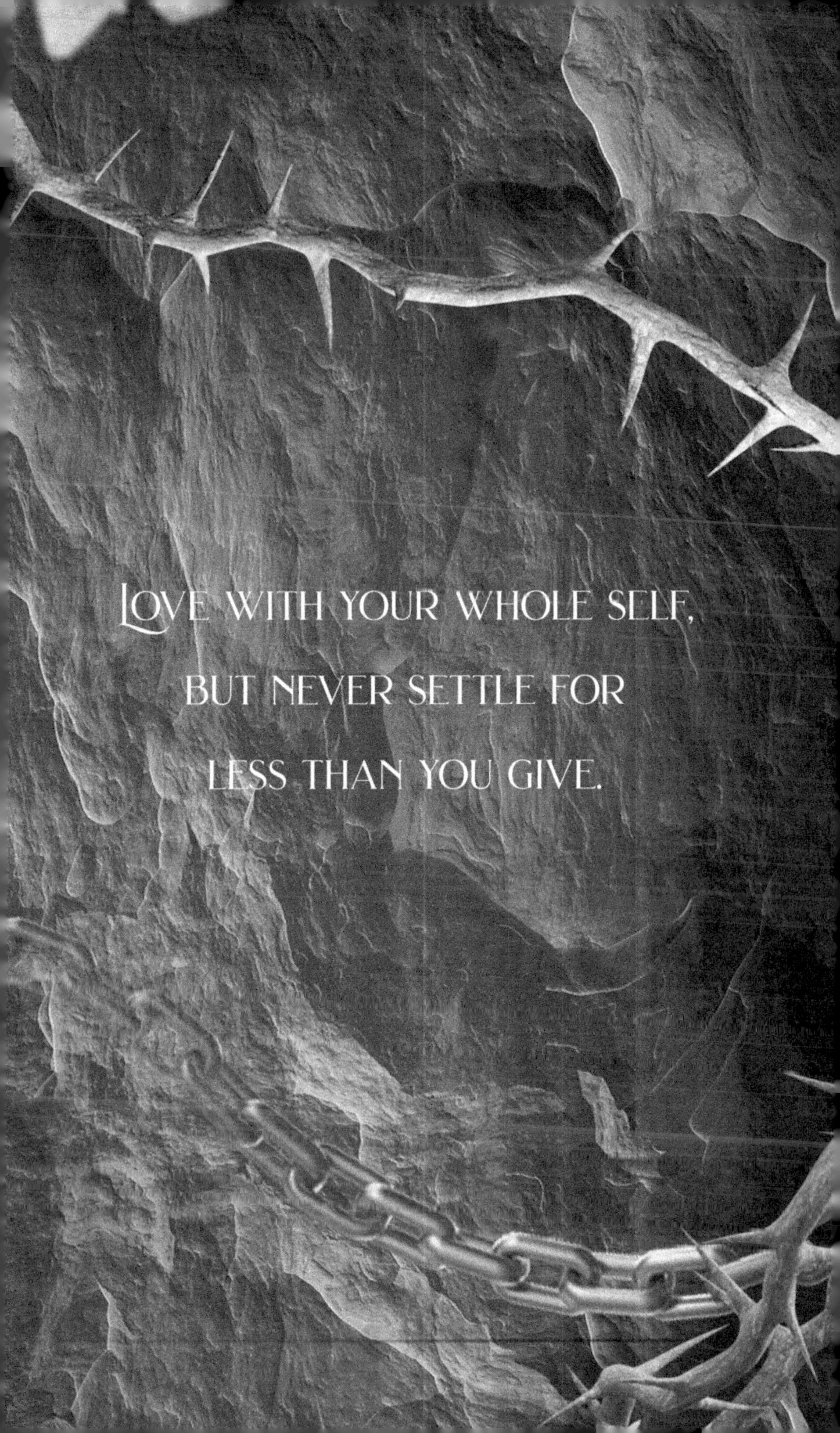
Love with your whole self,
but never settle for
less than you give.

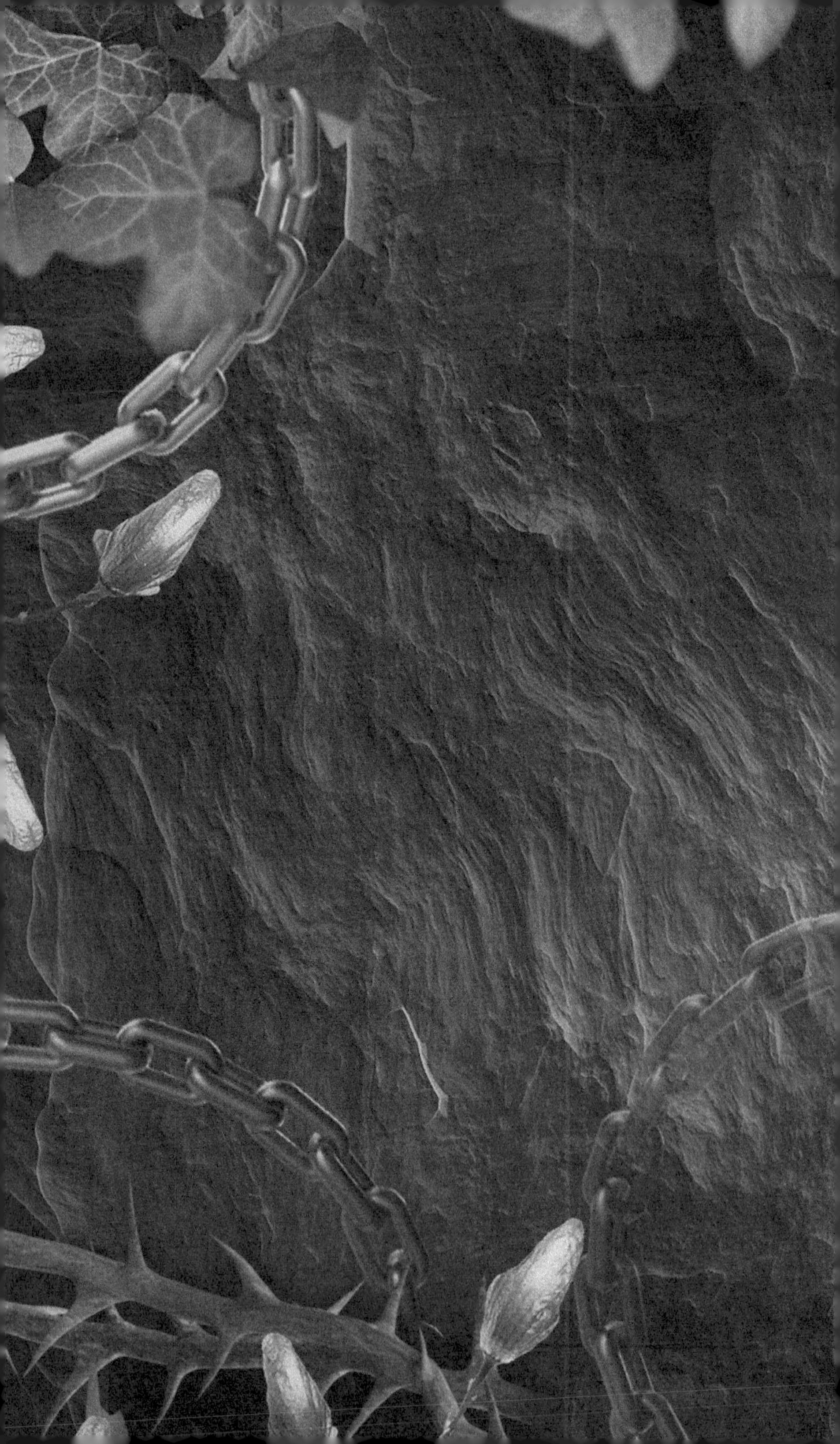

1

KATE

Run.

Hearing my brother's plea, my eyes snap open.

I gasp for breath as my back springs off my bed. It's dark, in the middle of the night, but the glow of the waxing gibbous moon shining through the opened window makes it easy for me to search every square inch of my bedroom.

Trez isn't here.

My chest sinks, and the ache behind my breast plate rapidly returns as I relive the memorial service we had for him two days ago. An unbearable sob threatens to rip from my throat, but I swallow the lump, knowing I have nothing left inside to give.

His ashes are still sitting in the middle of my father's dining room table a mile away. I wanted the urn, but Dick denied my request, saying the alpha's son deserved to be honored by being on display; not stashed away in the small, two-bedroom cabin Trez and I have shared since moving out of Dick's house two years ago.

My brother wouldn't have wanted to be Father's centerpiece, nor appreciated his remains being used as a trophy to gawk at during each meal.

My stomach rolls, the whiskey I've drunk over the past three days needing to purge. It's not like I can get drunk. Believe me, I tried. My shifter blood has burned through the good effects, leaving liquid sloshing around and making me nauseous.

The best I got was a strong buzz kicking, and that's only because I guzzled one hundred and twenty proof straight from the bottle.

I wouldn't have hidden my brother's ashes. I would have scattered them along the Oregon coastline, though I could never tell my father that plan. He would slaughter me himself if he discovered we've ventured south, across the Canadian border.

Three days.

Three agonizing days since I learned a hunter near the Canadian border had shot my brother in his wolf shifter form with a longbow. Why he was so close to Washington State is a mystery to me. We've only ever trekked that way together.

What's even more mysterious is it happened at the hands of a human. Wolf shifters have incredibly keen hearing. My brother would've been able to hear the hunter nocking the bow. We also have a large range of smell. Trez would have known how many people were within a half-mile radius.

It makes little sense that he wouldn't have picked up on a hunter within three hundred feet or fewer from him. The theory of the hunter being cloaked in deer piss to camouflage their scent? That's a dead giveaway to a shifter. The amount hunters spray on themselves is overpowering to our senses and reeks, not to mention Trez would've had to have been hit with a silver arrow.

Most humans don't know shifters exist and live among them, but there is a small population of *monster hunters* who think we're an abomination. Dick didn't claim they were responsible, so why would a regular hunter use a silver arrow?

That's another question I don't have the answer to, but what's odder is that Trez was with Henrik, our pack's beta. Trez hated our father's second-in-command more than he hated Dick, so I find it hard to believe my brother would go on a hunt with him.

Of course, my alpha didn't say it was a silver arrow either, and perhaps I shouldn't assume it was. Wolf shifters can be killed, but we heal so quickly that most wounds aren't fatal. Silver severely weakens us, which is why monster hunters use it. A shot through the heart or between our eyes can kill us. Getting beheaded is obviously fatal. If we're weakened enough and lose too much blood before our healing abilities kick in, we can also die.

Any scenario is possible, but Dick wasn't forthcoming with the details, claiming it was too hard for him to talk about so soon after the tragedy.

I call bullshit, not to mention Trez's body wasn't returned to the pack before he was cremated. On top of that, Dick had a memorial service less than twenty-four hours after telling the pack.

It was so much to process, but my brother had been acting strange for the past two weeks. He wouldn't tell me what was wrong either. Every time I asked, he played it off like I imagined something that wasn't there. I knew I hadn't. I knew my brother better than he knew himself.

He was my best friend, my littermate. We've had each other's backs since we were pups. Not that I remember anything from our first shift into our wolves, but I know it deep in my gut, the same as I knew Trez was keeping a secret from me.

Something big.

We didn't have secrets. We knew everything about each other, so for him to keep me in the dark after twenty years riled not only my human side but my wolf too. I wanted to teach him who the stronger wolf was, while I also wanted to ram my knee into his gut.

I was on the verge of starting a fight with him six nights ago when he finally admitted he was withholding information from me. The struggle I saw in his brown eyes was the only reason I held back. He asked me to give him a few days. Then he'd tell me everything. Trez said he just needed to go for a run to clear his head first. I expected him to return the next day, and when he didn't, I figured he needed more time in his wolf form to get his head straight.

Trez loved to run alone in the forest and along the coastline. I was the same way, so I understood. He needed space and time to process whatever was going on in his head.

Neither of us has felt the pull to run with our pack. We enjoyed each other's company just as much as we needed to be around the other, but that wasn't the same with the other shifters in the Marked Crest pack.

Our father is the alpha, so from time to time, Trez and I have had to play our part. We participated in all the things we were expected to do, but we never volunteered to do more. There were times I wanted to leave the pack to start our own. The problem was we were just two wolf shifters who had been raised in a pack to believe females weren't and would never be the alpha wolf.

The wolf side of me snarled at that thought. I've been itching for a long time to bare my canines at Dick while my wolf's paw was pressed against his chest, forcing him to submit. We don't have a good father-daughter relationship. It takes more effort on his part to force me into submission than it does the rest of his shifters.

In hindsight, I wish I'd had the courage to leave two years ago when Trez and I were eighteen. We could have formed our own pack hoping to find lone wolves that wanted to join. We're sociable creatures, even if neither of us cared for the shifters in our own pack. We get along with others just fine, and we prefer a warmer climate during the coldest weeks of winter.

For the last five years, we've gone on solo hunts for up to six weeks at a time. Dick didn't know we crossed the border. It was forbidden within our pack. We could go anywhere in British Columbia, but we weren't allowed in other provinces. Our father said it was because we were the alpha's children, and he couldn't take the risk.

The United States was strictly off-limits, which was why we traveled south all those years ago. There was a pull neither Trez nor I understood, so we chalked it up to defiance. Our dad was the alpha. It was natural for us to prove our dominance; me more so than Trez, but he wasn't weak. He would've made a powerful beta, and I swear he was born to be one. I also know I was born to be an alpha, but that'll never happen in the Marked Crest pack.

If we'd left, Trez would still be alive.

Run, Kate.

I stop breathing as a cold shiver races down my spine.

Trez? My brother's name rolls through my head in slow motion just before the beast inside me perks her ears.

It's impossible.

My grief is playing tricks on me. It's why I can still feel him. It's why when my alpha told the pack what happened, I called him a liar in front of everyone.

I'd know if something happened to my brother. I'd know if he was dead. We've always had a connection to each other that we didn't share with anyone else in our pack. That was a secret we kept between us.

To my knowledge, no other wolf in our pack could feel another wolf on a deeper level than the sense of smell or hearing them nearby. They couldn't communicate telepathically either, though Trez and I could only speak to one another in our heads during the phase of the full moon.

I glance out the window again. We're still two nights shy of the full moon, but there's also a lunar eclipse scheduled, and weird things always occurred with us when they've appeared over the years. We can hear the other in our heads for days leading up to a total lunar eclipse.

Does that mean I'm hearing him now?

Are you alive? I ask in my head while searching for the link we share. Maybe it's wishful thinking, but I'd do anything to bring him back. I'd trade places with him if I could. I need Trez to be alive more than I need my next breath. *Can you hear me?*

Run, he chokes out. *Go to Kane. Now, Kate.*

2

KANE

I scrub a calloused hand down my face. The smell of grease lingering on my palm overpowers all other scents in the bar. The odor of automotive lubricant generally calms the beast inside me. It's why I own and work at a restoration body shop, but tonight it's not cutting it.

Nothing gets under my skin more than dealing with rich assholes who think slapping a coat of shiny paint onto an old, rusted-out, beat-to-hell-and-back car is all there is to restoring a classic to its once-showroom glory.

They know nothing about the hours spent grinding out every speck of rust or the time spent hammering metal back into place, so the least amount of Bondo is needed to fill and shape a car panel or sanding and prepping the car before that coat of candy apple paint can be applied. The parts that must be searched for, bought, and then delivered with the hope they aren't damaged when you open the box.

Fucking customers.

A growl slips through the sliver of open space between my lips before I can swallow it back down. If I don't fuck soon, I'm liable to maul the next motherfucker that pisses me off. We're nearing the full moon—a lunar eclipse—and my body is on edge more so than usual.

Uncontrolled rage doesn't look good on any wolf shifter, especially when you're the pack alpha in an establishment with not only shifters but humans too.

Blow jobs aren't cutting it anymore, and I've amped up my daily runs to the point that I've dropped body fat I wasn't trying to lose. I'm giving my beta a run for his money against his vigorous cardiovascular routine. Jagger is the leaner one between us. He prefers running for longer periods than most wolf shifters, whereas I spend more time pumping iron than I do scouring the forest surrounding our land.

That doesn't mean I don't enjoy going for a run. I love it, but I prefer running with my pack than alone—or I used to. Then *she* came along, and I realized deer and elk weren't the only things I liked to hunt.

But I haven't allowed myself to devour my favorite prey yet.

And I can't.

Even now, I know it's wrong. She's wrong: the wrong fur, the wrong eyes, the wrong goddamn name. *She* isn't my fated mate. For that reason alone, Kate is off-limits. Not that it matters. I won't see her again for another eight months.

I've been in a foul mood since she and Trez left three months ago. They aren't part of the Bloodmoon pack. Hell, their alpha and their pack are enemies of mine dating back generations.

When Kate and Trez first trespassed into our territory five years ago, we allowed them to stay instead of chasing them back to the Canadian border. We decided it was better to make them think we were friendly, welcoming. At least, that was my dad's reasoning. I wasn't the alpha until three years ago. Plus, they were fifteen at the time; teenagers. I'm sure that was partly why my father allowed them the freedom to visit.

If their alpha had sent them here to spy on us for his benefit, I knew we'd figure out his angle eventually. Dad probably knew that too. But I hadn't counted on liking either of them, let alone both. I still remember the first time her scent tickled my nose. I smelled them both nearby, but Kate's scent hit me first. It was more overpowering than Trez's, but then she is the stronger of the two of them.

Jagger and I had been doing a perimeter patrol around the land our pack lives on along the coastal region of Oregon, with Ash trailing us. She wasn't on patrol duty, but my little cousin rarely missed the opportunity to scout with us even when she wasn't invited—and she was never invited. But Ashleigh was our shadow, and by this time, we'd gotten used to her tagging along on any adventure Jag and I set out to do.

I'd shifted from my blond, cream-colored wolf back into my human form and changed into the clothes we made Ash bring with her. If she was bound and determined to follow, she was going to be useful. Jag had changed too, but Ash remained in her red wolf form. Back then, she preferred four legs over two.

After a fifteen-minute hike that led to the beach, I saw them: a female with blonde hair so white and shimmery it almost looked unnatural. She was dressed in a black sleeveless crop top with army green, low-rise cargo pants paired with black combat boots. Her hair was straight and hung to the middle of her back. The guy with her had dark brown hair. They were both the same height, but he was bulkier. Though, I sensed her strength and spirit were stronger than his.

It made me suspect she was like my cousin, someone strong-minded and intelligent. She was clearly a female born to lead an alpha's army. Ashleigh only submitted to me, but she held so much respect for my father that it was easy for her to obey him without causing a riff in the pack. I knew long ago, when I became alpha of the Bloodmoon pack, Ash would be on my left side while Jag was on my right as my beta.

We watched the two young shifters for half an hour before letting our presence be known. I was about to step out of the woods when the girl looked over her shoulder, meeting my eyes with a smirk on her lips like she'd known we were there the whole time and had calculated the exact moment I was going to show myself.

My blood didn't simmer, it boiled. My wolf took it as a challenge. But I had at least fifty pounds on her. It wouldn't have been a fair fight. Besides, adolescents pose no threat to my pack or me.

We walked to where they had set up a makeshift camp far enough from the shore the tide wouldn't reach them.

From where I stood, her scent pissed me off just as much as it called to me. I knew the moment I scented them in the area they were Marked Crest shifters. They reeked of being silver wolves, but there was something deeper that I couldn't quite figure out that intrigued me. It made my beast want to claim her, and there was no way in hell I'd ever claim another unless she were my mate, who'd been kidnapped just shy of hers and my brother's second birthday.

My mother and Jag's mom are best friends, the same as our fathers are; like we are. They gave birth on the same day. Anna, my mate, is the little sister of my best friend. My brother Trey is Jagger's mate.

We discovered that when the babies shifted into pups for the first time just after learning to crawl. It was weird for Jag and me to learn who our mates were when we were eight years old and they only a year old. We were kids.

There was no instant love effect, but there was a bond, and it was strong. I vowed to protect Anna from that day forward. I knew in time, she'd be the only one I'd love the same way my dad loves my mom. Like I knew his beta loved Jag's mom. Anna was mine, and I was hers. Fate had declared it so.

I broke that vow a year later when she and my brother went missing. I failed her before I even claimed her. Before I truly understood what that even meant. At least I wasn't alone in my deficiency as a mate. Jagger was in the same boat. He'd made the same vow to Trey that I'd made to his sister.

Over the years, we've traveled the world searching for them, hoping we'd pick up their scent. Every being has a smell unique to them, and I knew Anna's. It's something I'll never forget.

Three years ago, our parents asked us to take over as alpha and beta so they could go on searches themselves. Our moms joined us over the years, but our dads couldn't leave our pack as easily as we could.

By the time I made it within three feet of the female, she reacted faster than I'd ever seen another shifter move. She lifted her knee and kicked her leg out. Her boot nailed me dead center of my gut. The next thing I knew, she swept my feet out from under me, and I was staring directly at the blinding sun, which was unusual for late January in Oregon with no rain clouds in sight.

Kate pissed me off before I knew her name, and she's been pissing me off ever since.

I was twenty-three at the time and struggling with an attraction to a teenager. I didn't want any part of the effect she had on me. For one, she was a shifter, and two, she wasn't my mate. And thirdly, she was a goddamn kid, and I was an adult. It was wrong. It wasn't going to happen—not then, not now, not fucking ever.

It wasn't like I was a virgin. I'd been fucking since I was her age, but I wasn't about to bed a minor, for Fate's sake. Had my mate not gone missing, I would have waited for her. But the fact was, she was gone, and I had no idea if I'd ever be given a second chance.

Teenage hormones were a bitch. I gave up my virginity to a human girl who was nineteen at the time. Jag and I snuck into a college party, and after that night, I never saw her again.

"Want some company, Kane?" I glance up, seeing Syn standing in front of me. "You look like you need someone to take the edge off." A smile inches up one side of her face as she bats her thick, painted black eyelashes.

I do. Fuck, do I ever, but it's not going to be her I screw.

"Come on," she continues. "For a night with you, I wouldn't even charge."

"Thanks for the offer, sugar, but it's never going to happen." I stand, making her step backward. I knew my wide, six-foot-eight-inch height intimidated her petite frame despite her being hungry for every dollar she could make. "You have a good night, though."

Stepping around her, I head to the bar, needing something stronger than the beer I finished a while ago.

Syn is a human and a local prostitute. Personally, I don't care what someone does to earn a living wage, but the last thing I need is for any of my shifters to see their alpha with one of the sex workers. If they want to pay for it, that's fine. Their business. They'll get zero judgment from me. But what I won't have is any of them bringing humans back to pack land just so they can get their dicks wet.

The shop I own, as well as this bar Ash owns, is on the outskirts of pack land, closer to the neighboring town. Our territory covers west Oregon to Freeway Five and up to Port Angeles in Washington state. Our pack property is near farmland and closer to Washington than California.

As I near the bar, seeing Ashleigh is the only one behind the counter, I flip the service entrance open and step behind it. With her tending to other customers, I'm not going to interrupt her to make me a drink. She'd stop serving everyone else to wait on her alpha. There's no point in her doing that when I can serve myself. Plus, she keeps the good shit hidden so she doesn't run out of the bourbon I prefer. Especially when it's so hard to fucking come by.

Dropping to my haunches, I open the cabinet under the register. While I'm reaching for the bottle, a delicious scent I'd recognize anywhere wafts up my nostrils, hitting every single sensory inside my body, making me freeze and lighting me on fire at the same time. Tingles tickle the back of my neck, telling me Kate is here.

But why?

They never visit this time of year.

What's strange is I don't smell Trez with her.

She's never come by herself. Why would she now?

3
KATE

Trusting my instincts hasn't let me down yet.

Trez talking to me last night could've been my imagination. I've never had to deal with grief before. We never knew our mother. She died within minutes of delivering us.

My brother is the first person I've ever mourned, so there's a chance I'm wrong, but there is also a chance he's alive. After telling me to run, to go to Kane, I had to sneak into my father's house first. I wanted the urn that my brother's ashes were in, and then I made a detour before crossing the border.

I had to be quick. Once Dick saw the urn missing, he'd know it was me that took them. My bike is fast, and I left five hours before anyone would be awake, but that didn't mean I had that much of a head start before he'd send his wolves to hunt me down.

Before he sent Henrik...

Anyone could have been awake and seen me leave. My

father likely has alarms around the perimeter of the pack that would have alerted him, but I had to scout the area where Dick said Trez was killed.

If Trez had been in the area recently, his scent would still linger. If blood had spilled, I'd know if it was my brother's. I also needed to know if my immediate distrust of Dick after he told the pack Trez was dead held merit. I've never trusted my alpha, and like Trez, I distrusted our beta even more.

I found nothing.

Not my brother's scent and not Henrik's either.

At that moment, I was glad I'd had enough forethought to steal the urn because something was amiss.

By the time I made it to Moonwake, Oregon, the sun had dropped below the horizon of the Pacific Ocean as far as the eye could see.

As I pull my racing bike into the parking lot of Ashleigh's bar, I'm exhausted. The bike isn't made for long-distance rides, which is why every place on my body aches. But it was fast, and I was racing against Dick or any male shifter in my pack who my father could have sent after me. Then again, maybe Dick was glad I'd left and hustling was for nothing.

I turn the bike off and take off my helmet. After snatching my key from the ignition, I toe the kickstand to the gravel rocks on the ground. Forcing my stiff muscles to move, I swing my leg over the rear and slip the key into my back pocket.

I'd stuffed the eight hundred bucks I had in cash from winning a bike race last weekend into the front pocket of a backpack, as well as a change of clothes while my brother's urn was zipped inside the main compartment.

Cracking my neck, I pull out the remaining six hundred dollars I have left after refueling and stash the bills in the front pocket of my pants before hanging the backpack from the handlebars. I'm not worried about it being stolen. Those who aren't afraid of Ashleigh's wrath wouldn't dare cross Kane, humans who frequent the dive bar included.

The bar doesn't have an official name. Patrons call it 'the bar' or Ash's place. There isn't a sign on the building either, but you get the idea of what's inside when the music hits your eardrums. Ashleigh purposely keeps it loud so that shifters can talk freely without worrying about humans overhearing something they shouldn't.

I square my shoulders and head for the door, the rocks crunching beneath my boots. Out of all the scents hitting me at once, I can always single out Kane's, smelling grease and dirt and the faintest new rubber smell from the tire inventory he keeps at his body shop.

I knew he was here before I'd pulled off my helmet. If I hadn't smelled him before I parked, I would have gone to his pack land instead, but I knew this was where he liked to wind down after a long day of working on cars. It's where his friends would be, where some of his pack members would be.

I reach out, grasping the door handle in my hand and yanking it wide open. My eyes connect with Jag's Nordic blue irises in less than a heartbeat. His eyes have always been such a contrast to his thick, black hair. There's something familiar about Jagger's eyes that put not only my wolf at ease but me too.

Kane isn't standing or sitting at the table where Jag is, but his beta will know his whereabouts. Though, I'm not sure I'm ready to find him now that I'm here. I know women fight for his attention. I used to be one of them, even if I'd never admit that fact out loud.

Stepping forward, I walk toward Jag. He's perched atop a picnic table with his boots on the wooden bench and his elbows on his knees like he's the center of attention. He stops whatever conversation he's in the middle of to track my every step until suddenly, my view of the Bloodmoon pack's beta is blocked as a burly man steps into my path.

I don't remember his name, but I've seen him before. He's a wolf shifter from Kane's pack, but he's an older man. He's older than Dante, Kane's dad and former alpha, with only a touch of gray in his strands of dark hair. He has a couple of inches on my six-foot height, but I don't have to look up to meet his angry stare.

"The stench of a *silver* doesn't belong here," he spits in my face, the smell of cheap beer and tobacco coating my lungs as I inhale, making my nose wrinkle. "Get out of here, little girl."

A silver wolf—his enemy. My pack has all gray wolves, but we're called silver because of the shimmering tattoo of a wolf's head that Dick proudly adorns on the top of his right hand. The alpha is the only one allowed permanent ink in the Marked Crest pack. It's forbidden for the rest of us.

"Last I checked, you don't own this establishment, so unless Ash sold it to you in the last few months, get the fuck out of—"

He snatches my black leather-covered bicep in his unnaturally strong grip, yanking me closer as a snarl forms on his upper lip while disgust seeps into his navy eyes.

My wolf growls from within me as I react, not giving the first fuck about where I am or the other shifters in the bar. I knee him between his legs, which loosens his grip. That allows me to twist out of his hold and swing my body around so that my elbow connects to the side of his face. I sweep his feet out from under him, and when his ass and back hit the ground, I tower over him, looking down and daring him with my gray eyes to get back up.

When I'm sure he isn't going to accept the challenge, I turn my back on him and step in front of Jag.

"Where's Kane?" I demand in a tone that tells the rest of the shifters and even the humans I'm not scared to go toe to toe with anyone who wants a piece.

"Probably getting a blowjob from one of the many alpha groupies sniffing around his dick." Jag smirks as he jumps off the table to crowd my personal space by towering over me with his six-foot-six-inch height. He's taller than me, but the half-of-a-foot difference isn't the slightest bit terrifying like I'm sure it is to others.

He isn't telling me this to be an asshole to the enemy wolf. He knows anything to do with Kane and other women gets under my skin, it riles up my wolf, and if there is one thing Jagger takes pleasure in, it's rubbing my attraction to his best friend in my face.

I know about his missing sister being Kane's fated mate. Damn near everyone in the Bloodmoon pack except Jagger has made it their mission to make sure I know I don't stand a chance with Kane ever since I turned eighteen and my wolf got restless.

Knowing his mate is out there somewhere should've dampened how I feel about him, but it hasn't; not in the slightest. If anything, every time I'm here, my desire for Kane grows stronger to the point I'm not sure how much longer I can put myself through the ache of him not being mine.

Every wolf shifter I've ever heard speak about fated mates wants to find theirs, but many never do. No one in my pack has found theirs. Me? I don't want a higher being to deem who I'm *supposed* to be with. What if they're a douchebag, or worse, a cruel person who takes pleasure in physically or mentally hurting another?

No, thank you.

I want a partner who has my back the same as I will have his. I want someone I can trust wholly, a man who doesn't see himself as superior to others, even if my chosen person ends up being the alpha of a pack. Because let's face it, that's the only shifter that'll be able to handle all of me.

As much as I yearn to live in Moonwake rather than on Rivermoon Mountain, I wouldn't be here if I hadn't felt the desperation in Trez's voice. The more I visit, the harder it is to leave. This is where I want to be when I'm not here.

Balling my fists, I peer up at Jagger. The smirk he's wearing is taunting me to react, but I'm tired, and I don't have time for his stupid games, so I do what I do best. Being as quick as possible in my current state, I grip the belt looped through his jeans to hold him in place, and with my other hand, I punch him in the gut as hard as I can muster. He doubles over to my right side.

"Where is he?" I all but yell.

"Behind you," he chokes out.

Whipping my body around, I see Kane in his rugged attire and all his six-foot-eight-inch height. His long, dirty-blond hair is pulled back into a hair tie, revealing his sinfully, neatly-kept beard and those penetrating amber eyes. A heartbeat later his long fingers close around my throat. His claws push through the nail beds of his fingers as if to warn me not to make any sudden movements.

"You better have a good fucking reason for being here,

Kate. That's two of *my* wolves you've put your hands on tonight."

His eyes visibly brighten as he brings his wolf closer to the surface. His alpha strength somehow paralyzes me, but it's different from my father's controlling power. Kane doesn't have to work up a sweat to force me into compliance. I don't even know how this is even possible. I'm not one of *his* wolves. He isn't *my* alpha.

The blood moon glow of his eyes though...

Calling on my wolf, I yank her close, pulling on her strength to fight Kane's power. It's the exhaustion. It has to be that I've worn my body down to the point I'd submit to another alpha if he demanded it of me.

"Trez," I choke out, but my brother's name causes the tips of his claws to sink into the flesh covering the back of my neck. It should be painful, but it's not. Instead, it sends a ripple of pleasure down my spine, all the way to the tips of my toes, making them curl. My thighs clench together while my core coils.

"What about Trez? Why isn't he with you?"

If fatigue wasn't threatening to buckle my knees, I think I'd enjoy the sensation of those claws wreaking havoc on my system. Kane's hold on me is the only reason I'm still standing and not bowing before him like the submissive, weaker wolf, and that pisses me off. So, I do the only thing I have the ability to do in this predicament. I use the alpha strength I know resides inside me to force my arms to move. Wrapping both hands around his forearms, I push my claws into his skin and say, "He's dea..."

I know my words fail me, but just before my eyes close and my body goes limp, I see the surprise in those brilliant eyes of his. My wolf retreats into the farthest corner inside me, pulling me with her into a coma-like state, forcing me to sleep.

I don't have the strength to fight it.

Darkness comes.

Then silence.

Then nothing.

4

KANE

Kate is an alpha wolf.

How did I never see that before?

It's the only explanation for her claws protruding from the tips of her fingers and penetrating my skin. It's not the ability to control what she lets shift that alludes me to think her wolf is a Luna wolf, an alpha female. Plenty of alphas, though not all, can control their shift. Only the strongest in mind and body can do it. It's even been recorded that a few betas have the ability.

Jagger can, but he's also stronger than most beta wolves, so it wasn't surprising the first time I saw him push his claws out without shifting into the giant black beast of his wolf.

In Kate's case, she was past the brink of exhaustion. I could smell the fatigue on her when she walked in last night, yet she didn't allow it to show through her expression or in her body language.

I didn't realize the depth of her tiredness until I was staring into her gray eyes. They were dull, almost lifeless.

Then I nearly fell to my knees following the words she wasn't able to finish.

It doesn't take a genius to figure out she was telling me her brother was dead before she went limp in my hand.

Trez is dead.

My friend is gone.

I can't tell you when it happened. When I started to think of Trez, and even Kate, as friends rather than the offsprings of their father. Richard Everhart is more than the alpha from a rival pack. He's our biggest enemy. Responsible for killing my grandfather, the alpha before my dad was the leader of our pack.

Years before I was born, the Bloodmoon pack and the Marked Crest pack were at war. It resulted in my father becoming alpha a few weeks past his eighteenth birthday following the death of his father and half of the pack. We still haven't regained the number of members we once had.

Wolf shifters aren't immortal, but we are immune to disease, and it's rare for a wolf shifter to die accidentally. Ninety-nine times out of one hundred, a wolf shifter is killed at the hands of another wolf shifter or another supernatural being. After we reach our mid-twenties, we start to age slower.

Trez hadn't even reached that mark. He was only twenty.

"You really think Trez is gone?" Ash asks from where the small of her back is pressed against the corner joints of the countertop to my right. I'm standing with my back facing the window above the kitchen sink while Jag is perched on a stool around the side of the island.

After Kate passed out, I took her to my pickup truck in the parking lot. That's when I discovered her racing bike with a stuffed backpack hanging from the handlebars. Her exhaustion made sense if she rode all the way from River-moon Mountain to Moonwake without rest. That's a sixteen-to-seventeen-hour drive; probably less the way she drives, but still too long on *that* bike.

She's had a love for riding motorcycles since the first winter they showed up. Jag taught her how to ride. The bike she showed up on is meant for a racetrack, not traveling between two countries. The only logical reason she'd drive it is if she were running from a supernatural being.

"She wouldn't lie, but..." my words trail off before my voice cracks.

Jag, Ash, and I are the only ones in the pack lodge with Kate while she sleeps on one of the oversized couches in the living room where I placed her.

There are two couches as well as a big recliner that all face a seventy-inch television hanging above the fireplace. The downstairs is open to the kitchen and dining room, making the space one large room with a hallway that leads to a full bathroom and the primary suite, which is where I've been living since I became alpha. There are five other bedrooms on the second level that only get used sparingly when we have guests visiting or lazy shifters who don't want to go to their own homes.

Kate's never been in the lodge before now. The only rule my father put in place when Kate and Trez started visiting was the lodge was off-limits to them. It was so a riff in the pack didn't occur. The fact is, they're from a rival pack, and several of our members didn't like them being here.

Ronnie, the old shifter Kate put on the ground last night, was the ringleader of the shifters that didn't want them in our pack. After becoming alpha, I kept my father's rule on the pack lodge being a no-go zone where they were concerned—until late last night.

It was after eleven when we returned to pack land. Eight shifters were in here drinking and having a good time. I kicked them out so Kate could rest. She's been asleep on the couch ever since.

"But we didn't hear the details either," Jag finishes for me, knowing exactly what I was thinking, or maybe I'm praying there was more to what Kate was going to say and Trez isn't gone in the *forever* kind of way.

"Uhhh," Kate groans. Our eyes snap to the couch facing away from us. Wrapping her fingers around the back of the sofa, she pulls herself into a sitting position. "Why is it so hot in here?"

"It's not," Ashleigh chimes in. "But it's June. You're probably not used to our weather down here."

Turning her head, Kate looks at each of us, her stare lingering before stopping on mine. She stands, cracking her neck as she steps toward the long, rectangular island in the kitchen. Slipping her leather jacket off, she lays it across a stool tucked under the counter before grabbing the backpack I placed on top of the island last night.

"What time is it?" Kate asks, her eyes on me.

Her cheeks are flushed, her hair is matted and dull, and there's no shimmer in her blonde strands. Neither diminishes her beauty. She is still the most stunning creature I've ever laid eyes on, but as she stands across from me, the island between us, I notice the dark strands of her roots for the first time. It strikes me as odd, making me wonder if she's been dying her hair an unnatural color this whole time.

"Almost six. At night," I answer.

Her head bobs in acknowledgment as her eyes go to the bag in front of her like there's something inside she doesn't want to face. I didn't plunder through her shit, but whatever is in the bag makes me think I should have looked.

"Tell us about Trez," Jag says, a strain in his tone that's rarely present.

"Is he dead?" Ash follows, pulling Kate's haunted expression toward my cousin.

"Yes. No. Maybe." She pulls in a breath, then quickly releases it.

"What the fuck does that mean?!" I blurt out, my tone harsher than I meant. I'm still on edge, and it's only gotten worse since *she* showed up. There's an itch to my skin I've never felt before last night.

"It means I don't know, Kane. It means I have my doubts about what Dick claimed happened to him." Kate's arms cross over her athletic chest as her back straightens into a steel rod. I haven't forgotten how she reacted to my alpha power. It rooted her feet to the floor, or maybe that was wishful thinking on my part.

Until now, I've always found it humorous how Trez and Kate call their father Dick rather than Richard or addressing him by any term of endearment meant for Dad. They claim to have a strained relationship with their alpha, and I've never had a reason not to believe that to be true. I've always been able to tell Kate dislikes her father, while Trez isn't as outspoken on the subject.

"Then explain," I growl, needing to know if the guy I've grown protective over in the last few years is alive or dead. If the latter, someone will pay with their life for ending his. "What did your father tell you?"

A low growl rumbles up her chest at the mention of her

alpha. Something about him always sours my stomach when it comes to Kate and her brother, which is why we've never officially spoken about Richard Everhart.

"He claims Trez was killed by a human hunter with a bow outside Vancouver," she spits out, and without a shadow of a doubt, I know she doesn't think it's possible for Trez to have been snipped with a bow and arrow. I have to concur. It is a hard fact to believe, but it's not implausible either.

"What makes you think there's a chance he's alive?" I ask, trying to control the rage festering inside me at the thought of Trez gone, taken from this world.

She glances down, looking at the zipped-up backpack in front of her once again. "Call it sibling intuition."

"Yeah, well, I'm calling bullshit on that." Her gray irises snap to my amber stare. "There's something you aren't telling us, so spit it out."

Kate reaches for the top of her bag. Grabbing the zipper, she pulls it open, revealing an urn. It's the last thing I expected to see, but I'm guessing it holds his ashes. This time, it's not me that lets out a low growl. It's Jag.

"That's not helping your case that Trez could be alive," Jagger tells her, and I have to agree.

Lifting it from her bag, she places the metal container on the counter, gently pushing it away from her to the center. I eye the shiny stainless steel canister, wondering why it's here if she isn't even sure Trez is dead.

"Before I left, I stole it with the hope that Dante could tell if the ashes are shifter or human. I have to know for sure."

"Dad's out of town. Don't know when he'll be back," I disclose, which is the truth. My parents and Jag's mom and dad left two months ago to search for our missing wolves. They likely won't be back for another few weeks.

"Could you smell the difference if the urn was open?" she asks, her tone hopeful but desperate.

I nod, then step forward. Reaching toward the center, I grab the urn and slide it toward me. Six tiny screws secure the lid to the canister, keeping it airtight.

Once, my father had to identify a shifter's body that had been killed by an organization of evil humans who call themselves monster hunters. The man's body was in such disarray that Dad had his remains cremated to bring back to his family.

Upon having the ashes given to us, Dad realized there had been a mix-up. The ashes he was given were human, not shifter. That's when he taught me how to distinguish between human scents and wolf shifters.

Wolves have a deep, earthy smell that humans don't often have from the amount of time we spend running and hunting in the forest. Plus, supernaturals have an unmistakable scent of *other* I'd be able to recognize.

"I'm going to need the smallest Phillips head screwdriver we can find." Looking at Ash, I say, "Can you locate one?"

Most of my tools are kept at work or in my shed at the secluded cabin I built close to a cliff that drops off to the sea.

"Sure." Ashleigh nods, then pushes away from the counter and heads to the front door.

"I'm going to take a piss while she's gone," Jag informs us before striding down the hall, leaving just Kate and me staring at each other.

Kate is the first to look away, and as her eyes roam around the open space, my stare dips to the flesh exposed between the waistband of her pants resting on her hips and the black top that stops an inch above her navel. Lifting her hand, her fingers grip the hem of her loose shirt, fanning the fabric back and forth from her abdominal muscles and making me swallow the nonexistent saliva in my mouth.

I wouldn't say Kate is slender, but then I wouldn't describe most female wolf shifters that way. The thing about wolves is we like to eat and indulge, but we also have an instinct within us to be the biggest and the toughest beast we're capable of being.

From what I've seen, there's no part of her flesh that isn't wrapped around strong muscles. Even as a teenager and eight years younger than me, she was able to drop me to my ass. The only other person to ever do that has been Jag, and even for him, it's rare when he can best me.

"I hear if you take a picture, it'll last longer," she chimes, making my gaze snap to hers. Her head is cocked to the side with one brow arched. There's a challenge in her gray eyes, making the beast in me rise to the surface before I push him back.

"When was the last time you ate?" I ask, ignoring her comment and the fact that her body has an effect on me that we've both danced around for years. But my question holds merit. I've been hearing her stomach rumble from hunger for hours. If she hadn't woken up when she did, I was on the verge of howling my dissatisfaction that would have woken her and alarmed my pack at the same time.

"About an hour before Dick tried to bring me to my knees by telling me my brother was dead in front of the whole pack." A growl slips past her lips before she clamps her teeth down and balls her hands into fists by her sides.

"And when was that?" I press for more information,

needing to know so badly it pisses me off. I shouldn't care. She's a grown fucking woman that can handle her own shit. She isn't mine to worry about.

"Four days ago." She rolls her eyes like it's not a big deal, but for me, it takes more effort and strength than it should to clamp a leash around my beast before he pushes through to shift, wanting to growl his displeasure at the fact that she hasn't fed herself.

"You haven't eaten in four goddamn days?!"

"Does bourbon count?" she tosses out, not the least bit afraid of my tone or the alpha vibes rolling off my heated skin like a thirty-foot wave about to crash into her, pulling her down into an abyss she can't come back from. "Pretty sure I drank three full bottles and had started on another when I passed out from lack of sleep."

The blood flowing in my veins rushes so fast through my system that for a split second, I see two of her. My beast is so furious it matches my human emotions. When Kate's lips part and an audible breath leaves her mouth, I know my eyes have flashed from amber to glowing a reddish-orange before returning to their true color, revealing my alpha temper.

All alpha wolves' eyes change color when we trigger the alpha power inside us, glowing a shade resembling an ordinary full moon. My pack, however, is affected by the lunar moon. When my eyes change, whether it's because I've pulled the power forward or an overpowering emotion triggered it, mine look like two blood moons.

Very few shifters have witnessed it from me. Like my father, I'm adept at controlling my reactions. It doesn't make sense that she's able to obtain that response as easily as she breathes. Sure, I can admit my attraction to

Kate, but that's all it is. She's just an itch I haven't scratched.

As if reading my thoughts, she rounds the island until she's standing toe-to-toe with me, looking up with a mixture of power and deep sadness colliding.

"Come fucking talk to me when Dante tells you Jagger was killed and then turns around in the same breath, forbidding you from tracking down the hunter that was responsible. Come speak to me then, asshole." Her palms meet my chest, shoving me, but my body doesn't budge, which shows exactly how weak she's allowed herself to become.

My fingers wrap around her throat, my claws extending, then sink into her flesh before my mind catches up with my reflexes. Just like last night when my hand was wrapped around her pretty neck and my claws pierced her skin, pleasure, unlike anything I've ever felt runs down my body, straight to the tip of my dick. If she hadn't passed out when she did, I'm sure I would have fucked her in front of everyone in the bar and not gave one fuck until I spilled my release inside her.

A moan slips from her mouth despite Kate's teeth biting down on her bottom lip. Her eyes flutter closed, and I have to force mine to widen for them not to mimic hers. Taking a step backward, I forcefully yank her along with me until I'm standing with my back to the range and vent hood. Kate's mouth is open as she tries to suck in the air I'm keeping from her lungs. Reaching behind me, I snatch a piece of bacon I'd cooked earlier and shove it past her lips.

"Eat," I command as I loosen my grip enough for air to fill her lungs and she's able to swallow once again.

She complies, but I can see the fight building in her eyes. My free hand flies between us, catching her knee before it nails me in the crotch. Shoving her leg down, I let her throat go, and then I flip her around so that her back is in the corner of the counter and I'm in front of her. Reaching for her waist, I hoist her up onto the countertop and force my way between her thighs.

"Get another piece and eat it," I order, unable to hold back the alpha power coursing through me, demanding that I feed Kate until her belly is full of food I've provided and not understanding one damn thing about why I'm doing this or acting like a jackass.

Wrapping her strong legs around my waist, she jerks me forward as her chin lifts and her eyes bore into mine. "Make me."

5

KATE

What am I, stupid?

When it comes to Kane Orion, that's exactly what I am: the stupidest bitch I know.

But in my defense, when he puts his hands on me, my brain malfunctions. When he goes all alpha, I'm torn between swooning with drool leaking from my mouth and wanting to bring him to his knees in front of me to prove which one of us has the bigger balls.

It's him, obviously. I can usually hide the weak bitch that wants to swallow his dick, but right now, I'm finding it extremely hard not to attack him and take everything I've wanted from Kane for five long years. The heat surrounding me isn't helping matters either.

"Baby, you're toying with something you can't handle."

This motherfucker.

"I've handled bigger beasts than you. Don't think for one second you know anything about what I can't handle," I lie through my teeth, praying he can't see through my bullshit. The truth is, I've never met a shifter bigger than him, but that doesn't mean I plan to let him know that small detail.

It's music to my ears when he growls and snarls in front of me, telling me I hit my mark exactly where I'd aimed.

"There may be bigger men out there than me, Kate, but there is no one that can tear up a pussy the way I can and make you believe you're experiencing both heaven and hell at the same time."

I open my mouth, but a second piece of bacon is shoved inside before my brain forms the words to tell him to prove it.

"Eat. Now."

His hand comes back to my waist, scaring my flesh and making it feel like his touch is a thousand degrees. But the sustenance his eyes are forcing me to chew and swallow is having the weirdest effect on me that has my wolf rolling over onto her back, showing her belly and submitting to *him*.

Bitch, we don't submit to anyone.

Kane shouldn't be able to coerce me into obeying him, but I suppose I've allowed myself to weaken *that* much.

With his eyes on me, Kane's hands slide from my bare waist and over the material covering my hips until they're sliding down my thighs, only stopping when he's wrapped his fingers around the back of my knees. Jerking me forward, he pulls my center flush with his hard abdominal wall. On reflex, my thighs clamp around his waist as my heart rate accelerates. My boots cross at the ankle, locking him between me.

"You smell good enough to eat," he murmurs.

Leaning toward him, I lick my lips, savoring the taste of delicious, greasy pork from the bacon before saying, "Seems to me, you're more talk than you are willing to eat someone, but so we're clear, I'm always on the menu for you, Kane."

Tilting my head until my nose is against the skin under his jaw, I inhale, pulling as much of him in through my nose as possible. With my neck exposed, he could take that as a sign of submission, but the yearning to sniff him is far greater than the need to assert my alpha side to another alpha.

He growls, but it's so low and deep within his chest that only another supernatural creature like me can hear it, and it's a joy to my soul.

"If you two are finally going to fuck, can we at least determine whether Trez is alive or dead first?" Jag rushes out, successfully ruining whatever ground I was covering with Kane. I unlock my legs and pull away, me nor the beast within liking it. Flicking my eyes over Kane's shoulder, Jagger's face is screwed up as if the sight of us makes him want to hurl everything sitting in his stomach. "And when *that* happens, give me a heads up so I can be miles away."

Kane lets out an angered growl a heartbeat before he jerks away from me, effectively telling and showing me, yet again, that I'm not his mate and he'll never be mine—not even for one night.

Thanks, Jagger.

What a fucking snatch blocker he is.

Way to piss all over my inner parade too because for a minute there, the anguish sitting on top of my chest was nonexistent. Now, it's returned tenfold. But even that doesn't tamper down the heat engulfing my body.

The front door flies open, and Ash walks back through, holding up the tiny screwdriver.

"Seriously, is the A/C not on? It's like a sauna in here." I hop down, pulling my loose top further away from my skin to get a breeze flowing up my shirt, but it doesn't help cool me down even one degree. If anything, my body temperature increases as the minutes tick by, and not in a good way.

"Yes," Kane answers and then turns away from me. "It stays on sixty-five year-round."

"Well, it feels like a hundred." I grab the urn as Ashleigh hands the tool over to Kane. Jag steps to the other side of the island and pulls out a stool.

"Maybe that's all the alcohol you're sweating out of your system," Kane says, waiting for me to hand the remains over.

"No," I argue while pushing it toward him. "That burned out over twenty-four hours ago. It's your house. Maybe it knows I'm not part of your pack and doesn't want me here."

"It's a house, Kate. It's not a living, breathing entity," Kane adds like I've lost my mind, but there is no way it's the temperature he said it was in here unless I'm the only one that can feel the difference, and for that to be the case, magic would have to be in play.

"Maybe your witch spelled it then. Whatever it is, it clearly doesn't like me."

"The pack doesn't use Storm like that. She isn't *my* witch. This is her safe haven for as long as she wants to call it home. She didn't spell shit," Kane spits out like he can't believe I'd think such a thing. But in my pack, that's precisely what Dick does. He just tries to downplay their coven living on the outskirts of pack land.

"Can one of you just open the motherfucker already?" Jag issues a low rumble of a growl, not liking our back and forth, but I shouldn't be surprised. Kane's mate is Jagger's little sister, though he's never been bothered before, so I'm not sure what's changed since I was here a few months back.

"Please open it, Kane," I ask, but even to my ears, I hear the whine of a beg in my tone. "I need to know once and for all that I'm not losing my mind, that he isn't gone."

I swear, I've died a hundred deaths by the time Kane places the screws on the counter. It's only by whatever strength my wolf possesses that I don't give in to my broken heart over the fact that my brother may very well be dead.

Tonight, we're due for a full moon, and if Trez were alive, he'd have spoken to me already. I've always been able to hear him, even when my body is in slumber. Waking me up before the crack of dawn on the day a full moon is scheduled is one of Trez's favorite ways to annoy me.

Where the hell are you, Trez? I scream inside my head, hoping he can hear me if he's out there. *I'm here. Why aren't you? Please don't be dead.* My words crack, but my brother is the only one who can hear my thoughts.

"It's other," Kane finally says, making my heart feel like it's stopped beating. An audible gasp slips from my lips, and there's nothing I can do to suppress it. Kane's head whips toward me, his amber eyes darkening and demanding mine to lock with his. "The ashes aren't from a wolf, Kate. It's not Trez. It's a witch."

"Ah, thank fuck," Jag breathes out a gush of air with his words, my heart echoing the same even though I shouldn't be relieved that someone else is dead, supernatural or human.

"He's not dead. It really was Trez in my head," I admit, not thinking before the words rolled off my tongue.

"In your head?" Ash is the first to catch what I said. "What does that mean?"

"I'd like to know that answer too, but first, I need to get these remains to Storm. She may know who this is." Kane's head tilts while he's looking at me, the wheels turning inside his skull. "A bigger question is, why did your father think this was Trez? Why did he want you and your pack to believe his son had been killed?"

"I'll take the ashes to her," Ashleigh offers. "She was at our cabin earlier, so she may still be at home. I overheard Maddy saying they were going out later tonight, but I doubt they'll leave without me."

"And we have to get going to make a perimeter run," Jagger says to Kane.

"Fuck. I wasn't thinking about the time," Kane curses as he runs his fingers and palm through the loose, dirty-blond locks on top of his head.

"I can go with Jag to check the land after we drop the urn. I've done it a million times. You stay with Kate and figure shit out," Ash offers.

"All right, but if there are any signs of that vampire's scent we sniffed out last week, one of you call me immediately," Kane instructs.

My wide eyes must give away my thoughts because Jag says, "There are all types of supernatural creatures, Kate. Doesn't your pack know this?"

"I know there are witches and humans-turned-were-wolves from a wolf shifter's bite, but . . ." I trail off, not knowing what else to say and not really caring at the moment. If I think about it, vampires existing, or any other creature isn't a stretch. If I hadn't just been told there's a good chance my brother isn't dead, I'd take the time to learn more about other beings.

"Just another reason your pack sucks," Jag comments.

"We educate all our shifters. We don't withhold shit or keep secrets."

"Never claimed to like mine, did I?" I say back as my feet start to step away from Kane. Flicking my eyes to his as they track my every step, I swallow the saliva pooling in my mouth. "I need a minute alone."

Turning, I quicken my pace until I'm down the hallway. The bathroom is to my left, so I dart inside and close the door. I flick the light and fan switch simultaneously, needing all the noise this small space has to offer. My breath catches in my throat a beat later. Dashing a long step toward the tub, I manage to turn on the shower a hair's breadth before the first tear falls from my eyes, a sob following.

I stink after riding on a motorcycle for hours yesterday, not to mention the sweat that has been coating my skin since I woke up half an hour ago.

Pulling my feet out of my boots and ripping off every stitch of clothing from my body, I get in the tub, letting the spray of cold water soak every inch of my flesh. Lowering myself to the bottom, I sit and allow the tears to fall. I cry until I have nothing left in my system to give, and I pray the rush from the shower pouring out water is enough to cover the ugliness coming from my mouth.

You have twenty-four hours to get your ass here, or I'm coming back to find you. Even if that means taking down Dad and any other pack member that gets in my way. Goddammit, Trez, say something. Let me know you're okay.

Please, just be alive.

I need you to be alive, brother.

6

KANE

Jag and Ash left twenty minutes ago to drop off the urn with Storm. By now, they should be roaming the lands in their wolf forms. I'm grateful to Ashleigh for going in my place. My head isn't in the right state to be as alert as an alpha has to be.

When Kate pulled that sealed vase from her backpack, the tissues that make up the organ in my chest squeezed so tight I thought it was going to burst. I shouldn't feel that strongly for another shifter who isn't part of my pack. It doesn't make sense. The thought of Trez being dead hurt and angered me.

We were never supposed to be friends—but we were. We are. But the relief I was gifted after I scented the witch's ashes was a fleeting moment. We still don't know where Trez is. If he's alive, hurt, or in danger. Worry crept in, sidling up next to my fury and mingling into something I don't have a word for.

Kate's father, her alpha, would have known those ashes weren't his son's. He would have been the one to have his body cremated in the first place, so what was Richard's end goal? Why did he inform his pack and daughter Trez was dead? What would he have to gain by lying?

"Kane?" she calls out, pulling me away from thoughts of her brother and where he could be. Her voice is low and hoarse, but I knew it would be before she shut off the shower less than a minute ago.

The second my hearing registered her shuddered breaths, sweat broke out across the back of my neck, and my wolf started pacing. It pulled me toward her until my boots stopped in front of the closed bathroom door in the hallway. Bracing my fingers around the unpainted wooden frame is the only thing keeping me from breaking the door off the hinges to get inside.

That earned me snarls, followed by low growls from my wolf. I can feel he thinks I'm not doing what we should be to soothe Kate's heart. I don't understand why he doesn't get that her heart isn't ours to heal, nor can I rationalize my chest aching with the need to do exactly what my wolf demands.

"Can you bring me my bag? It has clean clothes inside the front pocket," she informs me before I hear a thud against the other side of the door, making me think her forehead fell against it.

"Open the door." A growl follows my order as the sweetest scent I've ever smelled coats all the receptors in my nostrils, tickling my throat and sending a tingling sensation rippling down my spine. My fur sprouts before I force my golden blond hair to retreat.

The knob turns and the door opens from the inside, revealing Kate wrapped in a thick, navy towel. Whatever I smelled with the door closed hits me tenfold with her damp body standing before me barefoot.

My hands slip from the doorframe. I meant for my arms to drop to my sides and to take a step back, only I reach forward instead. Wrapping my fingers around the opening of the towel, I tighten my hand into a fist and pull. Kate flies toward me as the towel unwraps, falling from her and my fingers as my eyes cascade down the body of a goddess.

My wolf whimpers at the sight before us, and I can't blame him. Never before have I wanted to take to my knees in front of another until now.

Fuck.

She's more stunning than my imagination ever did her justice. The junction where the column of her neck connects to her shoulder has my canines aching; for what I haven't a clue. Her tits are small, but plenty to touch and tease and suck—and bite. Her waist tapers inward before flaring out toward her meaty hips. Her stomach looks so fucking soft that I want to squeeze my fingers around her flesh.

Reaching for the hem of my T-shirt, I pull it up, yanking it off my torso as quickly as I can, then I snatch Kate by her waist, pulling her to me until I'm able to reach her ass cheeks. Lifting her off the ground, she wraps her legs around me, and the feel of us flesh-to-flesh makes me lose every shred of control.

Stepping sideways and out of the bathroom entrance, I press Kate's back into the wall as I slam my lips down on hers. She whines, or it's coming from her wolf deep inside; either way, it's like a goddamn aphrodisiac that goes straight to my cock.

She kisses me back just as hard and brutally as I'm attacking her mouth. Her tongue, worshiping mine, is the most erotic feeling I've ever experienced, but then, I have five years of suppressed sexual frustration and need for this woman that maybe my head is making this more than it actually is.

Her pussy is already slick against my abdominal muscles. Feeling it is one thing. Being able to smell her arousal is something else entirely, and it's doing something to my wolf and me that I can't explain. He wants her to shift so that he can fuck her wolf, but that isn't happening. I've waited too long for this, thinking it would never happen. I'm having the woman before he gets the beast.

Going for the buckle on my jeans, I pull away from Kate's lips. A whimper leaves her mouth, but her eyes flick to mine, giving me exactly what I want.

"If you don't want this, you better stop me now," I say to her as I yank the zipper down on my pants and push my clothes down my thighs.

Kate's hand moves to my throat, her claws extending and sinking beneath my skin. My dick becomes harder as she looks me dead in the eyes, and for a moment, I swear the gray in her irises changes to a vibrant color that pricks at the back of my head. But then she says, "If you don't fuck me, Kane, I'm going to reach inside your chest and rip out your beating heart. Then I'm going to eat it," making me think I imagined it because when she blinks, her eyes are the same muted gray they've always been.

A low growl follows her threat, but before the rumble in her throat subsides, I shove my cock so deep and hard inside her that her lethal warning turns into a scream so loud there's no doubt in my mind the entire pack heard her cry of pleasure.

Kate won't go into heat for at least another year. Female

shifters don't come into heat until they are nearing their twenty-second birthday, and since we aren't susceptible to diseases like humans, there's no need for protection. Though this is a first for me since I've only fucked human women until her. With them, I always used a condom.

My wolf howls his satisfaction as I tighten my grip on her meaty ass cheek and pull my dick back to her slick opening, only to plunge forward with twice the force.

"Ah, Jesus, fuck, that feels good." Her moan vibrates from her throat down to her hot little pussy, squeezing my cock like no one before has managed to do. There's a pulse inside her, and it feels like something is nipping and licking the tip of my dick at the same time. It's like fucking two beings at once, and the reality is, that's indeed what I'm doing: fucking Kate and her wolf. Or, they're both fucking my wolf and me because she's giving just as much as she's taking.

"Tell me now that I'm not the biggest dick you've had in you, baby?"

I don't know where that particular endearment came from. I've never used it with a woman I'm fucking, or any woman for that matter, but then I've never fucked another shifter before now either, and apparently, I've been missing out. I usually have to let the girl I'm banging ride my dick to control the speed so that I don't hurt her, but with Kate, it's like I know she can handle anything I give her.

"Shut up and fuck me harder." Her claws sink into my shoulders as her heels dig into the meat of my ass cheeks, urging me to comply. "If you aren't the man for the job, bring your wolf to the surface. I bet he could fuck me harder than you."

A growl leaves my throat just before my fingers wrap

around the column of her pretty little neck. I shove her head toward the wall and slam so far inside her pussy that no man or beast will ever reach the depth I can.

A scream of pleasure and pain leaves Kate's mouth, but instead of pushing me away, she pulls me closer until her lips connect with mine. Her tongue and lips and teeth fuck my mouth equally as rough as my cock is fucking the best thing it's ever been inside.

Her pussy is an inferno I never want to leave. Her scent calls to me in a way I've only experienced when hunting prey, and although I do want to eat everything she's willing to offer me, I also want to protect her like she's more valuable than the rarest treasure. *Like she's more important than my pack.*

That realization should have me pulling out and getting as far away from her as possible. Kate isn't my mate. These feelings are nothing more than me projecting my longing for a mate I may never find into someone I've wanted for longer than is morally right.

Every dream I've had of my mate since Kate and Trez entered my life contorts into Kate's image.

Anna's blue eyes would fade until they turned into a shade of gray that matched Kate's. My mate's raven hair would lighten until it was blonde like Kate's long locks. Her tan skin, which I know would match her mother's complexion the way Jagger's does, would turn pale and snow-like to match Kate's fair skin tone. Kate is always the one I wake up in a cold sweat remembering.

Maybe this is what I need to get her out of my system and out of my head because, at the end of the day, she can't be mine, and I will never be hers. I've belonged to another since I was eight years old, and there is nothing that's going to change fate.

"Claws," she pants. "Sink them into me. Please, Kane."

My wolf doesn't wait for me to comply with her demand. Instead, he pushes his claws through the tips of my fingers and straight into Kate's flesh on the bottom of her ass and around her throat, piercing the back of her neck and making her eyes roll back. The most delicious moan I've ever heard slips from her lips.

While my beast holds her in place, I hammer in and out of her beautiful body, every dive inside better than the previous. It's a miracle I've managed to last this long without blowing my load. Jesus, she feels so fucking good that I'm almost convinced this has to be another one of my dreams.

Her muscles tighten around me, sucking me deeper, and whatever her wolf is doing to the tip of my dick has me seeing fucking stars. I have to bite down on my bottom lip to keep myself from sinking my canines into her like my wolf is trying his damnedest to do.

"Yes. Oh, fuck yes. Ahhhhh," Kate moans as her head tips forward. My grunts follow her over the edge of the best pleasure I've ever been gifted. My heart is beating so fast that it feels like it skips a beat as it trips over itself to slow down. My forehead falls to Kate's bare shoulder as shallow breaths leave my mouth. My claws retract back into my skin, leaving the only sound a mixture of our breaths coming in and out.

A growl rumbles its way up my throat, but it wasn't me that made a sound. My wolf wants what he thinks is his.

I let Kate's legs slide to the hardwood floor. My energy so

wholly spent that I don't have the strength to stop the shift I know is seconds from happening.

"Kate," I call out. My hands leave her slick body and plant them on the wall behind her as I push myself back to look her in the eyes. "Run."

7
KATE

I shifted into my wolf form as if I were following my alpha's orders. My wolf nor I have ever been keen on following anyone else's lead. That's something we've always been in sync with; besides, Kane isn't even *our* alpha. Still, I had to shake off the weird need and want brewing that she and I have when it comes to doing as Kane says while my wolf bolted through the sizable canine door built into the front door at the lodge.

The hot summer night air does nothing to cool the lava running through my veins. I took a cold shower, thinking that would help soothe whatever was happening inside my body, but that only cooled me down a fraction. The moment I opened the bathroom door and saw Kane standing before me, an inferno blazed to life like it was an entity in itself.

I step backward into a dark corner somewhere in my head as my wolf's paws speed up. She dashed through a thick brush ten minutes ago instead of taking the trail that loops through the forest on Kane's pack land. Taking the dirt road would have taken her nearly half an hour to reach his cabin atop a cliff overlooking the Pacific Ocean.

After being fucked against the hallway wall in the lodge, neither of us wanted to wait that long for round two. But we also don't plan to make this chase easy on the big beautiful alpha either. If his wolf wants us, he better push his legs harder. We've already put at least a mile of distance between us. Of course, I am the faster runner between the two of us. The only wolf I've ever met that can beat me is Jagger.

Just before the cabin comes into sight, our senses are overwhelmed by Kane's smell, a mix of him and his wolf; woodsy, automotive grease, and if alpha dominance had a scent, it would be pure Kane Orion.

Coming here is always torture in the best and worst ways. Over the years, I've spent many weeks lying in Kane's bed at night, alone, wanting and yearning for something I thought I'd never get. I don't know what finally made him give in tonight, but I'm not about to look a gift horse in the mouth.

Knowing what's coming, I step out of the shadows, then we shift. My wolf retreats as I change back into my human form just as my feet land on the top of the porch that goes from one side of the front of the cabin to the other. It's not a tiny home, but it's not the lodge, either. The lodge is at least six or seven times as big. There's only one bedroom, but it has a full bathroom. When Trez and I would stay here, he'd always sleep on the couch while I enjoyed Kane's queen-sized bed.

Here, he doesn't have a specialized wolf-sized door built into the main door like he does at the lodge, and I'd imagine he keeps it locked since most of the other homes are all closer to the lodge. Only the former alpha and beta and their wives live a little farther away, but their homes are on the other side of the pack land. It would take forty-five minutes to reach them if you were to take an ATV or side-by-side through the trail path.

I'm about to grab the doorknob to check if it's locked when the door swings open, making my eyes snap upward. Before Kane's massive height comes into full view, I'm snatched around the waist and pulled inside, then pressed against his hard chest before my brain catches up with him being here already.

"What the... How?" I say, my voice exasperated from the run, my shift, and being caught off guard. There's no way he beat me here. I took the fastest route. It's over two miles taking the dirt road.

"You think you know my land better than me, beautiful?" He laughs as he lifts my feet off the floor, wrapping my bare legs around his sculpted muscular waist. I've never been modest. I don't know many wolves that are, but that doesn't mean I actively walk around buck-naked. With Kane, I feel perfectly content in my own skin for the first time in my life.

Coming here, to Moonwake, to the Bloodmoon pack, it's like coming home from a long trip every single time Trez and I cross the border into Washington state. It shouldn't feel like that, but it does, and I don't have an answer as to why that is when it should be the opposite.

We're supposed to dislike them. Hate them. We were taught they are our enemies. One of the earliest memories I have is Dick making Trez, and I repeat over and over *death to the Bloodmoon pack.*

Our father's first mistake was ordering us to hate people

we'd never met. I've never jumped on *that* bandwagon, and I never will. It was one of the reasons we came down here in the first place. We wanted to see them with our own eyes, get to know them and decide for ourselves if they were our enemies. Instead, we made friends. At least to me, they've become our friends over the years. I know not everyone in Kane's pack like us. They don't trust us. They'd prefer we never come back.

"Trust me, Kate, no one knows this forest better than Jagger and me." He pivots, turning us as he steps forward, and with the back of his bare heel, he kicks the door closed. "I'd share my secrets, but I'm starving from the speed I had to maintain to get here before you."

He quickens his pace, walking behind the couch to his left and my right side. The cabin has an open floor plan, similar to the lodge, but on a smaller scale. With just one couch and a recliner, more than two shifted wolves won't fit in this small place, though it isn't as if I have anything to say.

My house back home is smaller than Kane's secluded getaway cabin. It's the smallest house on our pack land, but it was the only one Dick would allow us to take when we moved out, despite there being several bigger ones that are still vacant. I didn't fight him on the matter. I just wanted out of his house, away from him.

"If you think we're pausing for you to have a snack, you're out of your mind." The heat wreaking havoc deep inside my core is at a boiling point now that I'm back in my human form to the point it's almost intolerable. His giant, hard dick bobbing below my ass isn't helping matters either. I need more of him, and he'd better give it to me.

"Baby, I'm getting mine first, then I'll feed you all the

dick your greedy little pussy wants. I might even let your mouth swallow my cock, if it'll fit." He smirks, making the challenge in his tone hit its mark. He knows that making it seem like I can't do something will force me to prove him wrong.

Sitting me down on the countertop of the small island, he removes his hands from under me to glide his palms down the outer sides of my thighs, past my knees, and down the rest of my legs until he reaches my ankles, his hooded eyes on mine the entire time.

"Lie back," he insists, his wolf adding a growl to his demand, making a shiver run up my spine and along the base of my skull.

If he wasn't eyeing me like a starved animal, and I wasn't about to enjoy him feasting on me, I'd probably tell him to eat shit for issuing me another order. Instead, I obey and lean all the way back against the smooth surface as he plants my feet onto the stone.

"Grab your ankles." My eyes narrow on him, but I reach down, grasping onto the front of my legs, just above my feet. Kane grips my knees, and even with my eyes connected with his, I see the tips of his claws come out. "If you come before I say you can, your pussy is going to miss out on that dick you're panting so hard for. Wouldn't that be a shame for both of us?"

A growl seeps past my lips, and I do nothing to stop it, issuing my own warning. Without letting go of my ankles, I lift my back off the counter, coming to my elbow as I snarl at Kane.

"Don't underestimate my ways of getting exactly what I want," I tell him, and before he pries my legs apart, I open them, spreading myself as wide as I can.

He takes a breath, slowly inhaling my scent through his nose, savoring it. His lips part, and at the same time, his eyes drop to my center. The feral look in them makes a rush of lava cascade through me straight to my center. Without seeing exactly what he's watching, I feel the liquid leak from my body. That's the moment Kane pounces. Dropping the upper half of his torso, his mouth latches onto me: sucking, licking, biting hard enough that my shifter abilities will kick in to heal any bruises he leaves.

"Oh, fuck." My fingernails dig into the flesh around my ankles while my core tightens as his tongue enters me. Pulling out, he runs the flat part up my center, stopping at my clit.

Kane's hands roam up my feverish inner thighs as they begin to quake. The tip of his tongue flicks up and down at a rate that I swear is faster than my vibrator. Granted, he's a supernatural being, but this is beyond otherworldly, or maybe I just didn't know being with another shifter could be *this* good.

"Yes," I breathe out, my voice desperate for more. My back arches, and pushing on the heels of my feet, I lift my ass, trying to get more, wanting to control and take what I need as my muscles lock, and I know I'm seconds away from breaking apart, and it's going to be glori—"

What the fuck?!

His tongue stopped, and the vibration coursing through me fades, leaving so fast that a whimper escapes before I can stop the sound from breaking past my lips. The growl that comes from Kane's throat forces my eyes to snap to his as they flash reddish-orange, and because I can't blink, I watch in silence, fascinated as they change back to amber a second later.

"You think you can top me from the bottom, little wolf?" His left hand leaves my leg at lightning speed, and I don't realize his fingers are around my throat until his claws sink into me, eliciting a myriad of tingles that glide down my back until I feel them in my toes.

Jesus, was that an orgasm?

Standing back to his full height, he pulls me into a sitting position, making me release my ankles so that my legs drop and hang off the counter. Dipping his head, Kane smashes his wet lips to mine, pushing his tongue roughly inside my mouth. Somehow, tasting myself on him is making this hotter than when he was lapping my pussy like I was the last meal for a man on death row.

My arms lift, and my hands find his shoulders. I don't just love feeling his claws in me; I also like digging mine into his skin, which is exactly what I do. Kane's eyes flash like I knew they would, but before I can smile in triumph, his fingers enter me hard and fast, filling me. He doesn't give me more than a breath to get used to his thick digits before he begins pumping two fingers in and out in a fast but controlled rhythm.

"Your pussy is mine. Mine to give it what it needs. Mine to make come," he barks against my lips. Applying more pressure around my neck, he pushes back inside me with such vigor that not only do I feel his knuckles breach my opening, but I swear his alpha strength enters me as well.

My center quivers so violently that it takes more effort than it should to force words from my mouth. "Only if your dick belongs to me." A growl vibrates up my throat, letting him hear the seriousness in my words. He doesn't get me without me getting him. "Mine and no one else, Kane."

I want it all. I've wanted him for so long that I don't

remember ever not wanting him. I don't want to fathom a life without Kane or his pack. It's why I continue coming back year after year. But that doesn't mean I *can't* live without him. If he isn't prepared to go all in, then I'm wasting my time and risking my heart for nothing.

"Sounds like a fair trade," he says before pushing his tongue back into my mouth, making me feel overwhelmed, or maybe this is what drunken humans experience when they've had well over their limit.

Still, the fear living in the back of my mind persists. It doesn't matter how deep down I push, doubt continues to thrive inside me the same as my wolf does. Except now, a sense of foreboding is present too.

Kane may be telling me the words I want to hear, but that doesn't mean he'll still mean them tomorrow.

It's not a wolf's word that holds power. It's our bite. We're not wearing each other's mark for it to mean anything more than only one night together, yet my heart isn't getting the memo. Even now, I know he's all I'll ever desire. All I'll ever want, even if I'm not the one he needs the most.

How is he mated to someone else when I feel this so viscerally deep within me?

8

KANE

"Fuuuck," I moan into her mouth.

My fingers slide back inside Kate, slipping through her dripping pussy lips like it's a favorite pastime or maybe a newfound pleasure. It sure beats them being wrapped around my dick, that's for sure.

My eyes flick from Kate's one minute then down to her pulsing core the next. Breaking our kiss, I'm not able to keep myself from enjoying both beautiful views. There is nothing about her that's anything like any other woman I've ever been with. It's a fact I love more than I care to admit. It's why I've never allowed myself to indulge in another shifter or any other supernatural creature before now.

There's a gnawing feeling somewhere inside me that wants to give her everything. It's not just my wolf either. He's already on board with making Kate ours, but my head is at war, which is why I keep shoving everything it's telling me back to the furthest part those thoughts will go. Nothing will stop me from making her come, not even me, no matter if I know this can only end in a goddamned disaster. I'll have to live with the shame and guilt that she isn't my mate when that's precisely who I wish she were.

It just won't be tonight.

No, tonight I'm going to give her just as much as I plan to take, if not more. I want her to own every cell in my body, every organ, all the bones that make up my humanity and my animal. For tonight, we're hers, and if she'll give us her and that sexy wolf of hers, then we'll greedily accept and enjoy every second with them.

Slipping two fingers from inside her, I run the slick pads of my digits to her clit as I flick my eyes back to hers, finding them at half-mast.

"Kane." A whimper slips from her beautiful mouth. "I need more. I'm so hot. I'm burning up."

Grabbing her by the hips, I yank her body off the counter and fuse her to my front. Flipping us around, I slam her back against the stainless-steel refrigerator as something in the back of my head tickles the forefront of my brain, but her scent is making me too feral to care what it is.

Hoisting her ass up the front with my palms, I grip her tighter, and when her pussy is at mouth level, I dive forward, licking, sucking, biting, and trying to swallow everything her body is willingly giving me.

"When I said more, I meant your dick. I want your cock, Kane."

Pausing, I flick my eyes to hers. Kate's hands are braced on the two front corners of the top of the fridge. Her gray eyes pop open.

"Are my tongue and mouth lacking, baby?"

"Fuck, no," she declares.

"Then until you come on my demand, on my tongue, you don't get my dick." I growl against her opening.

Her head falls back to her shoulders as the muscle in my mouth sinks back inside her body. Her core feels like a coat of lava around me, squeezing and wanting more of what I'm giving her. As if my beast knows when to please her, my claws elongate and press into the meat of her ass cheeks and hips without me forcing them to change.

She tastes sweeter than any fruit that's ever graced my tongue. Kate is most certainly richer than any dessert I've ever eaten.

Kate bucks her hips, fucking my face with each powerful thrust forward. Her skin feels feverish to the touch. Sweat beads down her torso, the liquid disappearing into my hair-line from where my forehead is pressed against her belly.

"Come my fierce wolf. Come for me," I demand as I lift my head as much as I can without taking my mouth away from her, and without doing it with purpose, I know my alpha eyes are shining right up at her.

Locking her jaw, she grits her teeth and slams her eyes closed. I up the force my tongue is building inside her. She wouldn't be Kate if she didn't try to hold back. There's no doubt in my mind that my alpha abilities do not work on her. They only affect other supernatural creatures within my pack. It's impossible for me to force her to come using my dominance as the leader of the Bloodmoon pack.

She shakes her head. Then one hand slips, bringing her elbow down to the surface of the fridge. Her muscles tighten, constricting around me to capture my meaty tongue, capturing me in a similar way that I have her.

The claw on my thumb retracts back into my finger, making the corners of my lips tip upward. Knowing my wolf has his own ideas, I slip my tongue from inside Kate, licking her until I meet her clit, then I jut my digit into her with so much force, the pain in my balls intensifies as my dick pulses.

If I don't enter her soon, I'm going to wash my kitchen with cum.

A moan seeps through Kate's lips, and when she can't hold back any longer, her bottom lip drops then panting ensues, causing the most erotic tingles to glide down my spine in a slow path.

I can feel her abdominal muscles tighten against my forehead while her pussy tries to suck my finger deep inside her hot walls.

Her head once again tips backward, falling to her shoulder. Then she comes, screaming my name. The ceiling seems to light up in an orange glow, but I know it's nothing more than the clouds slipping away to reveal the Lunar moon I knew was coming tonight.

It's said my pack is more vulnerable during blood moons. Until tonight I didn't believe that theory. I always saw strength in a full moon—a lunar moon even more. But tonight, I let myself succumb to want and need. To a desire I've had for years, and in this moment, I'm not so sure I'd change the outcome of this. Of Kate showing up last night at Ash's bar. Trez's fate aside, I'm glad she's here.

Pulling my tongue back into my mouth, I retract the rest of my claws from her flesh and remove my thumb. Lowering my forearms, I slide Kate's back down the front of the refrigerator until her sweaty, beautiful face is in front of me. Her chest heaves, but her gray eyes lock on mine, holding them hostage.

I still wish they were a different color, her blonde hair black, even if she's somehow dyed parts of it darker. I'd noticed last night but never got a chance to say anything.

She's always had shimmering white-blonde locks, but it's as if her blonde is dull and the undergrowth, close to her roots, is darker.

Not wanting to think about mates or wanting a woman who'll never be the one whom fate deemed mine, I smash my lips to hers. If she's put off by tasting herself, she doesn't show it. She kisses me back with as much brute force as I'm giving her.

How is she not my match is the question I should be shouting to the unknown. Kate handles my strength like it's no big deal. Like she was born for everything I have to offer.

Dropping her feet to the floor, I rear back, releasing my hold on her. "My bed. Now!"

9
KATE

What the hell is wrong with me?

On top of being insatiable, the temperature inside me continues to climb at an accelerated speed. I know Kane doesn't have central air and heat here, but even if he did, I don't think it would help lessen the fire burning within. I know I'm not going into heat. I'm not of age.

Females weren't taught much in our pack except that we're only there to breed and obey, but the one thing I learned from the omega wolf that cleaned my father's house was I was safe until my first heat cycle. She told me it could happen just shy of my twenty-second birthday but not before and that if I were as smart as she'd hoped, I would run before that day came.

I still have a year before that happens, so it's not a heat cycle. And wolves don't get sick unless we've come in contact with wolfsbane or silver, which I've neither touched nor ingested. And believe me, I know exactly what wolfsbane feels like coursing through my system. Dick often used it as punishment on younger wolves to incite fear among the pack. For his kids, he uses it to weaken our strength.

Kane's lips rip apart from mine, leaving the taste of him mixed with me in my mouth. Sucking in a lungful of air, I tip my chin up and look him in the eyes.

It's dark in his cabin, but with no curtains covering the windows, the light from the moon shines bright, giving me the best view. Kane towers over me as if he owns me, and for whatever reason, that doesn't bother me. Maybe it's because I know he isn't like any of the men in my pack, certainly not like my father. Kane may be the alpha, but I've never seen him speak of any member of his pack like they're property, like they're a lesser being than him.

"My bed. Now!"

If I could reach inside myself and smack my wolf's snout, I would. I swear to the stars she fucking purrs before she rolls onto her back, showing her belly at Kane's demand.

We aren't feline, bitch.

When I don't jump at his order, he smacks my hip with his palm, the sting making me jump.

"There is no doubt in my mind you can take anything I dish out, Kate, but I'd rather not dent my refrigerator."

Gripping the back of my legs, he hoists me up and over his shoulder.

"Why not?" I say in a goading manner. "As much dirt is caked onto the top of it, you might as well buy a new one. When was the last time you cleaned it?"

"Way to tell me I didn't fuck you hard enough without telling me I didn't thoroughly fuck you, Kate." A low rumble moves through his chest, sending tingles racing up my back. "That's okay." He smacks my ass playfully as he strides down the hallway. "We can all improve, even me. By tomorrow morning, your bones will be jelly, and I guarantee you won't be able to walk without your thighs aching with the amount of time I plan on spending between them."

My body propels backward, and in less than a breath, my back lands in the middle of his plush bed. Before I can blink my eyes open, Kane rams his long, thick cock so far inside me that my heart skips a beat, and all the air in my lungs is forced out like a violent tornado took hold, ripping it from me.

My fingers find his shoulders, and without the thought forming, my wolf pushes her claws through skin and muscle, joining the fun.

The burning intensifies. It's everywhere, even inside my head, making it feel like my brain is cooking. It's too much. I can't take this. It needs to stop. It has to stop before...

"Kane," I cry out. "Please."

I've never begged a day in my life. Why am I doing so now? Furthermore, how is he supposed to stop whatever has seeped its way into me?

Did I piss off a witch?

It's been known to happen. Dark witches aren't bound to the same laws as light witches. If you cross their path wrongly, they're liable to curse you with whatever they feel like. With my shifter blood, we're supposed to be able to burn through hexes, but it's rumored that one witch is more powerful than any other to walk among the rest.

Maybe it was even the leader of the coven that lives on my father's pack land. I know he uses them in whatever cunning way works best for his gain. He probably knows I'm gone by now. He likely manipulated his witch to do this to me.

Kane pounds in and out. I can't even enjoy it for the

pressure mounting behind my eyes, at the base of my skull, the heaviness sitting on my chest, the ache in my bones, or the sound of my own blood rushing to only Fate knows where.

"Kane." My fingers flex, digging my claws deeper.

My vision blurs, but the feel of fur spouting between my digits is unmistakable. My back arches as my head tips back. My eyes slam shut, but the heat continues to climb, getting ten times hotter with my next breath. Squeezing them tight does nothing. *I can't breathe.*

Jesus Christ, what the fuck is happening?

Stars dance behind my eyes, and just when I've accepted it's all about to end, it does.

Teeth sink into my shoulder between my collarbone and deep into the muscles on the backside, claiming me. My eyes fly open while I pull with all my strength to keep Kane fused to me. I've always heard the claiming bite is the worst pain imaginable, but this is anything but. The heat left me the second his canines broke skin, my lungs filling with air again.

An orgasm so pleasurable rips through me, going on and on so long my mouth opens and unintellectual words spew out in a moan I'm not even ashamed of.

When everything ebbs away, Kane stills inside me. After a beat, he pulls away, then his face comes into view above me. No fur covers his flesh other than the hairs along his lower abdomen, his forearms, and the thick, trimmed beard on his beautiful face.

His eyes skate to his mark, but with the blink of an eye, his amber stare is back on mine. "Let's talk about that tomorrow. I need more, Kate."

There's more volubility in his irises than I've seen before.

He's always been a master at shielding his thoughts from me, but right now, everything is on full display. His guilt, for one, but so much more than just that. He does want me, and he's letting me see just how much. There's a settledness inside him but also need and desire. He does want more, and so do I.

Lifting my back off the bed, I stop a hair's breadth from his face. He's being real with me, so I decide right then and there to give him all of me as well. "I don't think I'll ever stop wanting more, Kane."

And with that truth, I grab his arms and flip us so that I'm on top, straddling his hips. Kane's dick hardens back inside me as if my words sent all his blood straight to his monster cock. Then I move. Slow at first, finding a rhythm that feels so good I don't ever want to stop fucking the man or the wolf under me.

So, we fuck.

We fuck so much that time stands still, or I lose track of the hours we're connected as one. I give him everything I have and still continue to push my limits, needing more. Wanting to claim him the way he marked me as his. But he said we'd talk about that tomorrow, so even though my wolf kept urging me to bite him back, I didn't. Even though my gums ached and my canines kept elongating, I kept my mouth closed except for when he was kissing me or had his dick plunging down my throat.

Fucking continued. Me on top of him, then him on top of me. At one point, Kane's dick was buried inside me, pumping in and out while one thumb was in my mouth and another finger was deep in my ass, fucking all of my holes so thoroughly that I never wanted it to stop.

We kept going at it for so long that fucking felt like it was much more than fucking...

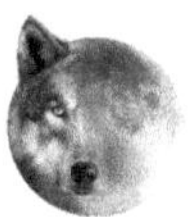

Hours later, when we're spent, and the sun has been up for who knows how long, and I'm lying wrapped in Kane's arms, I feel settled for the first time in my life. Maybe it's the claiming mark on my neck or the solace I feel being here among his pack, in his cabin. Or maybe it's the woods surrounding us and the seclusion they bring.

Then again, we have woods and an even bigger forest back home, so it's not that. Still, there is something right about this place, this land, Kane's people. The only thing missing is my brother.

You only have a few hours to show, Trez. I will come find you if I have to. Please be okay.

"Why don't you like your pack?" Back at the house last night, you mentioned that. I'm curious as to why?"

Kane's question flips my thoughts away from the doubt and dread running amok through my head.

"There's no one in my pack I like except Trez. The men are all chauvinistic assholes. The women are weak and afraid. The pups grow up learning how to be one of the two. Dick is the worst of them all, or maybe his beta is. They're a coin toss, but I do know we should have ditched our pack years ago. We don't fit. It's like we were born into the wrong pack, I guess you could say."

It's the truth. A sad truth, but a reality, nonetheless.

I may not easily bend to my father's will, but I still

stayed. I still obeyed to a degree. I put up with his bullshit rules for too long.

No more.

Never again.

"You hate your dad that much?"

A growl rumbles from deep inside me. "He's my alpha, not my father. Besides, Dick isn't for women's empowerment. How am I supposed to trust or follow an alpha who doesn't see my worth to the pack? If Trez and I had left, I wouldn't be wondering if my brother is alive or dead."

Or which lies my father fed our pack and me. Or why.

There's no way he wouldn't have known the ashes in that urn weren't his son's. I don't even want to think about the person that was inside. The witch. She likely had a family too. Do they know she is no longer part of this world?

Is Dick responsible for her life ending, or was Henrik?

"Trez can hold his own. He isn't weak, Kate."

No, he's not. And that's the only truth I know at this time.

"Doesn't change the fact that I need to find him and figure out what he wouldn't tell me a week ago."

"What do you mean? And what did you mean by Trez being in your head? I didn't forget that slip of the tongue." There is an edge to his voice. A hardness unmistakable of an alpha that's suspicious.

"Before my brother took off for a run, he told me there was something he needed to tell me. After he left, he never returned, so I have no idea what he knew, but I do know it was something big. There was sadness in his eyes, but fear and hatred too." I sigh and roll onto my back, Kane's arm trapped beneath me. "I should have made him tell me."

"And the other?" he questions, not letting the smallest detail go unanswered.

Rolling to his side, he pins me to the bed with his stare.

Blowing out a breath, I finally glance up and say, "Not something I have enough control to speak of without bolting to go find my brother. If he isn't here by nightfall, I'll tell you, and then I'm going in search of him, but right now, give me a few more hours of reprieve."

For several long seconds, we're locked in a battle of wills. Kane's instincts are telling him to demand an answer. Mine are begging him to let it go a little while longer.

In the end, I win out, or I suppose he lets me keep my secret because his head dips in acknowledgment a breath before his lips connect with mine. A heartbeat later, he rolls on top of me while his hand goes between us, positioning himself at my opening. Kane enters my body in a fast jolt forward, and once again, my head clears of everything and everyone except him.

And damn, is it more than I'd ever imagined in my dreams. It's a feeling I never want to lose. He was wrong when he claimed the way he fucks is both heaven and hell. This is pure bliss. It's heaven on earth.

The only thing I can imagine being better than the way he feels inside me is experiencing my teeth sinking into Kane's neck.

10

KANE

Hours after the sun has risen to its highest peak, my sated body begins to stir. A sense of calmness I haven't experienced in years settles in my bones. The heaviness in my chest is gone.

My wolf's head pops up, his cocky smirk staring back at me like I'm the dumbass that can't put two and two together. He huffs through his snout to drive his point home, which has my eyes popping open and my thoughts echoing: *what's changed?*

Delicate snoring tickles my eardrum to my left. My chest expands, and I pull in air through my mouth, her scent coating my insides.

Kate.

Everything from last night and this morning comes rolling back through my head. The way she feels when I'm inside her. The sexy sounds she makes. The taste of her skin, her essence. Our bodies joined, making me feel stronger than I ever have. Not having to hold back...

I roll onto my left side, putting most of my weight on my

elbow. She's sleeping on her front side with her long blonde locks covering her face and the top half of her back and shoulders. Her breathing is even as her back lifts and falls in a hypnotic pattern. I could stare at her forever and not tire of the sight before me.

Moving my right hand to the side of her face, I gently pull the strands of her hair away, allowing me to see more of her stunning beauty. She doesn't stir, and I can't blame her. The hours we fucked, it felt like we went at it for days. Being between her thighs blew every fantasy I've ever had out of the water.

My knuckles run across rough skin along her neck a beat before Kate's face turns into a grimace, and a whimper of pain slips from her still swollen lips. My eyes flick down. That's when the memory of my wolf forcing his way through me to bite her returns, flashing through my head. It happened so fast I couldn't stop him from claiming her, from forcing me to claim her.

He pushed me to make her ours, but I wouldn't do it. I still had enough sense about me to know I couldn't take it that far. Not to mention, it should always be a conversation beforehand, even with mates, to make sure both want the same thing.

I told her we'd talk about it today, but I still have no idea how to rectify what I've already done. And apparently, I'm even more of an asshole because I never healed her wound. The bite is deep. It's angry. My wolf didn't show her an ounce of mercy, and the last thing I want is for it to get infected because he refused to control himself.

Maybe I need to seek Storm out for advice. To see if she knows of a way to undo a claiming that neither of us agreed to. Kate isn't my mate. I'm not hers, but she bears a mark that

I'm responsible for. If I heal the wound soon enough with my saliva, that could mean minimal scaring or no scar at all.

It's odd that her shifter abilities haven't already kicked in to start the healing process, but then the bite was from an alpha wolf. Still, I need to heal it. It's the right thing to do. It's what I should have done as soon as I retook control from my wolf the second I'd seen the bite instead of forcing it from my head and continuing to enjoy Kate's heat.

Leaning down, I brush more of her hair away from the side of her face, sliding the strands across her back. My tongue inches out, licking her jagged, raw skin, but something on her back catches my attention. My eyes dart over her as a moan from Kate's lips tickles my ear. It's a tattoo between her shoulder blades.

The shimmering silver of a wolf's head makes me pause my aid to her wound. Lifting my head, I take in the whole of the design. A silver wolf blended into a full moon that I know all too well. Both are encased in a thick circle that's more faded than the beast and moon. There are familiar symbols inside the inked circle, though I can't place where I've seen them before. But it's the Marked Crest tattooed on Kate's back that rips a growl from me, not my wolf.

It's an almost copy of the Bloodmoon crest I have tattooed on the upper part of my left shoulder, only the full moon is reddish-orange and the wolf doesn't shimmer that sickening silver metallic.

For all her claimed hatred of her father and his pack over the years, the fact that she bears the silver wolf that represents Richard Everhart's pack speaks volumes above her words. Last night, she told me they don't fit in with their pack, that she and Trez were born into the wrong pack.

Clearly, that was a lie, or she wouldn't have had my enemy's wolf tattooed on her flesh.

Has she played me this whole time? I don't want to believe the thoughts thundering against my head, but the proof is inked on her skin.

A warning growl comes from my wolf, but it's not aimed at the woman in my bed. His issue is with me, and that pisses me off. He already sees her as ours, and that can't happen. He's protective of *her*.

"Kane," Kate whispers, her tone sleepy, but there's also contentment in her voice that's hard to ignore. My wolf notices it too. For her, he smiles. For me, he snarls.

Flexing her hand, she finds my naked thigh and runs her palm up my leg.

I jump off the bed so fast I would have gotten tangled in the covers had they been covering us instead of piled on the floor at the foot. Pressure builds inside my chest while the pounding behind my eyes thunders. I'm unsure if it's my wolf's doing or the guilt creeping up my spine.

I've never fucked another wolf shifter for a reason. My mate was missing, is missing. It was always supposed to be Anna. Not Kate. Not anyone else. Just Anna. Now, my stupid fucking wolf has screwed everything to hell. He bit the wrong woman. He claimed someone he did not have the right to take. An enemy, nonetheless.

Kate rolls over onto her back and sits up. "What the hell, Kane?"

My wolf growls, but only I can hear him. It's low but lethal. He's angry—with me.

There's worry etched across her beautiful face. The first instinct that comes to mind is to fix it. Take her concern away, but that isn't something *I* can do. It's not something I'm willing to do.

She should be worried.

My own anger swirls around me. It clouds my vision. The blood pulsing through the veins behind my ears roars. It's all I can hear as the noise grows louder with each passing second.

"What's wrong?" she asks, looking from me and then around the room as if she doesn't know what spooked me before her round eyes land back on my face. "Say something, Kane."

"Your brother isn't missing, is he?" My spine steels. My shoulders roll back. My chin lifts. Distrust sinks so deep inside me while my wolf pushes against the cage I trapped him inside. "Otherwise, you would have left last night after I told you the ashes weren't his."

The truth coils around me, choking me. She played me. *But why?*

Why plant the seed that Trez might be dead?

Was he even my friend?

"What are you talking about? Yes, Trez is missing. I don't know where my brother is. I told him I'd give him until tonight to show up, and if he didn't—"

"There you go again. So, you've spoken to him. You know he's alive." My tongue clucks as a humorless laugh falls from my mouth. "Why are you really here?"

"You know why."

"If I had to guess, I would say certain members of my pack were right all along. Your father sent you here for a reason. What reason was that? What did he have to gain? Is he looking for another war?"

Kate is off the bed so fast her naked body is standing in

front of me before I can blink. Her speed could rival a vampire, but it's her warmth that wraps around me, reminding me of every second I spent connected with her very much alive and beautiful body that makes me take a step away.

Kate follows, eating up the distance between us.

"Dick is not my father," she says so adamantly a growl rumbles behind her words. "Maybe technically he is, but I have never loved that man. Never respected him. Never obeyed him unless he forced me to do so." Her palms lift, and before I step back again, she shoves me away, my back connecting to the closed bathroom door. "Fuck you, Kane. Fuck you for whatever this is. For whatever has you regretting last night. At least be a man and admit your guilt. Don't accuse me of bullshit."

"Bullshit is tricking me into wanting you. You sure played the long game well. I'll give you that."

My wolf slams against his bars, my chest wall. The sheer force feels like a boulder nailing me center mast. It fucking hurts.

"*You* bit *me*."

"It was the blood moon. You are not my mate." My wolf snarls at me from within, disagreeing or pissed that I'm using the moon as an excuse. But it was him... not me.

"You claimed me!" Kate shouts, her mouth open and her eyes full of emotions that make my knees weaken. It takes loosening my hold on my wolf to prevent myself from going to the floor.

"I don't fucking want you. It wasn't real, Kate."

"You expect me to believe that you don't feel it?"

"I don't feel shit for you. My wolf wanted you, not me. It was the total lunar eclipse with the full moon. That's all."

"The only way you wouldn't be able to control your wolf, your instincts, Kane, is if I'm your fated mate." Her statement sends a shockwave with a magnitude that could level a building straight to my eardrum. Anger coils at the base of my skull.

"I know who my fucking mate is, and she isn't you." I reach forward, snatching her by the throat. My fingers squeeze, but my claws won't extend. Doesn't matter. I can still get my point across. "Get out of my house. Out of my fucking pack. And if you or any other Marked Crest wolf enters my territory again, I'll kill you myself."

I push her away before I do the opposite. Before I kiss her instead of running her off.

"Get the fuck out. Now!"

Standing feet from me, her shoulders roll back. She stares, her eyes darkening. "You're a fucking coward. I hate you."

"Good. Leave."

She turns. By the time I blink, she's no longer in my bedroom, but with my supernatural hearing, I hear every step she takes. They're like knives, stabbing me in the chest, over and over, faster and faster, deeper with each thrust.

When the front door slams, my knees finally give out. I go down fast, my wolf ripping me apart from the inside.

My head pounds.

My heart stops.

Everything goes dark.

11

KATE

I wasn't going to let him see me break, but as soon as the door closed and my wolf shifted, my heart shattered into a million pieces. The tears came. Then, the dam I tried to hold in broke.

I sank into the darkest corner of my head, and I cried. And while my wolf ran back to the lodge, I felt the weight of his rejection, the loss of the other half of me I'd never allowed myself to imagine existed. His words and the look in his stare ripped me apart.

Maybe Kane is right.

Maybe I'm not his mate. Maybe he's not mine, but that wasn't what my gut was saying. When he bit me, there was pleasure on a whole new level. A connection took root deep inside me that I'll never be able to sever. I'll never rid myself of the parts of him he left in me.

I wanted to mark him in return. Claim him as mine. But I cowered back into the girl I was at fifteen. The kid who was insanely attracted to a man she had no business feeling things for. The teenager who stupidly tried to repeatedly prove she could match his strength and intelligence better than anyone else.

Why can't it be *me?*

Why isn't it *me?*

I've never seen him or anyone in the Bloodmoon pack as my enemy.

I've never lied to any of them. It's impossible to lie to Kane. Something inside me won't allow it when it comes so easily with my pack.

Fuck him for insinuating that Trez and I came here all those years ago to spy for our alpha. Kane doesn't know me at all if he thinks I'd infiltrate his pack at Dick's order.

Fuck Richard Everhart too. We didn't ask to be born into his pack. We didn't ask to be saddled with him for a father.

Our pack has treated us like outcasts for as long as I can remember. I thought Dante's pack was different.

Before Kane and Jag ran the Bloodmoon pack, it was Dante and Elijah. They were weary at first but welcoming all the same. I didn't think they saw us as wolves from the enemy pack once they got to know us.

Annalise, Jagger's mom, was always the nicest to me. If anyone, she should have been the least open to me. She knew I liked Kane, and I knew she was his mate's mother.

She never held my attraction to Kane against me, but we also didn't speak about her daughter. Annalise taught me how to bake. Becca, Kane's mother, taught me how to apply makeup.

No one in my pack had ever made an effort with Trez or me. I learned how to love more than just my brother that first winter in Moonwake. The second winter here, I learned to love myself; to want more.

Every night since our first return to Rivermoon, I

dreamed I was born into this pack, not mine. But when daylight came, I could pretend no more. Like now, with the setting sun, the facade is over. I'll never be one of them, but I can't be a member of Dick's pack any longer either.

I have to find Trez.

I will find my brother, and when I do, we'll finally be our own pack, living by our own rules, finding our own path—together.

Just us.

We don't need anyone else.

"What's wrong?" Jagger demands.

After I ran through the wolf door and into the lodge, I snagged my bag that was lying on the floor where Kane must have dropped it and leaped into the bathroom to change. When I was as presentable as possible, I slung my backpack over my shoulder and walked back through the living area.

I knew Jagger was in the kitchen when I ran through, but out of all our kind, I couldn't shift back into my human form in front of him. Like Trez, he feels more like a brother than the rest of them.

Stopping in front of him, I toss my bag onto the counter and take the deepest breath I can force down my throat. His arms are resting at his sides. He's in jeans and a plain white T-shirt with motorcycle boots adorning his feet.

"I have to go." I sniffle, forcing my emotions to bottle back up. "But I need you to promise me something first."

"You're crying. Why?" His brows furrow.

"That's not important." I swallow the lump in my throat, unable to control the tremble in my lower lip. Overwhelmed with the need for something—I'm not sure what—I jump forward, wrapping both arms around Jagger's neck and squeezing like my life depends on it. To my surprise, he hugs me back, tightening his hands around my back.

"You don't cry, Kate," he says as if it's a fact.

If only that were true.

"No, I do—more than I care to admit. I just don't let anyone see my tears. Not even Trez."

"Then why are you letting me?"

Because if I don't let some of this pain out, I'm going to find myself in a fetal position, I think to myself.

To Jagger, I say, "If I had another friend besides my brother, you'd be it. I'm going to miss you," which is as true as the former statement.

"What are you talking about? We are friends."

"No, we're not, because... because I'll always be one of them. I'll forever be a Marked Crest wolf. I can't change my DNA, and that makes us enemies."

"Why the fuck are you saying this?" He pulls back but doesn't let me go. His piercing blue eyes find mine, his stare searching as seconds pass between us.

I don't want to leave.

"Because it's true. Your alpha knows it. Your pack even knows it, but if there is an ounce of anything akin to friendship, please don't let anyone hurt Trez. If he shows up here looking for me, swear to me that you won't let anyone kill him."

Jag jerks backward, blinking, but I can't go without his oath. I grab ahold of his arms, not letting go.

I know my brother is out there, and I will find him, but he could very well show up here before I can get to him first.

"Promise me, Jagger. Say that you won't allow anyone to cause harm to Trez."

"I won't let anyone hurt him." A growl leaves his lips. "For the record, I'd never let anyone in my pack hurt Trez, but you need to tell me how the fuck you just did that?" His eyes are wide, unblinking like he's seeing the impossible.

"I didn't do anything. I have to go now."

"You did, but, fuck, I don't understand how. I have to call Kane. You aren't going any—"

"Shhh." I put two fingers against his lips, silencing him. "Kane doesn't want me here. We shouldn't have come here in the first place. I'm sorry for that. Trust me, I'll be sorry for that for the rest of my life."

I grip him by the shoulders again and yank him to me, then wrapping my arms around Jag, I give him a final hug goodbye, squeezing with all the strength I can muster and hoping he feels the friendship I thought we had. The one I'll mourn for the rest of my life.

"Thank you for giving me your word. I'm going to hold you to it." My voice cracks. "I'm going to miss you, okay? Tell Ash I said bye, and tell your mom…"

I loosen my arms, and after a breath, I step backward, dropping them to my sides. Jagger's eyes are still wide, but he remains tight-lipped.

"I-I don't know why I mentioned your mom." I shake my head. "She was just always nice to me, I guess." I take another step back, waiting for him to say something, but when he doesn't, I turn and swipe my backpack from the counter, swinging it around both arms. "Don't forget me, okay?"

He takes a step toward me, his arms lifting to reach out.

"Stay," I say quickly, and as if I'd commanded it, he drops his arms. "Don't come after me. This is the way it has to be. I don't belong here, right?" When he doesn't respond, I nod in understanding as my eyes close. In the same breath, I swallow back everything I'm feeling, everything that's telling me not to leave. My wolf howls in protest.

I pivot, and I'm out the door before I do something stupid like run back to Kane's cabin instead of Canada. I jump on my bike and start the engine as the pressure in my chest intensifies, and something inside me tugs.

There's a howl in the distance that forces a shiver down my spine and has my eyes jerking in that direction. It's not just any wolf. There's only one I feel so far inside he can rattle the deepest part of my being.

Kicking the kickstand off the ground, I grip the throttle and twist. The tires spin the gravel underneath as the bike propels forward. There's another agonizing roar. The rumble of the engine lessens the impact on my ears yet does nothing to loosen the grip on my heart or the throbbing where his mark resides.

My wolf wanted you, not me.

That's what he said. His wolf claimed me. He didn't. He doesn't want me, and like hell if I'm going to trade one pack that doesn't respect me for another. Especially one that sees me as the enemy when I've done nothing to give anyone an inkling that I have ill-willed intentions toward the Bloodmoon Pack.

My worth is more than that. I won't settle for anything less than being a partner's equal. I want it all.

A best friend.

A lover.

Someone that'll have my back and know that I will have theirs just the same.

I want someone who chooses me.

Who takes my side above anyone else's, but also someone that'll call me on my bullshit when I need it. Not to embarrass or demean me but to help me see things from a different perspective.

I'd hoped that person was Kane, but clearly, I was wrong. It's not like I can dwell on that fact. I have my brother to find, and if Dick or Henrik did something, they will pay with their lives.

12

KANE

I don't know how long I was blacked out. Seconds. Minutes. Hours. I haven't the first clue.

By the time I came to, it was pitch black in the sky. I woke in the middle of the trail on pack land, naked and covered in dirt. Payback from my wolf for locking him inside my body like it was a prison cell. My throat was parched and sore. My calves and the top of my thighs were throbbing.

He must have howled and run a marathon the way my body aches. Not that it wasn't every bit of what I deserved.

Kate.

A sense of dread, or maybe foreboding, crashed into me as hard as the waves breaking against the rocks not far from where I was.

Everything that happened between us replayed in my head like a horror movie. The words I'd said to her like daggers driving into my chest one at a time, over and over.

My dad taught me when I was young to never say something I don't wholly mean. But that's exactly what I did. That wasn't the only thing I recall from my adolescence. At that moment, I remembered the time when my alpha taught a group of us about the Birds and Bees—shifter edition. It was a lesson on recognizing when a female wolf shifter is going into heat.

It was the cringiest moment of my life: my father describing my mom going into heat for the first time. I could swear on my life it would explain what happened last night between Kate and me to a T. Yet, I know that's impossible. She isn't of age.

Right?

Of course, I'm right. Because if I'm wrong...

Fuck, it would damn near be impossible for her not to have gotten pregnant. My wolf wouldn't have allowed us to stop going at it until he was sure his seed had fertilized her egg.

Mate or not, it's still possible and very likely to impregnate another shifter during her heat cycle. That was why we were taught the same thing year after year. Dad wanted to ensure his wolves knew the consequences of sticking our dicks inside another shifter if we planned to wait to start a family with our fated mate.

I thought for sure we'd eventually find Anna. We've scoured the world more times over than I can count, and still, she and my brother remain missing.

How can fate be that cruel? Giving me a mate, only for her to disappear and then dangle Kate in front of me like the forbidden fruit. Anna was too young. I never developed feelings for her the way I have Kate.

With Anna, my head tells me she's mine. With Kate, it's my heart that craves her every second of every day. When Kate isn't near, something in me is missing. I feel half-empty inside.

I can't have them both. Nor do I desire two women. I want Kate to be the one, my mate, but she isn't. And what if we do find Anna? I can't choose another over her. I won't do that to her. I made a vow I have every intention of honoring.

Even if I'm going to pine for another for the rest of my supernatural life.

AFTER I TREKKED BACK to my cabin, I showered and put on clean clothes. My wolf refused to shift, and I'd been closer to my hideaway than I was to the lodge.

When I finally take the steps up to the lodge, I hear a voice in a delicate female tone I've come to feel as protective over as I do any of my wolves.

Stopping in front of the door, I turn and watch Storm jog up the steps toward me.

"Got a minute?" she asks.

Ambient lights are strung across the front of the porch, along the ceiling and railing. It lights up her pretty face, showing me evidence of where she recently cried. A low growl rumbles up my chest in displeasure.

"What's wrong?" I demand in too harsh of a tone.

"The urn," she reminds me with a shrug.

I'd forgotten Jag and Ash dropped it off with her last night while I was with Kate, doing things I don't regret despite what I said, and deep down, I know she believed every word.

Fuck, I'm a royal dick and then some.

"Come inside." I gesture with a nod to the door as I press

the lever with my thumb, opening the door and waiting for her to enter in front of me. "Tell me what you discovered."

Closing the door, my eyes snap to the kitchen sink, where Jagger splashes water over his face and neck. Hearing us enter, he grabs the hand towel lying on the counter, then turns to face us as he scrubs the cloth down his face.

"Where the hell have you been?" His eyes are round with confusion but also anger is clouding his hardened stare. He tosses the towel behind him, and it drops into the sink.

I raise my arm, halting him with the palm of my hand facing him.

"Tell me, Storm," I say in a calm manner.

"Ashleigh said your wolf shifter friend from out of town brought it here. What pack is she from?"

"Kate is a Marked Crest wolf. That's common knowledge," I add, feeling defensive on Kate's behalf. I said she was my enemy, but that's never been true, even if it should be. Trez, either, despite my threat. It's the only one I've ever made that I'd never carry out.

I can't. I love them both for reasons I cannot explain to myself or my pack.

"I didn't know that," she claims. "I'm not exactly friendly with anyone besides Ash and Maddy, you know."

That's true. Storm is timid around most of the pack. She keeps to herself even though I've invited her to every pack get-together we've done except for when we run.

I suppose she's only sociable with Ashleigh and Maddy because she shares a cabin with them. Being roommates might make it difficult if you aren't on friendly terms. Storm and Maddy are the same age and have a lot in common, so it makes sense they'd be friends. Maddy is also a human who doesn't have supernatural strength like the rest of us.

I've always thought Storm's shy demeanor was a defense mechanism. Her eyes are brown and bold. Her long, sandy blonde hair, which she keeps covering her front, is straight. She wears long dresses that cover her skin except for her hands and neckline. Her appearance is guarded, but from day one, I've sensed great power within her. It's only grown stronger since she arrived three years ago, just after I became alpha.

"Did you recognize the remains? I know the person was a witch. A female. Did you know her?" I ask.

A thunderstorm flickers through her eyes, lightning flashing within her irises. Only witches that possess the water element can do that. It happens when their emotions are raw and uncontrolled. Storm has all elements: water, fire, wind, and earth. She's the least uncontrolled witch I've ever met.

"They're my mother's."

Jagger gasps at the same time a curse slips from my lips.

"Fuck. Had I known, I wouldn't have sent them over the way I did. I'm sorry. Fuck. I don't know what to say," I admit.

"Did you know she was..." Jagger trails off, not wanting to finish his question.

She shakes her head in reply.

"My former coven resides in Kate's pack territory. If they sent her to deliver the ashes then my coven leader knows where I am. It means I'm not safe here anymore. I have to—"

"Stop," I command as I grab her shoulders and squeeze them gently. "I promised you safety. I meant it then, and I mean it now. You are safe with us."

After a breath, she finally nods, but I see the lie in her

eyes. She doesn't believe she's safe, and that washes down my back like molten lava. Everyone in my care should feel protected by Jagger and me.

"Kate thought the ashes might be her brother's," I tell her. "She brought them to me to find out if his remains were inside. She didn't know they belonged to a witch. To your mom."

"Are you certain? Because if you aren't, I need to leave. For your pack's safety as much as mine." Her voice grows urgent. "Salem will use Kate's pack to get to me if she has to. She's the worst kind of witch, Kane. She's more powerful than you can imagine. She's pure evil. A dark witch."

"We're certain, Storm," Jagger answers for me as he walks toward us. "Kate isn't like her pack. Neither is her brother. They're our friends," he bites out, the edge in his tone telling me that last bit was for me, not the witch among us. Storm swallows as Jag flicks his blue eyes on me. "We need to talk. Now."

"I have a sister," Storm blurts out. "When I left, my mother wouldn't come, and Ivy was too young to decide for herself. I have to get her from them." Terror and worry swarm within her, the thunder in her eyes growing stronger, causing a gust of wind to open the front door, slamming it into the wall behind her.

"We'll get in touch with Kate. We'll help you find Ivy," I tell her, knowing I have to find Kate anyway. I can't leave things the way I left them. I have to right my wrongs even if she doesn't forgive me for what I said, for what I did...

"Are you sure about that?" Jagger spits, a snarl firmly in my place as he stares me down. "When I said we needed to talk, it wasn't a request."

"If you were anyone else, you wouldn't be standing right

now," I say too calmly for the rage he sparked. My alpha eyes flash. I see the color change in the reflection of my beta's eyes, but he doesn't flinch.

"If you were anyone else, I would have ripped your fucking throat out already."

My spine straightens, my eyes widening, shocked at his admission. Jagger's temper has always matched mine, but he's harder to rile up than I am. He's my voice of reason. It's why there was never a choice as to who would be my beta. My best friend knows me better than anyone, the same as I know him.

That's how I know he knows what happened between Kate and me, or he at least knows part of it. They've always been close, but for him to take her side without hearing mine? That's unacceptable as the beta of *our* pack. As *my* best friend.

A warning growl leaves my mouth through clenched teeth. A fight between us may be what I need. We've had plenty over the years, just none since we took our places as leaders of the pack.

"Should I leave?" Storm voices.

Neither of us blinks or looks away from the other. We may tie up in here tonight, but Storm has nothing to fear. We're coordinated fighters. She won't get hurt.

Jagger's claws extend, his growl louder, provoking me. My beast is nowhere in sight, still refusing to acknowledge me. He can stay mad all he wants. I don't need his help to defeat my beta, to make Jag submit. I can do that all on my own.

"You really want to do this?" I ask.

"No," he spits out, shaking his head slowly. "But you shouldn't have made Kate cry."

His admission is sobering, but at the same time, if you'd asked me two days ago, the thought of Kate crying would be laughable. But I saw her. I saw her eyes when I told her to get out, that I didn't want her, that I'd kill her if she returned. I hurt her worse than anyone else ever has. I damaged her the same as I damaged myself.

But by Fate, I hope we're not unrepairable.

Heavy footsteps behind me cause me to whip my body around to tell whichever shifter is here to piss off when I see my dad standing in the open doorway.

"We've found our wolves."

13
KANE

"You've found them?" I repeat, my voice coming out less like an alpha and more like the boy I was when Trey and Anna were taken. "Where? Are they here?"

News I waited so long to hear. Only there's no elation coursing through me the way there should be. Sorrow and a sinking feeling in the pit of my stomach are all I'm experiencing now.

There was a time when I begged daily for their return, for Anna and my brother to be found. Then Kate and Trez appeared, and I no longer prayed to a higher power for our mates to be located. We still looked. I had a sense of duty. I wanted to find them, but over time, Anna and Trey weren't my first thoughts when I woke in the morning, nor my last thoughts when I shut my eyes.

Kate was. And now...

"I meant, we think we know where they are. It's our last option. The only place left I know to search." My dad combs his hand through his dirty blond hair. It's longer on top than when I saw him nine weeks ago. His beard is still neat and trimmed, but he looks tired and worn out.

When words fail me, he answers my unspoken question. "British Columbia."

I swallow the lump taking form in my throat.

"That was the first place you searched," I say, knowing damn well he told us so himself.

"We had scouts comb *his* territory. We never stepped foot within those borders ourselves. Maybe if I had… Fuck." He sighs. "I need to talk to Kate or Trez. Both preferably. Do either of…" Dad steps forward, his shoulders pulling back. He sniffs the air. He smells her. He knows she was here.

"She isn't here. She's gone," I say more to myself than to him. Kate is gone, and now, with this news, she certainly can't ever return. I won't allow it. I won't bring my mate home only for her to be forced to live in a pack where *the other woman* visits each year.

"Then get her the fuck back here, Kane. There are things I need to know before I declare war on a pack that almost annihilated us thirty-five years ago."

"She isn't going to return for Kane," Jag states matter-of-factly, his attitude grating on my nerves.

I turn my head, eyeing him, wanting to knock the shit out of him even though he's right.

"You don't know what happened. Maybe you know her version of it, but why the fuck are you automatically pissed off at me and taking her side when I'm your goddamn alpha? Your loyalty belongs here, not to a Marked Crest wolf," I spit in his face.

"How old are Kate and Trez?" Storm asks almost too quietly, but with shifter hearing, she knows we heard her.

"Twenty," my dad answers while Jag and I are locked in a stare-down. Neither of us is giving an inch.

"If you'd shut your fucking mouth for a minute and hear me out when I said we needed to talk, then you'd fucking know, Kane." Jagger balls his fists at his sides, and knowing my best friend the way I do, he wants to hit me. Maybe more than I want to punch him in the mouth.

"Someone explain what the hell is going on," Dad demands, his former alpha role showing in his tone. "What happened when Kate was here?"

"The *alpha*," Jagger bites out, "fucked her and then kicked her to the curb after he'd had his fill."

My eyes flash, changing. A lethal growl, slow and measured with purpose, leaks from my mouth. Jagger's body goes deadly still, his arms locking to his sides. I snarl, increasing my control, making him feel the heaviness of my power weighing on his shoulders, his chest, the pounding thundering in his head so loud all he can do is grit his teeth and lower his eyes.

I've never used my abilities on my beta, my best friend. I never thought I would need to.

He can speak. I didn't cut off his breathing ability. He could even fight against my power over him if he wanted, and he does, but he also doesn't.

"She said that?" I ask.

"Let him go, Kane," my father says. I don't bother acknowledging the demand he no longer has the right to issue.

When my father stepped down as our alpha, he wasn't mentally ready to give up his leadership role. It wasn't his time to retire. He only relinquished because the need to find his younger son and my mate weighed heavy in his heart.

He's struggled for far too long, feeling like a failure in locating his wolves, our wolves.

When I became alpha, I felt his emotions as if they were my own. He truly believes he let down his wife, his best friend, Annalise, Jagger and me, the pack. He carries too much self-loathing regarding my missing brother and Jagger's sister. It wasn't his fault. No one should have been able to enter our territory without us knowing, let alone take two wolf pups without anyone aware it was happening.

I told him before he left this last time that he was never a failure, but he didn't want to hear it. In all fairness, I understand why he feels the way he does. I think the same. I haven't found them either.

"What did she say, Jagger?" I bite out.

"I'm sorry to interject, but is it possible for Kate and Trez to be your missing—"

"No." My father and I bark at the same time Jagger answers with, "Maybe," followed by a deep growl.

I pull the power back, releasing my hold on my beta.

Dad's stare flips to Jag, his eyes squinting, but he shakes his head and turns his focus back on Storm.

"Trez isn't my son. If he were Trey, I would know. Kate's spent enough time with Annalise. If she were her daughter, she would have felt it, smelled it, sensed it. They aren't our wolves," he says with such vigor that it's almost as if the force is meant to reassure himself, giving me pause for the briefest moment.

But then Jagger opens his mouth again, shaking the remnants of my lingering power off before stepping back and pulling my gaze to his.

"Unless they are, and they've been under our nose this whole fucking time." He grits his teeth and balls his fist so tight that his emotions send a shockwave down the inside of my forearms straight to my palms.

"Jagger, they aren't ours. I had their blood tested to be sure," Dad reveals, severing my connection to my beta.

"When did you do that? And how come I never knew about it?" I ask, not the least bit okay with being kept in the dark on something this important.

"You weren't alpha back then. Elijah asked me to do it when he saw Annalise getting too close to Kate. He wanted proof his wife couldn't ignore."

"Then explain how Kate placed her fingers over my lips, and suddenly my fucking voice was gone. Or how she told me to stay like a dog so I wouldn't stop her from leaving, or how I couldn't move my feet for over three goddamn hours."

I can shield my state of mind from my pack, but I can't always block experiencing their emotions, so when Jag's eyes go from my Dad to me, his feelings hit my chest like a ton of bricks. He's at war with himself, feeling like he's being split into two pieces. It hurts me the same as it torments him.

"That's impossible," my father answers while I stare, trying to figure out why he thinks he's being torn apart.

"Well, I guess it's not." Jag's stare flips to mine. "Her eyes glowed blood-orange. It only lasted a second, two at the most, but I saw what I saw. Explain that, *Alpha*."

"That would only happen if—"

"My wolf bit her," I say, cutting off my dad, knowing that's the only plausible explanation.

"You claimed her?" Dad's eyes visibly widen in front of me, shocked, perhaps even horrified, as they should be.

"No!" I shout, the word sour on my tongue. "I have a mate, and it's not Kate."

"You bit her and then rejected her?" Jagger growls, his face reddening as his blue eyes darken.

"Kate bears Richard's pack crest tattooed on her back. She claimed to hate her father but permanently inked herself as one of them. She is our enemy, the same as all the rest. No, I didn't reject her, but I didn't solidify the bond either. She didn't bite me. Nothing was sealed."

"What the fuck, Kane?!" my father says, all but screaming at me.

"My wolf wanted her and took someone that wasn't his. He didn't have the right. Yes, I told her to leave. She doesn't belong here. For all we know, she could have known where my brother and mate were all along. Kate isn't my fated mate. Her wound will heal. The claim my wolf wanted will fade. It's time for us to focus on finding our missing wolves. If any of them get in our way, we make good on the promise I issued before she left."

"Which was what?" Dad asks, anger laced in his voice.

"You really told her you'd kill her and even Trez, didn't you?" Jagger accuses.

"Yes. And I meant it." I didn't mean it, but fuck, it's the way it has to be. What's done is done.

My father looks horrified at my admission.

"That's a problem, brother." Jagger stares, waiting for me to push him further.

"They're our enemy," I say again, this time more adamantly. "I ignored that fact for too long. So did you. We made our pack ignore it. No more. Kate is one of them. But if I find out she did know about Anna and Trey, that she knows where they've been this whole time, you better believe I'll make good on that promise. I'll kill them all."

I'll have to. I'm the alpha. If it has to be done, it'll be done by me and me alone.

"Her pack may be our enemy, but she is not. Trez isn't. Let's be clear on that because my wolf won't allow anyone, even you, to harm them. That's something else she did," he informs me, a bitter taste on his tongue. "She used her alpha power to force me to promise I'd protect Trez from *you*. My wolf is now loyal to her."

"That shouldn't be possible." My dad combs a hand through his hair as he looks between Jag and me.

"Then I suggest you fix whatever spell or hex she put on your wolf before I force your beast on his back. You're both loyal to the Bloodmoon pack and to me, or you're both not. I can't have a beta whose wolf wants to rip my throat out."

"There's no spell or any magical element at play against Jagger or the wolf inside him, Kane," Storm tells me. "I'd know if there were."

"Then how is it possible for one of our wolves to be controlled by someone who isn't *his* alpha? If a bond wasn't formed, how is magic not in play?" Dad begs Storm for an answer, the same one I desperately want. Need.

"I can't answer that," she says, her head moving from side to side, "except that I'll ask again: are you sure Kate isn't Kane's fated mate?"

Steps on the patio past the open front door save me from snapping at Storm. I turn to see who it is. We all turn.

My body goes rigid. A beat later, a single word falls from my lips, but it's the relief I feel at seeing him that confuses the hell out of me.

"Trez."

14

KANE

He stumbles over the threshold, his face drained of color. Trez is shirtless, missing his shoes. His jeans ride low on his wide hips, unbuttoned like he barely had them on before having to run for his life if his ragged breaths are an indicator.

His brown eyes lock with mine, the whites of his eyes bloodshot.

I step forward, something inside urging me to reach him. Jagger growls from my right, but I ignore my beta, prepared to deal with him later.

"My sis…" Trez starts, but his eyes roll back into his head as his knees give out. His head tips back while his body falls forward. Even with supernatural speed, I'm not close enough to the entrance to catch him.

My father is, though. He catches Trez under his arms. I take another step, intent on taking him, when my dad jerks around, yanking Trez away from me. My eyes flash, the alpha in me wanting to make my father submit, but before I do anything, I see the darts. One is lodged in Trez's right shoulder, another lower on his back, closer to his waist.

"What the fuck?" Jagger spits before the exact words fall from my lips.

I close my distance, yanking them from his body, and suddenly, I'm angrier than I was earlier. It's not lost on me that I'd never be able to make good on my threat to Kate. I could never hurt either of them. He's my friend, and... fuck if I know what she is because there isn't a word for how deep she's embedded under my skin. Especially now.

But what if I have no choice?

I bring the tips of the darts to my nose and sniff. A rumble so loud leaves my throat that there isn't any doubt the entire pack heard my anger.

"Kane?" my father says, his hold around Trez growing tighter.

"Wolfsbane," I answer, disgusted and pissed the fuck off at the same time. Whoever dared to trespass on my land and use poison on another shifter will pay with their life before the end of tonight once I find out who did this.

Silver is more lethal, but Wolfsbane hurts far worse. A shifter wouldn't keep something like this on their person. At least one that didn't intend to harm another of our kind.

"Trez," I bark out through gritted teeth as I step toward him, needing to know who did this.

Jagger sidesteps me, then twists around, blocking my direct line of sight.

"Back up, Kane." Jag's teeth smash together at the same time his head twitches, and I know it's because his wolf wants to be released, but he pushes his beast back.

"I only want to know who shot him," I force past my lips as my blood boils.

"So the fuck do I," he snarls, and when Jagger blows air from his nostrils, steam follows.

"They're mine," I clarify. I'm alpha. It's my responsibility to protect everyone, shifters and other, on this land.

"No, brother. They're motherfucking mine."

"He isn't your mate," I say so slowly I wonder if it's more for me than him. "Don't tell me you've forgotten what yours smells like because I haven't."

I comb my hand through the loose strands of my hair.

"Look," I start again, knowing from the way his eyes soften that he does remember, "we have shit to figure out with Trez. For starters, who thought it was okay to pump him full of poison. We deal with that tonight. Tomorrow, we find our wolves once and for all, even if we have to tear apart an entire providence to do so. I need you with me. I need your wolf with me, Jagger. Can you give me that?"

His canines extend behind his lips, but without agreeing, he turns his back to me, facing Trez and my dad.

"Give him to me," Jag bites out, his emotions all over the place and on full display.

"I can help if you'll allow me," Storm says quietly from behind me, reminding me of her presence. She's always been too silent for my liking, mouse-like, and it doesn't suit her. Not when I can sense all the power residing inside her.

"How?" I ask, twisting around to face her. Her backside sits against the arm of the couch, her right hand squeezing the dangling necklace at her chest.

"I can draw the poison out using this." She unwraps her fingers, showing me the blue crystal. "Bring him over here."

Looking over my shoulder, I nod to my father.

"Dante," Jagger says, a clear warning in his tone, "give him to me. Please."

I can't blame Jag for the way he's acting. He gave into his attraction sooner than I did. I don't think my beta has fucked anyone else since Trez left months ago. His possessiveness started long before whatever it is he and Trez started over a year ago. Like my feelings toward Kate, his started the first winter they showed up too.

Dad presses Trez's back to Jagger's chest and releases him, but it's evident in his stare that he doesn't want to. My beta wraps his arms around him more securely as Dad bends, gripping Trez by his ankles.

"I'll help you carry him to the couch."

Why my father is reluctant to let Trez out of his care, I'm not sure. They were never close when Trez would visit, but then my father is the one who taught Trez how to properly track and hunt prey in wolf form. Perhaps he cares more than he's ever let on.

Back when my father and Elijah were our leaders, they quickly realized the Marked Crest pack hadn't taught Kate or Trez shit. I'm not sure how they survived the trek from their pack to ours that first time. By the time they left, they were deadly creatures in animal form and human, thanks to our fathers.

Recalling that memory does nothing to help me solve the turmoil in my head. Maybe Richard did send them and kept sending them, but then perhaps they learned from us and realized we weren't the enemy they'd been taught. Maybe they kept returning year after year because they enjoyed it here and have been our friends this whole time.

I don't fucking know, and I hate that I'm questioning shit I stopped asking myself a long time ago. Either way, I don't see a good outcome where we can remain friends. Not if Dad is right about Anna and Trey.

"Lay him with his back," Storm tells them as her backside comes off the arm of the couch. She turns, rounding the sofa.

I move out of Dad and Jag's way as they hoist him over. When Jagger's back is next to one end of the couch and Dad's is at the other end, they lie him down. Dad steps back, stopping beside me while Jag slides in behind Trez's head.

Since becoming my beta, Jagger's protective instinct has matured. Mine did too when I accepted the alpha role, but this is different. It's *more* with Jag and Kate's brother to the point the night before they left, Trez was bitching about Jagger to me.

Trez may yield to Kate easily, but like me, his temper flairs when anyone else tries to tell him what he should or shouldn't do. It makes me wonder how their alpha dealt with their insubordination because, knowing them both, there's no way in hell either were obedient.

Dad crosses his arms, his eyes fixated on Trez. I'm about to open my mouth when Storm beats me to it. "Is everything all right, Dante?"

"Yes." He nods. "Do whatever it is you need to do to pull that shit out of him. We need him awake to find out who's responsible."

"It had to have happened close by," I say to no one in particular as I stare at Trez, his eyes closed. Sweat beads against brows that are drawn tight. The pain is evident even though he's passed out. "He wouldn't have made it to the lodge with two tranqs still lodged in his back otherwise."

Storm lowers herself, kneeling on the floor next to the couch by Trez's side. "I need a towel. The thicker, the better."

Dad steps behind me before I can move to retrieve one

from the bathroom. Storm pulls the necklace over her head as he disappears down the hall. She places the crystal on Trez's stomach, above his belly button, and then lets the chain go.

"Jagger, will you put your hand on top of the stone? Make sure it touches," she instructs.

Jag's brows turn inward, then his eyes flick to mine, but he complies without question.

Dad stops behind the couch, handing Storm the folded towel, then he places a second on top of the middle cushion. "An extra, just in case."

"Thank you, Dante." She nods, then proceeds to close her eyes as she drapes the folded towel over Jagger's hand. A breath later, she flattens both palms on the Terry cloth and presses down.

Her lips move, but even with my keen hearing, I can't hear the words that leave her mouth.

I feel Jagger's unease before his mouth opens and snap my eyes back to his.

"What the hell is happening?" His back straightens, and then his free hand wraps around Trez's shoulder in an unmistakable form of protection and possession. His upper lip starts to curl.

Dad steps next to me again. I feel his eyes on me in question, but my stare remains on Jagger and Trez, wondering what alarm bells are going off with my beta when it's Trez she's supposed to be helping.

"Storm?" Jag questions, his voice firm.

She glances at me first, then at Jagger. "Anger is a toxin too. Your wolf is filled to the brim with it toward your alpha. I thought it might be best for the pack to draw it out before..." She leaves her words hanging in thin air, but we all know where she is headed.

Before he and I come to blows over how I treated Kate and the threat I vowed.

"It feels weird," Jagger admits, his eyes on the towel now darkening in color as the substances Storm is pulling out soak the cloth. "Is this what it feels like for him?"

"I'd imagine the pain is so great for him that either his wolf forced him to black out, or they both did. If Wolfsbane is anything like Hemlock, then it's the latter. For witches, Hemlock can be both paralyzing to us and painful at the same time," Storm informs us.

"I'm sorry about your mother. I should have said so earlier when..." Jag's eyes flick to mine as Storm reaches for the other towel.

"When you were mad at Kane," she finishes for him while replacing the Terry cloth with the clean one.

"I'm still mad at him."

"But now your head isn't as clouded with rage, is it?" she asks, tilting her head to the side.

"It's not. I feel lighter." He relaxes back against the armrest of the couch.

"You can remove your hand now. I think you're good," she tells him.

"Thank you. I am sorry that I didn't consider your loss. If there is anything we can do, all you have to do is tell us," he ensures her.

"He's right," I add. "Whatever you need, we are here for you. This is your home as much as it is ours. We're your friends, Storm."

"Thank you." She nods, and after a deep breath, she

closes her eyes again, murmuring words my supernatural ears can't pick up.

"Why is this towel getting wetter?" Jag's nose wrinkles. "And that smell. Jesus."

"I drew your toxins out first. I could have done you both at the same time, but then your hand would have come in contact with the poison. I didn't want to chance hurting you."

"Thank you," he says, breathing his relief at the thought. "How long will it take to get it all out of Trez?"

Storm doesn't answer right away, but there's no doubt she heard his question. Instead, she pulls the saturated towel away and grabs the one she discarded on the floor, putting it back on Trez's stomach where liquid was pooling around the glowing crystal.

"Storm?" I call out when her brows pinch together.

Her stare immediately finds mine, and what I see in her eyes is alarming.

"I'm going to need another towel. Quickly," she adds.

Without waiting for my Dad to retrieve one, I step toward the bathroom. Grabbing the one hanging from the towel rack, I take it back to the living room and hand it over.

"What's wrong?" Dad asks before I voice the same thought while I remain standing behind the couch.

"There are more toxins in his system than the amount that would have been in the two tranquilizers he was shot with," she tells me, her eyes flicking up to find mine. "Remember when I said magic wasn't at play with Jagger?"

"Yes," I growl as a slow prickling effect dances down my spine while foreboding twists my gut.

"That doesn't apply to Trez."

15
KANE

"What the fuck does that mean?" Jagger fumes as his temper flares again, and likely flooding his system with the same toxins that Storm removed.

"Now that the Wolfsbane is out of him," she explains, "I can feel the energy around him, and I can feel his aura, but I can't see it, which is concerning."

"Why is that?" Dad asks, pulling her eyes from where they snapped from Jagger to his.

Pushing away from Trez, she stands, taking the soaked cloth off Trez's abdomen along with her crystal necklace, and then snatches the other towel off the floor. Glancing at me, she asks, "Do you want me to toss these?"

"Please," I say, and follow with, "Thank you." The remnants of the poison would wash out of the material, but I'd rather throw the towels away than be reminded of what they were used for.

After placing the towels in the trash, she walks back

over. Sitting on the end of the other couch, she slips the long chain over her head and pulls her strands of hair from beneath it.

Tilting my head, I give her my undivided attention while Trez is still passed out.

"What do you smell?" Her warm eyes go from me to look toward my dad and then to Jag. "Any of you. What can you scent besides the lingering Wolfsbane?"

"I'm practically sitting in this shit with him," Jagger tells her. "All I smell is poison burning the inside of my nose. It's almost enough to make me run outside to inhale fresh air, but my wolf doesn't want me to move."

Dad's eyes pinch together, his stare fully on where Trez lies on the couch with his head in Jagger's lap.

"There's something heavier within him, but…" Dad trails off.

"But what?" I ask, wanting to know what he can scent that Jagger nor I can.

Sure, he was alpha longer than I've been. My father is more experienced than me, but that doesn't mean I'm okay with knowing less than him. I was born to be the alpha. I've known for as long as my earliest memory that I'd be alpha one day. That doesn't mean I recognize that there are and have been better alphas than me. I just don't like that fact.

"It's always been part of them," he informs me. "From the first day you brought them to meet Eli and me, Kate and Trez had such an overpowering scent of their pack that it made Eli nauseous. I wanted them out of the pack at first because, although it didn't make me sick to my stomach, I didn't like it. It made me remember things I wish I could forget. Things I wish had never happened."

"Then why did you let them stay?" I ask curiously.

"We're getting off-topic," Storm interjects. "Look deeper than their overpowering Silver scent. Their Marked Crest. Of course, their scent is overpowering. What else do you smell?"

"Earth," Dad responds almost immediately. "And…"

"Darkness," Storm adds when he trails off like he can't pinpoint exactly what he can smell on Trez.

"Are you saying Trez has evil within him?" I ask, forcing the question past my lips and unable to fathom it at the same time.

Jagger growls a warning that vibrates off the walls at my suggestion.

"In him? No," Storm confirms, her eyes darting to Jag and then back to me. "On him? Yes. He's cloaked in more dark magic than any Marked Crest wolf I've ever met. It's what hides his aura from me. Makes me wonder if his sister is shrouded as thickly as he is."

"Are all Marked Crest wolves fueled by dark magic?" Dad questions the same thought filtering through my head.

"Not so much fueled as they're cursed with it," she answers. "How else would a false alpha control a pack of wolves without magic being involved?"

"False alpha?" the three of us ask in unison.

She cocks her head to the side as her eyes move between us. "Why do I get the feeling none of you know how Richard Everhart became alpha of the Marked Crest wolves?"

I'm about to admit I don't know when my dad opens his mouth, but before words pass his lips, movement on the couch pulls my attention back to Trez. His face contorts as if he's in agony.

"What's wrong?" Jagger questions urgently.

"Trez," I call out, and almost immediately, his eyelids pop open.

For a heartbeat, he holds my stare, but whatever pain lingers isn't letting go easily. He bolts up, then jumps off the couch and away from Jagger, but falls to his denim-clad knees.

"Fuck. Fuck, it burns."

His arm lifts, his palm meeting the flesh between his shoulder blades, and that's when I see it. That goddamned tattoo. Trez's claws extract, piercing his skin, digging into his flesh like he's trying to rip the pain out.

"Jesus," Storm says as a rumble leaves my throat, forcing all eyes to turn toward me.

"What is it?" Jagger asks, concerned but also weariness in his tone, questioning the anger noted in the growl that left my mouth.

"That fucking tattoo." I throw up my hands, the heat from Kate and my argument coming back to me. "Kate has the same one. Hers is a bit faded, though. The black in his was gray on her. It's what made me blow up. It's why she's gone. I lost my shit when I saw the silver wolf on her back."

"What the fuck are you talking about?" Jag says the same time Dad says, "What tattoo?"

"Trez doesn't have tattoos," Jagger adds.

"Except the one between his shoulder blades." *Are they fucking blind?* It's right there for the whole world to see.

"I don't have a tattoo." Trez grits his teeth. "What happened with my sister? Where is she?"

"Okay, you fucking liar." I shake my head and flip my eyes to Jagger and then to my Dad. "Have both of your visions fucked up in the last few minutes? It's not small, so what the fuck?" I ask, ignoring Trez's mention of Kate.

"They can't see it," Storm answers.

"I'm sorry?" I ask, knowing that's not possible.

"It's not a tattoo, Kane." The line between Storm's eyebrows deepens. "The question is, how can you see it?"

"With my eyes, the same as you."

"Fuck!" Trez yells in agony. "Why won't he stop?" His eyes focus on the ceiling.

Glancing down, Storm steps next to Trez. "Put your claws away, please, and give me your hand." Trez is reluctant, his eyes going from Storm's to Jag's, where he remains on the couch; only now, both of Jagger's feet are on the floor, and he's facing Trez and Storm. "Trust me."

Slowly, he reaches up to her. She takes his hand in both of hers and closes her eyes. Her lips move, but no sound leaves her mouth as she says a spell.

Trez's body goes from coiled to relaxed within seconds, a harsh breath leaving his open mouth.

"Whatever the fuck you did, thank you," he says, gratitude genuine in his voice.

"I'm not able to take the effects of the mark away fully. I flooded your system with coolant, so to speak. The pain will come back if *she* keeps calling you home. You have an hour of relief at the most," Storm tells him, but I haven't a clue what she means or who she's talking about.

Storm steps away from him, her eyes snapping to mine, then my dad's, and finally back to me.

"I can see the marked crest because it was placed on him by a witch from my coven. The only person outside my coven that can see it is the shifter's alpha. It doesn't make sense, Kane, unless . . ." she trails off, her eyes flicking to Trez once again.

"Unless what?" my father asks, the demand in his tone so palpable Storm swallows as she stares between him and me.

"You mentioned Kate having the same mark." Storm's head tilts. "You have two missing wolves, Kane. So, unless you have other missing wolves I don't know about, Trez is one of them."

"He's not," I growl.

"You are his alpha. If you see the mark, and you saw the same one on Kate too, you are, in fact, their alpha, Kane," she argues, her tone more assertive than it's ever been before.

"He's my son."

"Stop. Everyone, fucking stop." I roll my head, looking at the side of my dad's face. His eyes are wide. They're on Trez, taking all of him in. "Dad, he is not your son. You said it yourself, you tested them."

"You aren't shocked," Dad says to Trez, ignoring my statement. "You knew."

Trez remains seated on the carpet, not saying a word, just staring at me.

"How can he be my mate if I can't feel the pull of the bond?" Jagger asks, his question aimed at Storm, and all I can think is why the hell is he questioning a non-shifter on shifter shit. She's a witch. A good witch in every way. She is skilled in her own right, but she isn't one of us. She doesn't have a fated mate like we do. It's different for them.

"It would be covered by the sheer magic that's rooted into the marrow of his bones," Storm tells him, then she looks my way, sadness in her stare. "You don't know why Richard Everhart's pack is called the Marked Crest, do you?"

I shake my head.

She looks at my father. "Do you, Dante?"

"No. I don't recall any significance to their pack name."

"Trez?" she questions.

He shakes his head too.

"Richard isn't a true alpha. He's only an alpha by the magic bestowed upon him in the form of a crest. The shimmering silver wolf on his hand isn't a tattoo. It's a mark given to him by a powerful witch that disappeared over a century ago."

"Are you fucking kidding me?" I spit out while Storm continues.

"The way he controls his shifters is by the same crest on them too, but Trez's mark is surrounded by circular runes. The more rings the crest is encased in and the thicker the circles are, the more magic it takes to control the wolf. It's the only way he could make them submit to him. Otherwise, they wouldn't. He's too weak to be an alpha."

"None of that explains why you believe I'm their alpha or that Trez and Kate are our missing mates," I say to her.

"You are their alpha. It's a fact whether you believe me or not. Only the shifter's alpha can see the mark. And since you saw it on Kate and now Trez, that means you're their alpha, Kane. The magic in the rune can also glamor whomever it's been placed on. The appearance we see may not be what Trez looks like, or the magic could have altered him forever. Salem is that powerful. Not as powerful as the witch that made Richard an alpha, but she's close."

"Then remove it. You want me to believe Trez is my

brother, then take it the fuck off and let me see myself," I demand.

"How about you slow your fucking roll, Kane, and tell me why Kate isn't here." Trez jumps to his feet, the color in his skin finally turning back to his normal complexion. "What did you do to make her leave? I specifically told her to come here. She would have waited for me. What did you do?" he repeats.

"What happened between Kate and me is between us. Stay the fuck out of it."

Part of me is embarrassed by the way I acted toward Kate. She didn't deserve my anger or for me to snap at her over a tattoo or a crest if what Storm says is true. The other part is still trying to catch up with everything Storm laid at my feet.

There's no way my mate and brother have been coming here every year and none of us knew it was them. I can't fathom it. It's impossible.

"You've been under my nose this whole time," Dad mumbles, his eyes wide, still on Trez. "And you knew. Why didn't you say something? Come to me? Tell me?"

"I didn't know when we were here." Trez runs a hand through his hair. "I still didn't know for sure. A few weeks ago, I overheard something I wasn't supposed to hear."

"What did you mean by, you told Kate to come here? She mentioned that but never explained. She told us you went for a run and never returned. Then Richard told the pack a hunter killed you. How exactly did you tell Kate to come here? Because nothing that either of you has told me is adding up."

"That's a me and Kate thing. It doesn't concern you," he snarls as his jaw locks.

"If we've ever been real friends, then you will tell me, and you'll tell me right fucking now."

"You can talk to her in your head," Dad states, and as soon as his words fully penetrate, a cold shiver runs down my spine.

They're celestial twins.

Trez is my brother.

And Kate...

What the fuck have I done?

16

KATE

After exiting off the 101 half an hour ago, I pulled into a roadside diner in a town I haven't the first clue where I am except that I'm in Washington state. At the speed I rode my bike, I'm far enough from Kane, but I still have a ways to go before I'm close to the border.

I don't plan on leaving the States until I'm certain my brother isn't here despite Kane's threat. I shouldn't have left Oregon until I was sure Trez wasn't close, but I couldn't breathe being in the same state as Kane.

If you or any other Marked Crest wolf enter my territory again, I'll kill you myself.

Was he serious?

Did he mean the words he yelled?

I'm not entirely sure. It felt like he meant them down to the center of my heart when he broke it. I told him I hated him, and I do, but I also don't.

I can't.

For all my bravado, I told myself yesterday that I could live without him, but now I'm not sure that's true. My wolf retreated so far inside me that I can only feel her when she pines for someone she'll never wholly have.

And if we can't have both, then it's neither Kane nor his wolf.

Kane made it clear he wouldn't settle for anyone who wasn't his mate. It's admirable. I should respect that, but I can't when I'm in love with someone fated to another. And being the other bitch isn't in my future.

"Are you sure there's nothing else I can bring you, hun?"

My eyes flick up, seeing Peggy pull my ticket from her pad and place it on the counter next to the plate of food I scarfed down. I started with two steaks, six eggs, and a double order of hash browns. After I polished off that meal within fifteen minutes, she brought me a stack of pancakes. I counted them. There were eight, which I devoured. A few minutes ago, she told me the peach pie was on the house.

Who was I to refuse such a generous offer?

I ate the pie too, not that it helped anything except curb my hunger. It did nothing to soothe my soul or the raging headache pounding against my skull.

"Yes. I'm good. Much better than when I walked in here. Thank you."

The food was delicious, but I was also starving. After the marathon sex session Kane and I had, the energy those two pieces of bacon provided was gone. I was running on empty.

"You be safe, dear."

Pulling cash from my bag, I place enough bills down to cover the meal and her tip, then I swivel around on the stool. Hopping down, I step away from the counter.

Pushing against the glass door, I head toward my bike. I paid the attendant for fuel before going to the diner, so I'm good, but I still don't have a plan to find my brother. I don't even know where to start.

Where the hell are you, Trez?

I can't feel anything except the Mount Everest size heartache breaking me apart. I don't know which direction to go. I could have already passed him, or what if he never left Canada? What if the night I spent with Kane was my only chance to find him, and I gave into my stupid desire for a man who doesn't want me instead of searching for my brother?

A real alpha would have put her brother first instead of her selfish wants. Maybe I'm not really an alpha.

Doubt and self-loathing settle in the pit of my stomach. Usually, my wolf is there to growl some sense into me when that happens, but she's lost in her own pity and heartbreak to bring me out of mine.

As I near my bike, I pull my keys from my pocket, then stop dead in my tracks. I'm ten feet from my motorcycle when my nose catches a smell I know all too well.

The attendant I paid is nowhere in sight. There were only humans inside the diner. I made sure I pulled in the surroundings before shutting off my bike to ensure there weren't any supernaturals around.

How did he find me?

A white van, dirt covering every viewable surface, is parked at the pump in front of my bike. There are no windows except for the cab facing away from me.

I glance to my left, then my right, seeing trees across the street and behind the diner and service station. I know I have to run, but which way?

I pivot, but something sharp pierces my chest before I

take the first step. I rip it out as the man holding the gun comes into focus.

Then I feel it, and my breath catches. The poison begins to spread, and anger grabs ahold of me as acutely as the burning blooms inside my body.

"I'm going to rip out your throat," I seethe. My teeth clamping together, the pain latching onto every nerve.

He fires the air gun again, and this time, the tranquilizer penetrates the muscle in my shoulder. I yank that one out, but another stabs my forearm and then my stomach.

Pulling the one in my arm out, I stumble forward and toss the dart to the ground.

"Katie," his stentorian voice echoes behind me, telling me he's closer than when I saw him step from the front of the van into view. I've hated that nickname since I was a child, and he knows it.

It's worse than when my alpha calls me Katherine, refusing to acknowledge Kate as my only name. Both Katherine and Katie grate on my nerves. They both piss me off, but the way Katie rolls off Henrik's lips is possessive.

Whereas my father is narcissistic and pretentious, his beta is calculating and devious. Henrik is patient but ruthless. My father treats me like I'm dirt under his boot. When the alpha looks at me, it's with hatred in his eyes. When his beta's stare is on me, it's the confidence of someone who owns the thing they're gazing at.

"Kill her already," the disloyal coward standing behind the rifle shouts, his raging navy eyes looking behind me where Henrik stands, waiting for me to drop to my knees.

My keys slip from my grasp, falling to the ground.

"That's not our plan at all," says a sickly-sweet voice

behind me. "I need her alive, and Hen was promised a compliant little plaything."

"You're not a wolf," I spit out. "You're a snake in the grass, and if I don't kill you first, Kane will do it for me." The poison clouds my vision, but I take another step and then another, my strides short. I can already see two of him, and I'm not wholly sure which version is correct.

Another shot pops off, but this one is louder than the noise the air rifle made. The sound cracks all around me a nano-second before the bullet hits its target. The fire at the back of my thigh hurts like hell, the pain too great for my willpower to withstand. I go down. The knee of the leg that the silver bullet pierced hits dirt and gravel hard.

"That'll be hard to do when you're kept on your back, where bitches belong, cunt," says the traitorous mother-fucker as my other leg gives out, the minerals in the silver zapping the remaining strength I have left that the Wolfs-bane hadn't smothered.

"Time for you to skedaddle, mutt." The woman with Henrik steps from behind me and into view. I can only make out her petite stature, a long dark-colored dress, pitch-black eyes, and black inky lines covering her hands and disappearing beneath the sleeves. "It's your job to kill your alpha's brother before he makes it home. I suggest you hurry."

"Kane's brother?" I choke out, my heart spasming. "Trey?"

If Trey has returned home, does that mean . . . *No.*

"Trey," the witch coos. "Trez. They're one and the same, *Anna... Kate.*"

17
KANE

Is the one woman I've wanted and refused to allow myself to have my mate?

Could Kate really be Anna?

Guilt presses against my chest plate as the same panic that jarred me awake an hour ago claws at the back of my neck.

Everything inside me is at war. Well, everything except my wolf. He's still MIA, and as lonely as that feeling is, it's pissing me off too.

Kate can't be Anna. It's impossible. But fuck if I don't want her to be. And that fact makes me the world's shittiest mate. I want another woman to be my fated mate rather than the one I was gifted twenty years ago.

How fucked up is that?

I can't think clearly to even begin to analyze everything.

My skin prickles and itches with unease. My hackles are up, and it's not just because I'm mad at my wolf for putting up a wall between us. Something else is triggering my senses. My instincts are telling me to run, to find Kate, but my head is telling me to stay the fuck away from her. She's not Anna. I can't have her.

Storm is wrong. I'm not Kate's alpha. I'm not Trez's either. They aren't *them.*

"Goddammit, A.K., where the hell are you?" Trez bellows from where he's standing, staring out the open front door. My gaze flicks to his back, his hands braced on each side of the doorframe.

Who the fuck is A.K.?

He took a shower half an hour ago to wash the remnants of the Wolfsbane and smell off his body. We're close in size, though I have several inches of height on him. The pair of worn jeans and loose Carhartt T-shirt he grabbed from my closet fit him perfectly. Even my boots look like they belong on him.

That was one of the first things I noticed about him years ago. We wore the same things. Everything he was wearing the day we met was the same brand, down to the color of the material, as the ones in my closet. Back then, the only difference was he was smaller than me.

Now, he's not, and I'm unsure when that happened. The second year they visited, he'd put on weight and grew a few inches. The year after that, the same.

"What did you say?" My dad steps from where he'd disappeared down the hall to contact my mom after Trez came from my bedroom.

Dad said he wouldn't tell Mom that Trez was her missing pup, at least not until it's confirmed, but I know my father. If he thinks Trez is Trey, then he won't keep those thoughts from his wife, the love of his life, his fated mate.

"Who's A.K.?" I ask the same thought that flickered through my head before my father opened his mouth.

Trez swivels his head, looking over his shoulder, first at my Dad, then at me. His mouth opens, and my supernatural hearing picks up the swoosh of air forced between his lips instead of an answer.

"Kate," Dad replies for him, his eyes never veering from Trez while I'm left baffled as to why my father would assume that when I've never heard Trez call his sister anything other than her name. "I'm wondering, does my son know why he called her by that specific reference."

"Jesus, Dad. You don't even know—"

"I'm certain." My father interjects, his former alpha side showing in his tone as his head whips toward me, not liking that I can't accept his certainty as a factual statement. "They're initials, Kane. They're Anna's initials." He sighs, his breath more ragged than his spoken words would have you believe. His eyes leave mine, his head shaking ever so slightly I wouldn't have noticed if I hadn't trained my unblinking stare on him.

"My sister's initials are A.H. for—" Jagger starts to argue, but Dad cuts him off.

"Anna Hayes, yes, Jag, but you're not putting two and two together. Neither is Kane." He swallows, his amber eyes flicking back to mine. "Fuck, I didn't either, and it's been staring me in the face for years. Her name is Anna Kate Hayes."

Pins and needles prick the back of my neck, stabbing a path down my spine. The air in my lungs rushes out of my mouth.

How did I not know that?

I glance at Jagger, his eyes as wide and round as mine. He shakes his head, telling me he didn't know either.

"A wolf won't answer to any name other than what its

mother named him or her," my father explains, reminding me of the time I learned that lesson in middle school.

"Is this where you tell us that Trey was also called Trez before he was kidnapped?" I ask, knowing I sound like I'm smarting off and not giving one fuck.

This isn't possible.

Kate and Trez aren't our wolves.

She is not my mate.

He isn't my brother.

This is too farfetched to be a reality.

Dad has lost his fucking mind.

"No, Kane," he barks. "But Trez is close enough to Trey that at the age he was, your brother could have been manipulated or…"

"Beaten into believing it," Trez finishes when my father pauses for too long of a beat.

"I'm going to rip that motherfucker's throat from him if it's the last thing I do," Dad vows.

"Not if I beat you to it." Jagger's voice is a whisper.

Dad pivots on his heel, turning to face my beta. "He's *my* son. That is not a kill you'll take from me."

"He's *my* mate," Jagger says, his teeth bared.

"And *he's* standing right here," Trez adds. "*He* doesn't need either one of you to fight *his* fucking demons. You both want a run at Dick Everhart? Get in fucking line. Besides, what he's done to me over the years doesn't compare to what he's put Kate through." Trez turns his back to us, going back to watching the outside from where he's standing just inside the door.

There's a powerful force inside me that wants to stalk the four steps it would take to reach Trez to force him back around to face me, to make him spill everything that anyone has ever done to harm or wrong Kate and make them suffer a long, slow death. But then another side of me still refuses to believe any of this make-believe. That part of me is also running scared because *what if...*

No. There is no what if. Only proof and that isn't something I've been shown.

"You're going to have to do better than closely related names to get me to buy this nonsense, Dad."

"You want proof, Alpha?" Jagger says in an almost menacing tone, making my fists ball at my sides. He stalks forward, his hard gaze on me as he storms between my father and me, stepping toward Trez's back. "So be it."

My head doesn't catch up with what my eyes witness. Shock cements my booted feet to the floor. My father's too. It happens before I can blink. Jagger's head tips to the side, one claw comes out, ripping the T-shirt down the center of Trez's back as his teeth sink into the flesh covering Trez's neck.

I blink, and it's done.

Jagger pulls away, but Trez flips around to face him so fast that multiple emotions pass before a growl rumbles from his throat.

"What the fuck did you do?" he accuses.

"What was bound to happen sooner rather than later," Jagger answers, licking his bloody lips. "Kane wanted proof, and if his bite faded Kate's mark, then mine should fade yours."

"That's not a gamble you take," I chastise, almost yelling in his ear now that he's backed away from Trez to stand between my father and me. Dad is silent, and that's an admission by omission that he's okay with Jagger's actions.

But I'm not.

Trez reaches for the shirt collar, barely hanging from his shoulder. Fisting the material, he yanks the shredded cloth from his torso.

My wolf isn't obeying my commands, but that doesn't mean I can't put my beta on his back. That's my sole intent when Trez rushes forward, shoving his hand against Jagger's chest and pushing him backward.

"You think that was your right to take what I didn't offer?" Trez demands, his tone bordering on lethal.

"You're mine." The possessive wolf inside Jagger growls in agreement. "I made that clear the last time you were here."

A warning growl, low and calmer than I know Trez is right now, seeps from his mouth, followed by a beat of silence long enough for me to anticipate his next move. Jagger does too, but my beta does nothing to stop Trez from pouncing on him and taking them both to the floor, Jagger on his back with Trez straddling his hips.

"You think a bite makes me yours?" Trez's head dips to Jagger's neck quicker than a blink of eyelids. A guttural growl leaves my beta's lips, his hands going to Trez's waist as teeth tear through skin. "That two bites bond us together by fate?"

Three audible gasps sound at the same time Trez leans back up, Jagger's eyes wide as he stares up.

"Fuck fate. I'm only yours if *I* decide I'm yours," Trez declares, his words as clear as the flesh no longer marked by the curse that existed on his back seconds ago. "And fuck you too right now."

"You. You look..." Jagger stammers.

"Am I seeing this?" Storm says, but it's more to herself

than any of us. She's been silent the entirety of the time we've been arguing.

"Your hair…" Dad's words fail him too, but they make me take in more than the blank canvas of Trez's back.

"Is just like Dante's," Jagger says. "You look like Dante."

Trez pushes from his knees to his feet, then steps back while Jagger stares from the floor. Turning, Trez meets my father's eyes, then flicks his gaze to mine, a question waiting for me to answer.

I nod, confirming Jag's claim. Staggering to the side, Trez's unblinking eyes on mine, he turns and dashes down the hall to the bathroom, my guess to look in the mirror.

"He's my son. He's really my son," Dad says, but all I can do is take a step back, away from everyone. "Trey is finally home."

My feet move again, taking another step back.

Jagger pulls himself to his feet. He looks toward me, then rolls his head to see the open bathroom door. A beat passes, and his eyes are back on me.

Trez is my brother, which means…

"Kane," Jag calls out. He takes a step forward but stops. "We're going to find her."

Trez comes back down the hall, his fingers running through his lighter hair. The change is a lot to take in, and now I can feel everything he's feeling on top of everything running through my head.

Confused.

Overwhelmed.

Relieved on one level, but also fear tainting that tiny bit of joy that he isn't a silver wolf, that he isn't a Marked Crest wolf.

Then there's his worry and mine knotting together to the point I don't know whose is whose.

Kate is gone. I ran her off.

I kicked my mate out of my pack. Out of *her* pack. Her home.

Acid coats my tongue.

A mountain sits on my chest, pinning my soul in Hell.

How did I not realize?

My head thunders with my pain, my agony, my fear, my failure. My father's disappointment in the son he made an alpha rains down on me like icicles piercing my skin. But I feel his elation too that he's trying so hard to hide. Trey is home. He should be happy. I should be thrilled. We should be celebrating that one of our wolves made it back.

But Kate isn't here, and that's on me.

Jagger wants to punch me as much as he wants to take my burdens from me. He can't fix it. I'm not even sure I can fix this.

My mate is still missing, but she isn't the only one I'm responsible for who's out there somewhere.

I glance up as a shadow catches my focus, giving me a momentary reprieve from everyone's heavy emotions. If only it stopped my own from clawing at my insides.

Jagger stands in front of me.

"It's only been a few hours. She wouldn't have made it to the border yet. We will find her. You know Kate. She won't leave until she makes sure Trez isn't here. We'll find my sister, Kane."

"My sister!" Trez corrects, a snarl on his lips. His too-familiar eyes flick to mine. "There's something you aren't telling us. Spit it out."

"Kate's pregnant."

18

KANE

"Come the fuck again?" Trez grits out, his eyes hardening as his jaw locks.

Jagger's brows furrow, his mouth slowly opening as if he wants to refute my knowledge of that fact. That it's impossible to be true. After all, we both know it can't happen to a wolf shifter unless she's in heat.

But Kate isn't who we thought she was.

She isn't as young as we thought, either.

As if my beta had the same revelation I did, his eyes round, widening in shock.

"Everyone, get out," Jag seethes, his eyes locked on me, his words for everyone else.

"Kane," Storm calls as she lightly steps my way. "I have to find my sister. I have to go tonight."

"Wait and leave with me. I'm going that way. You might as well come with. Just give me time to speak to Jagger first," I tell her, hoping she takes me up on the offer. I may not cross the border if I find Kate first, but at least I'll know Storm will be safe while she's with me.

She nods.

"I'll go pack a bag." She turns, sidestepping Trez to skip out the open door.

Trez crosses his arms, his feet shoulder-width apart, telling me he doesn't plan to move from that spot.

"I said get out," Jagger repeats.

"No," Trez deadpans.

"Not happening," Dad adds. "How the fuck did she go into heat, Kane, and you not know it? You, of all people, know the signs of a wolf going into fucking heat. Explain."

"With all the respect I have for you, Dante, it was an order, not a request. Out. Now!" Jagger barks.

"Give us a minute," I tell them. Flipping my eyes to my dad, I jerk my head toward the door that Storm left open, ordering him to follow.

"Fuck. That," Trez spits, snarling at us.

His insubordination crawls my skin, but it's the missing growl that should have rumbled up from my throat that grips the muscle in my chest like a vise that bothers me more.

My wolf is nowhere in sight. We've never had a wall between us. I can't help the sinking feeling in the pit of my stomach, wondering if he's gone; blocked from me forever over what I did to Kate.

It's what I deserve, but he doesn't.

Jagger growls when I don't.

My mouth opens, about to piss off my father and my *brother*, but before the words form, my name is called, pulling my attention outside.

"Kane," Ash calls, urgency in her tone.

An unnerving sensation creeps inside me, but before I can step in her direction, Trez whips around. In the blink of my eyes, he's through the entrance and outside. I follow as fast as my legs will move. By the time I reach the edge of the wooden deck, Trez jumps off, tackling someone to the ground. Ashleigh steps back but doesn't move to stop Trez in his attack.

Jogging down the steps, I reach for Trez, pulling him off, but not before he lands one hell of a punch to Ronnie's jaw. I force him up the steps as Jagger descends them. My dad stops at the edge where Trez tries to plow through me to get back to Ronnie.

"Stop." I plant my hand on the center of his chest, pushing against him. Luckily for both of us, he actually obeys.

Turning around, Jagger hauls Ronnie to his knees while Ashleigh stands with her arms crossed and a look of concern as her eyes roam over my shoulder to where Trez remains, noting the change in his appearance.

When I cut my eyes to the shifter kneeling in front of me, I see silver-coated cuffs connected by a thick iron chain wrapped around his wrists, binding them together and burning his flesh if the stench is any indication. Ronnie's shirtsleeve being the only barrier between himself and the metal, weakening him while his body spasms involuntarily.

They were made by my grandfather's father over one hundred years ago. I've never used them. I've never had a reason to. I can't imagine why Ashleigh would have them locked around his wrists. I knew she carried them on her person often, but to shackle them around one of our own demands an answer.

"What is the meaning of this, Ashleigh? It better be good," I seethe.

Trez growls from behind me as he takes a step down, my ears picking up his quiet movement.

"He's the one that poisoned me," my brother says as he stops to the left of my back.

My eyes flash blood-orange as rage billows up my throat.

"It's true," Ashleigh confirms, not that I wouldn't have believed Trez. "I was running solo when I picked up his scent. I took off in his direction, but never once did I smell *him*." Ashleigh juts her chin toward Ronnie. "When I got close, I saw him aim and hit Trez in the back. He had a bag full of tranqs, Kane."

She tosses a brown canvas bag on the ground inches from my feet.

Trez knocks my shoulder while passing me, but I grab his bicep and yank him back, turning to face him at the same time. "Don't make me put you in your place."

"Go ahead," he bites out, his angry eyes challenging me. "Nothing I'm not used to."

Knowing he's referring to the Marked Crest alpha who raised him, who stole him and my mate, my jaw locks as my fists ball at my sides. I'm so mad I want to rip someone apart, but that anger must wait.

Ronnie has to have a reason for doing what he did. He wouldn't have used Wolfsbane unless he thought he had to. For the life of me, I can't fathom any reason he would have or why he'd have darts filled with poison.

Turning back around, I eye Jagger, making sure he doesn't do something on his mate's behalf before we hear the man out.

"Stand him," I tell Jag. When Ronnie is on his feet, I

breathe through my nose before saying, "Speak for yourself. Explain this to me."

"You said that if any Marked Crest wolf entered *your* territory, they'd be killed. I was doing exactly—"

"How the fuck would you know that? I never issued that order to the pack." My guilt over threatening Kate returns, but I jerk my head, trying to shake the feeling. I can't deal with those emotions until I find her. I can't right my wrong until she's back.

"I-I..."

"You would've had to have been near my cabin to have overheard that, Ronnie." I step forward, and as if on reflex, he takes a step back. Ashleigh is on him before Jagger, stopping him and then shoving him forward. "Only a few are allowed that close to my cabin. You aren't one of them."

"Alpha, I was..." he trails off. I can feel his fear, but there's also something else I can't pinpoint. He smells funny. Almost like burnt fuel or dirty motor oil.

"You were what? Trespassing. Not following your alpha's explicit orders." I snarl. I growl too, but it's all me, not my wolf. "Explain. You have one fucking chance."

"Kane," he says quickly. "I wanted to make sure you were fine. Kate showing up this time of year wasn't right. Wasn't normal. I was afraid for my alpha. When I heard your orders, I knew she wasn't to be trusted. That *he* wasn't to be trusted." Ronnie looks to Trez, then back to me. "I was protecting the pack when I saw him running through the woods, heading toward *our* alpha. I thought I was protecting you and following your orders. I'm sorry, alpha. I thought..."

His voice cracks, but a cold shiver runs down my back at

the same time. That doesn't explain why Ash couldn't pick up his scent when she smelled Trez.

"Please, alpha. I wouldn't have done it if I didn't think I was following your orders," he adds.

"I should banish you for using Wolfsbane on another shifter, for bringing it onto pack land." I turn to Ashleigh. "Take the chains off."

He knows the rules. I don't have to reiterate them. He's been following them longer than I have. But he's also right. I did say what I said. At the end of the day, this was my fuck up, no one else's, and I'll take responsibility.

Once the metal falls from his wrists, relief on his face is instant.

"Get out of my sight before I change my mind. And if you ever bring Wolfsbane back here, you won't be banished. I'll kill you myself." I hold his stare so he knows my promise is true.

Backing away, he holds my gaze for a long beat, then cuts to his left, running in the direction of his home. The one he shares with his sister and niece.

The moment he's out of sight, I'm shoved forward, stumbling, but I recover and whip around, my eyes flashing at the audacity. I know who it is before Jagger tries to step between Trez and me.

"That's how you handle that piece of shit?" Trez's mouth is agape. "Are you for real? He poisoned me, Kane. He wanted to kill me, in case you missed the stench he was drenched in."

I didn't miss it, but we don't execute our wolves. It was a misunderstanding on his part. That doesn't mean he should pay with his life. This isn't the Marked Crest pack. I don't kill unnecessarily. I can't even recall a time we've ever banished a shifter. That shit doesn't happen in my pack. We have each other's back. We respect pack rules and value everything we've built.

"It was my fault, Trez. He shot you because of me."

That's the truth. Still, there was something amiss about what Ronnie did. I can't tell my brother that or admit I don't know. Not while my father is here, looking at me like he's angry and disappointed at the same time.

"His actions are on him," Trez argues, but he's wrong.

"Not this one. My orders. My pack. My responsibility. You want to take out your anger, take it out on me, but let's find Kate first. That's an order from your alpha, Trez."

"You're no longer Alpha, son." My stare cuts to my father. He still stands on the porch deck, his arms crossed, his eyes with an orange tent coloring the whites. "I'm taking it back. When Eli gets home tomorrow, he'll be beta again. You and Jagger are going to step down."

Jagger starts to pass me, but I jut out my arm, halting him.

My father doesn't know me if he believes I'm going to do what he says when he says jump. I'm the alpha of the Bloodmoon pack. Me. Not him. He had his time, and though it was short, that was his choice.

"Dad, there is no one that I have ever respected more than you. I also know when you stepped down so that you and Elijah could hunt for our missing mates, it wasn't either of your times to do so, but you still did it. That was your decision and Eli's. I'm not stepping down as alpha. Jagger isn't stepping down as my beta. If you want the role, you'll have to challenge me. But it won't be until submission. You'll have to kill me."

19
KANE

Telling my father he'd have to challenge me for the alpha position isn't anything I would have ever thought I'd say in my lifetime. My mother would be as appalled as she would be shocked if she had been here and heard the words from my mouth.

The only evidence of Dad's surprise was the flash of color in his eyes. He flicked it away so fast that if I hadn't been staring into his eyes, I would have missed the tinge of orange. He put up a wall to block his emotions from me in the next breath, but not soon enough that his hurt, anger, and pride didn't take hold of my heart before vanishing in the blink of an eye.

I dashed up the steps and past him after that, going straight to my bedroom and then the closet. I packed two duffle bags of clothes, one for me and the other for Trez. Storm should be ready by now. The sooner we get on the road, the closer we'll get to Kate. Wherever the fuck she is.

I will find her.

I'm not losing her again.

Stomping out the door and onto the porch, my gaze snaps to Trez. His ass is pressed against the railing with his hands braced on the wood. I throw the duffle at his chest, ignoring where my father is seated to my left in one of the Adirondack chairs.

There are four dark gray chairs on each side of the porch with my father occupying one of them on the side where Trez stands while Jagger is sitting on another to my right.

"You're coming with," is all I say as I jog down the steps.

"He isn't going. Take Jagger and Ashleigh," Dad says from behind me, his voice final. My feet halt as the back of my neck pricks. Jag follows me, stopping next to my side and twisting to face me while I look forward.

Ash catches my stare from where her back is leaning against my black four-door pickup truck that's rarely taken off pack land. It's not the preferred vehicle I usually drive. That's a restored 1970s Ford. Ashleigh made the right call. This truck will carry more than three people, and once we find Kate, we'll need more room. I don't want Storm leaving if I can talk her into coming back with us.

I look over my shoulder, my gaze going to Trez, then cutting to my father, but before I open my mouth to say something I may regret later, Trez beats me to it.

"*He* can speak for himself." Trez stops at the top of the steps and, rolling his head, he meets our Dad's gaze.

Our father.

Fuck me. I don't know how to feel about Trez being the brother I've been looking for, for so long. I haven't had time to process it after the truth came to light before my eyes.

"And *he* is going to find *his* sister," Trez finishes, his feet dropping down the steps in slow motion as the words tumbled from his mouth.

Jagger growls, and all I can do is shake my head. This is going to become a problem for me as much as it will be for Trez, which is one of the reasons Jag isn't going with us. Jagger doesn't like to share what he deems as his. With my brother being his mate and mine being Jag's flesh and blood, it's going to turn my beta into an even bigger asshole than I am if Trez continues to call Kate *his* sister.

That's a problem for another day.

"Your mother will be here by morning. She needs to see you, Trez," Dad says, his voice more alpha than it should be, pissing me off more than I already am.

I turn fully around so that I'm facing my brother and my father. Flicking my eyes to Trez, I say, "Get in the truck."

His tongue clucks, but he doesn't argue as he bypasses me, never once looking Jagger's way. I don't see Storm, so I'm guessing she's already inside the cab since I can smell her nearby. She has a unique scent. It's like rain, fresh-cut grass, and an aroma of different flowers invading your senses all at once.

"This is your way of being an Alpha?" Dad questions. "Thinking of yourself and not the pack as a whole? Your mom needs to see her son, Kane. She's dreamt of this every night for over twenty years. You're really going to deny her that reunion?"

Fuck you, Dad, I think to myself, but instead of letting the words easily roll off my tongue, I take a breath instead. I should curse him, but I'm not going to. I'm not one to hold back no matter who ticks me off, but this isn't the time.

"What I do is based on each pack member's individual need, and right now, Trez needs to get the fuck out of here. Mom will get to see him soon enough, just as Eli and Annalise will see Kate when we find her. But the longer you fight me on everything I do, the farther she gets from here. We're leaving, and in case it wasn't clear, Jagger and Ashleigh are in charge while I'm gone."

"I'm coming too," Jagger seethes, his voice a low rumble. "She's my sister and he..." Jag breathes. "He's mine."

Turning to face Jagger, I snatch the back of his neck and pull him toward me until his forehead touches mine. Wolves are touchy-feely. Shifters are no different. We need contact. I've always seen Jagger as much my brother as I've thought Trey to be.

"If you don't curb this shit, you're going to fuck up like I did," I say to him, breathing my words into his mouth as a whisper so that only he hears them. "I know *he* is yours like *she* is mine. Kate, being mine, trumps her being your sister and your parents' lost daughter. But Trez isn't Trey, and Kate isn't Anna. Not in the way we remember and have always thought of them as. You have to let him breathe. Right now, he's overwhelmed and feeling too much."

"I know what he's feeling," he spits back at me, his voice as controlled as he can manage. It's at that moment that realization dawns on me. He can feel Trez's emotions as clear and palatable as I can taste them. Their mate bond was completed, unlike Kate and me. "But what do you want me to do? My restraint is nonexistent. You're trying to take him away, and it's pissing my wolf off."

I know exactly what he's feeling. He's a mate before he's a beta. It's how I feel too, but I haven't acknowledged it until now. My pack is supposed to come first, but all my instincts tell me the opposite.

Not wanting anyone, especially my father, to hear the following words, I close my eyes to concentrate, momentarily shutting the rest of the world out, focusing all my senses on Jag.

"They are ours. They're our first priority. I agree, but the pack is ours too. I need Trez to find Kate. I need you here for the pack. The pack needs you like I need you to be here for them while I'm gone. Without Trez, I don't know that Kate will come home with me. I won't force her, and if she doesn't come..." I trail off, not wanting to solidify what I know to be true. Facts I don't want anyone other than Jagger to know.

The pack doesn't know that Jagger and I can speak telepathically at will. I'm fairly sure our parents do after dad figured out that Kate and Trez speak to each other in their heads. But with Jagger and I, it's always been our secret. We've never told a soul, not even Ashleigh.

It's not like we can hear each other's thoughts. We have to actively be speaking to each other to even communicate. It's how I woke up a few hours ago. Jagger was calling out for help inside my head, but as soon as my eyes were open, all I could think about was Kate and that damn spelled mark disguised as a tattoo on her back.

Fuck.

I have to get out of here. I need to find her because who knows what she's thinking right now.

"You won't come back either," he finishes for me. *"I'm not an alpha. If you don't return with her, you know I'll abandon them to come after you. If she doesn't come back, neither will Trez. I'm not losing him again. Not when I've just found him, and let's face it. He may be my mate and the bond may exist, but I don't really have him. Not yet, at least."*

"You'd make a great alpha if I weren't around."

"I make an all right stand-in." We open our eyes and lock

onto the other's stare. *"And I'll do it, but you better bring them both back. Storm too. She's one of us."*

A deep growl from inside the truck pulls Jagger and me out of our heads. Cutting my eyes to the porch, I find my father watching us. There's no curiosity in his stare, but I wouldn't expect there to be. This isn't uncommon for Jagger and me. We've always done this, acted in this manner with each other.

"Maybe you have him more than you think," I say, locking eyes with Jagger again while the jealousy in Trez's tone eases a fraction of the ache in my chest. I don't *want* to leave my pack. But I need Kate more than the need and will to honor the vow I took when I became alpha.

"We'll see," is Jag's reply.

"I need you here, Jagger." I raise my voice, tugging my alpha power forward. Looking over, I meet my father's stare and his snarl once again. "I wouldn't want our parents staging a coup in our absence."

Rolling his head, Jagger finally acknowledges our former alpha. "I got this."

Knowing the pack is dealt with, I walk away and round the pickup to the driver's side. I climb into the cab and shut the door, my gaze set out the window.

"You have something to say?" I press the brake pedal and push the engine button to start the truck.

"Don't touch my shit," Trez replies, his head facing forward as I put the gear in drive and release the brake.

"Everyone in the pack is *my* shit. Get used to it, little brother."

20

KANE

After we left, Ashleigh texted me with the address of a diner, saying Kate had been there for over three hours. When I replied, asking her how she knew that, she simply said she had her ways. I knew about the tracker Ash has been planting on Kate for a few years, but I wouldn't have thought she would have gotten the chance to do it this time.

I guess I underestimated my third in command, which is exactly why Ashleigh is just that in our pack.

It took two hours to get here, breaking every speed limit law posted along our route, but the pull to find her, to get Kate back, to... fuck. What am I even going to say to her?

I'm sorry I kicked you out of your own pack.

I'm sorry I bit you without your consent.

Turns out, you're my stolen mate, and I'm a complete fuck up of a man and alpha that I didn't realize you'd gone into heat last night.

Also, I probably got you pregnant.

None of those excuses will go over well with Kate, and

they shouldn't. Granted, she didn't know she was in heat either. But I can't worry about what I will say to her. I have to find her before she crosses the border. It's a gamble, but I'm banking on her not leaving until she's certain Trez isn't here.

I thank the fates she's an alpha female, knowing it'll drive her to find him. She's always been protective over him. It's in her blood. It's a force at the center of her being. Even if she weren't a Luna wolf, Kate would still search for her best friend—the person she believes to be her brother. He's her family. It's who Kate is.

Knowing I need fuel, I park my truck next to the gas pump closest to the diner and shut off the engine, noting that I don't see Kate's motorcycle anywhere. It's late, with only two cars parked in front of the brightly lit restaurant.

"I need to call Ash. Kate isn't here."

"We don't know that. We haven't checked," Trez replies as he unbuckles his seatbelt.

"Do you see her bike anywhere?" I ask.

"Why don't I go inside and ask if anyone's seen her?" Storm says from the backseat behind Trez.

"Do you even know what she looks like? You said you'd never met her."

"No, I said, I didn't know they were from the Marked Crest pack. I met Kate once, two years ago," she informs me. "Plus, they'll likely tell me more than they would you if Kate's been here."

"Fine. I'll ask the gas clerk."

When Storm steps down from the truck and shuts the door, I stare out the window, waiting for the fuel attendant to notice us.

"Want to talk about it?" I ask Trez, his head turned away

from me as if he's watching Storm or eyeing inside the diner as she pulls the door open and slips inside.

"Jagger? No," he deadpans. "Being mated? Fuck no. Being not me? Also, no."

"You're still you. Finding out you're my brother and one of the missing shifters from the Bloodmoon pack doesn't mean you aren't you."

"Is that even my name anymore?" Finally, he twists his head, his eyebrows arched.

"It is until you say otherwise."

"You sure about that?" He shakes his head. "I don't even look like me. I look like *your* father."

I roll my head, taking in his profile while he goes back to looking out the window. I take a moment to really *see* the changes in him for the first time. I saw it when it happened, when the marks disappeared from his back, and the pigment of his skin darkened. His appearance changed drastically, but he's still the same being he's always been.

"Your bone structure didn't change. You're the same height and build. Your eyes are the same brown they've always been. You are you, Trez. You just didn't know the *you* that you were born as. Neither did I. Jagger didn't either, but that didn't stop him from realizing the signs I refused to see."

"Didn't stop him from staking claim without asking me if I wanted it first," he growls, but there's a lack of heat in his tone that doesn't go unnoticed by either of us.

"You wouldn't have bitten him back if you hadn't wanted it," I reason.

"Like you wouldn't have bitten Kate if you hadn't wanted her?"

Could I have stopped my wolf from biting her if I'd wanted to?

He pushed through so quickly that I'm unsure, but maybe that's the excuse I told myself to absolve some of my guilt. Either way, it doesn't matter. I fucked up. I handled everything wrong from the moment I smelled her heat and pounced on her until my beta proved that Trez was my brother and Kate's my mate.

"Where the fuck is this guy?" I say, ignoring Trez's question while exiting the truck. My brother is right, but I can't bring myself to acknowledge it.

I round the front of the truck at the same time Trez jumps out and does the same, meeting me at the bumper corner on the passenger side.

"Oh, so you want to talk about me, but not you and my sister, even though we're out here looking for her because you were a dick?"

"How about, where you were? What you overheard that you weren't supposed to hear, and the reason you didn't tell Kate? Why let her think you were missing, dead? She thought you were fucking dead, man. There was a goddamn urn with ashes inside it." I step forward, intent on crowding his space when I abruptly stop and jerk my head to the side.

"What is it?" he asks, suddenly as alert as I am.

I smell the night air as he whips his body around to face the threat he saw on my face, but it's not what he's imagining. Pins and needles prick down my spine.

"Kate," I whisper as my throat clogs, dread weighing me down.

"Where is she?" Trez looks in the direction of her scent, but he must not be picking up the smell that I am.

"I smell her blood," I tell him as acid burns my throat and a sinking feeling takes root in my gut.

Darting around him, I quicken my pace, stopping fifteen steps past the back of my truck where the scent is the strongest.

"Just her blood, or do you smell Kate too?"

Trez halts behind me to my right side while I drop down on my haunches, looking at the dirt. It's dark, but I have the eyes of a predator, and among the dirt, gravel, and even a penny, I spot droplets of dried blood.

"You've got to be fucking kidding me," Trez whispers.

My feet twist, swinging my knees around as he swipes something off the ground. He holds the empty dart in the air, a scent of poison and shifter hitting me at once.

"Look familiar?"

21

KATE

I remember the first time I felt Wolfsbane enter my system like it happened yesterday. The thought always sends a tremor through my body. It's never the prick of the needle or the liquid being forced down your throat that sticks with you no matter how many times you've been poisoned with that vile plant.

The internal burning is the worst of it like you're being cooked from the inside out. Then the fever hits, and suddenly, you're colder than the coldest winter night. Your insides are like ice while your skin sweats the poison slowly from your body. Depending on how much you've been given, it can take hours or days to fully recover.

It took forty-eight hours to heal the first time Dick punished me using Wolfsbane. I was four, almost five years old. Trez had gotten in trouble the day before for breaking a vase while we were playing hide and seek inside Father's home. He punished my brother by withholding food, so I snuck down to the kitchen later that night and stole several slices of bread from the pantry.

I was caught, but it was after Trez had finished eating. We both had to suffer without meals for three days. Luckily, it was only me that had to ingest the Wolfsbane.

At least that time, anyway.

Eventually, Dick moved on to more physical forms of punishment. He favored striking his subordinates using silver-coated brass finger knuckles over the herb his witches turned into specialized poison. Only the top outer portion of the finger knuckles was coated in silver, but he wore gloves to make sure his skin didn't contact the metal that weakens us.

Shifters in my pack weren't allowed to hit the alpha back. Doing so was breaking *his* law. Punishment was having your head cut off or a silver bullet between the eyes. I've never seen him use a sword, but he did shoot a shifter once for arguing with him. No one toed out of line, except for me and sometimes Trez, in fear of what Dick would do to them. He was never challenged for his position. His shifters were too afraid.

Other times, he would force submission out of me in front of the pack. He'd make sure they knew I wasn't stronger than him. I despise Dick for using his alpha power on me the most. Unlike when Kane did it, my father's control felt unnatural.

My belief that my father is wrong is what keeps me from challenging him. I'm not afraid, but I am biding my time. I will be stronger than him one day, and he will roll onto his back and show his neck to me if it's the last thing I do.

But first, I have to find Trez.

That was the plan when... Henrik.

A bone-chilling sensation pricks its way down my spine, remembering he found me.

With Trez missing and after what happened with Kane, I'd forgotten my pack was likely searching for me. I hadn't expected any of them to cross the border, though.

Doing so could start a war.

Why would my father risk that? It's not like I'm of any importance to him. But then... it wasn't just Henrik that discovered my whereabouts. Dick's witch, Salem, was there too, and what did she call me? What did she say about my brother?

My head is fuzzy from being shot with copious amounts of Wolfsbane. A growl rumbles its way slowly up my parched throat, but it's not my wolf. She's still curled in a ball in the deepest part of my chest, unconscious, suffering the remaining effects of the poison.

My eyes snap open, thoughts of my shooter clearing some of the haze. Why was *he* there?

"Don't get up," a whispered voice says urgently. "Please don't move."

I jerk my head in her direction, smelling the witch who's feet from me. Shock must be evident on my face when I realize the girl isn't Salem. She's too young — a child or early into her teenage years.

"I'm Ivy," she says, her words shallow. "I mean you no harm. I swear it." Her voice is strong despite her teenage years.

Her eyes are brown with flakes of green and yellow, her hair a long shade of sandy blonde. She's huddled in the corner, her long dress covering knees that are pulled to her chest with one arm wrapped around them and the other flat against the floor. Even the sleeves of her dress are long.

Moving my eyes, I look left and then up, seeing steel bars closed around us on all four sides and above. We're caged, the earth our floor, and if the smell is an indicator, we're in a horse barn, yet I don't sense any animals among us. They'd be restless and spooked with a predator in their confinements.

"Where are we?"

I glance to my right, seeing Ivy with her back to the bars while my thoughts go turn toward Moonwake.

Ashleigh and I have an unspoken agreement. She places a hidden GPS device on my bike before I leave, and I don't destroy it until I'm fifty miles from Rivermoon Mountain. For some unknown reason, it gives her peace of mind to know we've returned home safely. Why I play along is lost on me, but I allow her to continue tracking us anyway. Anyone else and I would have beaten their ass.

Now, I don't know how I feel about it. A part of me hopes she did it this time, but the rational side knows she wouldn't have even if she'd known I would be leaving so soon.

Kane doesn't want us there. He doesn't want me there.

He threatened to kill any Marked Crest wolf, so despite the friendship Trez and he has, that goes for my brother, too. I just pray Jagger holds true to his promise because now that Henrik has me, I won't be able to easily escape to search for my brother.

That doesn't mean I won't try.

My father's beta will have to keep pumping Wolfsbane into me or shoot me with another silver bullet if he wants to keep me prisoner.

"Near Port Angeles in upstate Washington is what I heard a few days ago," she tells me, pulling my focus back to the here and now.

"Days?!" I ask, my tone giving away my shock. "How long have I been here?"

How long was I unconscious is what I should have asked.

Shit.

But the girl said we're in Washington. Why are we still in the States? Why didn't Henrik take me home to face my father?

"We've been here almost three days, but you've been out for four."

I can hang up any rescue attempt. Ashleigh definitely doesn't know where I am. Even if she'd tracked my bike, I doubt Henrik brought it with him when he took me from the diner, and well, let's face it, even if she did, Kane wouldn't have cared.

I'm not his mate.

He doesn't want me.

And that's fine. I'll figure my way out of this and make my father's beta pay with his life.

My only priority is getting out from within these bars and finding my brother.

"Good. Our little momma is finally awake."

"Salem." Her name falls from my lips without thought.

I shouldn't be surprised my alpha sent his witch to fetch his daughter. She probably used her magic to find me.

"So, you have heard of me, or has our little Ivy girl filled you in about me?" There's a giddiness to her tone that doesn't match her dark, haunting eyes. They're slate gray, but if you'd asked me the other day, I would have sworn they were black, the same as her long, straight hair.

I take notice of her hands and wrists peeking out from her long-sleeved dress. They're free of the black ink I saw.

How is that even possible?

Were they not tattoos?

"She hasn't told me anything," I say, suddenly feeling protective over a young witch and unsure why. I don't know Ivy, but there's something so innocent and sad about her that makes me want to shield her if this dark witch means her harm. Ivy is, after all, caged with me.

Make no mistake about it. Despite the black, inky markings missing and her eyes not as dark as I thought, this woman is very much into dark magic.

"I doubt that." Salem glances from me to Ivy. Something softens across her face, but it's gone within a blink of her eyes when they pop back to mine. "She's a talker like her mother was."

Ivy's abrupt intake of air through her lips tells me there's a story there and not a good one, and by Salem's words, that must mean her mother is dead.

"Was?" I can't help asking, my curiosity getting the better of me. Hell, it's not like I'm going anywhere. My ankles are shackled. Though they aren't made of silver, so my strength may get me out of them, but the bars won't be so easy.

Salem's eyes flash, darkening with a hint of red coloring the whites as her jaw locks. After a beat, she breathes and tilts her head, cracking the bones in her neck. She blinks and her eyes are dark gray again.

"That is neither here nor there. Frankly, wolf, it's coven business. You are not coven. Your pack has been searching for you for four nights now. Your mat—"

"Why would my pack be looking for me when Henrik found me? I'm guessing I have you to thank for that."

The real question is, why are we still in the U.S. and not

back home?

I'm about to ask her when she inserts a key I hadn't noticed in her hand. The latch releases, and the door creaks as it opens. Reaching into the pouch resting on her hip, she pulls out a bottle of water.

She tosses it at my face, and I catch the plastic container on reflex.

"Drink it. You must be dying of thirst from the amount of herbs you absorbed. Not to mention that nasty gunshot wound had gotten infected by the time we arrived."

I'd momentarily forgotten I'd been shot with a silver bullet. Henrik, if I had to guess, though, I suppose there could have been other men from my pack with my father's beta to apprehend me.

"The bottle is sealed. It's just water," she adds when I don't immediately drink the liquid.

She isn't wrong. I'm thirstier than ever, but I won't allow her or anyone else to know that.

Twisting the cap off, I lift the bottle to my lips. The second the cold fluid hits my throat, I have to suppress a moan and force myself not to guzzle the contents.

Parched doesn't come close to describing the way my throat felt while I'd been speaking. It was like a desert took up residence in me. My mouth was dry and my stomach ached from emptiness.

It still aches, but nothing I haven't experienced before. All part of surviving as a Marked Crest wolf for the two decades of my life.

I pull my bottle away before it's half drunk, knowing from experience that it'll only make me sick if I drink the whole thing too quickly.

"Wolfsbane is poison, not an herb," I tell her, then lick

my lips of the remaining water.

"One person's allergy to a plant is another person's healing medicine," she comments like it's not a big deal.

"We'll have to agree to disagree on that one."

Stepping just inside the door, she kneels down and extends her arm toward me, and says, "Take my hand."

I stare back at her, not saying anything and certainly not touching her. Who knows what she plans to do to me. I'm not going to help her. She wants to subdue me? Let her try. I won't go down without a fight.

"I'm not going to harm you. I'm doing you a favor," she says like it's an annoyance. Like my unwillingness to cooperate is futile.

"My father sent his witch to escort me home. I've been shot up with two types of poison and lost four days of my life. I'll pass on your offer. I won't be indebted to a witch."

"First, that was Henrik, not me. I was simply playing a part. And secondly, the most important thing you need to know: I am not Richard's anything. He doesn't own me or my coven."

"Not how he tells it," I say because it's the truth. He's used Salem's powers as threats against the pack many times. The pack is as afraid of her abilities as they are the Alpha's.

"Place your hand in mine, and I'll show you how I tell it. I'll show you the truth he's kept hidden from you for twenty years."

History got it wrong, or maybe the saying got messed up over the years. Curiosity didn't kill the cat. It slaughtered the fucking wolf because I lift my hand and extend my arm. Reaching out, I slip my fingers along Salem's icy palm.

Grasping ahold of me with a strength she shouldn't

possess, I go to rip my hand from hers but can't. Her hold on me is more secure than the metal latched around my ankle.

"We aren't continuing our conversation until I'm looking at the real you. The girl I concealed years ago."

Before I can demand she explain what the fuck that spiel meant, an icky warmth washes over me. Whatever she is doing makes any remnants left in my stomach roll. Nausea hits me instantly, as though someone snapped their fingers to make it happen. My mouth pools with saliva as fire bursts from my back, so suddenly it steals my breath. If I weren't already sitting on my ass on the ground, I'd be on my hands and knees.

A scream works its way up my throat, but I clamp down hard on my teeth, refusing to release the sound she's aiming for. It's a pain unlike anything I've ever experienced. It's worse than anything Dick has put me through.

Sweat beads across my forehead and washes past my brow. The water I swallowed threatens to come back up. Unable to keep my mouth closed, my lips part, and I pant.

"Make it stop," I beg.

My torso tumbles over, my free palm smacking the ground, making loose dirt jump into the air. My claws jut from my nail bed and dig beneath the compacted soil.

"Salem, you're hurting her," Ivy says. I barely registered her words from the ringing in my ears. My heart beats faster, hammering against my breastplate as the heat intensifies. It feels like I'm being branded.

"It has to be done," I hear the witch say.

When smoke wafts up my nostrils, stinging me, I force my head back. My wide eyes land on my bare arm, the limb of the hand still captured in Salem's firm grip.

My head twists, seeing eerie black lines flowing from

behind my shoulder and down my arms like a river with a slow current, crossing onto Salem's fingers, moving up her wrist, and disappearing beneath the cuff of her sleeve. It's the same markings I recall seeing outside the diner when I was on the ground looking up at her.

The furnace roaring on my back eases, the burning fades, and finally, my heart rate slows back to regular beats. That's when I notice the inky, slithering lines vanishing from my skin as they continue slithering just under the surface of Salem's skin.

"That's better," she draws out. "Black looks good on you. Prettier than that sickening unnatural blonde I saddled you with all those years ago. And your eyes... Stunning. I'm almost jealous of that vibrant shade of blue."

What is she...

I glance down my chest, seeing the ends of my hair covering my breasts. Strands that used to be blonde are now a shiny shade of black. The color reminding me of...

"What did you do to me?" I demand, yanking my hand back. She lets go, and my back crashes against the cage's bars.

"I turned you back into you, Anna Kate." A jet-black brow on one side of her face arches.

Goose bumps erupt along my arms as a chill races down my spine.

"Wh-why did you call me that?" Before she opens her mouth, I remember and say, "That's not the first time you've called me by two names. You said it the other day too."

"Would you prefer me to call you Katherine?"

A growl seeps from between my lips.

"I didn't think so. Why do you think that is?" She doesn't wait for a reply, and I don't have one to give. "Until you and

Trey, I had no idea that wolves wouldn't answer to any other name except the one their mother gave them."

"Trey?" I say, his name coming out slowly. "Kane's... brother?"

"Technically, yes, he is your alpha's brother. But you've called him Trez since I taught you how to speak."

"What the hell is going on?" I demand, jumping to my feet. "Kane is not my alpha." I ignore how my tongue suddenly tastes sour, the need for answers more pressing. "And how is Trez... Trey?"

"Well, that's quite a tale. See, there was a very powerful and determined *being* nearly two hundred years ago, before my time, who fell in love with a woman who was fated to someone else. That woman was a wolf shift—"

"What does that have to do with Trez and me or Kane's pack?" I ask, interrupting, the need to know if the thoughts adding up in my head are even possible because...

"I'm getting to that, but you should hear the full story. It might save your son from suffering a fate worse than the one you endured."

"My son?" *Is this witch crazy?* I think to myself. "I'm not having a—"

"You went into heat during a full lunar eclipse. During a blood moon, as your pack calls them. Your mate's wolf not only claimed you—nice bite, by the way—he knocked you up, dear."

"That isn't possible. I'm not of..."

My words fail me as my senses search out the link connecting me to my wolf. She was distant earlier, and I thought...

She wasn't curled into a ball to protect herself. She's protecting our baby, our pup.

22

KANE

Pressing my foot against the brake pedal, I come to a stop and shove the gear shifter into park in front of the lodge. We drove seven hours back home after spending a week driving up the coast of Washington and then over to Seattle, turning north until we reached the border. We went east again, but I turned us back not long after.

There was no sign of Kate anywhere. The closer I got to Seattle, the more my instincts told me I was going in the wrong direction.

I never once picked up her scent. Neither did Trez, so here we are, empty fucking handed and back where I started with a mate lost.

Only this time, it's wholly my fault she's missing.

"I'll run to my house to get everything I need for scrying. I'll let you know when I locate my sister." Storm pulls the handle on the back door behind Trez and slips out, leaving just him and me in the truck.

"We should still be out there looking for her instead of

being back here," Trez grumbles, his elbow digging into the padded fabric next to the window seal, his head resting in his palm, and his eyes staring out the windshield. Since we left home last week, we haven't stopped longer than to take a quick shower and get a few hours of sleep.

"We're going to find her. One way or another. Like I said yesterday, if I have to enlist help from the Yukon pack, I'll do it, and we'll cross the border."

But I don't think they took her to Canada. I told him that hunch yesterday, but he didn't want to hear it.

After I picked up the scent of Kate's blood outside that diner and Trez found the remnants of wolfsbane from a discarded tranquilizer, I had the manager of the eatery show us footage from their surveillance camera. I damn near lost my shit when I saw Kate get shot four times with poison-filled darts.

From the angle where the camera was positioned, it didn't show her attacker, but I knew who *he* was. His scent was all over the dart Trez picked up. That fueled not only my anger but pissed off my wolf too.

I should have been elated that he'd dropped the wall between us, that I could finally feel him inside me again. But seeing the Marked Crest beta emerge from the driver's side of the van, following Kate with a handgun aimed at her back, the fucking air was knocked from my lungs as my heart plummeted.

Then he shot her.

And my wolf raged.

She went down to her knees. I couldn't tell exactly where she'd been shot, and not knowing scared the fuck out of me. A witch appeared next, and Storm's sudden intake of air told me exactly who the dark-haired woman was before her name tumbled from Storm's mouth.

Salem Delvaux.

The darkest witch of our time, or so Storm claims. I don't know much about Salem besides a few stories she's told me since landing in Moonwake.

After the video ended, I went back to the parking lot to search for the item I noticed fell from Kate's fingers. Within a minute of looking over the ground, I found the key to her motorcycle. It had been partially covered by loose dirt. That's when my wolf decided my punishment wasn't over, and like pulling in a breath of air, the wall between his mind and mine was rebuilt and locked. I couldn't stop it from happening or the loss I felt when he was no longer present.

But that wasn't something I could dwell on at the time. Trez and Storm searched behind the diner and the gas station while I went inside to speak to the attendant. My tank had been filled. I saw him walk toward my truck when I'd entered the diner fifteen minutes earlier, and since I'd unlatched the fuel door after I'd put the truck in park, he wouldn't have needed me until I was ready to pay.

Only paying for fuel was the furthest thing from my mind. I wanted to see his surveillance in case we missed anything or if there had been anyone else with Henrik, like his alpha or other traitors I needed to know about.

I was about to ask him when Trez pushed past me to the cash register counter, demanding to know why the bike behind his building was hidden out of sight and where the woman it belonged to was.

The name sewn onto the guy's blue shirt read Ian in an italic font. His eyes widened, and he took a step away from the counter. When he didn't say anything, he only stared at Trez, then glanced my way, I growled loud and menacing.

"Answer him," I ordered, my words coming out slow but laced with the authority of an alpha.

"I don't know. The motorcycle was abandoned," he told us.

The problem with that statement was that I could smell his lie, his breath rancid as he spoke. Even from where he stood, the smell wafted up my nose, making me itch to get away from him.

When Kate was pleading with me before I said unforgivable things to her, I should have known she was telling the truth. She said that she didn't know about the mark on her back. That she wasn't playing me for a fool or here because Richard had sent her. If I'd paid attention like an alpha is supposed to, I would have known she wasn't lying.

Instead, I allowed my guilt to fester since entering her body back at the lodge. Thinking I'd betrayed my fated mate with another shifter made the need to hurt myself by hurting Kate the only thing I could see.

She may not forgive me—and I wouldn't blame her—but I will find her if it's the last thing I do. Henrik and that witch are going to die. They signed their death warrants when they took Kate. The back-stabbing bastard who put four tranqs in Kate... his time is coming to an end soon, but not before I find Kate.

No, I want him to see her and realize he failed at whatever he was trying to accomplish. Maybe he thought he was protecting me, but if that were the case, Ronnie would have come clean when he saw who Trez really was.

My brother.

One of our missing wolves.

But he didn't.

He didn't say shit about what he'd done before he shot Trez. No mention that he followed Kate, or that she's been taken against her will.

A rumbles courses up my throat, but I swallow the sound back down before it crests my lips.

I knew something was off with his smell, but I hadn't put two and two together. I still don't have all the details, but Ashleigh has been working on that since I called her to fill her in.

So far, she hasn't found anything to tell me why he'd help the Marked Crest pack. I don't plan to ask him until I get Kate back. Without further proof that he betrayed his people, I don't want to alert him that I know any more than what he claimed he was doing, which is why I'm not showing that video to mine or Jagger's parents yet.

Then there's Richard Everhart, the false alpha, as Storm called him. The only thing she knew was a former coven leader, another dark witch, had given him the strength and power of an alpha well over a century ago.

The desire for revenge sits heavy behind my eyes, but it's not my top priority unless that motherfucker has my girl—and then I'll rip him limb by limb to get to her. He doesn't deserve mercy, and his time is coming, I just don't know if it'll be me that rips his throat out or if it'll be Kate.

His crest is too similar to the symbol of the Bloodmoon pack: a reddish-orange full moon, a blood moon, with the head of a wolf faded into it. I've always said it can't be a coincidence. I still believe that now, and it makes me wonder if Richard was once a part of the Bloodmoon pack.

This isn't the first time that thought has come to mind. I

once asked my father years ago when I was a teenager, but he promised me there was no evidence of Richard ever being anyone except the Marked Crest alpha. But every alpha is someone before they become an alpha. My father has never cared to find out, but I will. Now that I know he isn't a true alpha, I'm determined more than ever to find out who he really is.

Wolf shifters are born with their wolf. You're either alpha, beta, gamma, a pack warrior, or an omega. A beta can rule a pack if there isn't an alpha leader, but it's rare. Most packs want an alpha and will seek one out until they find one.

The Yukon pack is an example of that. Caleb was a born beta. Their alpha was killed, though no one knows how or why. Caleb leads them, and to my knowledge, their pack is happy with him and does not wish to find an alpha. Betas have a similar power to alpha shifters; it's just not as strong, and they can't make their alphas submit like an alpha can their beta.

Pushing all that shit to the back of my mind, I release the latch on my seat belt. Trez does the same.

"You still haven't told me where you were when Kate thought you were dead. Or what happened before you showed up here," I say to him for at least the tenth time this week.

"If I were you, I wouldn't hold my breath for answers."

"Trez," I say his name like a warning as a growl rumbles from deep within my chest and up my dry throat.

"Give it a fucking rest and drop it, Kane. You brought us back to deal with your pack, so go do it."

"I brought us back because your *mate*—my beta—was about to abandon the pack to come find *you*."

"And so Storm could do her witchy shit and find *her* sister when we should still be looking for mine," he argues.

"Which could also help us find Kate." I pause, taking a needed breath before I blow up and force him to whine in submission. I've allowed his attitude to go on too long. I've had enough.

"Who is not your sister, by the way," I grit out. "Because you're *my* goddamn brother."

Storm reached out to another witch in her old coven two days ago. According to her friend, Storm's mother went into town for supplies early last week and never came home.

That coincided two days before Richard Everhart announced Trez's death, which explains the ashes. Not why he killed or had Storm's mother killed, though. Storm believes Salem was involved and that it was retaliation for her leaving the coven without their leader's permission.

The thing is, that scenario only makes sense if her mother's ashes were going to be given to Storm. How would her coven leader know Kate would steal them? How would Salem be so sure that Kate would bring that urn to the Bloodmoon pack?

No one besides my pack knew where Storm lived. She hadn't left pack land since arriving here—until five days ago.

There's one plausible explanation. If that's the case, then Kate isn't the only person's safety I have to worry about. I have to keep Storm safe too, and that means she can't cross the border in search of her sister without me.

The witch that Storm spoke to told her Ivy was last seen with their leader, but Salem had left to deal with a traitor of the coven. Whether or not Storm is the traitor her friend mentioned is still to be determined. What we do know is that Henrik and Salem were both in the Pacific Northwest five days ago when they took Kate.

Ashleigh hasn't found any evidence of them crossing the border into Canada, so I'm hoping they're still here. Somewhere. I just don't know why they wouldn't have taken Kate back to Rivermoon Mountain.

"We are going to find Kate, but you can no longer avoid our mother or your mate. Heads up, because he's about to—"

Before I can warn him, the passenger side door swings open with such force that metal slams into metal and I know without looking that Jagger bent my fucking door.

"You're going to fix that," I bite out.

Jagger flicks his blue stare toward mine. "You're the auto body technician, not me."

No, he's not. He's the motorcycle mechanic, but that doesn't mean he doesn't know how to repair damaged door panels because he's just as good as I am.

"You fucked it up, you're going to repair it."

"It'll have to wait. The pack is assembled in the pavilion. But you're on your own tonight. I have a bond to consummate that you kept me from doing." Jag rolls his head to Trez. "Let's go."

"Fuck you," my brother snaps.

Jagger jumps onto the running board and gets in Trez's face, a cocky snarl already formed on his lips.

"I plan to. Until the sun comes up. Now get out of the fucking truck before I drag you out, *baby*."

That purposeful endearment sets Trez off. Reaching up, he snatches my beta by the throat, his claws extending and piercing Jag's skin. "If anyone's going to be fucked, it's going to be you," Trez tells him.

Uhh, fuck me.

I slam my head back against the headrest. "Can you both get the fuck out of my truck?"

I don't have a problem with my best friend and my brother being together. They were always meant to be; just like Kate and me, but I'm not into voyeurism—or having them get it on in my truck.

Wrapping his fingers around the material on the front of Trez's t-shirt, Jagger yanks him out of the cab.

I wait a beat, then get out myself. Music coming from the pavilion hits my sensitive eardrum. Every Thursday night, the pack goes for a run, hunting deer or elk, then we roast a meal over the fire and spend most of the night partying and hanging out with each other as a family.

Shutting the door, I hesitate before I head toward the pack, knowing I'll find Annalise and Eli there, and I'm no closer to finding their daughter than when I left.

Where the hell are you, Kate?

23
KATE

Twenty-three hours after Salem revealed my supposed *real* identity, I'm still shell-shocked.

I'm Anna Kate Hayes, not Kate Everhart.

Jagger's younger sister.

Eli and Annalise's daughter.

Kane's fated mate.

It's too good to be true... and tragic at the same time.

There's no possible way for there to be any truth to her claim—except for the pregnancy part. I can see my wolf protecting our pup. I can feel them both inside me.

Unless...

Unless it's a spell and the witch has her own agenda for me returning to the Bloodmoon pack. I can only be pregnant if I were of age to go into heat, putting me at least a year older than the twenty-year-old I believed I was.

Sure, when I woke on Kane's couch, I was overwhelmed by the temperature of his house. Never once did I think I was in the midst of my first heat cycle.

Isn't that something a woman would know or realize was happening to her body?

Then again, I've never wanted to think about that approaching time. It wasn't something I wanted to face within my pack. Dick always decided which of his wolves would mate and with whom. He never allowed anyone the chance to find a partner of their choosing or their fated mate. When his female shifters reach fifteen, he pairs them with a male he selects.

He decided who Trez would be with when my brother was seventeen. We've never spoken of it, but I assumed Trez knew I'd never let that happen. At least not until he wanted it, and I knew he didn't want a lifetime bond with someone he didn't have feelings for. Like me with Kane, my brother has been in love with Jagger just as long as I have with Kane.

He may not admit it, but Trez likes Jag's possessive side as much as it irks him.

I used to wonder why Dick never selected a mate for me. I figured it was because it wasn't worth the fight he knew I'd put up. No one will ever force me to be with anyone not of my choosing.

I never submit to Dick Everhart without him physically breaking out into a sweat, working his alpha powers extra hard to be able to force me to comply. I won't willingly submit to a man or anyone who doesn't offer me equal respect. *And genuine love.*

Which is why I can't believe, even for a second, that I am who Salem claims I am. If I were Kane's mate, his wolf wouldn't have allowed him to emotionally hurt me as deeply as he did. He broke my heart.

I don't feel shit for you, he spit at me.

The force of that statement sucked the air from my

lungs. I'll be damned if I hand over my heart again to be trampled on, stabbed, or sliced into a million pieces.

But what if Salem's warning that Dick *needed* me impregnated, and not by just *any* alpha wolf but by Kane specifically, was true? That Dick and Henrik had two separate plans for me.

One wanted me for himself and had planned to vanish with me.

The other wanted the wolf pup inside my womb as an offering to the devil himself.

Both wanted to cage me.

And one of them would have achieved their goal had Dick not ordered the murder of one of Salem's witches for her ashes. According to Salem, he needed to make sure I believed my brother was dead and to send a message to her and the coven that resided in his territory.

Salem was his... Her magic belonged to him. Her purpose was for him just like the one before her.

Richard Everhart angered the wrong witch by killing Salem's sister. When Henrik executed Ivy's mother, it broke the hold the dark magic had on Salem, though, it hadn't freed her, just cleared the fog from a part of Salem that she thought she'd lost long ago—her light side.

That didn't suddenly make her a good witch again. No. Dark magic still thrives inside her, feeding on her feelings for a sister who is no longer part of this world, and Salem wants carnage and revenge.

Crossing said dark witch is what got Henrik captured early this morning before dawn.

Last night, after Salem removed the cloaking spell—a glamour she called it—she explained how Dick came into possession of a power he was never gifted with at birth. Then she fed Ivy and me.

I was starving after the poison wreaked havoc on my system, leaving me unconscious for days. The cold, leftover food Salem sat in front of me was bland, but I ate it like it was the best I'd ever had on my tongue and in my belly.

It wasn't. Far from it.

When I finished eating, she revealed why Dick needed my baby so desperately. Ice-cold fear danced down my spine following her words. The contents in my stomach threatened to come up, but I managed to swallow the bile back down the best I could, my vocals silent, unsure how to react in her presence.

She is a dark witch, after all. And one that isn't on my side. I didn't know how far I could trust her or if I was being set up for a bigger fall. I knew I had to get out of the shackle she had me in and outside the bars she caged me inside. My only option was to return to Moonwake.

If it wasn't a spell, if I am pregnant, then Kane deserves to know. That doesn't mean I'll stay in his pack. He probably won't believe I'm his fated mate anyway, and I have no intention of claiming to be *her*.

Salem told me Trez was already in Moonwake but didn't reveal how she knew that information. She did, however, tell me that Trez had overheard a conversation between herself and Dick about the two of us. That it had been done on purpose, and my brother played into their plan how they'd hoped.

Trez's wolf had been near a cave at the bottom of River-moon Mountain. A cave that has always been off-limits to our pack, forbidden to be within half a mile of its entrance.

As pups, we used to be curious about what was inside,

so we snuck in once, but it spooked my wolf, so we never went back. There was nothing out of the ordinary about the cave other than a bone-chilling feeling once inside.

Salem said she tugged on the rune on his back just a smidgen with her magic. That made Trez come to the mouth of the cave, but he didn't go inside. With his supernatural hearing, he picked up on their hushed conversation about two kidnapped wolf pups from two decades ago.

The seed was successfully planted is what she didn't have to tell me. I wanted to ask more: where'd we go when he disappeared, who took him, did anyone hurt him? But I wasn't going to push my luck with a witch. She could turn me into whatever she wanted. I didn't know her magical limit or if witches even had one.

So, I pulled my shoulders back and asked her what I needed to do for her to let me go.

A slow smile spread across her lips, the sparkle in her eyes wicked. She knew she had me where she wanted me, that I'd do anything to put as much distance between Dick and my pup as I could. Being in Port Angeles, I was too close to the border, only a ferry ride away from Canadian land. But in my mind, I wasn't anywhere close to being far enough from Rivermoon Mountain to feel safe.

"You'll escort my niece to Moonwake," she announced yesterday. "Take her to the witch that has made herself part of your alpha's pack. Ensure Ivy makes it safely into Storm's care, and you'll never see me again. Don't..." She paused for a hairbreadth, just long enough to cause a shiver to shoot down my spine. "You'll die a hundred deaths before your soul leaves this earth, mutt."

A low growl slipped from my lips in warning, but I didn't

say anything back to her. In that moment, I knew better than to use words.

An hour afterward, I watched a team of Monster Hunters torture Henrik to the brink of death for sixteen hours. It got to the point that it was so brutal I almost felt sorry for him. That didn't mean I did. It was the methods they used that rolled my stomach. At one point, my wolf lifted her head and urged me to run, to get away before they picked up our scent and came for us.

Before they finished Henrik off with a beheading, they kept him shackled in the silver-coated iron they're known for. They injected him with potent amounts of wolfsbane every half hour. They shot him several times with silver bullets. They interrogated him, wanting to know where others like him were. There were three of them, and they each used a blade made of silver to slice through his skin.

Even with my supernatural hearing, I wasn't close enough to hear more than Henrik's shouts, his whines, and the begging he did in the end. After the Marked Crest beta was dead, they removed the shackles, stuffing them into what looked like a tool bag you'd find at a local hardware store. Then they ripped the old horse farm apart, starting with the house and then the barn I'd woken up inside.

By then, Salem, Ivy, and I were watching from the thick forest that surrounded the farm. Salem assured me that they wouldn't find us. She told me when they first arrived, she'd been the one to tip them off. It was payback for Henrik killing her sister, for taking Ivy's mother from her.

When they lit fire to the barn, we turned away and trekked down a narrow dirt path that Salem said would lead us to the white van I'd seen from the diner.

Salem brought us close to Seattle, where we'd need to

sneak onto a freight train that would take us to Portland. Before Ivy and I got out, Salem produced my backpack. For whatever reason, she washed the dirty clothes I'd stuffed inside that I'd left on Kane's bathroom floor. Surprisingly, the money I had in my pocket was inside the pack.

Salem left us at a truck stop after that. She had plans for Richard Everhart, which meant she had to get home. Part of me was fuming that he would perish at her hands or by her use of magic. I wanted to rip his throat out with my canines because, until now, I hadn't fully realized that Dick may *not* be my father.

If what Salem told me is true, that he is the one that had the Moonwake pups kidnapped twenty years ago, then shouldn't it be me that gets to kill the Marked Crest alpha, not her?

I understand her need for vengeance, but shouldn't I also get retribution? Then again, maybe that's a selfish thought.

Does it really matter who kills him as long as his life ends?

There's another part of me that's relieved. If she takes his life, then I won't be putting my pup at risk to sate the dark voice inside me urging me to go north rather than south.

In the end, my wolf was the voice of reason, and in her way, telling me I had to make better, safer decisions for the baby growing inside me.

She was right.

So, I turned my back on the vehicle as it disappeared out of sight. Ivy and I went inside, we ate, and then we each showered, making use of the facilities offered to truckers and travelers.

"Let's go," I say to Ivy as she exits the shower room, clean and her wet hair hanging down her chest. "We have a freight train to stow away on."

My hands go to my abdomen, pressing lightly against the exposed skin between my cargo pants and the black crop top I changed into. I lost my padded leather biker jacket and my racing bike when I was poisoned and kidnapped from the diner, so the fastest way I know how to get back to Moonwake is by stealing a ride in one of the cargo containers.

"I promise I'll get you safely to your sister."

With that, she nods, and when I drop my hands to my sides, Ivy slips her fingers through mine.

24

KANE

"Where is he, Kane?" My mother's supernatural grip tightens, her arms squeezing around me.

After Jagger pulled Trez up the steps to the lodge, my brother jerked out of his hold and slammed Jag's back against the door. When their mouths crashed into each other's, I turned away and started walking toward the music.

The entire pack, minus Jagger and Storm, was hanging out, shooting the shit in their usual groups. Maddy was sitting in an Adirondack chair next to Ashleigh. Across from them on the other side of the campfire, my parents and Eli and Annalise looked deep in conversation. Ronnie was standing with one foot perched on the picnic table bench with his elbow braced on his knee and leaned over, talking to his sister and a few others.

Ash noticed me first but didn't move. My mother was next. The second her eyes met mine, she jumped to her feet and rushed to me, pulling me into an embrace without saying a word.

"He's with Jagger," I tell her.

Her chest deflates. I feel her disappointment through our pack bond and because I'm her alpha, it sends a sharp ache through the organ in my chest.

"Does he not want to see me?" Her voice is a whisper next to my ear.

"Of course he does." I tighten my arms around her, hugging her back. "Trez is still adjusting to every—"

She pushes away from me, her brows furrowed, her mouth hanging open. "Why are you calling him by *that* name when he's Trey?"

"Mom," I start. "I know you've been waiting a long time, too long, to find him, to see him, but you cannot start calling him Trey just because—"

"The hell I can't," she barks, cutting me off again. Her eyes harden as her temper flairs to life. She steps back but holds her chin high. She isn't an alpha female, but you'd never know that being the strong woman she is. "I named him Trey, and that is who he is. I will not call him by any other name again."

"You will until he says otherwise, and that's an order."

In my twenty-eight years of life, I've never spoken to my mother with the breath of authority. Sure, I've been her alpha for over three years, but that doesn't mean I lost my respect or no longer value her opinion. I'm the man I am today because of the way she raised me.

My father shaped me in many ways; he made me strong and ruthless when I needed to be, while my mother ensured I knew the importance of listening to my pack, to consider what they needed on an individual level.

Which is exactly what I did with Trez.

"I don't—"

"You do take orders from me." I stare down at her. Despite being five feet ten inches tall, she's still a bit shorter than me. "So does everyone in this pack."

At that, my father and Eli jump to their feet, having heard the authority in my tone. An angered growl hums through my head, Jagger no doubt picking up on our confrontation.

Annalise's eyes are wide, her expression worrisome.

I take a breath, hoping it calms the rage building inside me as my alpha side pushes me, wanting to make my mom submit. Maybe she hasn't accepted that her husband isn't the alpha any longer like I thought she had. She pledged her loyalty to me the same as everyone else in the pack.

Ashleigh moves quickly, standing at my back in case this goes south. Maddy isn't as fast but runs over, halting next to Ash. Being human has never stopped Maddy from being one of us. She's trained with shifters her own age since she was a small child. Granted, everyone knew they better not hurt her or take it too far, or they'd face me and not like the consequences.

"I'm sure your *husband* told you I took Trez with me to look for Kate because he was overwhelmed by the mate bond, and yes, he did need a breather from Jagger, but the main reason I kept him from here was because of you. Because I knew this is what you'd do."

Maybe I'm being a dick and not fully considering her feelings, but Trez is the one who just found out his whole life thus far has been a lie. His sister, whom he loves more than anyone, isn't even his sister. That the place he's pulled to visit, the people he's come to know as friends are his family, that here is where he was always meant to grow up. Where they were supposed to be this whole time.

It's a lot to come to terms with, not to mention the mate bond that was forced on him, though that piece of him is more settled since we got back, even if he hasn't realized it yet.

"My son was taken from me, Kane. It's been over twenty years. I never thought..." Her voice catches in her throat, and it makes me want to pull my mother back into a hug, but I can't do that yet. I have to get her to understand, to take a step back from her emotions as a mother. She needs to see Trez as the man she's watched him become, not the loss of a son she's pined over for two decades.

"I know he was. He was taken from us all. They both were." I step forward and place my hands on top of her shoulders. "If you rush to mother him before he's ready, you may regret it."

"You should have waited before you left with him. Your father is right," she says in anger. "You're not making the right decisions as alpha, Kane. You need to st—"

A growl echos all around us, the trees moaning and swaying as limbs rub against each other just before Jagger appears beside me in only a pair of jeans. Scratches and dried blood dot his torso and arms. Those marks will be gone within an hour after his healing abilities kick in.

"You're out of line, Becca," he seethes, his bright eyes hard and trained solely on my mother.

She jerks away from me, taking two steps back. My father and Eli come to stand on each of her sides.

"Where is Trey?" she asks, an order in her tone when she speaks to her beta. "Where's my son, Jagger? The two of you have—"

"He is Trez to everyone in the pack unless he tells us otherwise," Jag says slowly, speaking to her but making his voice carry so that everyone in the pack hears him. Then he folds his arms across his chest.

At that, my mother crosses hers as well and pushing her shoulders back now that she's standing between my dad and Elijah.

"I wasn't convinced at first, but now I am. You're both going to announce to the pack tonight that Kane is no longer our leader. Dante and Elijah will—"

"That isn't going to happen, Mom," I say, tired of this shit and hating that I have to put her in her place because she's my mother, but doing exactly that so the pack knows I will not stand for this, not even from my mother whom I love more than I could ever put into words.

"I don't think you want that, Becca," Jag follows. "You're hurt and lashing out because neither Kane nor I are telling you what you want to hear. Don't push this. Don't make yourself a widow and your sons fatherless. Trez is my mate, and until he's ready, which may never be, you and everyone else will call him Trez, not Trey. Am I clear?"

"Watch it, Jagger," Eli warns his son.

"Elijah," Annalise reprimands her husband as she joins our crowd, or standoff is more like it, before turning to face my mother, her best friend. With her back to me, she says, "Kane is alpha whether the three of you like it or not. Jagger is beta. None of you get to decide they aren't fit for the roles we raised them for. Why don't you ask yourself *why* they're adamant on this, Becca, instead of fighting against it?"

Mom steps forward, closing the short distance between her and Annalise.

"I've waited twenty years to see my son, and they act like Trey is still a..." She takes a breath, either unable to or refusing to say a Marked Crest wolf.

She's wrong, but I don't tell her that because it wouldn't help defuse the situation.

Sure, I fought the truth that Trez couldn't be my missing brother at first, but that had more to do with my guilt over Kate and how I treated her after the best hours of my life were spent between her soft, perfect thighs. I threatened her and kicked her out of the pack while the whole time I'd been staring at my mate.

"So have I," Annalise cites. "But we've also gotten to know them and them us over the past five years. You cannot expect either of them to start calling us Mom overnight, Becca. How do you think Trez feels? He's barely an adult and just learned he's been lied to his whole life while the person he's closest to is missing and who knows where. On top of that, she isn't the sister he believed she was. Now he has an entire pack expecting him to be someone he doesn't even know. Trey may be Trez, but that doesn't mean Trez is Trey. Give the boy time to adjust to this while we find Kate."

"Speaking of my daughter," Eli interrupts. "Where is she, Kane? All we know is that she showed up here, and then the next day, she took off to look for... him." Elijah juts his chin up, gesturing behind me.

I cut my eye down to my side. Trez stops, closing the corner between Jagger and me, his eyes on our mom while his arm flies out, his hand smashing a t-shirt against Jag's chest. Reaching up, Jagger snatches the material from him and pulls the shirt over his head and through his arms.

I'd heard him stomping toward us, but Annalise was on a roll, and it's rare you hear her speak her mind. She's always been reserved, whereas Jagger is more like his dad. Apparently, Kate is more like Eli too, now that I know she's his daughter.

I glance in my father's direction, meeting a stare already on me and asking a silent question. Elijah doesn't know what happened between Kate and me. If he did, he would have made it known just now. The slightest shake of his head answers me, telling me he didn't share the fact that Kate went into heat while she was here or how I reacted the following day that made her leave.

Now, I'm curious why he wouldn't tell his best friend.

Did he keep that from my mother too?

"Tre…" Mom stops herself, her eyes snapping to mine in the briefest of moments before they glide back to her younger son. "You're here. I—"

"Annalise is right, Becca," Trez points out, causing my mother to gasp in a breath through her open mouth at using her nickname instead of mom or mother. "You'll only upset yourself more if you expect me to be someone I'm not. I'm still the person I was when I was here in February. The same man the year before that. Call me by the name you know me as, or don't call me anything at all."

"You don't know who you are because you were stolen from us." The heartbreak on my mother's face is too transparent to go unnoticed. I feel the agony in her voice as though it's my own. "This is precisely why Dante is the alpha our pack needs, the leader you need in order to find the person you were meant to be."

Jagger and Ashleigh growl at the same time.

"Me and mine stand behind the true alpha and beta of the pack," Ronnie states, gesturing to my father and Eli while his old eyes meet mine, his chin raised too high in the presence of his alpha—me. He and his small circle joined the crowd after Annalise confronted my mother.

His sister nods in agreement while his niece's mouth

hangs open in shock. Laney looks between me, her alpha and her boss, and then her uncle, unsure whose side to stand with. After a beat of silence, she steps closer to my side, picking her alliance.

"Enough," I yell. At this point, I've been quiet too long. I've allowed this to go too far.

Something has to be done, but without my wolf present, fueling my alpha power, I'm not sure I can bring all of them to their knees. I'm about to have no choice but to tap into my reserves, and who knows how long that'll last. I don't need to use any unnecessary strength while Kate is missing.

I don't have a problem being challenged. I welcome it and every pack member's opinion. This, however, is disrespect. The nearly two hundred people watching this play out can't see me weak.

Luckily, my father saves me from having to decide.

"Rebecca." Dad's voice booms before he steps forward. His face is hard, but his arm reaches up, his fingers gently taking hold of his wife's chin and tipping her head back. "I love you, baby, but this stops now. You'll only divide the pack, and that's the last thing we need. Kane is alpha. He will be alpha until his last breath or until he steps down like I did, handing the role to his son."

Or daughter, I think to myself. Jagger snickers, letting me know he heard my thoughts.

I'm not old school or have a warped way of thinking. Kate is proof enough that a woman can lead in the same way as a man. I've watched Ashleigh grow into a fierce fighter. Even Maddy, our human who wishes she were a wolf shifter, is resilient. She may not match a supernatural on the same level, but she's the strongest human I've ever seen. And if I have an alpha-born daughter, that's exactly the role I intend to shape her for, provided she wants it.

But first, I have to find my mate and convince her to forgive me.

Even if that means groveling until my last breath.

Because that's exactly what I'll do, on my knees, in front of her with my neck bared if she wants it.

For her, I'll submit.

25
KANE

The next night, we're no closer to finding Kate or Storm's little sister Ivy. There haven't been any reports of descriptions that match Henrik or Salem crossing the border.

I should be happy about that, but they could have boarded a ferry or a ship. It would be easy to pay off someone and be a stowaway, and no one would be the wiser.

Her being in Canada feels off, but there isn't a reason I can fathom to keep her in the States. She has to be there, yet my gut says to keep searching here.

Since waking this morning, there's a heavier weight pressing against my chest than last night. It's as though she's closer than she was. I felt the same way while driving through Seattle a few days ago. I thought I could feel her, but I know that isn't possible.

She wears my bite, but I don't wear hers. There isn't a solid bond connecting us... except she may be pregnant with my pup.

Still... I can't run off of a gut feeling alone.

I need a fucking break.

Something.

Anything to guide me in her direction.

So far, Storm scrying for her sister's location isn't panning out like she was so sure it would.

"This is Caleb," a gruff voice greets me, my ear pressed against my smartphone.

"Kane from Moonwake," I reply.

"And what can I do for the Bloodmoon alpha?" There's a smugness to his tone, but I expected that. My father warned me that the Yukon pack alpha was a cocky son of a bitch, despite being a born beta. "Ready to take me up on the offer I made to your parents two weeks ago?"

"No," I deadpan, being honest with him. "But I need to know if it comes to that, do I have you as an ally?"

A beat of silence follows my question, a pause too long for what Dad and Eli assured me he was willing to do. *Bringing war to Richard Everhart's territory.*

"Do you want to find your mate and brother, or is it Everhart's daughter you'd rather have more, Orion?"

I swallow the growl that tries to rumble past my throat, the flutter in my chest telling me that my beast heard his mention of Kate. My finger goes to my lips when Trez opens his mouth. To say what, I don't know, but I don't want Caleb Drake to know my brother is listening.

Alphas have an unspoken rule amongst ourselves. When we communicate with another alpha, we do so in private. Should we choose to relay the details of our conversation to another, that's on us. It's meant to be out of respect and because we're of the same rank, but I've always included my beta when dealing with pack business. If it concerns my pack, it concerns Jagger too. He can't do his job if I keep him out of the loop, and since he took Kate's bike to my shop this morning, he hasn't returned.

After we found Kate's racing bike behind the gas station building, I didn't want to leave it. Trez helped me lift the bike into the back of my truck and strap it down.

"Kate," I say with noticeable irritation, "is no concern of yours."

"I don't know about that," he quips. "From everything I'd heard, she sounds like my type. Maybe I want Richard's territory plus his daughter as payment for my help."

"Touch her, and I'll rip your fucking throat out."

My fingers tighten around the device clutched in my hand so tightly that the crack in the glass muffles his warning growl.

"Take that however you want to, Drake. Kate is mine," I declare. "If you're looking for pussy, look somewhere else, or we're going to have a problem that can only be solved one way."

I don't want to start a war with him or his pack. Not when the potential of another is so high. Caleb could easily swap sides and help Richard defeat us instead of allying with my pack.

"Careful, Orion. My pack numbers triple yours. I'm not an enemy you want to make."

He sounds so sure of himself that his voice is starting to piss me off.

"You aren't my only option, and if you go sniffing around a woman I've already claimed, it'll be me who you don't want as an enemy of yours."

I yank the phone away from the side of my head, bringing it in front of me. Sure enough, the screen is shattered, but the end call button is still viewable, so I tap it and hang up on the motherfucker.

I wasn't bluffing when I told him he wasn't my only option. Miles McKenna wants Richard's territory as much as he does. The Alberta alpha has never shied away from spouting off his dislike for all Marked Crest shifters.

McKenna and his wife are friends with my parents as well as Elijah and Annalise. Once a year, in the Spring, Miles travels to our pack for five days, and my parents go to his land in the Fall. He never understood why my father allowed Kate and Trez to visit, whereas his wife, Addy, thought differently. I once overheard her tell my mother that it could be a sign of a change to come in the future.

"So now *you've* claimed Kate, not your wolf?" Trez remarks, making my gaze flick to where he stands, his arms crossed, his back against the post. We're outside the lodge on the porch, me sitting in one of the chairs and him across from me, irritation marring his face. "My sister would likely kick your ass if she'd heard that declaration."

"Probably," I agree, ignoring the fact that he continues to refer to Kate as his sister every chance he gets. I don't know if he wishes the truth about who they are wasn't ever revealed or if he's holding on to the only thing he's ever known.

Kate.

The only family he's truly ever had until now.

I know what he's feeling, but I don't have a clue what he's thinking. He's overwhelmed, but above everything, he's worried about Kate, so he continues to push everything else to the back burner.

"We're going to find her," I say, my eyes never leaving his amber ones.

"She'd already be here if you hadn't flipped out on her." His arms drop and he turns, giving me his back while bracing his hands on the railing. "There's no telling what our... what Dick is doing to her."

An audible exhale leaves his mouth, then his head shakes ever so slowly while his fingers tighten around the wood and his claws extend.

I'm standing in the next breath. Taking a stride forward and then another, I mirror his stance beside him. There aren't any shifters in the lodge tonight. They've been giving me a wide berth since the confrontation with my mother last night.

"She isn't there."

Saying the words out loud feels right, but I can already tell Trez doesn't share the same intuition before he turns, facing my profile. His anger coats my tongue and burns down my esophagus.

"Well, she isn't here either. Why are you so scared to cross the fucking border anyway? If we stand a chance to find her, then we actually have to go look. I'm done waiting on Storm when it's Kate I care to find. No one else."

I don't disagree with him. We should be out there looking for Kate. I only came back because Jagger couldn't mentally handle being away from his mate any longer. Finding Kate is my top priority, but I'm still the alpha of Bloodmoon. I have to balance what's best for the pack and everyone in it. I didn't know which direction to go that would lead me to find her, whereas I knew where Jag was, so I gave him and Trez what they both needed.

"My reasons for staying out of British Columbia have nothing to do with being afraid," I finally answer. "I want to rip that motherfucker from limb to limb so bad I can almost taste his blood coating the inside of my mouth."

"Then what's holding you back? If you want to kill him, do it. Do something, Kane. You're the alpha of the pack he stole two shifters from. He took your mate, and now you have the confirmation you've been searching for, yet you're here doing nothing."

"If I cross the border between his territory and mine, I will hunt him down, and there is no one that will stop me. I will slaughter anyone who gets in my way. That's why. But whether I like it or not, what was done to me, to Jagger, to our parents is nothing compared to what Everhart did to you and Kate. His life isn't mine to take. It's yours, or it's Kate's."

"You want it to be yours," he states, like he can easily feel my emotions the way I can his now that the mark he wore on his back is gone, and maybe he can. It's a two-way link. The pack can feel me if I allow them, but shielding my feelings has always been second nature, except with Jagger. I don't even let Ashleigh in that far. With Trez and Kate, I never needed to put up a wall because I believed they were Marked Crest wolves.

"Of course I do. He tried to destroy this pack before I was born. Because of him and that fucking witch of his, I fought everything I've ever felt for Kate, thinking those feelings were wrong. I've been at war with my wolf just as much as I have been at war with myself. I don't just want to kill him, brother. I want to make him hurt. I want to make him regret what he did a thousand times over. I want him to beg for mercy, knowing he won't find an ounce of it from me."

"Kate can have Dick. I want his beta," he bites out as a bitter taste coats my tongue at the same time.

He doesn't say more, and when I hear the wood creak, my eyes flick down to where he's gripping the railing.

"Something there I should know about?"

"No," is all he gives me in reply.

"Trez," I say, dragging out his name as the hair on the back of my neck stands and anger rolls inside my chest, knowing whatever reason that caused him to hate Henrik Hale so much is one I'm not going to like.

He once told me Richard's beta caught him fucking another shifter, but he didn't really go into it, only that he and the other guy, another shifter, both lost their virginity to each other. All I know is that it happened right before the first time they showed up in Moonwake.

Maybe I should have pried more, but he didn't act like it was a big deal.

"You know I can make you tell me, right?"

I'd only force the truth from his lips if I thought I had to know to ensure his safety, but I'd rather him tell me because I know it isn't *nothing*, that's for damn sure.

Fear and guilt, with remnants of sadness and a mountain of hatred, all wash through him within seconds.

"You probably could, but don't." He turns to face me. "It's my shit. Just let this one go."

"Tell me why first. Are you ashamed of something, because if that's—"

"It's not that, but if I tell you, if you find out, then it would only be a matter of time before my sister finds out. Kate is who I don't want to know. I won't put that on her. Ever. So, I'm asking, Kane, let it go. I'm fine. I'll be even better if I'm the one that kills Hale. But if not, dead is still dead as long as that's the end result."

"Fine," I concede, and with a sigh, I say, "Then let's go pick up Jag. Being here isn't going to find Kate."

I push off the railing and start toward the steps. "We get her back first, and then we go after Hale and Everhart."

Trez says something, but whatever it was gets drowned out when Jagger's voice inside my head stops me in my tracks.

Kate's in Portland.

"Are you sure?" Trez says out loud, which tells me that Jagger is speaking to us both, using his mate link with Trez and with me through ours.

"How do you know she's in Portland?" I ask, saying the words out loud and in my head before flipping around to face my brother. Usually, I'm protective over my link with my beta, but it wouldn't be right to keep it from Trez.

"What the fuck?" is out of his mouth quicker than his eyes flash with jealousy. "You heard him?"

His jaw firms as his teeth gnash together.

"Just get in the truck." I turn and jump from the top step to the ground. "We're coming to get you, Jag. You still at the shop?"

The sound of a motorcycle engine roars in the distance, too close to have been my body shop, but the sound is unmistakable—*Kate's bike.* Trez and I look at each other when he leaps off the last wooden step.

I'm going after my sister.

A growl comes from Trez's mouth.

"Come on," I tell him. "With her bike, he'll beat us there no matter how fast I drive."

"Wait." Storm halts us before we climb into the cab of the truck. "I found her."

"Ivy?" I question, confused by how Jagger suddenly

knows where Kate is, but Storm has been scrying for her little sister since we got home yesterday.

"No. Kate. My sister's location is still hidden, so I tried looking for Kate. I found her almost instantly."

Storm lifts her hand, and I see her holding Kate's leather jacket. When we found her bike, her jacket had been draped over the handlebars.

"Get in," is all I say, and before her door is latched, I gas it.

I'm going to find you, Kate. I just hope you have it in you to forgive me for all the damage I've done to us.

26

KATE

"Why are we staying here?" Ivy whines.

"I told you," I remind, *for the tenth time*. "We need a real meal and some sleep. Plus, I have to figure out how to get us to Moonwake... unless you can morph into a four-legged creature who can run for hours at a time."

"You call *this* a real meal?" She holds up the two paper bags she's carrying. I'm toting the other four. "Are shifters not susceptible to heart disease? Because witches are."

"What happened to the kid I met two nights ago? She didn't complain."

That's all she's done since we hopped onto the train that brought us from Seattle, Washington to Portland, Oregon. Before Trez and I started racing street bikes, which is how we bought our first set of wheels, we'd jump different transits to get here. From Portland, we'd shift and travel the rest of the way on paws. Sometimes, we lucked out and found local trains running through smaller towns.

"I'm not a kid," Ivy snaps back.

She is, but nothing I'm going to say to her will convince Ivy of that fact. I was the same way at fourteen, maybe even worse.

"Look, the cost of food and the motel room for the night took most of the money I have. It's not like we have many options. The only thing I know to do is steal someone else's ride."

"Then let's do that and be on our way," she chirps up, sarcasm rolling so thick off her lips it makes me cluck my tongue in annoyance.

"It's not that simple."

"It is. You just don't *want* to get there. I thought you wanted to find your brother, or is seeing your mate what has your panties twisted?"

"Okay, miss know-it-all, tell me the easy way because I'm not carjacking anyone."

With my luck, I'd give an old man or old lady a heart attack and have to live with that on my conscience for the rest of my life. No, thank you.

And maybe I'm ignoring her remark about Kane.

She may have a point, and I don't like that a part of me is scared to go back to Moonwake. The closer we get, the more prominent the ache in my chest gets.

"We use magic, of course."

I look at her like she's grown two heads.

"Yeah? Exactly how is Earth magic going to start an engine? Huh?"

She rolls her eyes, continuing to act every bit of her annoying and defiant age.

"I know other magic besides drawing from my elemental magic," she confesses.

"Light or dark? Because if you say dark, you can forget

about it. I've experienced enough of your coven's witchy shit to last a lifetime."

Just the thought of the magic Salem pulled out of me sends a chill down my spine. I've never felt that much pain in my life. Not even brute force could amount to the grip she had on me. I was paralyzed in the literal sense until she released me.

"Not all dark magic is bad, and if you only use it—"

"No." I cut her off, then veer left, walking the path to the room I rented for the night.

Ours is room twelve with two double beds. I'm starving. The sooner we scarf down the burgers and fries, the sooner I can get some shut-eye and leave dealing with finding a vehicle and adding theft to my rap sheet for tomorrow.

Dark magic is out of the question, and I'm about to reaffirm that stance with Ivy when the hairs on the back of my neck stand, alerting me to something.

But what?

I turn, doing a one-eighty to face Ivy. Her eyes widen, but she stops before plowing into me. I shove the bags in my hands out for her to take, then pull the key from my pocket.

"Go to the room. Don't open the door unless it's me," I order her.

"Why? What's up?"

"I don't know. Something is off, or we're being watched." That feeling dawns on me.

"You shouldn't have taken the crystal off your wrist like I told you." She huffs, struggling with everything gripped in her hands and resting on her arms.

"The time for *I told you so* can wait."

After Salem did her voodoo, she made me wear a bracelet with a lone crystal wrapped in leather around my wrist. Ivy already wore a similar smoky quartz on hers. She's still wearing it, along with an amethyst stone on her other wrist and a necklace with a white crystal dangling from it.

I tore mine off during the train ride and tossed it out the open cargo door into the passing wind with a *fuck you and your dirty magic* salute.

"Looks like I get two for one."

I whip around to face the parking lot while shoving Ivy behind me and backing her up against the brick wall between rooms four and five.

A guy in jeans and a dark T-shirt stands twenty feet from us between two sedans parked on the second row of parking spaces, an empty spot between the two vehicles.

He cocks his head to the side to peer around me, a handgun dangling between his fingers at his side. There's a tattoo on his neck, and with the street lamp shining at the right angle, I can see the symbol clearly.

The mark of the slayer of monsters.

A monster hunter.

The tattoo is mostly black, a shotgun pointing down with two daggers crossed behind it and a bullet on each side of the X. Red ink drips from the tips of the blades like blood.

"What are you, sweetheart? You're too small to be a werewolf."

"I'm a wolf *shifter*, you dumbass, not a werewolf," I reply, even though it's Ivy he was speaking to.

I should have smelled him before he'd opened his mouth. Their scents are all the same like their members are required to wear their own brand of monster-killing cologne.

"Same difference, bitch." His human brown eyes snap to mine.

"It's not, but call me a *bitch* again, and I just might become feral like one." My hands go to rest on my hips.

"You're a smoking hot wolf bitch, I'll give you that." Then he snickers. "I might have to take my time with you. Find out if you're just as hot on the inside as you are on that fine exterior."

He nods his head in my direction as he licks his lips, making bile threaten to come up my esophagus.

Gross.

"There you go, using that *word* I warned you not to say." I smile, despite knowing there are definitely going to be silver bullets in the gun he's waving around, and getting myself shot again is not on my bingo card tonight. "The only thing you're going to feel is my claws ripping you to shreds."

If I can't be the one to kill Dick, thanks to Salem taking that luxury from me, then maybe I can take out all my years of aggression and hatred for the man I thought was my father on this douchebag. Maybe even send a message to his friends that I'm the wrong supernatural creature to fuck with.

"No, I'm the man whose dick you're going to swallow just as soon as I pry all those sharp teeth and claws from your body, dog."

"You should have gone back with the werewolf name-calling. It's more of an insult than being called Fido, you dickless twat."

With his free hand, he cups himself between the legs and jerks his hand and junk upward.

"Oh, I've got di—"

Before he finishes that statement, a sharp intake of air comes from Ivy's mouth a hair's breadth before claws sink into the side of his neck. My eyes never blink, watching the whole scene.

His throat is sliced open, blood spilling over ripped flesh.

Then, his deceased body is shoved sideways, landing ten feet from the man standing in the hunter's place.

Our stares lock.

"Jag."

27
KATE

My body is as still as a statue, my eyes mirroring his unblinking stare.

Is that relief in Jagger's blue gaze?

A choked scream from behind rips me out of the trance I'm stuck in, my body jerking around to face Ivy. The horror in her eyes looks through me as the sacks of food fall from her arms.

"H he sliced t that guy's th throat," she stutters.

I grab the sleeves of her dress, pulling her into an embrace.

"H-he's dead, i-isn't he?"

"He was a hunter, Ivy," I inform her. "He was going to kill us both." I squeeze her and then pull away so that I can look her in the eyes. "Jagger saved us. He's my friend. You don't have to be afraid of him."

Her heart pounds so fast I can feel the pulse in my ears. A minute of silence passes when her eyelids snap up, her shell-shocked eyes meeting mine.

"I've never seen a..." she trails off, her gaze peering around me.

"But you were there when we watched Henrik get killed," I say, confused.

"Salem told me not to watch. I didn't see it happen. Plus, my eyesight isn't like yours. I wouldn't have seen whatever you saw from where we stood."

Her body tenses up a hair's breadth before a squeak slips from between her lips as she backs fully against the brick wall. That's when his steps register from behind me.

"Kate," he whispers.

Warmth envelops my chest at the sound of his voice. My wolf perks her ears, having heard him too. There's a pull inside of me, but not like a command; more like a connection fusing together, like recognizing like.

Slowly, I turn, and when I'm facing him and my eyes land on his, he jerks me forward. Banding his arms around my waist, I can't do anything other than wrap mine around his shoulders.

"After you left, I thought I'd never see you again," he admits, fear in his tone, but I'm too stunned to respond, so I hug him back. For the first time since I left Moonwake, I find breathing easier.

A minute passes when he slowly pulls away. "Don't ever do that to me again." When I don't respond, just continue staring, Jagger adds, "Do you hear me, little sister?"

"Sister?" I say, but it's more to myself than to him.

Why would Jagger call me little sister?

I know what Salem said, but it isn't fathomable.

It just isn't.

My focus veers off in thought because what if I'm not allowing myself the option to consider what Salem said as the truth? But then my gaze catches on his throat, and my mouth drops open, that train of thought forgotten as my feet retreat, stepping away from him when I see the claiming mark.

"You're mated. But…" My chest deflates as air rushes out. "I-I don't smell Trez. I smell someone else."

My heart rate kicks up a notch at the realization. No, he can't be. My brother loves him too much for Jagger to have found someone else. And I thought…

"You smell different too," he says as if that's an answer to the question I haven't asked.

"What?" I bite out, a growl following as anger coils inside my head, making my neck stiff.

A smirk takes up residence on his face. It relaxes him and shows me the side of my friend that I'm used to seeing.

"You smell like one of us now. So does he. I'm mated to Trez, Kate. There was never going to be anyone else." The way he says it is like he's stating the obvious. Relief is almost instant as his words wash over me, and that's when I take in the *whole* bite.

"It's an interesting placement for a mark," I tell him when I don't know what else to say.

I mean, it is interesting being in the center of his neck. Without wearing a turtleneck, there's no covering that scar.

Jagger laughs. "And you and everyone think I'm the possessive one."

"Trez made it after I left?" I ask, and without waiting for an answer, I continue needing to know more. "Kane didn't hurt him?"

"Kane knows Trez is his brother, Kate, but even if he weren't or he didn't know, Kane would never have followed through with his threat. Not to Trez. Not to you either."

His brother? Trez is my brother.

I step to the side, needing distance to think and not wanting to crowd Ivy at the same time. My head swings away from him, my focus landing on the motorcycle I thought I'd lost as I try processing everything.

"My bike," I say in lieu of the shit running rampant in my head.

Little sister.

His brother.

"We searched for you." Jagger's voice snaps my focus back on him. "Well, Kane and Trez did. For a week, they scoured everywhere between Moonwake up I-5. They found the bike where Hale took you from."

Does he know what happened in the parking lot of that diner?

"Here," he says, and my eyes flick downward, seeing Jagger reaching into his blue jeans pocket, where he pulls out the key to the motorcycle.

"No." I hold up my hand, stopping him from handing it to me while taking another step away from him and Ivy. I glance at her and then back to Jag as I step back again. "You can take Ivy to her sister. I promised I'd get her to Storm. You can take her on the bike and get there faster than I would have made it."

This works out better than me taking her there. He can do it, and she'll be safe with him. I trust Jagger.

"Kate, no." He shakes his head. Worry and something else—concern or fear—seep into his features. His legs move, but he only takes a short cautious step toward me. "You're coming home with me."

A tingle runs down the left side of my neck behind my ear as my vision becomes brighter.

Jagger is in front of me before I can take my next breath. "Shut it the fuck off. Don't you dare open your mouth right now." His palm suddenly covers my lips and half of my face. I jerk away, shoving him while he continues. "Do you even know?"

"Know what?" I bark while I keep backing away when what I really want to do is lash out at him for putting his hands on me. Something inside me pushes at the back of my skull to make him submit.

He doesn't tell us what to do.

Jagger's arm lifts, his fingers gently grabbing the ends of my hair. On reflex, I swat his forearm away.

"You couldn't have looked at yourself in the mirror and not seen exactly who you look like, Kate. You have Mom's hair and eyes just like I do, but you look so much like Dad in the face. You've had to have realized who you are by now."

"She knows," Ivy speaks for me, her voice less afraid. "But she hasn't looked in the mirror. She's too scared. She doesn't want to believe it."

"I'm not scared," I say through clenched teeth, my fists balling at my sides. Closing my eyes, I bite harder, locking my jaw so I don't yell at her.

"Kate," Jagger says, and I hate the caution in his tone like I'm an animal he needs to calm down.

My eyes pop open, and as he goes to step forward, I take a longer stride backward.

"I-I have to..." I look to Ivy and then back to Jagger. "Please get her to Storm. I need..." My words die off at the sound of squealing tires.

My body twists around, seeing a black truck with headlights shining directly on us. I know that pickup. It's the one Kane rarely drives.

The truck suddenly comes to a halt, and a door swings open, pulling my gaze off the windshield. With the head-lights shining in my eyes, I can't make out the people inside, even with my supernatural sight. But then I see a massive body jump from the passenger side. My unblinking gaze follows, and when I see my brother, my feet are running before my head catches up with me.

It's when I wrap my arms around his neck and crush myself against him that I realize Trez is really okay. He's here. My brother is alive.

Tears leak from my eyes, so I slam the lids closed to make the moisture disappear.

"You're really here, right? I'm not dreaming?" I ask.

I feel him nod as he pulls me closer, his arms banding around my middle, and he squeezes so tight it feels like I can't breathe, but I don't even care. My brother is alive.

"Fuck," he breathes through my hair, fanning the now dark strands. "It's really you."

The click from the truck's back door forces my eyes to pop open. I see a woman around my age slip to the ground. Her ash-blonde hair so much like Ivy's.

She must see her sister because her warm gaze is on me for a split second before her eyes flick past me, a scream falling from her lips, then, "Ivy," in the next breath before darting past Trez and me.

"He told me you were dead," I confess, not sure if Kane or Jagger told him, my heart aching when I think back to that moment and the gleam in Dick's gray eyes. "Where were you?"

"The cave, but let's talk about that later." He pulls back but doesn't release me. I can't seem to let him go just yet, either. "Did Henrik or that crazy bitch do anything to you? Did they hurt you?"

I'm guessing he's referring to Salem. Jagger admitted they looked for me, so cameras must have been on one or both buildings. It's the only way they'd know Henrik and Salem were there. It makes me wonder if Kane knows *who* else was there.

Wouldn't he have to?

Not ready to linger my thoughts on Kane, I shove him and the rest as far back in my head as possible and focus on my brother.

It's now that I'm hit with the full force of Trez's appearance. To say it's a shock is an understatement. He still looks like himself but has a different shade of hair and eyes, like he is wearing colored contacts. He has a warmer skin tone, but his jawline is still the same. Square, just like...

Jesus.

I'm staring at a literal replica of Kane's father, of Trez's Dad, which means...

It's all true.

Everything Salem told me was right.

Not that I didn't kind of believe her, wanted to believe her even... Then, how Jagger's eyes looked at me like they would jump from their sockets at any moment told me what I'd been too afraid to face in the mirror.

I'm not Kate Everhart.

Trez isn't Trez. He isn't my brother.

"Kate," Trez calls out, his tone cautionary as I'm warring with the fact that I don't know if I'm even supposed to call him by that name, or if...

My thoughts trail off when my brother tightens his fingers

around my back, but before he can latch onto me, I jump back. His eyes widen and then flick somewhere behind me to where Jagger is standing, I suppose. Some silent message passes between him and whoever is behind me, then his warm eyes are back on me as he steps forward. "Kate, what's wrong?"

Everything is wrong, but I can't tell him that, so I hug my middle as the need to shift festers, my bones aching to break, yet my wolf is holding me in my human form.

"I'm happy for you," I say, and I am. I'm glad he and Jagger discovered they're mates, but I... *can't be here.* I have to go.

Kane is here. I feel him like an invisible string tugs at the base of my skull, urging me to seek him out, to find him, to go to him.

But I can't.

I won't.

My vision starts to haze, my view of Trez clouding. It's either that or he's glowing an orangish red.

Fuck, I'm losing my shit.

"Whatever you're thinking right now, shut it down, Kate," my brother... no, Kane's brother says. "Everything is going to be fine. We have a lot to talk about. Let's just—"

"No," I cut him off, but he advances toward me, so I take two steps back. "Just stay put. I need a minute. I need..." My words fail me when I feel his warmth behind me, towering over me a hair's breadth before his hand grips and squeezes my hip.

"Don't make me do this," Kane pleads, his palm shaking against the material of my pants.

"Do what?" I bellow as I whip around to face him. He's so close I'm forced to tilt my head back, and that's when it happens.

His hand wraps around my throat while his other one finds my waist. At the same time, my stare locks on his, but in place of his amber eyes are two literal blood moons shining down at me. His alpha power takes hold of my mind, then my body, and lastly, my soul, freezing my limbs where I stand. I couldn't run right now if I wanted to. I couldn't even take a swing at his insanely hot face if I tried.

What's surprising is that I don't want to do either of those things. That's when my wolf decides to roll over onto her back with her tongue lolled to one side, showing her belly—to *her* alpha.

You goddamn traitorous slut, I seethe through the link inside my head. *He broke our fucking hearts. Get up!*

Something unlocks from inside my chest, and it catches me completely off guard. It's as if an imaginary key was inserted, then turned, making the door squeak open and the word *Mate* is whispered all around me, echoing. A gasp falls from Kane's lips, and I know he heard it too, felt it.

"Don't fight it, baby. Just close your eyes. Take a nap for me," he commands, but his tone is soft as he coaxes me to comply with his wishes.

The sheer power coming from him and into me feels like the warmest blanket wrapped around bare skin on the coldest night. It's hot, but it isn't suffocating like I'm used to when Dick turns his alpha power on me. This feels good, making my anxiety slowly dissipate into nothingness.

My eyes droop, my body relaxes.

"I got you, Kate," is the last thing I hear, a breath before my eyelids lose the fight to stay open, and all the remaining strength in my body vanishes, and sleep takes hold of me.

28

KANE

I've heard my parents recount the moment it happened to them a hundred times in my twenty-eight years. I know Eli and Annalise's story just as well as Jagger does. Maddy's parents are fond of telling their own during times of pack gatherings, but I hadn't expected the mate bond to catch me by surprise when Kate turned around and I locked my alpha stare on hers, exuding every bit of strength and power within me to keep her from running.

When I pulled into the motel parking lot, my headlights shone directly on where she and Jagger were standing. My breath caught, and I had to slam on the brakes because my heart started to beat too fast.

It was after Trez bailed from the passenger side and stole her attention that I noticed the lifeless body on the pavement. Blood pooled around his nearly severed head, which told me it must have been Kate or Jag that sliced him from ear to ear.

Storm and I got out of the truck at the same time, her to

run to her sister and me to move the corpse to a nearby dumpster.

I didn't have to see the tattoo that had been ripped to shreds by claws to know he was a hunter. I make it a priority to know every single member's face and commit them to memory. He'd been their newest recruit. Still young and too green. Dumb too, if he thought coming up to one of us alone was a brilliant idea.

The alpha in me recognized Kate as pack immediately, even with my wolf failing to show for the occasion. Like with Trez, I could feel her emotions as if they were my own.

Her heart hammered against her breastplate. Her anxiety was running at levels I'd never experienced before. She was scared and elated at the same time. The latter for her brother and Jagger, I'm sure, and the former because of me.

I could feel her anger too, but above all, it was her heartbreak that crashed full force into my being that hurt the most. The magnitude almost brought me to my knees right there in front of her, but I knew at any moment she was going to shift even with her clothes on to get away from me. I felt it before Trez told Jagger to tell me to do something to stop her.

I didn't want to use my alpha power on Kate, not my Luna wolf, my mate. But I knew the second she flipped around to face me, her eyes glowing a dull orange, there would be no talking her into coming home with me. She would have shifted, and then she would have ran. I couldn't let that happen when I couldn't chase after her in my wolf form.

The only reason my alpha strength overpowered hers was because she hasn't accepted her place in the Bloodmoon pack yet. When she does—if she does—she'll be one of the strongest beings alive that walk the earth.

A Luna wolf is rare. I only know of four in the world, and that now includes Kate. There are likely more, but they're coveted, and Monster Hunters are the least of their threats. Wolf shifters either worship them or want to use them. There are alphas who seek to mate a Luna wolf solely for the added power it's rumored the mate bond provides, boosting a male's dominance.

Other supernaturals fear them, while vampires have an addiction to their blood. Other shifter beings loathe them and think they're an abomination when, really, it's their power and strength they envy. Demons may not be able to possess the body of another supernatural, but they can feed off them. I don't want to think what could happen if one were to get ahold of a Luna wolf. They'd be unstoppable.

"Couldn't you have just talked to her?" Trez's voice yanks me out of my thoughts, my eyes snapping to where he stands a foot from the front quarter panel on the passenger side of the truck, Jag on his other side. "You didn't have to knock her out... or whatever you did."

"She was going to run," Jagger responds before I do. "Kane did what he had to do."

I pulled her front against mine when she lost all bodily function. It was the only thing I could do in that moment to keep her from slipping from my grip. If my fingers hadn't been wrapped around her throat so firmly when she and her wolf lost consciousness, she would have fallen to the ground, and that would have been yet another thing to add to the long list of shit I've failed as her mate.

I poured everything I had into Kate to get her to comply. It took every ounce of strength I had left without the added bonus of what my wolf provides as backup. At this point, it's clear he has no intention of lending a paw to help, so now, my hands have a slight tremor to them and my vision is seeing double of my beta and brother.

"What did you do to her?" A voice shouts from my left, her chucks stomping the ground as she nears.

Without giving Storm's sister my attention, I hook an arm behind Kate's knees and hoist her into my arms. Half a breath later, stars dance in front of my eyes, and I'm hit with a sudden case of vertigo, so intense pain triggers behind my eyes, ringing stings my ears, and nausea churns in my gut.

"You're her mate, aren't you?" Ivy presses. "No wonder she didn't want to come back. I get it now. You're a—"

"Ivy," Storm scolds, embarrassment evident in her high-pitched tone. "You will not finish that statement, and you will not speak to Kane with such disrespect."

Storm's sister pivots, giving me her back to face her older sister, and even with dizziness surrounding me, the night air is suddenly thick with uncontrolled power floating all around us.

"You've been gone for more than three years. Don't think for one second you get to tell me what to do. You aren't my mother."

Storm gasps at her sister's mention of their mom, her eyes widening as they round.

"Ivy, Mom—"

"I don't want to talk about her right now. I'm not ready for that conversation."

"But you know?" Storm says weakly.

"Yes," Ivy bites out as her fists ball at her sides a heart-beat before a crackling sound snaps my gaze to where Ivy stands. Fatigue cracks spread outward around her.

"Shut it off, girl," I order, my voice gravel, my patience worn thin.

I don't know anything about Ivy's magical abilities, but if I had to place a bet, I'd say she possesses the earth element inside her. It's rare for witches to have all four like Storm, and it's unlikely that sisters would have that in common. Most witches only have one element unless they turn dark, and if they do, then they have a treasure chest full of unbridled abilities at their disposal.

Ivy whirls around, her long hair brushing across Kate's legs from where I'm holding her in my arms.

"As soon as Kate wakes up, I'm leaving with her. Don't think because you're the alpha that you can stop us," she threatens.

A growl vibrates up my throat, but it isn't my doing, proving that my wolf is still paying attention even if he's hiding behind an invisible shield he's erected deep inside me. My canines elongate, also his doing, but I don't fight him even though I can see the fear in her eyes.

I don't make it a habit to scare children, not even the ones in my pack. Sure, I demand obedience, loyalty, and respect, but I'd like to believe I've earned that from every member of the pack. I want to be their safe space, for each of them to know they can come to me about anything and I'll listen without judgment, that I'll protect them with my life. But Ivy isn't pack, and spouting off that Kate is going to leave won't win her points with me or my wolf.

My eyes dip when sudden movement draws my attention. Her fists unball, her fingers straightening at her sides, as a light breeze kicks up around us, quickly turning thick and suffocating at the same moment her eyes narrow on mine.

"Don't make me repeat myself, little girl."

My fingers tighten around Kate's unconscious form, my instinct to protect her above anything and anyone else a reflex.

The bones in Jagger's neck crack like he's about to shift when Storm's arm lifts in the air and her wrist flicks while her fingers, one by one in quick succession, fold into her palm. The wind vanishes, the cracks spidering in the pavement abruptly stop spreading, and judging by the surprise in Ivy's eyes, I'd venture to say her magic was cut off.

She whirls around, knowing the only person capable of stealing her magic is her sister.

"How did you do that? It's impossible. Not even Mom had that ability," she shouts, it sounding like an accusation.

"I'm older than you, I'm stronger than you, and I have more magic than you do, little sister," Storm informs, her voice thicker, more assertive. "Attempt to use magic against Kane again or anyone else in his pack, and I'll do more than shut the faucet off. I'll spell your magic where you can't touch it without me allowing you to use it."

And just like that, the sliver of my wolf's presence disappears while Storm and Ivy hold each other's stare. Whatever energy I had remaining within me flees with my beast, leaving me to run on fumes alone because the adrenaline I had minutes ago died out when Kate fell against me.

"You two, get in the damn truck," I say to them while my stare holds Storm's gaze for a beat longer. "Let's go home. Trez, you're driving."

"Jagger can do it," he says, then flips around to face his mate. Holding out his hand, he says, "Give me the key to the bike."

"What?" Jagger jumps back. "No. You're—"

"Don't fight me on this." Trez's head jerks from side to side in quick succession, his nostrils flaring. "Hand it over, or I'll take it if I have to," my brother promises.

"Then do what you think you have to do, *mate*. You aren't getting it. We're all going home, so get in the—"

"I never said I wasn't coming back to Moonwake. I just need..." He slams his jaw shut and tips his head back to look at the starless night sky.

"Trez?" I question, wanting him to tell me without having to ask what he's planning to do. His emotions are all over the place, but I don't get the feeling he'd run in the opposite direction without Kate, and no one is taking her from me. At least not while she's unconscious. It's still her choice to be with me or not. I'd never force her to stay, to be with me, but she is the one and only person I'd beg to choose me, to forgive me.

"I'm going to see Becca. Okay? Jesus." He inhales through his mouth before blowing a harsh breath out. "Key," he says through gritted teeth.

My head tilts, feeling too heavy for my shoulders, but I force my stare to move on to Jagger.

"He isn't lying. Give it to him and let's go," I order, knowing that if I don't climb into the backseat in the next few seconds, I'm going to crumple to the ground and be taking a nap along with my mate.

"You think I don't know that?" Jagger says, his tone as angry as it is accusing. "I can feel him more accurately than you can, so butt out, Kane."

Snapping my teeth together, my jaw hardens. I have to close my eyes so I can concentrate in order to drop the wall of my emotions for only Jagger to feel.

"Fuck." Jag shoves his hand down the front pocket of his

jeans, pulls the key out, and then slams it in Trez's outstretched palm. "Here." My beta goes to step away but turns right back and jabs his finger against Trez's chest. "Don't take all night. I'll come drag you home if I have to."

Trez rolls his eyes before turning his back on his mate without a reply.

Jagger turns toward me, but his head rolls to where Storm remains. "You're in the passenger seat," he informs her, but when he speaks to Ivy, it comes out more like he's barking. "Go around and get in the back behind the driver's seat."

She crosses her arms defiantly, and I'm quickly losing my patience. She's lucky I'm on the verge of passing the fuck out.

Storm grips her sister by the elbow and pulls until she complies. Continuing her adolescent behavior, Ivy snatches her limb from her sister and stomps around the front of the truck.

Jagger's head rights, his eyes snapping to mine. "Hand Kate to me."

If I had the strength to pull her closer to me, I would have done so, but instead, a growl works its way up my throat and out of my mouth.

"You can't get in the truck while holding her. You know it, and I know it, so stop being a stubborn ass and give her to me."

I know he's right, but I'm not going to admit that out loud. I do, however, allow him to take her from me without gnashing my teeth at him. He should consider himself lucky. The fact is, he's the only being I do trust with my mate.

It's not that I don't trust my brother, but with Trez, I'm

not certain he wouldn't leave with Kate if she chose not to stay in Moonwake.

Take us to the cabin, I tell him in my head. When he nods, I continue, *Don't alert the pack that Kate is back. If anyone noticed we tore out earlier, tell them Storm found her sister. That's where we went.*

Jagger purses his lips, followed by a strong huff of air flaring his nostrils as he exhales.

He doesn't have to agree with me, he just has to do what I say. I'm the alpha above everything else except for when it comes to my mate. So much is about to change for the pack, for me, for us. But only when she's ready.

Until then, my beta and the rest of them can keep their mouths shut. My sole responsibility isn't just to the pack anymore. I smelled the change in Kate the moment I opened the truck door and was hit with Anna's scent. The one I remembered from all those years ago, as well as the barely formed pup growing inside her.

When Kate is safely secured in Jagger's arms, I step around them and pull the rear door open, not in the mood or the state of mind to argue with him. I know he wants to tell his parents—they have a right to know—but they aren't my concern. If Kate wakes up and she wants others to know, then so be it.

The effort it takes to climb into the truck is shameful, but I make it. Once I have Kate on my lap and my arms around her, I sigh in relief with one thought in my head. *Thank fuck, we found her.*

Now that I can breathe again, my lights are out before Jagger rounds the truck to the driver's side.

29

KANE

I awoke fifteen minutes ago to the sun shining through the window and a light sheen of sweat coating my skin. I figured it was mid-morning, but without a clock in my bedroom, I wasn't sure.

I rolled onto my back and caught sight of Kate's sleeping form to my left. It was then that I saw the difference: her hair black and shiny with life, her skin tone a bit warmer with an unmistakable resemblance to Elijah in her features.

Watching her made me realize all the worry sitting heavily on my chest over having not found her was gone. The panic I've lived with since losing her and my wolf wasn't so desperate anymore. I could breathe easier.

Apprehension still lingered. Detachment from my wolf was still growing between us, and having not shifted in over a week was taking a toll on my body and my mental state. *A shifter without his animal can't survive*, but I shoved that thought out of my head and climbed out of bed.

I showered, trimmed and cleaned up my beard, brushed my teeth, took a piss, and then pulled on a clean pair of jeans. I didn't wake Kate. A part of me too afraid to face her just yet after what I did, while the other needed to ensure she got as much rest as she and her wolf needed.

Leaving the bedroom, I ease the door closed as quietly as possible and pad my bare feet down the hallway, hearing the voices that woke me up to begin with and itching to slam my fist into my beta's mouth for defying my orders.

Motherfucker.

Stopping where the hallway turns into the living room with the kitchen to my left, I take in the sight of them all in. Trez is asleep, his massive body stretched out on the couch with an arm flung over his face, covering his eyes to block the light. Jagger is perched on a stool at the island, his back to his mate while facing Ashleigh. She's sitting crisscrossed on the counter along the back wall next to where the kitchen sink is center of the window.

"Ahem," I say, clearing my throat to gain Jag's attention despite them knowing I'm here. With our hearing capabilities, it's impossible not to have heard my movements. After a beat, his spine straightens, and then he lets out a prolonged breath before his neck rolls and his amused stare finds mine. "Are you for real?"

I cross my arms over my bare chest while pinning Jagger with a hard stare, my eyes flashing orange to drive my point.

"I thought we agreed not to tell anyone until Kate was ready?"

"I'm not *anyone*, stupid," Ashleigh huffs as her eyes roll on their own accord. Her legs unfold, then she slips off the counter, her booted feet making a thud against the hardwood floor. "Besides, you tell me everything anyway."

Her attitude over the past week is beyond grating on my nerves. She was pissed after she learned how I treated Kate and the threat I vowed. She had every right to be angry. Kate's her friend too, but I let shit slide with her that I wouldn't ordinarily despite her being one of my closest friends. I'm her alpha, and it stops now.

I took responsibility for what I did and made it known to the whole pack days ago when I told everyone that Kate and Trez were our missing wolves. Ashleigh had found out the night it went down, but my speech seemed to piss her off again, and every day that passes, she gets bolder with her childish name-calling.

The only person's opinion of me I give a damn about is currently sleeping in my bed. To her, I have a lot to make up for. To my cousin, she can kiss my hairy, wolf ass, but she will still show me respect, especially when she's in my house.

My glowing eyes snap to hers, but unlike when my gaze was locked with Jagger, I pour my alpha power into her whole being, forcing her to feel my strength and almost surprised at how recharged I am.

My stare paralyzes her in place. She can't shift. She can't speak, she can barely breathe air into her lungs.

Stepping between the refrigerator and the island, I slowly walk toward her, and with every step, I add just a little bit more power into my hold on her and her wolf. Ashleigh's wolf has already rolled onto her back, submitting and showing me her belly. My cousin, on the other hand, is fighting it. I'd be surprised if she weren't.

I stop when I'm four feet from her and re-cross my arms, knowing she'll tire out before I do.

"Was wondering how long you were going to put up with that bullshit?" Jagger comments nonchalantly, then he picks up a can of soda before bringing it to his lips and tipping his head back to swallow the contents like this is an everyday occurrence.

It's not.

It certainly isn't something I take pleasure in, but it's also something I can't continue to let slide.

Ashleigh's knees wobble, and then her eyes lose focus, fluttering rapidly. She grits her teeth, fighting the inevitable. After sucking in a breath through her mouth, her knees buckle and slam against the floor. Closing her eyes, she tilts her head and bears her neck in submission.

Jagger stands and leans forward, peering over the side.

"For the record," he says, his head cocking to the side, "we don't tell you everything."

"Stand," I command as I release my hold, making it her choice to do as I say or not, and hoping she chooses right because I hate this fucking part of being the alpha.

After waiting with bated breath, she jumps to her feet, her hands down by her sides.

"Are you done with your bullshit?" I ask. "Acting like you're twelve again is beneath you."

Her tongue clucks at my remark, and she folds her arms over her chest. "I'm allowed to be mad at you, Kane."

"You are, cousin, and by all means, if you have something you still need to get off your chest, do it now and do it here. I'm done with your attitude in front of the pack." I step back. Turning, I give her my backside while walking to the refrigerator, continuing our conversation. "It's pissing me off, and it's giving everyone mixed signals. We have to be a united front."

Opening the fridge, I find it stocked with meats already thawed, and I know without asking it was Jagger who took the frozen venison and elk out of the freezer, knowing I'd want to feed Kate.

Thanks, I tell him through our mind link as I grab two vacuumed sealed packs of meat. He responds the same way, but Ashleigh's raised voice drowns out his thoughts.

"Just because I think you're a dick for rejecting your mate doesn't mean I don't have your back."

I slam the refrigerator door closed so hard that the stainless steel machine jolts, slamming against the wall behind it. I whip around to face her, the bag of meat at my side, while my free hand lifts and points at her. "I did not reject my mate. Do not ever insinuate that I did."

"But you kind of... *actually* did," she argues, her snarky words biting as they hit every nerve ending in my body.

Using more energy than it should require, I force my claws to extend from my empty hand and use the one on my index finger to slice through the plastic wrapped around the meat. I turn my back on her, facing the stove, so I'm not tempted to force her into submission again.

"He didn't know she was Anna. None of us did," Jag interjects. "Until you find your mate, stay out of that discussion. You have no fucking idea what you're even talking about."

I sit the raw meat on the counter with it still inside the bag while I pull out a cast iron skillet and turn the biggest burner on the gas stove on to high to heat the pan.

"I know that when... *if* I find my mate, I'd never forgive him if he did anything remotely close to what Kane did."

Pins and needles prick my skin as the sensation climbs my back until it feels like someone took a sharp blade and jabbed it into the base of my skull.

I turn on my heel, but when I'm about to open my

mouth, the front door of the cabin swings open. Even annoyed with Ashleigh, I should have heard her approach, but then again, Annalise has always been a more silent predator than others in the pack.

The smell of freshly baked cookies hits me before her scent follows. My stomach growls, recognizing her delicious-smelling cookies.

"Who pissed off our alpha?" Her fingers clutch the white platter, giving away her nervousness that her steady voice doesn't show. Being the wife of the pack's former beta for so long, she's perfected how to mask her feelings. It doesn't work on me despite her trying to erect a wall between us.

Forcing my gaze back on Ashleigh, I say, "Mine and Kate's business is between me and Kate. You've stated your opinion. I don't want to hear it again. Go do a perimeter check, then make sure every member of our warrior group is fight-ready. Up everyone's training. Also, see if any recruits want to join the team. They still need to be adults and willing."

"Jagger and Trez already ran the perimeter this morning," she says, her arms crossing. "My team is always fight-ready. Don't insinuate that we aren't. Besides, there has been no intel that The Marked Crest pack plans to invade our territory."

"Now isn't the time to question me. Do as you're told and get the fuck out of my sight." When she doesn't move, I growl and bark, "Now," at her.

Without a word, she turns and leaves, not even acknowledging Annalise or grabbing a cookie on her way out the door.

"Do you really think we'll go to war with them again?"

Annalise closes the door and then walks over, stopping next to her son and placing the tray on the island.

I turn back to the stove as Jagger snatches a cookie and shoves it into his mouth. Smoke filters up into the vent hood, telling me the pan is hot enough for the meat. Grabbing a set of tongs from the utensil canister, I pull the elk from the bag and place it in the skillet as I try to answer her question to the best of my ability.

"I've had much time to think since we discovered Kate and Trez were our stolen pups. Everhart wouldn't have allowed them to get close to us, let alone visit yearly. He had a reason, but I haven't the first clue as to what that reason is or why. We need to be prepared if they come looking for a war."

I turn around to face them, my eyes landing on my beta.

"I didn't tell her either." His tongue clucks in annoyance. "But... she's a mom. She's psychic. She knew Kate was here yesterday."

"I'm not psychic, son. You're just complete shit at keeping secrets and telling lies."

"Yesterday?" I question, knowing it would have been late or even early morning when we returned.

"You and Kate have been out for a day and a half. It's almost noon."

"What must a guy do to get some sleep around here?" Trez remarks as he pulls himself into a seated position behind Annalise and his mate. Standing, he runs a hand through his dirty blond hair.

It's still bizaare getting used to him looking so much like our dad. Even spending nearly a week with him when we were searching for Kate wasn't enough to not be taken aback every time I look at him.

It makes me wonder if it's going to be strange getting used to seeing Kate with black hair and blue eyes. It's such a contrast from how I once thought she looked like Richard Everhart with her matching blond hair and gray eyes.

"Maybe try sleeping in your own bed and not on my couch," I say as I flip the meat to cook the other side.

"Hard to do when my bed is in Canada," he says, and for a split second, I contemplate if he said what he said to get a rise out of Jagger because if so, it worked.

A deep growl rumbles from my beta's throat so loud the stainless-steel tongs rattle against the cast iron skillet.

"Can you stop pissing me off?" Jagger's head swings toward his mate, his jaw firm and his eyes heated.

"Can you both take it to another room in another house?" I follow. "If Kate wasn't awake before, she is now."

Sure, I wanted her to wake up, but I wanted the smell of the food I'm preparing for her to do the job for me, not Jagger's over-possessive bullshit.

"Better yet," I say to Jagger, "go make sure we're stocked on all the essentials. We don't need to only be ready for a fight, we need to make sure everyone has plenty of food and water. Take your mate with you."

"Gladly." He chirps up, a smirk seeming to form slowly on his lips before his whispered words in my head make me turn away from them annoyed. *If he hates my bed so much, we'll see how he likes it on the hay in the barn.*

Leave, I growl out as I pull the meat from the pan.

"Let's go, mate," Jagger grits out, obviously hurt by Trez's comment.

As I wrap the elk in aluminum foil to keep it warm, it hits me that Trez's comment irritated me too. His bed will never again be in Marked Crest territory.

Make sure my little brother understands he'll never see that bed again.

I was planning on it. Once I'm done with his ass, he'll never want to leave my bed.

The latter wasn't needed.

"I'm going to take one of these," Jag says to Annalise as I twist back around and cross my arms over my chest.

"Did you forget how to count? That's three," she scolds.

"I'm a growing wolf." He shrugs his shoulders.

"You're twenty-eight," she deadpans, arching an eyebrow while pursing her lips.

"My mate isn't, and he needs all the extra energy he can get for what I have planned." He lifts his arm and pops one full piece inside his mouth, a smirk firmly in place on his smug face.

"The only thing I'm going to do is find another bed."

Looks like you're bunking in the lodge tonight, I comment to my best friend, and with the look my brother throws my way, he knows I'm having a silent conversation with his mate.

"Plenty of beds for you to choose from in the lodge. Knock yourself out—after you help *your* beta," I say. "That's an order."

Don't bet on it. Jagger chuckles, likely figuring out the cause of the sour look on Trez's face. *My bed is his bed, and his ass will be in it even if I have to pin him down to keep him there.*

Good luck with that.

Keep all the luck for yourself, Kane. You need it where my sister is concerned.

Get the fuck out already.

Jagger tosses one of the cookies in the air to his mate, then jerks his head to the door before stepping toward it.

Trez snatches it mid-air, making it disappear into his mouth as he follows his mate out.

Once the door is closed, I train my eyes on Annalise. She hasn't moved from the spot next to where Jagger had been seated. She isn't sitting on the stool but rather standing behind it with her forearms resting on the stone counter.

"You're quiet," I state my observation.

I did want them gone, and if I'm honest, I want Jagger's mom to leave too, just not before I do what needs to be done. A shifter's alpha can alleviate most of their emotional pain, grief, and even depression. A mate, on the other hand, can pull some or all of it into them, giving their fated mate total relief.

"Jagger told me she almost ran." She isn't looking at me. Her head is bent, her eyes on the tray. "That if you hadn't used up all your gifted power, she likely wouldn't be here."

"Annalise, come here."

The base of my skull tingles as I pull on the power within. Every time I use it, the area behind my earlobe tickles and a dull ache forms at my temples. It's not exactly a fun experience, which is why I only do it when it's truly needed.

When she doesn't move, I walk to her. When I'm close enough to touch her, I extend my arm and wrap my hand around her bare skin just above her elbow, then I pull her into a hug, wrapping my arms around her while she closes hers around my waist.

"Thank you for bringing her home, Kane."

If I hadn't fucked up, Kate would've already been here, but I don't say that. This isn't about my guilt, and at this point, I'm done owning up to my wrongdoing to anyone other than my mate.

"Look at me," I coax, forcing my tone softer and void of my alpha power. I want her to comply with her own free will. It's what comes next that requires the gift my alpha abilities give me.

Pulling back, my hands slip to her shoulders. Her head tips back and her blue eyes halt on my glowing gaze. I pour my energy into her, but this differs from how I used it on Kate.

"Kane, you don't—"

"Shh," I whisper, sinking my claws into the muscle behind her shoulders. I can pull her emotions to me without drawing blood, but doing it this way is the quickest. "Let me take it from you."

I'm not hurting her. She's a beast, the same as me. We have a high tolerance for physical pain.

She doesn't fight me, and almost immediately, years of feeling like a failure as a mother shoots through my veins like acid, burning my insides. Her worry over not knowing if her daughter was being mistreated or if she was scared. Despair, longing, and heartbreak of just missing her pup.

Each emotion feels and tastes different as it courses through me. The pain that Annalise was carrying around was far worse than any of my own. The amount of depression inside her makes me regret not doing this sooner. It raises questions I want answers to.

"Why hasn't my father ever taken any of your pain away? Why hasn't Eli?" I growl, angrier now that I see so much relief wash over her face, the stress lines gone, her eyes clearer, her anguish tamed.

Seeing Annalise once again looking the way I remember her from when I was a small child pisses me off more toward my dad than when he made the assumption he was going to become alpha again and that I was going to step down like the boy he apparently still sees me as.

Fuck that.

He doesn't take care of *my* wolves like *I* do.

"They were different leaders than how you and my son run the pack." She shakes her head lightly. "That doesn't mean Dante wasn't a good alpha, Kane, or that Elijah wasn't the beta the pack needed then. You and Jagger are just better and right, and that has everything to do with the way the four of us raised you boys. You saw what worked and what didn't and adjusted your ways. I know you didn't know him, but you're more like your grandfather than you are Dante. He used to do this too. He was compassionate but fierce, like you. When he thought someone was sad, he'd siphon those emotions from them. He was a great man and the best alpha. So are you. I hope you know that."

She takes a deep breath, pulling air in through her mouth and exhaling the same way.

"It feels so good to breathe again. To feel like me again."

"I'm sorry I can't take it all, but trust me, I'm going to have a word with your *mate*."

It's probably a good thing I can't shift because I'm not wholly sure I could hold back from ripping him apart. Annalise is like a second mother to me. She and Eli are fully bonded, so unlike Kate and me, he can feel every emotion that goes through her like it's his own. The least he could have done was shoulder some of it even if he was feeling some of the same things she was, and I know he was.

I can't imagine waking up and your child no longer being where you tucked them in to sleep the night before. Losing a mate I hadn't fully developed feelings for was hard enough.

"That's not needed, Kane, but I appreciate the thought."

I'm about to tell her I don't give a shit if she does or doesn't want me to say something to Eli when we both freeze while looking at each other.

A low growl with lethal promise sends a chill down my spine.

My eyes flick over Annalise to find the most beautiful, solid black wolf I've ever seen staring back at me, her teeth bared and the front of her body crouched, ready for attack.

Fuck, she's gorgeous.

30
KATE

His scent hit me before my eyes opened.

Kane.

It was intoxicating and warm, overwhelming, yet it felt... like home.

That was the moment awareness smacked me in the face. The firm feeling against my back, the buttery softness against my skin, and the cushion under my head. I was lying in Kane's bed, pulling him into my lungs with every breath.

My eyes snapped open.

The room was bright. Rolling my head, I looked out the window. I couldn't see the sun, but his bedroom faces the west, the same way the window in his kitchen does. You can see the ocean in the distance and smell the salty air. The window was closed, but there was a hint of it inside the cabin. That smell also lived on Kane.

I didn't have to turn my head to the other side of the bed. I knew Kane wasn't there. I also knew he'd slept beside me.

I could hear voices coming from the front of the cabin. I didn't try to eavesdrop. I wasn't ready to face him or anyone else in the pack.

You're not ready to face yourself.

But I did need to relieve myself, so I crawled out of bed and padded my bare feet into the bathroom, avoiding the giant square mirror hanging over the vanity. Afterward, I could smell myself now that I wasn't lying in Kane's scent, and it wasn't pleasant. I desperately needed a shower, but something else decided to come to the forefront of my mind right then, making the fact that I stunk unimportant.

Kane used his alpha power on me.

The memory from the motel parking lot slammed into me at full force, and it pissed me right the fuck off. My wolf growled from deep inside, which surprised me, considering she always rolls over onto her back when he's around.

Finally, the bitch is on board, I thought.

Leaving the bathroom, I walk to the door and ease it open enough for my wolf to walk through, then I shed my clothes and shift as easily and swiftly as drawing air into my lungs. We don't shift like werewolves. For them, it's a painful process of bones breaking and them usually turning into a feral beast as a result.

Usually, I'd take a backseat and let her do her thing, but I'm curious what she'll do when she sees Kane. Her claws click with every slow step down the hallway, then her ears perk when we recognize the other voice.

Annalise.

Jagger's mother.

My...

No. I'm not going there, not yet, not when I don't know

what I believe anymore other than who my mate is. From the second I woke up, I could feel the connection—a tether, though weak at best, is still real, nonetheless.

Shouldn't that tell me everything?

Jag called me his sister, referred to Trez as Kane's brother, and told me I smelled like them—the Bloodmoon pack.

So why can't I believe it?

If Salem glamoured us to hide our true identities, who's to say she isn't doing it to make Kane think we're his missing wolves?

My wolf stops where the hallway turns into the open living room and combined kitchen space. What I see at first makes me almost shift back into my human form. For some unknown reason, I hold back even though Kane is using his alpha power on Annalise. The anger I felt when I remembered he did the same thing to me triples seeing him do it to her.

When Kane unleashes a low growl, I see his muscles bunch, tensing in anger. My wolf's ears flick back, flattening.

"Why hasn't my father ever taken any of your pain away? Why hasn't Eli?" His questions come out hard, demanding an answer, yet it's also in a warm, caring way toward her.

That has my animal tilting her head in observation.

It takes longer than it should for me to catch on that he's pulling her raw, suffocating emotions into himself, relieving her of whatever she's been carrying around for who knows how long.

She lost her daughter, stupid, my conscience reminds me

while I realize Kane's anger was toward his father and Annalise's mate.

Although I've never seen it done, I know an alpha has the ability to draw emotions from any wolf he's connected to, which would be anyone in his pack. I know this only because I learned it from Annalise herself. So, if Kane's question holds merit, and he would know, why hasn't the former alpha or her mate ever given her the relief Kane is doing now?

If I had the same ability Kane does, that Dante still has, that her mate has always had since their bond was solidified, you better bet your ass I would've yanked those crippling feelings from her in a heartbeat.

Who wouldn't is a better question?

A leader's job is to do what's best for their people. Compassion costs nothing, so why hasn't anyone shown her any until now?

Those questions burn inside my chest like acid. My wolf can feel my emotions the same way I can feel hers, and she always reacts to mine, so when the rumble starts deep within her chest, I'm not surprised. Her growls never fail to startle me, though. It's deeper when she does it versus when the sound releases from my throat in my human form. Hers sounds ferocious.

Kane's eyes snap to us, widening just before his breath —so audible in the now silence—lodges in his throat.

Annalise whips around, pulling away from Kane's grip. She sucks in a quick breath, then her hand covers her mouth as tears well up in her pretty eyes. Dashing toward me with a quickness I didn't expect, her knees slam against the hardwood, and then her arms wrap around my wolf's neck, squeezing us.

"I'm so sorry." Her body shakes, and even though it's against my wolf, I can feel her through my wolf senses. "I should have known, Kate." A shuddered breath goes down her throat, and in this moment, I wish I were in human form so I could hug her back. "I-I'm sorry."

It's okay, I want to tell her, because what else am I supposed to say?

It's not like I even fathomed the possibility. Sure, the first time we arrived in Moonwake, I was overcome with a sense of home. Provided I stayed clear of a few specific pack members, it felt like I belonged here. But never once in five years has the thought crossed my mind that Trez and I could be one of them. That we were their missing kids who disappeared over twenty years ago.

"Annalise," Kane says with a softness I've never heard from him.

She pulls back but keeps her fingers buried beneath my wolf's fur.

Fur that I've yet to acknowledge is black, not shades of silver and gray.

"I brought you clean clothes yesterday. They're on the arm of the recliner. If you don't like them, it's fine. I just wanted—"

"Annalise," he says with more authority this time, his voice laced with his alpha power as he cuts her rambling off.

My wolf's head tilts, telling me she's picking up on the same thing I am from him, and it makes her want to challenge him.

Dropping her hands, Annalise pushes off her booted toes and stands, stepping away from my wolf.

"Come here," he tells her, his voice coaxing and soft.

"No, Kane. You've done enough, far more than..."

My wolf's snout lifts when her voice dies down. She's staring at me with a mixture of sadness and heartbreak but also... warm, motherly love. I want to embrace her in the same powerful hold she had me in moments ago. I'm just not sure if my reasoning would be for her needs or my own.

"I'm here, Kate. When you're ready, that is."

Swallowing, she turns, pivoting quickly and then dashes to the front door like if she doesn't leave quickly enough, she won't be able to go.

My breath catches at the same time my chest physically starts to ache. I don't want her to leave. She's in pain and Kane can take it away. She doesn't deserve the suffering she's endured, and seeing more visibly than ever, I hope I never experience the torture of losing a child.

"Stop." That one word from his mouth is a command directed toward the woman who may very well be my *mother*, halting her hasty exit. Annalise's feet remain inside the open door, her back to us. "If it gets to be too much, come see me."

Her only reply is a nod of her head, then she steps over the threshold, pulling the door closed, leaving my wolf and me alone with the only man who makes my heart race, whom I want nothing more than to jump into his arms and knee him in the dick at the same time—the only person who's ever broken me.

Kane's movement pulls my wolf's attention to him, but he isn't looking at us.

He grabs a plate from the cabinet and sets it on the counter next to the stovetop. That's when my wolf sniffs the air, both of us recognizing the smell.

Meat.

Especially raw venison and cooked elk.

My stomach growls and contracts like we haven't eaten in days.

Turning and giving us a full view of his bare chest, he steps to us, plate in hand. Bending, he sets the plate of raw deer meat on the floor.

"Eat, my pretty little wolf."

She snarls, releasing a low warning growl while baring her canines.

Good.

She's pissed, like I am, instead of swooning over him. Maybe my anger is more debilitating heartbreak, but the emotions are close enough.

This motherfucker is going to get bitten if he calls her little again. There is nothing petite about my wolf or me.

"Whether you're happy about it at the moment, *Kate*, you are mine." He folds his thick arms over his chest. "And I'm yours, *mate*."

I would have given almost anything to have heard him call me his mate a week ago. Now…

Now, I don't even know who the fuck I am.

What I do know is that I don't want a partner who can so easily use harsh words and threats to hurt me. I have twenty years' worth of that treatment accumulated to last multiple lifetimes.

Mate or not, I won't take more. The days of biding my time and holding my tongue are over. Never again will I be someone's doormat to kick and stomp their feet on.

He drops his arms and squats down again, this time nearly at eye level with my wolf. Cupping her large head in both hands, he holds our stare.

"Eat, wolf. Then shift so that Kate can eat too."

Kane turns, walking back to the counter. With his back to us, my wolf scarfs down the raw meat, practically swallowing the chunk of meat whole, and I can't blame her. I'll probably do the same. Just thinking about the cooked elk waiting for me to devour it has my mouth watering and my teeth aching to tear into it.

But I can't bring myself to shift.

I'm not ready to face him as me yet. Maybe that makes me a coward, and if so, so be it.

I just want to eat, shower, and find my brother; Trez, not Jagger, though if Jag is my real brother, I won't be upset by that fact. Trez, being Kane's brother, is a different story.

I don't want to think about any of it. It's too much for my brain to handle.

I've never gotten a headache in my life, but the pounding against my temples and above my eyebrows must be what that feels like, and I have to say, it sucks.

Hearing a scraping sound against the counter, my head snaps up, and I see Kane sliding the plate onto the island. It's the cooked version, and it smells divine.

"It's cooked the way you like it," he says, talking to me, not my wolf.

Leaning his hip against the side of the counter, he crosses his arms over his chest. As mouth-watering as the meat smells, watching Kane is more appealing. Too appealing, so my wolf huffs out an annoyed breath through her nose.

"Don't act like I don't know how you like things cooked, mate. Every meal you've ever eaten in Moonwake over the last five years has been cooked by me."

That can't be true. *Is that true?*

"Besides these, that is," he adds as he drops his arms and reaches across the counter. Lifting the object in his hand, he shows me a cookie, and I immediately know who made it. It also makes me wonder how they got past my sense of smell. "She made you a whole batch, but I'll take offense if you eat them before the elk steak."

I'm all about Annalise's cookie, but meat trumps sweets any day.

Sighing, Kane tosses the cookie back onto the platter, then shoves his hands down the pockets of his jeans.

"You aren't going to shift with me here, are you?"

His head tilts back, and after a long beat, he nods as he pulls his hands from his pockets.

"Fine. I'll leave you be for now. We'll talk later." He bypasses me, walking to the door without finding a shirt to pull over his head or boots to cover his bare feet. With his back to me, I shift. "I'll be at the body shop after I go to the lodge to change. If you need me, come find me or ask Jag to contact me."

"Don't turn around," I say, hoping he gives me the courtesy, but not because I'm embarrassed by my nakedness. I'm not, but being bare in front of him will not lend me any willpower should he march back over here. "I don't want the rest of *your* pack to know I'm here."

It's relief and torture at the same time when he doesn't turn around. Instead, he pulls open the door, giving me a view of his side profile. Still, he doesn't turn to look at me or even flick his eyes to the side.

"Your parents already know; mine too, probably. Ashleigh was here earlier. She knows. *Our* pack is going to find out sooner or later."

"You can either agree, Kane, or by the time the sun comes up tomorrow, I won't be here."

I'm not sure I mean those words. It's not like I have anywhere to go, and I still haven't told Kane about the baby—our pup growing inside me.

"Agreed," he bites out as his hand tightens around the doorknob. "Okay. No one will know. Just don't... leave," he says, only this time, his voice doesn't hide the brokenness and pain he carries inside. Watching him visibly swallow, I'm overcome with wanting to wrap myself around him, but I don't move to do it. Then he exhales, only to breathe back in through his mouth before saying, "You know where I'll be."

My heart plummets, but why?

He pulls the door closed, leaving me staring at it and alone.

I don't want to be alone.

A whimper slips from between my lips, and I wrap my arms around my naked middle, fighting the need to go after him to sink my teeth into his neck. My canines haven't stopped tingling since Kane's scent was sucked down my throat upon waking.

The muscles between my neck and shoulder ache, but not in a painful, hurting type of way. There is a want... no, a need inside me that throbs to feel his teeth sink into my flesh again.

That can't happen, though. I can't mark him, and he can't bite me again. Not when I'm so unsure of everything. Not when I need to know what's real and what has been fabricated. But I also don't want to find out what I feel for Kane was a spell created by a dark witch doing another man's bidding.

My heart and soul ache for Kane. I want him to be mine, the same as my wolf pines for Kane's wolf to be hers. But he damaged my heart.

It isn't even what he said that hurt so much. It's how he acted. He regretted being with me, and I don't know how to get over that.

31
KATE

The steak was better than I'd imagined it would be. Kane really did know how I like it cooked, and though a bit cooler than I would have preferred, it was the best thing I'd ever swallowed, with the exception of his cock a week ago.

Or maybe it's been a week and a half. I don't even know what day or time it is. Hell, I don't know how long I slept.

After inhaling the slab of protein, I devoured every cookie on the platter. They were delicious, and I swear, they're always better than my previous memory of eating Annalise's baked goodness.

With a belly full, I took the longest shower of my life. I scrubbed everywhere and shaved my legs and underarms. It took the longest to trim my snatch using Kane's spare trim tool he keeps in the cabinet under the sink.

Once done, I dressed in the clothes Annalise left me: a pair of black denim overalls and a sleeveless white cropped top. I wasn't putting dirty underwear back on, so I swiped a pair of Kane's boxer briefs and forwent a bra. It's not like I have much that needs to be held up anyway, and dealing with the heat, I could get used to never wearing one again.

I stole a pair of clean socks, too, before shoving my feet into my black combat boots.

When I'm walking down the hall, not sure what to do and warring between leaving the cabin or not, the door opens, and Jagger steps over the threshold.

"Where's my brother?" is the first thing that slips past my lips.

I instantly regret how I phrased those words as disappointment stops him in his tracks, as evident on his face, when he forces a smile and says, "Standing right here, little sister," while closing the door.

"You know I meant Trez."

I don't want to hurt Jagger's feelings, but I'll never not see Trez as my brother, and I won't pretend otherwise.

He walks closer to me but stops at the other end of the couch across from me.

"Said he was going to the shop to help Kane." He clucks his tongue and slides his hands inside the front pockets of his jeans, rocking on his heels. "But I think he's just avoiding Becca and Dante."

"Or he's avoiding me." I arch an eyebrow, silently asking if that's the case.

I still want to know what happened to him when I thought he was dead, but unless he comes to talk to me, I'll never find out if anyone hurt him. *Why didn't I think to look in the cave?*

"He slept on the couch here last night," Jagger enlightens me, snagging me out of my dark thoughts, "waiting for you to wake up." He juts his chin down, and my eyes follow, seeing a discarded blanket that hasn't been folded. "He's in the same boat as you are, wanting to believe the truth in front of his eyes but not allowing any of it to fully penetrate. Even knowing I'm his mate and feeling it beyond the bite on his neck, he can't let go of the lies you both were fed."

Were they lies, though?

"How do you know that's how I feel? Only an alpha can read their pack's emotions, right?"

That's not something I learned from my pack, but a truth I learned from Dante years ago that even Eli has backed up multiple times. Elijah can't feel or sense anyone's emotions other than his mate's, which means Jagger can't feel mine.

"Not exactly, but I don't need to feel your emotions to know what's going through your head. It's reflected in the tension and doubt in your eyes."

"What's *not exactly* mean?"

"Trez is your brother in the same sense that Kane is mine. We're celestial twins. We're connected differently than others. I can talk to Kane in my head like you can with Trez. I can feel what Kane feels if I choose to or if he forces it on me."

"What are celestial twins?" I probe, curious, while my head spins with the realization that Trez and I aren't the only beings connected like we are.

"Any supernatural children born to different mothers on the same night and at the same time during a passing comet."

"Sounds a little witchy," I say flatly, not liking where this is headed. "I've had enough of that shit to last a lifetime."

"It's fate, not sorcery. Celestial twins are rare. Well..." he pauses and pulls in a deep breath of air. "That may not be true. It could be like Luna Wolves, just not spoken about within packs. No one knows that Kane and I are connected like that. We've never even told our parents, but like me, Kane thinks our parents are aware. Plus, Dante figured out you and Trez can communicate telepathically. My guess, he's already told Becca and our parents, so you're aware."

"We can only talk like that one day out of the fucking month. It's not even that big of a deal. I don't see anything special about that."

"Only Bloodmoon shifters who are fated mates have the ability to speak telepathically, Kate. I've never heard of another pack having the ability."

"Well, I wouldn't know. We don't have any fated mates in the Marked Crest pack."

A low rumble slips from Jagger's mouth, making my eyes squint.

"You aren't one of them," he snarls.

As much as I want that to be true, getting my hopes up isn't worth it. I blow out a breath and roll my eyes.

"Maybe," is all I offer back.

"Have you looked in a mirror yet?" He crosses his arms over his chest only to drop them to his sides in the next breath.

I stare back, not opening my mouth.

"That's a no," he grits out as he sidesteps the end of the couch, then steps behind it as he walks my way. "And we're going to remedy that right now."

"Yeah?" I laugh. "How are you going to do that? March me in front of one?"

So what if I haven't looked in the mirror yet? It took a lot of effort not to peek at my face when I pulled the shower curtain back and dried off. The shower in Kane's bathroom is dead center of the vanity. It wasn't an easy feat with that big ass glass mirror that covers the wall.

"That's exactly what I'm going to do, little sister."

His hand juts out faster than I can jump back, snatching my wrist into his grasp. I yank hard, but Jagger is stronger than me. Then again, it's not like I put much effort into pulling out of his hold. So, maybe I want someone to make me see the proof I've been avoiding.

Tugging me behind him, he relaxes his fingers more gently around my wrist as he stalks the short distance to Kane's bedroom and then inside the connecting bathroom. Flipping the light switch on, he pulls me to stand in front of the sink while he stands behind me, staring into my eyes as I stare into his through the mirror.

"Happy?"

"Depends. What do you see?" He arches an eyebrow.

"The same as you see." I shrug my shoulders because what else does he want from me?

"Kate," he drawls out, irritation laced in his tone.

"What do you want me to say? That we look alike? Okay, we look alike."

We look a lot alike. So much so that I wasn't expecting that much likeness, but he was also right when he said I favor Elijah.

"You see it, but do you believe it?"

"I don't know what to believe or what's real or fake." My eyes flick down to the porcelain basin. "If a spell can hide my identity and change the way I look and smell, then who's to say what either of us is seeing is the real me or that I'm even your sister?"

His hands grip my bare shoulders, squeezing my flesh reassuringly.

"I know you are my friend, Kate. I believe you're Kane's mate without any doubts in my mind. And yes, I'm certain you are my sister, but do you want to know how I'm so sure?"

I nod.

"We're pack animals, loyal to our alpha. My wolf has always been devoted to Kane, the same as me, even before he became alpha. There isn't anything I wouldn't do for him. I'd give my life to save his."

"Pretty sure he feels the same way."

"He does, but my point," he continues, "is my wolf isn't loyal to just one alpha any longer. Neither am I."

"I don't understand. Did Kane step down?"

I shake that thought. He wouldn't. I know him well enough to know if someone wants to take his position, they'd have to do more than challenge him and win. Kane would never submit to anyone, not even his father. You'd have to kill Kane to take the Bloodmoon pack from his leadership.

"Stepping down isn't in Kane's future until he has a son or daughter ready to take his place like he took Dante's." Jagger sighs heavily. "You're not this slow, little sister." He shakes his head and sighs like he shouldn't have to spell it out for me. "We're loyal to you too now."

"Why? Because you *think* I'm your *alpha's* mate?" I purse my lips and cock an eyebrow.

That's the last type of loyalty I want from anyone, especially from someone who may be my big brother.

I jab an elbow into his middle to drive my point home. He pinches my side through the open side of my overalls, making me yelp. I flip around to face him, but he jumps out of my reach as he backs against the narrow wall next to the tub, pressing his back to it and crossing his arms now that there is a little distance between us.

"I *know* you're my *alpha's* mate, but that isn't why. Not even close, Katie Bear." The smirk twitches on his lips.

"What the fuck did you call me?" I gasp while delight lights up his entire face like it's Christmas morning and he has just opened the present he'd been wanting.

"Too soon for a nickname?" His chuckle burns fire through my veins, and I'm not even sure why it's pissing me off. "You're right. It doesn't fit. You're a wolf, not a stupid bear... lil' pup."

My bottom lip drops open at the audacity, and my eyes widen, momentarily clouding with a haze before narrowing and coming back into focus, only this time, my view is crisper.

Jagger sucks in a breath of air, then his back leaps off the wall.

"Turn around, Kate. Now," he demands, his beta attitude no longer playful.

My wolf comes alive inside me, urging me to make him submit, to show him there isn't one damn thing little about us, which makes me pause and look at him... because, what the fuck?

We've always done this.

Jagger picks and ticks me off to the point we end up coming to blows, but not in an all-out brawling way. It's more grappling and controlled roughhousing until he's on his back laughing, and I'm on top of him, bruising his ribs.

He's always submitted.

"Not this time, little sister." He shakes his head, and before I realize it, he advances on me. His hands go around my arms, and in a motion that makes me dizzy, flips my entire body around so that I'm once again facing and staring into the mirror.

My eyes widen, but they aren't the electric blue I saw minutes ago. The irises resemble blood moons, lunar eclipses.

Holy shit.

"That. That right there, Kate. That's why my loyalty, my devotion, is now split between you and Kane. You're our alpha too. You're our Luna wolf, little sister. You have the same ability to make us submit that Kane does."

I push away from the vanity, but the wall of Jagger's chest stops me from moving more than a couple of inches. His hands release me, dropping to his sides.

"This isn't possible," I say, my head barely swinging. "It has to be a trick. Salem. She must have done this. I'm—"

"An alpha, Kate. You're an alpha, and this is real. Come on, being an alpha isn't a new realization. You just didn't know the extent of it or what pack you were born to lead." Jagger takes a long breath, his eyes holding mine in the mirror as the reddish-orange fades, the blue that matches his returns. "Salem did a lot of things, but you being a Luna wasn't one of them."

"I don't know how to believe any of this is real," I admit. Then, forcing my spine to relax, I turn around, pressing my ass against the edge of the vanity and cross my arms.

"There's a bonfire tonight. The *whole* pack will be there. You should come. Let *everyone* see you."

The way he says the whole pack and everyone makes me narrow my eyes. *What did that mean?*

"No." I'm not ready for that, but mainly, if I go and see that old fucker, I'm not sure what'll happen. I'm almost certain my rage will come out and payback will—

Wait a minute. *Does Jagger know?*

It's on the tip of my tongue to ask, when he says, "Mom and Dad—"

But I quickly cut him off, not ready to go there yet. "I saw Annalise earlier." Well, she saw and hugged my wolf, but that's almost the same thing. Maybe tomorrow I'll be ready to face her as me. "She brought me clean clothes."

Speaking of those clothes. They were mostly maternity leggings and loose tops, which tells me far too much, but I need to know for sure.

"Jagger?" I cock my head and jab the inside of my cheek with my tongue.

"Yeah?"

"If Annalise knows I'm pregnant, does that mean…"

"Yes." His voice sends a ripple of tingles skating down my spine. My head swings to the door so fast it feels like whiplash. "I know my baby is inside your belly, mate."

The weight of Kane's admission to knowing I'm pregnant has played on repeat in my head for over a week now, not letting me forget the way he said it or the way his words made me feel.

Jagger ducked out of the bathroom seconds afterward, leaving me alone with my mate, staring at him mere feet away, his height nearly as tall as the door frame. He looked too good to be true.

The way *my baby* slid off his tongue made me weak in the knees.

The heat in his eyes as he stared back made me almost run straight into his arms while a need I didn't understand pulsed inside me.

But if I'd done that, it could very well set in motion a life where assholery is acceptable when it is not. I certainly don't want my son or daughter to be raised in an environment where that's the norm, either. No one should be subjected to that upbringing. I know firsthand how that story plays out, and I will not put my child through it.

But instead of acting like the adult I am and talking with Kane like I should, I'm still ignoring him. I can't get past wanting to climb onto his lap and punch him in the dick at the same time. I should just do the latter and get it over with. It might make me feel better. Maybe it would cause this tightness in my chest to loosen.

Footsteps on the deck of the porch snap my attention to the cabin door as it opens.

Kane left early this morning after he cooked me breakfast. This morning, he went all out with stacks of pancakes, eggs, and two steaks cooked medium rare. Since I've stayed in my wolf form when he's here, he also plated raw animal meat that I'm confident he hunted before daylight.

I couldn't ask since I'm still giving him the cold shoulder like a five-year-old.

"How long are you going to make Kane grovel?"

"Is that what he's doing?" I ask Trez, watching him close the door behind him. He turns to face me, then crosses his arms as he stops on the other end of the couch.

I finish folding the blanket Kane used last night when he slept on the couch, then tossed it on top of the pile with the rest beneath the window.

In the wild, a pack of wolves will snuggle with each other to keep warm in the winter. Wolf shifters aren't any different. We crave touch from our pack, and when that isn't available, a soft, warm blanket is about the next best thing. We're known to hoard them.

"You know that's what he's doing. The question is, how long are you planning to draw this out?"

"What are you doing here?" I ask, changing the subject. When I'm ready to speak to Kane, I'll do so, and it'll be on my terms. Maybe that's childish, but frankly, I don't care.

It's not even all about Kane. It's the pack, Annalise and Elijah, an accidental pregnancy, a traitor among us, and I don't know what to do about any of them.

"I'm not welcome to come hang out with my sister?" He drops his arms to his sides as he sits on the end of the couch arm.

"Can you not?" I ask, huffing out air and gritting my teeth at the same time. "All that does is make the fact that you aren't my brother more real, which in turn makes me want to rake my claws down someone's chest."

"Mine or Kane's?"

"Richard's," I snarl.

"Why do you have to bring up Dick? I thought you said that bitch... I mean, witch, was taking care of him."

"Maybe." I sigh. "But I don't trust her any more than I trust our kidnapper."

"So, you've accepted that we're Bloodmoon instead of Marked Crest?" He doesn't allow me time to respond. "That you and Kane are fated mates?"

"It's hard to ignore you and Jagger being mated when he comes by at least twice a day. Or the hopeful, desperate look on Annalise's face every time she shows up."

"I thought you didn't believe in fate deciding your destiny?"

"Fate can go fuck herself. If I end up with Kane, it'll be because I decide I want him."

"We both know you want him, Kate. The other question is, why are you making him sleep on this couch, which, by the way, isn't that comfortable for someone our size." He huffs air out through his nostrils to drive his point home like I don't know exactly how this couch sleeps. It's okay for a nap. It very much sucks for attempting any real rest.

"I'm not making him do shit. He's chosen to sleep right here every night." I point down. "If he wanted to sleep in his bed, then he could have slept at the lodge or kicked me out of his bed here. He's the alpha, after all."

"Is he, though?" Before I open my mouth, he continues, like he didn't just insinuate that I'm Kane's equal and also an alpha of his pack. *I'm not.* "We both know Kane isn't going to kick you out of his bed or either of his houses."

"Oh, really?" I laugh, but it lacks any humor. "Because you weren't here when that's exactly what he did almost three weeks ago."

"Because he thought he betrayed his mate. You, Kate. He thought he betrayed you and was ashamed of himself."

"Whose fucking side are you even on? Not mine, apparently," I add, hearing the saltiness in my tone.

"Stop sulking and mark your goddamn territory already."

"You mean like you did?" I throw up my hands. "I don't even know how you didn't rip out his throat."

Trez smirks, and I immediately know he's proud of *his* mark on his mate.

"Jagger pissed me off, but he also made me so fucking hard it felt like my dick was going to combust. That was the only thing I could do to ebb the pain and ecstasy I was feeling, not to mention my fucking body was so drained from all the Wolfsbane."

A low rumble bubbles up my throat, the nail beds on my fingers and toes throb, the need to shift and shred flesh so intense and compelling I have to squeeze my fists together and curl my toes to stop my wolf from breaking through.

She needs to run. It's been too long... but there's a reason I haven't left the solace of Kane's cabin. It's more than not being ready to face the fact that I'm Annalise and Elijah's daughter, Jag's sister, and Kane's mate. More than not being a Marked Crest wolf.

Kane has a traitor in his pack. It's why I told him not to tell anyone I was here.

I should have told Kane what happened at the diner by now, but I didn't know how he'd react or what he'd do about it. Before, when Kane thought I was a shifter from a rival pack and had laid that old fucker on the ground in Ashleigh's bar, he snatched me around the throat and got in my face like I didn't have a right to touch one of *his* wolves when it was Ronnie who'd put his hands on me first.

Back when Trez and I first came here, Dante and Eli made it clear that we couldn't cause trouble or we wouldn't be allowed to return. Ronnie is older than Dante, which means he was in the pack back when Kane's grandfather was alpha. Maybe he has more of a right to be here than I do.

But maybe he shouldn't have shot me with four tranqs filled with poison, especially after I'd left. For all he knew, I wasn't coming back. Unless… Kane had him follow me to make sure I left, but I don't think he did.

It happened so quickly, and although I've thought a lot about it, I'm betting Ronnie is the reason Henrik found me.

What did he demand of the Marked Crest beta when I was on my knees? *Kill her already.* They knew each other, but they would have, I suppose. They're members of rival packs, after all. Yet, Ronnie didn't act like he hated Henrik. There was hate in his stare, but it was directed at me.

His hatred from the first day we arrived in Moonwake had always been directed toward me, but I still don't know why. I've never done anything to him. I've never even come onto Kane in front of anyone in his pack other than Jagger and Ashleigh.

I thought Ronnie and a few of his friends, his sister even, didn't like that Kane had a fated mate somewhere in the world, and to their knowledge then, I wasn't her.

But I am. Even if I haven't admitted it to Kane, I know now that we're mates. I feel it deep within my soul. I've always felt it. I just didn't know that was what I was feeling.

A few days ago, Trez told me Ronnie also shot him that same night when Trez was headed here to meet me, and I almost lost it. That's when I told Trez about the diner incident. He went into more details, telling me they searched for me, but I wasn't ready to hear any of it. This is the first he's brought that up since.

"Come to the bonfire fire tonight." Trez's comment jerks my eyes to his.

"There's another one?" I arch an eyebrow.

"There's one every other night. I guess it's what they do during the summer months, but this one, *everyone* will be there. Ashleigh even closed the bar. You can thank me afterward." He tries to force his lips to remain in a straight line but fails, and a sly smile breaks free.

I cock my head in thought as my mouth opens. "By everyone, you mean—"

My question is cut off when the door opens, and Jagger steps across the threshold, a backpack slung over his shoulder. His blue eyes land on where I'm standing and flick down my attire and then back to my face.

"She doesn't look ready to join the *festivities.*" Jagger purses his lips and crosses his arms before blowing out a dramatic breath.

"I'm not joining anything, and trust me, Jag, you do not want me to come to that bonfire."

"So you're going to continue staying here, wearing your jammies?" Before I open my mouth to respond, he holds up his hand. "My bad. Let me rephrase. I meant wearing Kane's shit even though you don't want Kane to know you're wearing his clothes."

His laugh puts a scowl on my face. My tongue clucks in annoyance.

Wolf shifters are pregnant for a fraction of the time humans are, and frankly, I view that as a plus. I still have at least five, maybe even up to eight weeks left. Humans have to endure pregnancy for forty weeks. No, thank you. I've had enough already, and I'm not even big yet. But I finally understand why Annalise brought me multiple pairs of overalls in two different sizes because I wake up every morning to a bigger belly than the previous day.

Maternity leggings are the easiest to slip off, but they're not my style at all. They itch my stomach, so I've been wearing Kane's boxer briefs and his t-shirts. Unless he's here, then it's just black fur, and he gets to listen to my wolf's low-key growl at him every time he makes a noise.

Okay, maybe I need to go for a long, therapeutic run. It's undoubtedly overdue. Perhaps it'll improve my mood, and I'll finally be more apt to speak to Kane without wanting to unsheathe my claws whenever he's near. That conversation is overdue at this point too. We probably need to discuss the baby before he or she is born.

"For your information, little sister, he knows."

"Because you told him, you fucking narc."

Seriously, is no one on my side?

His lips spread wide across his face before his head shakes rapidly.

"Not me," he says as his eyes skate over to where Trez sits several feet before him.

"Really?" I ask, turning my stare to Trez.

Ignoring me, Trez twists around to face Jagger, then stands. "My sister needs to go for a run. Why don't you go with her? I have other shit to take care of."

"I'll gladly go for a run with *my* sister." Jagger takes a step, closing his distance to Trez. Leaning forward, he says, "And I'll make sure she shows in a bit too."

"Good luck with that," I say despite neither paying any attention to me.

"You better… because *it's* getting handled tonight one way or another," Trez says in a low tone, but with supernatural hearing, I heard him clearly.

I just don't know what he meant.

Handle what?

Why does my presence even matter?

Trez sidesteps Jagger and is out the door without even telling me bye.

"Can we go already?" Jagger stresses when I stand there silent, looking at him and waiting for him to explain. "With Mom staying at the lodge and my mate refusing to sleep at my house, I've eaten my weight in cookies this week. I need this run more than you do, little sister."

"Why is Annalise staying at the lodge?"

That's weird. She hasn't mentioned that, and she's here within minutes of Kane leaving every morning.

"She's mad at Dad and refuses to sleep anywhere near him," he admits.

"Doesn't that just hurt her too?" I've heard fated mates

tend to pine for one another when they're apart for too long. Kane and I haven't completed the mating bond, but sleeping without him when he's so close makes my chest ache and my anxiety skyrocket. I'm about to ask him if that's true when another thought pops into my head. "Wait. Did he make her leave her own house?"

"Of course not. Dad would never do that."

"Then why didn't he go sleep somewhere else?"

"He did. He's been staying at Dante and Becca's, but since their houses are next to each other, that's too close for Mom. She knows she'll give in and isn't ready to be over it yet."

"Over what?" He gives me a look like it should be obvious, but it's not. I grit my teeth. "Tell me, or I'll make you."

"I should have never told you about that." He slips the backpack from his shoulder and tosses it to my end of the couch.

Yesterday, he revealed I'd used alpha power on him the day Kane ordered me to leave his pack and never return. I knew Jagger wasn't lying to me, so I spent two hours yesterday and nearly another hour today staring in the mirror, trying to spark something. Anything. But nothing happened.

"You're going to use it against me every time you want your way, aren't you? You don't have to be a brat, not when I'm the one who has to live with the fact that my best friend is banging my little sister."

"First, Kane isn't banging anyone, not even me. Secondly, you couldn't care less if Kane bent me over the armrest in front of you right now. We've had this convo before, remember?"

A few years ago, just before Kane became alpha and him

beta, I asked Jagger if it bothered him that his sister was mated to the one person he was the closest to. He surprised me by saying, not in the least.

"I didn't care until you put it that way." He shakes his head like he's trying to knock the image out. It makes me chuckle until he says, "Just because Kane isn't fucking anyone, it doesn't mean there aren't others trying to get him to."

"Excuse me? Who," I seethe.

"Doesn't matter. I only need you to maul one person tonight, not anyone else. Now," he jerks his chin upward, "put a change of clothes in the bag, and let's go run off some calories."

"Fine, but I'm going to need all my calories and more replaced when we get done."

"Not a problem. There will be plenty of food and then some waiting on us when we return." He takes a step back. "I'll be outside. I'll leave the door open. Shift in here, please."

Pulling the door open, he disappears outside while I'm left wondering what he meant.

I only need you to maul one person.

What does that mean, or more over, who does he want me to attack?

And why?

Maybe Jagger knows Trez told me what the old shifter did, and he's testing me, or Kane's testing me to see what I'll do.

That isn't smart on their part if they're expecting me not to go for his throat.

Given the chance, that's exactly what I plan to do. If Kane has an issue with that, then that's his problem. Ronnie wants to see me dead, and if it's him or me, then I choose me.

Besides, if I do stay in the Bloodmoon pack, I will not do so while he's part of it.

I don't trust him.

He'd kill me or hand me back over to Dick—if he does still have a beating heart, that is.

It's best if I stay away from that gathering tonight.

But now I'm not so sure I want to.

Even if it's to see the look on Ronnie's face.

33
KANE

During summer months, with kids out of school, we gather more often as a whole pack than at other times during the year. We feast for hours as the sun sets on the night of the full moon, we run for at least two solid hours, then we return and eat some more.

Tonight isn't a full moon. We still have nearly a week until then, but that doesn't mean we don't run together as a pack at other times or in small groups. We do, but I've brushed off running with my parents, Jagger, and even Trez. Ashleigh hasn't said anything, but her looks speak volumes. She suspects something is wrong.

I overheard Laney asking Ashleigh why I hadn't been coming with them. Since she started working at the body shop for me a few months ago, she asked if she could join Ashleigh, Jagger, and me on our once-a-week group run, and I allowed it once. That turned into her showing up to them all, but I didn't want to be a dick and disinvite her, so the three of us started running on Saturday mornings while the rest of the pack slept in.

As the next full moon nears, I still haven't figured out how I'm going to get around not shifting or leading the run. I doubt I'll be able to use the same excuse as last month when Kate and I fucked each other into a coma, and I got my mate pregnant.

She's yet to say one word to me.

At this point, I'd take a *fuck off, Kane,* just to hear her sexy, raspy voice again.

My one saving grace this week is that as each day passes, I can feel more of Kate's emotions when before I couldn't feel her at all. That tells me she's starting to accept being part of the pack. I can sense her in ways I can the rest of my pack, but her emotions aren't ones I can easily shut off like I can the rest.

Perhaps that's because she's my fated mate. I know if our mate bond were complete, I'd be able to know the direction she was in just by sniffing the air. I could communicate with her in my head like I can my beta. Maybe then I'd know the right thing to say to get her to see that I know I fucked up, that I'd do anything to take back the words I spewed, the way I acted, how I treated her. To earn her trust again.

Fate knows I would do anything to earn her forgiveness.

The bathroom door down the hall opens, the sound turning my head and pulling my gaze toward it to see steam billow out at the same time Trez comes into view. He's dressed in a pair of dark wash denim, my jeans, because he's yet to leave the pack to buy any of his own, not that I'm bothered by it. His feet are bare, he hasn't put on a shirt, and his dirty-blond hair is still damp as he turns right, coming my way instead of the bedroom he and Jagger have been sleeping in.

The oven door slams hard, making my eyes skirt over to

where Annalise sets a tray of goodness on top of the stovetop.

"More cookies?" Trez screws up his face in distress.

"Shut up and don't ruin it for the rest of us," I chime in before bringing a bottle of beer to my lips and letting the contents fill my mouth.

"Easy for you to say." He blows out a dramatic breath. "You don't seem to have a problem not eating them."

"Moderation is key, little brother. You should learn it."

"Where's the fun in that?" he comments, not looking at me as he swipes a chocolate chip cookie from the tray while Annalise is turned away, washing her hands. It crumbles between his fingers because he didn't wait long enough for it to firm up.

Impatient dumbass.

We three are the only ones in the lodge. With her staying here, I haven't let our rowdier bunch of shifters hang around, not that Annalise would care. She'd likely mother them the way she has been doing all of us. Jagger is more thrilled than I would have expected that she's here instead of with Eli.

She's been baking all day, only breaking when she went to visit her daughter for an hour this morning, like she's done every morning since Kate has been back.

I get why she's upset with my dad and her husband, and now my mother, since she took their side in all this. I'm angry with them too, but I'm pissed off at myself more than I am anyone.

I should have known Kate was my mate. Spell or no fucking spell, I should have known, felt it, and goddammit, I did. I just ignored the signs, telling myself it was simply an attraction. And sure, it was that as well, but I was drawn to her from the first moment I smelled her nearby. Never in a million fucking years would that have happened with anyone else if she wasn't the one person fate chose for me and I for her.

"Did I say those were ready to eat?" she seethes in a way a mother does when she's both annoyed and happy that someone can't wait to devour something she made. "Shoo."

She fans her hands, chuckling when she swats him in the side. He turns to face me, stepping to the island's edge to my right.

"Lay off the little brother shit, the brother calling altogether, unless you want Kate to slice your junk off with her claws," he offers.

"She likes my dick too much to go to those extremes."

At least, I hope she does, but I keep that thought locked behind the smirk on my face.

As many times as I made her come that night and filled her full of my cum, I like to think I pleased her before I went and fucked it all to hell.

"That's just the attitude to have. I'm sure my sister can't wait to jump back on the Kane train and tell you how much she forgives all of your douchebagness." He shakes his head.

"It's more like a roller coaster that tips at four hundred feet in the air and plummets at a ninety-degree angle. Speed mixed with adrenaline and a force you'll only ever dream about... little *brother*," I snicker, enjoying the easiness he and I share around each other.

Growing up, I was just as eager to find my brother as I was my mate, but that was because my parents were heartbroken and never stopped grieving for their son, and the fact that he was my best friend's mate. I never considered that we'd one day become friends. He was seven years younger than me. I didn't see it happening. Ashleigh is three years younger than Jagger and me, and for the longest time, I saw her as an annoying brat who just wanted to play with the older boys so the rest of the pack didn't view her as weak.

It makes me wonder, *would Trez and I have the friendship we do today had we grown up together, had I always known he was my brother?*

"Okay, that was too much for my ears," Annalise says, sounding as grossed out as her eyes portray. "I'm going to see if Storm and Ivy need any help with the meat pies."

After the door closes behind her, I roll my head over to find Trez back in front of the stovetop, a cookie in hand traveling to his mouth.

"I thought you said you'd get her to show?" There's irritation in my voice, but it's not directed toward him. Everything about the situation with Kate comes back to me and me alone.

He devours the chewy goodness in one swallow and then twists to face me. "I planted the seed. Kate is too curious not to come tonight. She'll be here. Trust me. I know my sister, Kane."

"I hope you're right." I strum my fingers on the island. "I can't go another day looking at that motherfucker, knowing he had a hand in those bastards taking her."

It's taken mental strength I didn't know I possessed not to wrap my hand around his neck, sink my claws in, and rip his throat from his body. Being unable to shift into my wolf makes it impossible to kill him with my teeth. I'm lucky I can still force my beast's claws through my nail beds.

"You and me both," he replies while I lift the beer bottle to my lips and tip it back, letting the contents flow into my mouth and down my throat in one swallow.

The sound of the rubber flap attached to the wolf door opening causes me to twist around to see which shifter came through. I find a black wolf with blue eyes staring at me, but it's not the one I was hoping for.

Jagger shifts, then shakes his head in a jerky motion like he's trying to knock something loose or rid water from his ear. I can smell the saltwater residue from his naked flesh, telling me he recently took a swim or at least ran through seawater at some point. I'd take a bet it was the former.

Whereas most wolves don't care to get wet, Jagger loves it. Swimming in the ocean or a lake or running through a rainstorm are things he enjoys doing. Summer is his favorite season. It's my least favorite, but I'll admit, that's because I only get to see Kate in the winter.

"She said she was coming." Jag raises his arms above his head, stretching.

A frustrated sigh falls from my open lips.

"But," he continues, "there wasn't any conviction in it like she was asking herself rather than telling me she wasn't coming. Give her time, brother. She'll show up tonight. I feel it in my gut."

"Do you think your gut could tell you to go put on some fucking clothes," Trez grits out as he steps around the island toward us. Crossing his arms, he leans his lower back against the edge, the same as I'm doing.

"You worried your big brother wants this?" He motions down his body, a smirk forming as Jagger tilts his head, his eyes on his mate. "He's seen me in my birthday suit more than you have. We used to take baths together before you were even born."

Jag doesn't remember that and thank fuck, neither do I. If it weren't for Annalise having a picture as proof, I could have gone my whole life without knowing that ever happened. I definitely don't need to be reminded of it.

A low rumble vibrates up Trez's throat and past his lips.

Jagger bellies over with a haughty laugh, proud of himself, while I swallow the last ounce of beer from my bottle.

"Give me ten minutes to shower and adorn some coverage so my mate doesn't get jealous and show his true colors," Jagger's eyes flick to Trez, then back to me, "and we'll find your mate. We can drag Kate kicking and screaming to the gathering if necessary."

"Her kicks don't feel that great. I wouldn't advise it," I note.

"Neither do her punches," he adds, triggering a memory of when she nailed him in the stomach after she showed up at Ash's bar looking for me those few short weeks ago.

"Make it quick. I need a beer, and if I go outside to grab one from the cooler, there's a good chance I will ruin everyone's night."

I want to give Kate time to deal with shit on her terms, but my patience is waning. The longer he remains in the pack, the more time he has to infect others with hatred. Hell, for all I know, he already has, and I still don't know why he did what he did.

I need him alive until I find out.

I know that, yet it does nothing to dampen the desire to end his life for hurting my mate.

Maybe it's a good thing she didn't come back with Jagger.

Part of tonight's festivities is ensuring everyone is near the lodge so Ashleigh can get into Ronnie's house to search for any information we've missed. She's been combing through his emails and online activities since I discovered he was at the diner the night Kate was kidnapped.

It doesn't take a genius to assume he followed her when she left here and was likely the source that tipped the former Marked Crest beta to her location. Ivy was the one who told me of Henrik's death. According to Storm's sister, their coven leader was the one who saved Kate and why she returned to me.

Storm isn't buying into her sister's claim that the dark witch isn't pure evil in every sense of the word.

I haven't made up my mind one way or another. I can't. I've never met the woman, so I'll leave my judgment open until I do, but frankly, I hope we never cross paths. Because if she had anything to do with my brother and Kate's disappearance when they were pups, I won't care whether she's a bad person or goddamn saint, I'll end her life.

Something else Ivy admitted to her sister was that Salem knew Henrik murdered her sister, Storm and Ivy's mother, and the reason she allowed monster hunters to dispatch him, doing what they do best: eradicating shifters from this world in the most painful ways imaginable. Ivy also said Salem held Richard responsible for their mom's death because it was his order Hale carried out.

It sounded to me that had Salem's sister not been killed, she wouldn't have had a reason to let Kate go when she went back to Rivermoon to end the British Columbia alpha.

If he were dead, I would know it. I would have felt his death. Or maybe not, Everhart isn't a real alpha.

Alpha wolf shifters all across the world have a single connection with each other through Fate. When one dies, there's a violent pop that happens within our heads, signaling the event. We don't know which alpha, only that their spirit is no longer on earth.

I've felt that volcanic headache once when Caleb Drake killed his own alpha. At least that's the rumor, but he's never confirmed it as fact to my knowledge.

"Want me to fetch her?" Trez asks, suspending my thoughts just as the shower faucet from the hall bathroom shuts off. "You have murderous vibes rolling off you."

"It's not a vibe if it's premeditated."

"Which will turn into a crime of passion if you take this kill from Kate."

"Do we really want this on her hands?" I turn, pressing my hip against the edge of the island while facing my brother. "What kind of mate am I if I let him continue breathing after he literally served her up to a wolf?"

"One that knows she's also an alpha, his equal, and knows she's capable of handling herself. A mate that recognizes she doesn't need or want a man to come to her rescue."

"Shut the fuck up. No one asked you," I grumble because he's so fucking right that I want to punch him in the face. Instead, I narrow my eyes on him and bare my teeth.

That's the moment the door squeaks open and Trez's eyes skate over my shoulder. Jerking around, I see her standing at the entrance, her hand on the knob, her smile bright.

"There you are."

34
KANE

My shoulders drop with so much disappointment I can barely suppress the whine that tries to work its way up my throat before I swallow it back down. I'm not entirely sure if the reaction was me or my absentee wolf.

"Laney," I breathe out, not bothering to hide my annoyance at her presence.

I gave her half the day off today because she was getting in my way more than doing the job I pay her to do.

I hired her a few months ago to answer the phone, deal with customers, take inventory twice a month, and order parts and materials. I was reluctant then, and now, I know I made a mistake.

Once I returned to the shop regularly after we found Kate, Laney started offering her assistance to help me work on my jobs. I blew her off at first, then allowed her to apprentice twice, thinking if she got her hands greasy, she wouldn't ask again.

I was wrong about that too.

I know she has a crush on me. I learned that fact when she was ten. Back then, it was cute and innocent, not something I'd ever reciprocated, even if I'd never found my mate. I see Laney the same way I see Maddy. The only difference is I enjoy being in Maddy's company. Like my cousin, Maddy might as well be the other little sister I never knew I wanted.

I'm not the only one Laney annoys. She gets on Ashleigh's nerves by just opening her mouth, but then Ash is the leader of an army of wolf shifters I hope I never have to use. She's skilled in hiding her emotions and thoughts from everyone except me. Sometimes, I think she could put up a barrier between us if she wanted, but she chooses not to.

Maddy, on the other hand, has never gotten along with Laney and doesn't hold her tongue. They're the same age, and when they were younger, Laney used to pick fights with her just to show everyone she was stronger. Of course, she was and still is stronger than Maddy. She's a supernatural creature, whereas Maddy is human.

Though, Maddy is only human in bones and blood. Her mind is as strong and determined as the rest of us.

I can't count how many times Maddy has begged me to turn her, and even knowing it's what she wants more than anything, I can't bring myself to do it. Not every created werewolf turns feral, but taking that chance isn't something I'm willing to do. I can't stomach the thought of one day having to put her down.

"Hey, Boss," she greets with an eager smile and a beer bottle in her left hand.

She's twenty, but the way I see it, Laney is an adult. As long as she doesn't leave pack land or drive any type of automotive vehicle, including an ATV, her choice is hers to make. I don't attempt to father my shifters, not even the ones like

Laney, whose Dad is absent. I'll only advise them should they ask my opinion. Otherwise, they make their own choices. Jagger and I were sneaking beers at fourteen, so even if I wanted to disagree with her choice of beverage, I'd be the pot calling the kettle black.

When she started working for me in March, she went from referring to me as Alpha to Boss instead of calling me Kane like most of the pack does. A handful of shifters refer to my title, and that doesn't bother me like hearing her call me Boss.

"What do you need?" I ask, cutting to the chase.

Once Jagger comes out, we're going to locate Kate, even if it's so I can put eyes on her for the first time today. After I cooked her breakfast like I have every morning, I left before she came out of the bedroom. The only glimpses I've gotten of her in human form since she slammed the bathroom door in my face have been while she slumbers... naked in our bed.

Luckily, my view has been of her meaty ass and smooth back. Had her legs been open, or had she been flipped around, I'm not sure I could have kept my distance standing in the doorway watching her rest. I've yet to see the proof growing in her belly that I badly want to feel with my hands. I can sense him within her, and that's amazing in itself, but to touch her while she's carrying our pup is something else entirely and the one thing I've longed to do since I woke up beside her weeks ago.

But I can't. I won't without her permission.

If it takes the rest of my life to atone for my fuck up, then that's what it takes.

"The fire is going. Everyone has started chowing down, but our alpha is missing." Her body twists marginally as her head turns to look over her shoulder and out the open door before she rights herself, her gunmetal eyes returning to mine. "Uncle Ron wanted me to see if you'd hang out with our group tonight."

My fingers tighten around the empty bottle in my hands. It's the only visible sign her mention of Ronnie bothered me and not one she would have noticed with her eyes fixated on mine.

My brother slides down the side of the island I'm standing against, stopping when the side of his bare foot meets the side of my boot. Somehow, his closeness relaxes me.

"Trez too, of course," she quickly adds, her stare darting to him. Then she blinks, and her eyes are back on me, another smile climbing up her face.

"What about me? Am I not invited?" Jagger walks down the hall, pulling a black t-shirt over his head, and when I see the design on the front, I know he helped himself to my closest as well.

"You're always invited, Beta. In fact, your dad was talking with Uncle Ron when I walked in about heading out for a run a little earlier than usual."

"Dad should probably run that by his alpha, not *Uncle Ron*." Jagger's jaw locks as he forces a tight smile. Jagger drops a pair of boots in front of Trez, then holds a shirt out to his mate.

He likes having his mom here. They've always been close, but he's angry that his father hasn't attempted to make amends with Annalise or gone to see his daughter once since she's been back.

I'm pissed about it too, but I also feel his guilt despite Eli trying to shield his emotions from me. He pines for his mate the same way Annalise has for him. He knows it, and so does she. The guilt he's harbored since learning that Kate is his missing daughter, that she's been within arm's length every year for the past five winters, is slowly eating away at his mental health.

Elijah's heart hurts maybe more now than it did when they first discovered my brother and their daughter missing. He blames himself because he was the one who urged my father to stop focusing their efforts on Trez and Kate after those blood tests came back as not a match for Trey and Anna.

Apparently, our moms had sought out a powerful witch from New Orleans that first year. I learned that tidbit of information last week while trying to get Annalise to open up about feelings she was still trying to hold inside.

I hadn't expected her to drop that bomb on me.

Had they followed through, maybe wasted years could have been avoided. I wouldn't be alpha, nor would Jagger be my beta. I'd gladly trade my role as a leader to have had my brother and mate back with us, back where they belong. Kate and I could have been better friends had I not kept her at a distance.

"Maybe the old crew could go early, and we'll go when the Boss wants to go," Laney offers, her eyes trailing back over to where I'm leaning against the island.

"We have more important issues at hand," Jagger replies. "I believe our alpha told everyone weeks ago that he wasn't leading a run until my *sister*, his *mate*, was found." He pauses, letting his acknowledgment of Kate sink in. When Laney flinches, he continues. "Can't have an official pack run without our alpha, now can we? That doesn't mean everyone isn't free to run in groups, but Kane and I won't be joining."

"Or me," Trez adds, lacing his shoestrings, his head pointing to the floor while in a squatted position.

To the pack's knowledge, we're still searching for Kate, though I suspect Maddy may have insider information since she and Storm live together. I can't feel either of their emotions, but with me, Maddy is a shit liar. She's been avoiding me, which makes me think she knows that Kate is on pack land.

"Noted," Laney draws out like she isn't sure which response to give Jagger.

"If there isn't anything else," I jut my head toward the exit behind her, "we have somewhere to be."

Trez stands and pulls on the t-shirt his mate brought him from my closet.

"Of course, Boss. If there is anything I can help with, let me know."

I tip my head but remain silent. After a beat, she twirls around and steps back over the threshold, pulling the door closed behind her.

"You still haven't fired her?" Trez inquires, his tone low to ensure she doesn't hear us.

"I can't fire her. She didn't do anything wrong."

"You don't call wanting someone else's mate wrong?"

My reply to my brother is on the tip of my tongue, but the tickle behind my ears, a feather-like starch so soft I barely noticed it, has my eyes flying out the window behind Jagger.

I don't have curtains hanging in the lodge either, so I have a view of the setting sun through the tall trees. They once hung above every window in the lodge when my father was alpha, but I took them all down when this became my primary home, preferring the sunlight and nature it brings indoors.

"You felt her, didn't you?" Jagger questions, his head tilting, and then I hear him in my head. *Kate, I mean.*

"It's impossible. The bond isn't complete. She hasn't marked me."

But I felt something.

I just don't know what that something was. It was the oddest sensation and one that felt... pleasant.

"What if it's not?" Jagger says in thought as his eyes flick to where Trez is next to me. "What if we've always been able to feel them when they were near? Maybe we were just too stupid to recognize the signs."

"Maybe," I say, not really believing the possibility, but also not stopping to give it much thought as goose bumps cascade down one side of my neck, then over my shoulder and down my arm.

My feet move on their own accord, eating up the path to the door in long, fast strides. When I'm standing on the other side, looking off the raised patio, I see roughly twenty percent of the pack, but not one of them is Kate. Sure enough, as Laney mentioned, Eli is chatting with Ronnie and one of his buddies. Jagger's dad is sitting, relaxed against one of the Adirondack chairs next to Pike, the backs of their chairs facing the lodge. Ronnie is standing in front of them both, a beer in his right hand that's hanging by his side.

Jagger steps to my left side and Trez to my right while my eyes scan the trees and tall brush. It takes mere seconds for me to spot her, or rather her wolf crouching low in the brush as if watching her prey and waiting for the perfect moment to strike.

She's perfect.

All black fur that seems to glisten in the rising moonlight. The sun hasn't entirely dipped below the horizon yet. Within another ten minutes, we'll be shrouded in darkness save for the ambient lights strung around the courtyard that are weaved through the surrounding trees and hung onto the porches nearby the same way they are here at the lodge.

We have several spots on pack land where we gather for these types of events that are meant to bring the pack closer. I decided to have everyone gather in front of the lodge tonight, where we have picnic tables and Adirondack chairs scattered about in multiple different groups with a bonfire in the center away from trees. Grills of different varieties have been smoking and grilling meat for hours, the smell of burning wood thick in the air, enough to cloak an approaching predator.

A feeling in the pit of my gut forms, but instead of a sense of foreboding, I'm stricken with anger as well as relief at the same time.

Kate creeps forward, her paws slow and measured.

I could stop her if I wanted to, and maybe a better alpha would. I never claimed to be the best choice for my pack. At the end of the day, I just want to be the best man for *her*.

My mate.

Anna Kate Hayes.

My gaze shifts, looking to see if anyone else has noticed her. No one has.

At least, they hadn't until everyone freezes in place at the sound of her low growl. It sends a shiver down my spine. A reaction that only another alpha could produce, one only a stronger alpha than myself could do to me.

A whimper slips from Jagger, then Trez, as over half of everyone standing is forced to their knees.

Ronnie's spine visibly straightens as Kate's black wolf lowers her head, another rumble bringing the rest of the pack, the shifters not seated, to the ground. Her wolf's eyes glow.

Only myself and Maddy remain standing, her eyes wide, but not frightened in the least. My limbs tremble, threatening to do the same, as the old man slowly turns.

Then Kate's wolf lunges.

35

KANE

Her paws push off the ground, propelling her into the air.

My lips part, my eyes unblinking as I watch the attack unfold. It's beautiful and so goddamn tragic at the same time.

I wanted this for her. For Kate to get retribution for Ronnie's ambush in her kidnapping. At this point, his reasoning doesn't fucking matter, and perhaps that's unreasonable on my part.

Do I care?

No.

I watched him shoot a debilitating poison into my mate multiple times. He's lucky I was more worried about finding Kate and having the restraint to give her this moment.

Because it was one of the hardest things I've had to do, and if it had been me, I'm not sure I wouldn't have dragged his death out.

Her wolf's jaw hinges open, her teeth sinking into flesh, muscle, his jugular veins, then her mouth closes as Ronnie falls backward with wolf paws on his chest and the top of his jean-clad thighs.

Before they crash into the shifter sitting beside Elijah, Kate's father jumps out of his chair, his eyes wide with horror. He grabs her wolf, banding his thick arms around her middle while every nerve in my body pinches. I jump over the railing before my mind catches up with my reflexes.

In Eli's attempt to save Ronnie, he shoves her wolf back, and I see motherfucking red.

But it's too late.

Everything of importance within the structure of his neck was ripped from his body as Kate's wolf flies through the air. I experience Kate's shock as if it were my own. The surprise catches her off guard and forces her to shift into her human form a beat before she slams to the ground, landing on her tailbone with the contents from Ronnie's neck beside her.

"What did you do?" Elijah bellows, his mouth hanging open, his hands covering the sides of his head in disbelief.

I'll deal with him in a minute.

He isn't my priority, and I know if I go at him now, Ronnie won't be the only shifter to perish tonight. I'll kill my best friend's dad—my mate's father—without thinking my actions through.

I yank my t-shirt over my head. When I'm close enough to Kate, I squat down in front of her to help shield her naked body from everyone while I use the balled-up material to wipe the remnants of blood from her mouth.

Kate stares wide-eyed at me.

"Kane, I—" A whimper slips from her lips.

I shake my head while handing her the shirt to put on,

unsure if she'd let me do it for her and not wanting to push for more than she's ready to give me.

"It was over quickly. He was given better than he deserved."

She pulls the shirt over her head and down her torso. As she comes to her knees, I push off mine, taking a moment to breathe in through my nostrils and blowing out through my mouth. I slowly turn to face the pack, my eyes going straight to Elijah, and the restraint it takes not to unleash every last bit of alpha power that remains charging me is almost more than I can hold onto.

I stalk toward him.

"Kane," my father calls out from ten yards behind Eli, my mother beside him.

I don't even glance in his direction. Instead, I force a rumble from deep within my chest as warning enough. If he chooses to intervene, then thank fuck I'm his alpha because if the roles were reversed and someone had laid their hands on his mate the way Elijah did mine, he wouldn't have hesitated in unleashing all his alpha power on top of his physical strength the way I'm restraining myself from doing.

Hell, a part of me wishes my wolf would jump out of my skin to handle him like a feral animal's instincts, showing no mercy. At least then, I wouldn't have pause, because I wouldn't be the one in control of our actions.

"She can't—"

Elijah begins, but he's cut off when I snatch him by the shirt and yank him forward within inches from my pissed-off face. "If you were not like a second father to me, I swear on everything... you would not be breathing right now."

"She attacked a member of the pack. She can't do that no matter whose daughter she is or who her mate is."

"You put your hands on my mate," I say, clenching my teeth so that I don't let my canines elongate and tear his throat out.

"Goddammit, Kane, she fucking killed someone."

Try not to kill him, would you? Jagger says in reason in my head.

"My pregnant mate," I finish.

His face pales as he swallows, his eyes growing round with surprise before his expression turns grave and he darts his gaze over my shoulder. I let him go, releasing my hold, but I don't step away from him.

Female wolf shifters aren't treated differently than the men in our pack. We play rough, train aggressively, and we fight dirty. They would kick our asses harder for even thinking about treating them delicately, and being alpha, I'd sense if the pup inside Kate was harmed. That doesn't mean I'm okay with the way Elijah handled her.

He interfered.

He sided with the wrong shifter without asking questions, and maybe he did so unknowingly. But Kate is his daughter, and he tried to prevent her wolf from killing Ronnie without pause as to why she'd do something that permanent.

I glance over my shoulder, seeing Trez pull Kate to her feet, my T-shirt covering down to her mid-thigh while Jagger firms his stance on the other side of his sister as he stares at their father. My beta's eyes flash a vibrant tint of reddish-orange, which is rare for him. He doesn't usually allow that side of him to come to the surface in front of the pack.

"Eli, what did you do?" Annalise calls out, and my head

whips back around, seeing her standing on Ashleigh, Storm, and Maddy's porch.

Only a small bunk-style house separates their cabin from the lodge. From here, I can see her emotions across her pretty face, as well as feel how raw they are, more so now than they were when I eased her heartache.

I changed my mind. Make him hurt before I do. A low, angry growl follows the words Jagger bit out inside my head.

I tilt my head, my eyes falling back on my mate's father.

"She can't do what she did, no matter the reason, Kane. I was trying to stop her before it was too late."

"He's right, Kane," my father adds, his voice seemingly closer than before. Still, I don't turn or seek him out with my eyes. Instead, my gaze remains on Eli.

"Kate's a Luna wolf, the alpha's mate," I continue addressing Elijah, my voice slow and elevating with every word to make sure not only he hears me but so Kate and the pack does too. "Technically, *she* can dole out whatever fucking punishment she deems adequate in *her* pack."

"It doesn't work like that, Kane." My father's tone is starting to grate on my nerves.

"Jagger, you want to explain to the former alpha how it works, and if he doesn't like it... well, the world is a fucking wide open space. Have at it."

I'm aware that our pack has never had a Luna wolf, at least not to my knowledge anyway, so it's fair that no one here has ever been lead by a female shifter. They wouldn't know how to deal with a change like that. Neither my mom nor Jagger's mom weighed in much when it came to Dad and Eli's rules unless they did so in private. I know my father values my mother's input, so I wouldn't think he'd share old-school ways of thinking or be closed-minded.

"I could elaborate that a Luna wolf outranks everyone, our alpha included, but I'm still pacing back, wondering why the hell no one told us my sister was a goddamn Luna in the first place," he spits out.

"We don't belong here. You know that, right?" Kate follows, her words like barbed wire wrapping around my heart with every syllable that falls from her lips.

I can only assume she's speaking to Trez because I can't bring myself to turn my head to look. Instead, I swallow the lump in my throat and continue to stare Elijah in the eyes. His jaw unlocks, and a barely audible gasp escapes the sliver of space between his lips.

"Maybe she wouldn't think that if you've paid her a visit," I whisper so low that only he can hear me.

"She killed my brother," Ronnie's sister screeches from my left side, her banshee voice causing my ears to ring. "Murdered him, and you aren't going to do anything about that? What kind of—"

I turn my head and unleash a roar so intense that the ground shakes beneath my feet. Veronica sucks in a sharp breath, her eyes going wide and freezing in place when my alpha power wraps around her throat. I only hold it in place for the length of two slow breaths, enough to catch her attention. Without my wolf aiding me, I would have gone to my knees if I'd held her any longer.

Laney dashes in front of her mother, shielding her, I presume, not that it would do anything to protect her from an alpha's wrath. Lucky for V, I'm not the type that takes out his anger on undeserving people.

"Kane," Laney starts, her voice soft with a whine. "He's... *was* her brother. Come on, go easy on her. Uncle Ron was the one who—"

"Traded two lives for two lives." A chill runs down my spine as Ashleigh's words sink in.

I hadn't noticed she'd joined the gathering crowd while focused on too many things at once, but as silence follows the bomb Ash dropped, Veronica's eyes double in size. Her bottom lip drops in surprise, giving her away despite me not feeling the emotions her face isn't hiding.

Boots stop next to me on the right, Ashleigh's sleeveless arm brushing against mine.

"Are you saying what I think you're saying?" I ask, my eyes never blinking away from V.

Laney takes a step back, closing the distance between her back and her mom's front, but Veronica is taller than her daughter, so V's suddenly scared expression is on full display to me, as well as everyone else.

"Yes, alpha," Ashleigh confirms, using my title rather than addressing me at ease and showing me just how serious the situation is.

"You discovered this information inside his cabin?"

Jagger steps forward on my left side, his wolf on the edge of jumping from his skin.

"No," she answers. "His house was clean. An asshole beta playing alpha supplied the info when I called him fifteen minutes ago."

There's a bite to Ashleigh's tone that makes me think there's more to her call with Caleb Drake than she's saying, but it's neither here nor there at the moment. Not when there is other pressing information I need to know.

"Kane," Laney all but breathes out while shaking her head. "I don't know what's going on, but my mom wouldn't have been involved with anything you're thinking my uncle did. Right, Mom?"

"Riii-ght," V stutters, her eyes finally flicking down and off me, showing her submission, but something feels off. I just have no fucking clue what.

"Who?" is the only word I can muster out of my mouth without growling as I continue to stare past Laney at her mother, the alpha power inside me vibrating with a need to strike out and not having the person I know to be responsible for my mate and brother's disappearance alive to target. I'm not a man who would ever knowingly harm an innocent person, which is why Veronica remains standing.

"His sister's life, as well as her unborn baby, in exchange for two wolf pups of greater value," Ash informs.

Before my foot comes off the ground, Eli is in my face, his palm displayed across my bare chest, pressing against me with the slightest amount of pressure.

"Kane, that isn't possible." Elijah's head swings back and forth. "I was with Dante when he grilled everyone. And I do mean everyone, so before you do something you'll regret, remember she's pack. Drake isn't," he tries to reason, making my blood boil.

Before I can blink, my father is next to Eli, his bulk moving Ashleigh back a step. She growls but doesn't assert herself like I'd prefer her to do in this circumstance. When it comes to my dad, she always hesitates, and I guess that's because he used to be her alpha.

"Caleb also wants Richard's territory more than anyone, son," Dad adds. "Who's to say he isn't saying this to further his gain, to make us help him fight the Marked Crest pack."

"Drake may be a dick, and he doesn't just want that providence, he needs it for the space his pack has outgrown, but he in no way needs *our* help to get it," I tell them. But I can't say I'm not curious as to how Caleb came to have this information and didn't share it with me on our call a few weeks ago. Then again, I did hang up on him. "They have enough shifters to fight The Marked Crest pack on their own. Not sure why they haven't done so already, but I don't care either way."

I throw my hand up, my forearm connecting with Elijah's outstretched arm.

"Move," I order, and luckily for him, he takes a step back and then another. Dad follows and it's then I see my mother a few paces behind her husband, but it's not my father who holds her attention. She's staring at Veronica, an expressionless mask on her pretty face. If it weren't for the conflicting emotions warring inside her, I wouldn't think she was affected by what's taking place right now.

"Ask her, Kane," Ashleigh says too nonchalantly that I know she has an agenda up her sleeve. "You're alpha. You can taste our lies on your tongue."

"Which is why I know she isn't guilty of anything," my father states. "I don't know why Kate did what she did, and I expect you to tell us her reason for attacking a pack member, Kane."

"She showed him more mercy than I would have, so you should thank my mate for a quick end. Ash, show them the video from the diner since they're reluctant to trust that the punishment he received fit the crime he committed."

"Already texted it to the entire pack. Everyone should know what a piece of shit traitor he was, after all."

"Wha-at did my brother do?" V speaks up. Stepping slowly around Laney, my eyes going back to hers. "Ashleigh is correct. You can tell when any of us aren't telling the truth. Ask me anything, alpha. I'll tell you. I swear it."

"Come. Here," I bite out.

With every slow step forward, my heartbeat kicks up a notch. I called Caleb Drake a dick, but at times, I can be just as big of one as he is. That doesn't mean I take pleasure in hurting others, and if I find out she betrayed my parents the way I wholly believe her brother did, I'm not sure I can refrain from killing her in a similar manner as Kate killed Ronnie.

"What the fuck?" Eli's head snaps up from his smartphone.

"He did the same to Trez and I let it go, chalked it up to a mistake. The same can't be said after watching that video, now can it?" I don't wait for a reply, one isn't needed, and anything out of Elijah's mouth other than he fucked up will not go over with me in this state of mind. "He led her to them. Had Henrik not fucked over a dark witch, Kate would not be here. Your daughter would still be missing, and who the fuck knows if we'd have ever found her. Let that sink in... to you both," I spit out and then cut my eyes to my dad.

"We're missing something," Dad says. "I'm not saying you're wrong about Ronald. But something isn't right. I questioned him. I questioned Veronica. They never lied to me. I asked them multiple ways. Neither could have lied to me."

"Alpha, please, I—"

"Did you have any part in my mate or my brother being kidnapped twenty years ago?"

"No!" her reply is instant, no hesitation, no sour taste pooling onto my tongue. She's being honest.

"Did you know that Kate was Anna and that Trez was Trey at any point before I announced it to the pack?"

"No, of course not, alpha." Her bottom lip wobbles but the answer she gave was an honest one.

"Did you know Ronnie shot Trez with Wolfsbane weeks back?"

"I did. He told me it was a misunderstanding. That he thought you banished him and his sister from here."

Hearing that again stings, but it's nothing I didn't explain to the pack when I revealed Kate was Anna. That she and Trez had been spelled, that I fucked up and missed every small detail that pointed to them being one of us. Like the connection Trez and I had from day one or mine and Jagger's intense attraction to shifters we believed to be from an enemy pack.

"Did you know Ronnie followed Kate when she left after I was an asshole and kicked her out?"

"I didn't know that. I'm sorry, alpha. If Ronnie betrayed anyone, I wasn't aware."

I roll my head, my frustrated gaze finding Ashleigh's calculating green eyes staring back at me. "You want to help me out here?"

"I think you should repeat every one of those questions again, or maybe just the fir—"

"Enough of this," my father butts in, cutting her off. "You interrogated Veronica. She answered. Be done. We have a pack member who needs to be prepped for a funeral despite what it might look like in a video you seem to have had for weeks, yet you're just now sharing with the rest of us."

"Or, you can do that. Go ahead, tell her she can leave, Kane." Ashleigh shrugs her shoulders, up to something, but clearly playing a baiting game with prey.

"You're free to leave, V," I say, eyeing Ash the whole time and silently ordering her to tell me what the fuck she's doing.

"I-I can't m-move," V announces.

My head whips around, seeing her body swaying, but her feet rooted to the ground like they're cemented in place.

A snicker comes from my right side, but Ashleigh's amusement isn't having the same effect on me. Instead, it's slipping under my skin. Theatrics aren't usually her thing, at least not since adulthood, but I know she wouldn't be making an ordeal of this without purpose.

"Guess you won't be leaving just yet," she quips.

"What's the meaning of this, Kane?" Dad voices, but since I don't have an answer, I look to my cousin, who better supply a good fucking reason to be playing with Ivy's earth element.

There is no way Storm would have assisted without checking with me first. Her sister, on the other hand, is far too impressionable and much too eager to use the magic in her veins.

"Ash?" I grit out slowly.

"You're no fun, you know that?" She steps forward, her eyes losing every ounce of humor and hardening into two emerald-like stones.

Pushing my father and Eli out of the way, much like my father bulldozed her several minutes ago, and not bothering with pleasantries to excuse her manners, her eyes remain locked with mine. Jutting her arm out with lightning quickness, Ashleigh snatches something from beneath Veronica's open flannel-covered t-shirt.

V gasps and tries to grab the item back, but she lacks the controlled speed Ashleigh has mastered. When Veronica's wolf claws extract, Ash's head swings toward her as her fist tightens and a warning growl releases from deep within her chest before the tips of V's nails touch my third in command.

Veronica yanks her hand back, her claws disappearing under her nail bed just before a shuddered breath leaves her open lips, her gaze darting to mine. Her body starts to tremble as sweat beads down her brow.

Needles prick the base of my skull, and one by one, they stab down my spine in a slow cadence, the sting increasing in intensity along each nerve.

V swallows. Laney, standing next to her mother, wraps her hands around V's long-sleeve-covered arm just above her elbow and huddles close to Veronica. In fear for her mom or herself, I'm not sure. The emotions pouring out of Veronica overload anything coming from anyone else around me, and it's now that I realize I've never felt V like this; this magnitude of feelings coming off her, slamming into me like waves.

Kane, what the fuck is going on? Jagger's thoughts push through my own. *Why does she feel different... like—*

Like there was some kind of cloak around her, and now there isn't?

From the corner of my eye, I see Ashleigh lifting her arm. My gaze drops to where her fingers are balled into a fist, a gold chain spilling out the sides dangling from her hand. Seconds tick by, the sound of a non-existent clock clicks inside my head, then her digits unfold.

"What is it?" I ask while looking at a flat gold pendant, unfamiliar symbols etched into the metal.

"A talisman." Ashleigh holds it out for me to take, her voice thundering against my eardrum. "If I'd have to guess, it was created to hide someone's deceit, their lying tongue," she grits out, her own anger so sharp it could slice through stone. "Betrayal to their pack, their former alpha who openly welcomed *her* back into the pack after she'd been gone for five years... or so I'm told. Did you know that, Kane? That V ditched The Bloodmoon Pack for a period and just so happened to return months before your brother and mate went missing?"

I snatch the jewelry from her palm as my eyes seek out my father. "Is that true?"

There isn't any doubt in my mind that the information is false. Ash wouldn't have told me if it were rumor or hearsay. She would have confirmed those details before bringing it to me.

"Mom, tell him that's not true, that it's only a coincidence," Laney urges, but V's lips remain fused shut. If it weren't for her heavy breaths and the tremors racking her body, I would think more than just her feet are stuck to the ground.

"Yes, Kane. It's true."

My father's claws slowly push out from his nail bed as a change in the air crackles around us, but that confirmation didn't come from his mouth. My gaze shoots over V's shoulder, finding my mother suddenly behind her.

I blink, and then Veronica is yanked away from her daughter's tight hold, my mother's hand wrapped around her throat with her claws sunken into flesh, shattering whatever spell Ivy had holding V in place.

"No," Laney screams, her hands going to her mouth. "Becca, please don't."

"I haven't done anything... yet," my mother tells Laney as her volatile eyes land on mine. "Ask her again, Kane. I want to hear it from her mouth despite knowing the answer. I felt what Dante did. I know."

I hadn't expected my mother to say that, but I suppose I shouldn't be shocked. My father doesn't keep anything from her, not even his emotions.

When a pack alpha chooses to step down, to hand his title over to another instead of through a challenge to the death, it is done through a ritual during a full moon. We lose the power to control the pack, not the alpha abilities we're born with. Those we learn to harness over time. He's still an alpha, just not the pack alpha, which means he felt the same facade vanish when the enchanted necklace was ripped off, exposing her deception.

"Did you have any part in my mate or my brother being kidnapped twenty years ago?"

Spells are tricky. It's all about the way you phrase a question, which is why I didn't say Kate and Trez or Anna and Trey the first time nor now. Kate is my mate. Trez is my brother. Those are facts.

When she doesn't offer anything up immediately, I close my fingers around the talisman and squeeze as I release what little power I have left. I'm running on empty, but I'll use it all if that's what it takes.

Veronica's legs quake, but she doesn't drop to the ground like she would have had my mother not had her locked in her grasp.

"I didn't have a choice, Kane." She gasps when my mom's razor-sharp claw sinks deeper into her neck. "He... the Marked Crest alpha would have given Laney over to the demon king if I hadn't given him what he demanded."

The king of the underworld is what humans refer to as the devil. Wolf-shifters don't serve a purpose for him. Why would we when he commands legends of hellhounds who are a hundred, maybe even a thousand times stronger than us? We might as well be newborn puppies in comparison to those creatures.

"Why did he want us?" Trez asks from over my left shoulder, his voice making me forget the confessions coming out of Veronica's mouth.

If he's behind me, where is my mate?

When she was close by, there was a tether connecting us. I felt it when I was in the lodge, and when I walked outside, it strengthened a fraction. When I was in front of her, handing over my T-shirt, it was the strongest it's ever been.

Now... nothing.

Like she isn't here.

The muscle in my chest seizes.

The chatter around me fades away, replaced with a glass-shattering ringing vibration.

I swing around, my eyes flicking everywhere at once.

"Where's Kate?"

36

KANE

I swear on everything, my heart stopped.

When I realized she wasn't in sight, I damn near lost it.

I didn't give a fuck about Veronica or what she was admitting. It didn't matter. Nothing without Kate matters. Even my wolf can go fuck himself.

I started running without direction.

When had she left?

I had no idea where she was and that was the worst feeling I've ever felt. It was ten times, no, a thousand times worse than when I realized how badly I fucked up and had kicked my own mate out of *her* pack.

I can't lose her again.

In hindsight, I should have jumped inside one of the side-by-sides or ATVs parked around the lodge. A machine would have moved faster than my slow-ass human legs.

Panic consumed me and wreaked havoc through my head. All I could hear was her voice saying, *we don't belong here,* playing on repeat, slamming against my ribcage.

Fuck.

Fuck, fuck, fuck.

Until recently, these out-of-control feelings, along with the pressure piling on top of my chest, were foreign. My mate had been missing for so long that I never allowed myself to believe I'd find her. Then I discovered she's been within my reach only to turn out to be the man who hurt her.

I can't lose her.

But I don't deserve her either.

I barrel into the door so hard wood splinters as my weight slams against it before my hand presses down on the handle. It opens, and I stumble inside, my breathing ragged.

"Kate." To my own ears, I sound frantic.

I don't fucking care.

I race down the hall of our cabin and into our bedroom. My eyes don't process the open bathroom door with steam billowing out before I've halted just inside the opening of the bathroom.

Kate's head snaps up, her hands freezing with the towel half wrapped around her wet body.

I charge forward on autopilot, not thinking any of my actions through. My right hand goes around her neck, squeezing as I force her to scramble backward while my other hand finds her terrycloth-covered hip as her shoulder blades press against the back wall. My forehead meets hers. She's hot to the touch from the shower.

"You *do* fucking belong here," I whisper, my breath fanning her face, my eyes staring into her guilty blue ones.

"I shouldn't have said—"

"But if you leave, I will follow you." I loosen my hold around her neck but tighten my grip over her hip bone.

"Don't say dumb things," she chides. "You couldn't if you wanted to, and you know it. You're the alpha."

"I don't give a fuck about any of it. The pack can live without me. My dad and Eli can have it. I cannot live without you. Or maybe I could, but I'd be a miserable fuck, and at that point, fuck life too. I just want you and... you and our son. Please, Kate. I need you, not because fate made you perfect for me, but because you're you, and I want to give you everything in the whole goddamn world. Please don't fucking leave me," I beg unashamedly. "I'm sorry for it all; for all the angry words I said, telling you to leave. Even without knowing you were my mate, I shouldn't have treated you the way I did. You didn't do anything wrong. It was all my fault, and I'm so fucking sorry. I—"

My vision of her clouds as the tears rush to the surface, my nostrils stinging.

I don't fucking care.

I need her to see how the thought of her not being here, not being mine, makes me feel. I can't go through that again. My soul feels like it's being ripped from inside me.

I drop to my knees, my right hand mirroring my other on her hip, then bow my head, tipping it to the side to bare my neck in complete submission.

She's the only being I'd ever do this for, and it's not even shocking that it feels right to submit to her.

"Wh-what are you..." She gasps from above me. "Kane, what are you doing?"

"This pack is yours, Kate. I know it may not feel that way, but you *are* one of us," I say, knowing I sound mad, but I'm far from it. "You were born here, the same as me. You fucking belong here the same as any one of us."

"G-get up," she demands, shock stumbling her words.

I tip my head back and lift my eyes. She's staring down at me, her lips parted and both hands clasping the towel to the front of her chest with droplets of water dripping from the ends of her dark hair, her eyes unblinking, the mark on her neck barely visible with her hair in the way.

"I don't know how else to say I'm sorry or show you that I know I fucked up." My shoulders start to shake. She doesn't have a reason to believe what I'm saying, but fuck if I don't want her to, need her to. "I'm both sorry and not sorry for claiming you. I shouldn't have done it without asking. My wolf had no fucking right, but goddammit, you're mine, and I fucking need you to want me the way I want you. I want you, Kate. Not my wolf. Me!"

A whimper falls from her lips, and that's when I feel the slightest tremble in her limbs, but Kate must realize it too because she goes stark still. Her gaze flicks over my head, then snaps up toward the ceiling. Her bottom lip wobbles, but it's the scent that swarms around us that pulls a growl from deep inside my lungs.

Her arousal is a beacon straight to my dick, hardening the muscle tucked behind the zipper of my jeans and making me ache as it pulses against the stiff material, seeking out her delicious smelling pussy.

Kate shivers, then drops her head, her eyes hooded. Her blue gaze looks as raw as I feel as a tinge of orange glows in and out like a flickering light bulb, her need almost palpable.

"You're a Luna wolf, Kate. Whether you believe it yet or not, you are, and if you want something, you demand it, right here, right now," I growl deeply, edging her courage to step up.

She licks her lips, her tongue slow to retreat inside her mouth.

I don't blink, not wanting to miss a second of watching her need me the way I need her, the way I crave only her. I can't breathe a full breath without her nearby, and I'm not wholly sure I have until she reentered my life those five short years ago.

Her fingers flex enough that the ends of the towel slip from her grip. I drop my hands to let the cotton fall to the floor and sit back on the heels of my boots, waiting for her, giving her all the time she needs.

My gaze drops to her small, rounded belly, and it's everything I can do not to drop a whimper from my lips. It's the first time I've seen the proof of my baby growing inside her.

Our son.

And I can't wait to meet him.

I've known now for a week that she's going to have a boy. It's one of the alpha abilities my father taught me how to tell in a lesson years ago. It's not only wolf shifters it works on. I can smell when any species is pregnant early on and once they're far enough along, I can scent what they're going to have.

My hands react on their own, reaching out and palming her soft, warm skin. Leaning forward, my lips brush across her flesh. I breathe her in, then lay slow kisses below her navel to both sides of her stomach. Kate pulls in a sharp breath through her mouth. My eyes flick up, silently begging her for a command.

The ball is in her court.

"Fuck me," she whispers, too uncertain for the strong

woman I know she is, and it makes me think I did this to her, made her feel unsure of herself.

My palms slide to the tops of her thighs and hook around the back of her legs as my head sways to my right, her left. My lips trail across her belly to where her hip and thigh connect, kissing her skin and breathing her in at the same time. My mouth opens, sucking on the meaty part of her flesh. My canines tingle as I lightly bite down while my eyes watch every reaction she has to my touch, and the feeling of how each one slams into my chest is more than I deserve.

"Fuck you how?" I whisper, knowing every slow syllable off my tongue produces goose bumps along her skin. "Fuck you where, baby?" When she swallows but doesn't answer, I keep probing. "Your pretty little pussy... your tight ass... or that heated wet mouth of yours." I flop my tongue out and swipe at the spot I bit. "Where do you want to be fucked, Kate?"

A mewling whimper slips out of her mouth as her knees lose some of their stability. My fingers tighten to steady her. I should move her to the bed so she doesn't have to stand, but fuck if I don't love kneeling in front of her like this.

"All of them." She breathes hard, her chest heaving.

"I only have one dick, baby, but it's yours." I smile against the apex of her thigh. "How do you want me to make you come? Tell me like an alpha," I growl, the front of my teeth pressed against her skin.

Kate's fingers dive between the loose strands of my hair on the top of my head, my ponytail holder missing in action. It was yanked out somewhere between racing through the brush and arriving at the cabin. At the time, I hadn't cared that it got caught by a limb. Now the too-long strands are driving me fucking crazy and getting in my way of watching my mate.

Her nails, or fuck, maybe her claws scrape my scalp, and it feels so fucking amazing. She tangles her digits around my hair, pulling it taut, yanking my head back and away from her sweet body. Looking up, I wait.

I wait for her direction.

Her order.

"Eat my pussy, Kane." She growls, and it goes in both ears and down my spine. My dick pulses, and it's almost too much pressure. I'm on the verge of exploding. "Shove your pants down. I want to see your cock in your hand while you lick me."

"Whatever you want." My words are strained, and the second my hands leave her body and Kate loosens her fingers, I get pissed at the loss of her touch, but I work my belt buckle as fast as I can, needing my hands back on her and my tongue inside her.

I push my jeans down my thick thighs, the zipper barely down an inch. My dick springs out, and I grab it with one hand while snatching Kate's foot up to my shoulder with the other to open her up to me.

The quick position change grants me an eye-level view of her slick pussy, already dripping wet. Her scent makes me lightheaded and my mouth water.

Fuck, it's so pretty.

Before I can dive forward, Kate jerks my head back and my eyes up to hers.

"Stroke it," she grits out, almost angrily.

"Fuck me," I heave.

"No," she growls, the rumble of her words rolling down my chest. "You're going to fuck me, mate. And you're not going to come until I do. So, fuck me, Kane. Fuck me so hard that I don't know if it's your tongue getting me off or your big dick doing the job."

Fucking hell.

My eyes roll to the back of my head, her words sucking the breath out of my lungs.

I stroke myself.

Then I stroke my dick again, only this time, I force my eyes to open and look at Kate, but she's biting her bottom lip and her stunningly blue gaze is between my legs.

A whimper leaves her parted lips, making her fingers loosen. I take that as my cue to lean in, burying my face in her needy, perfect little cunt. The soft curls tickle my nose as her scent works its way down to the tip of my dick. I can barely control it from painting the wall between her legs with my cum.

I lick her wet snatch as I stroke my cock, and either her leg is already shaking, or my whole body is. She tastes so goddamn divine that I want so badly for every ounce of Kate to coat the inside of my mouth, to drain down my throat. I'll never have enough of her. I'll always need more... want more... crave more.

"Yes." Her hands wrap around my head, and her hips buck into my face. "Oh, God, yes. Just like that, Kane."

Knowing all her weight is on one leg, I move the hand that isn't pulling on my cock to between her legs, to brace her ass. Wanting to give her what she wholeheartedly demanded, I dip my middle finger inside her wet pussy, coating it first. Then, pulling out, I press the blunt digit to her asshole as my tongue dives inside her snug entrance.

Kate's fingers flex, and I feel her wolf's claws at the base of my skull. Tingles erupt across my neck as I push my finger inside. She moans loud enough that my ears ring. It spurs me on, so I press deeper into her hot ass and then slowly pull out.

As I push back in, I pull my fist down to the base of my cock and squeeze. Kate's claws sink into my flesh. I suck in a breath, forcing Kate's scent into my lungs like she's the air I desperately need to live.

Fuck, she's going to kill me.

If I die right here, it'll be the happiest death imaginable.

Her muscles contract around my finger.

My tongue slips inside Kate's pussy, my fingers fucking her simultaneously as I continue stroking my dick like she told me to do. My tongue swirls around her clit.

Kate's torso bends over me, but I keep working her, my fingers going in and out, faster, harder. Her breaths quicken, and her hands move down my bare back, her claws scratching my flesh.

She begins to pant, her hot breaths fanning my back.

Her foot slips from my shoulder, and Kate's pussy walls start rapidly contracting. The sound of her coming makes my dick swell even more. She keeps coming while I suck her clit harder, wanting this to last forever, needing her to feel all the pleasure she so fucking deserves.

When her body sags over me and her breaths slow, I reduce my speed and let her clit slip from my grasp.

I pull my fingers out, kissing above her mound. Then, where her belly begins to round, I continue kissing the flesh protecting our son. I keep trailing light kisses up Kate's stomach and lifting myself to stand as I go. I keep stroking because she hasn't told me to stop... or come. And fuck is it torture.

Kate's back smacks the wall, her chest still heaving by

the time I'm standing to my full height above her. My eyes attempt to roll to the back of my head while my knees try to give out, but I keep stroking.

Because that's what she said to do.

As if realizing I didn't come, Kate's eyes round, and then those pretty blues flick down and back up to mine so quickly I think I may have been seeing things. I have no idea what she's thinking right now, and my brain isn't working enough to figure it out before her hand is flat against my chest and my feet are moving backward.

She's pushing me, even though I don't know how I'm still standing. The bathroom door slams, wood splinters, and then my back is against said door. The heat in Kate's eyes is throwing me off. I can't figure out what it means, and it's scaring the fuck out of me.

My heart starts to pound hard. My dick aches so fucking much, it's throbbing, but then her hand knocks mine away, and before I can blink, I'm encased in her soft palm.

I suck in a breath. My ears thunder, or maybe the earth moves. *Was that a fucking earthquake?*

Her hand moves up and down, the way I was imagining mine as hers, and the ache eases to pleasure like I've never felt. Her claws drag down my shaft, the palm of her hand pressing against the tip of my dick.

My hips buck.

Oh, fucking fuuuuck that feels so good.

My vision blurs, and then a beast's teeth sink deep into my neck.

I come un-fucking-done, exploding as the tips of her claws grip me tighter.

I see stars.

Goddamn motherfucking stars.

37
KATE

He keeps coming and coming, spilling through my fingers. His release is scorching, hotter than the blood gushing into my mouth, or so it feels. It could be in my head. I could be making this more than it is, but I don't think I am.

I never imagined it could feel like this.

Our connection. Solid. Impenetrable.

I can feel what he's feeling like they're my own emotions, a pressure so heavy my chest may cave in on itself.

Kane is wrecked. He's experiencing pure bliss. But there is so much doubt that it's breaking my heart all over again.

Was biting him, claiming him as mine, not the right thing to do?

It felt right.

It felt like I was going to die if I didn't clamp my teeth over him and break skin.

It was euphoric. Better than the drawn-out orgasm he triggered throughout my whole being.

When he came, it was like I was coming again too. If my teeth hadn't been holding me in place, I'd be a puddle on the floor right now. It was so intense my body is still shaking.

Kane's thick arms band around my back, pulling me closer and anchoring me to him as a shuddered breath leaves his mouth, fanning the side of my face. His wet cock slips from my hand, my claws already retracted back into my nail beds. My small breasts press against his upper abdominal muscles, his heart beating in rhythm with mine.

His lips make contact with my forehead in the softest touch I've ever been given, his kiss smooth like velvet. Kane lingers against me, his chest finally slowing, his breathing warming me like a campfire without smoke billowing in my face.

After a beat, his arms unwrap and his palms move up my bare arms, stopping at my shoulders. He pushes me away from him, our eyes locking on each other's stare.

"Did you do it because it's what *you* want?" He swallows, his eyes unblinking and reddish-orange with emotions that have nothing to do with the alpha power inside him. "Did you claim me as yours for yourself, or did you do it because..." He chokes up and jerks in a breath. "Because you feel trapped here with me like it was your only option."

"Kane—"

"I won't force you to stay here." His big hands cup my cheeks, the bottom of his palms resting on the column of my neck as his head shakes so slowly that I'm not wholly sure it's even moving. "I wouldn't make you be with me if you didn't want me, Kate, but I wasn't lying before either. If you leave, I leave. You'll never be free of me, and now that our mate bond is solid, I'll always know where you are."

"If I wanted to be free of you, I never would have claimed you, asshole."

I use the space between us to smack him in the stomach with the back of my hand, hoping to get my point across, but all it does is make me feel like shit when he sucks in another sharp breath like I sucker punched him. It's now that I see just how tired Kane looks. Like he's barely holding himself upright.

My brows knit with concern, and something scratches at the back of my skull like I should know something that I don't.

Is something wrong with him?

"I'd rather be dead than be here without you. Be anywhere without you. You're my always, Kate. Please, fucking forgive me. Don't hate me. Don't stop talking to me again."

His words make me lose my train of thought, and my chest starts to burn with an intensity I've never felt before as tension stretches across my back.

"Don't say that." I'd hit him again if I wasn't sure it would knock him out this time. Something is up, and I don't think it has anything to do with the silent treatment I was giving him over the last few weeks, but I can't dwell on it when he's talking about death.

I'd lose my shit if anything happened to him. Not when I just discovered who I am, who he really is to me, or why it felt like there was something just out of reach from the second I smelled his scent five years ago.

"We may be bonded for life, Kane, but you and I are anything but solid. You crushed my heart. You could have set my body on fire, and it would have hurt less. You fucking..." I jerk away, taking a step back and heaving as the memory comes back tenfold all over again.

Does no one understand that words often hurt much more than physical pain? It fucks with your mental health on a level that doesn't make sense. Once they're spoken, you can't take them back, and the person you lash out at hears them over and over like a bad song playing on a loop.

I want to forget I ever heard them from his mouth, but I can't.

"If you tell me it felt like I rejected you, my mate, it'll fucking kill me, Kate."

He yanks up his pants in haste, covering himself, but he doesn't button them or pull up the zipper. His belt buckle remains dangling.

"Do you want me to lie?"

"Never." He shakes his head. "I'd feel the lie. I'd taste it in my mouth. It would be pointless, but even if it weren't, you never have to lie to me." He swallows again, then his arms raise, his hands going to the top of his head and criss-crossing his wrists. Kane grips his dirty-blond strands, pulling them taut like he's trying to cause himself the pain I feel, and maybe he is.

He hurts because I hurt.

I know he does. I can feel his agony as deeply as he feels mine.

When I bit him—claimed Kane for myself—I hadn't been thinking about what it would do to us. How it would connect our feelings. It makes me wonder if our thoughts are connected too.

Ever since Trez told me that he and Jagger can speak to each other telepathically, that it's supposedly a benefit of being mates, I wondered if Kane and I would have that ability too. I've wanted it. I even dreamed that we could a few nights ago, and when I woke up, the disappointment made me want to cry.

Or maybe that was pregnancy hormones. Still, I wonder...

Can we?

I don't hate you, I say in my head, not really sure how it works with someone else who isn't my brother.

His eyes widen, surprise opening his mouth and giving me the answer I wanted.

We can talk to each other like Trez and I can during a full moon. But there is no full moon now. Not for another week or maybe a few days. I haven't exactly been staying up to date on what day it is or what phase of the moon we're in. I only just ran earlier with Jagger, but the moon hadn't crested the sky yet.

I could never hate you when I love you.

Whatever had been holding Kane back after I tore myself away from him breaks. It shatters in front of me and... inside me. But it's also as if a cauldron within us fills to the brim and firms into a gelatin of sorts.

Kane takes a long step toward me, and before I can blink, his hands wrap around my butt cheeks, and he lifts me. I have no choice but to wrap my bare legs around his waist, my hands going to his shoulders.

"I more than love you, Kate. You're my oxygen, my heart-beat, the blood in my veins. I don't want to do this life unless it's alongside you."

Tears pool into his amber eyes, or maybe it's my own because my vision of him blurs, but when Kane staggers with me in his arms, his hands pulling me tighter to his chest, I blink.

What the hell?

I know Kane's abilities. No matter how thick I am and pregnant, I am but a twig in comparison to his supernatural strength. He could hold me for hours and never tire out, but that's exactly the first thought that came to mind. But instead of opening another can of worms, I lean in, fusing my lips to his, wanting to give him my energy, and I kiss my mate until my lips go numb.

I kiss Kane until my eyelids grow weak.

I kiss the one and only man I've ever wanted until he's the only thing taking up space in my head.

I kiss my always until I forget I killed a man today.

I kiss my unborn baby's father until I'm not sure if we're still two beings or if we're now one.

38
KATE

I don't remember falling asleep or Kane moving us to the bed, but that's where we are when my eyes crack open.

I'm lying on my back, still naked, with half of Kane's front draped on top of me and the other beside me on his bed—or our bed, if I look at it like that.

I'm not going anywhere, at least not willingly. Then again, I killed someone in a pack I never knew I'd once been a part of, even if it was only for a short time.

Ronnie deserved what he got, but it's possible I made a rash decision taking his life. Maybe the rest of The Bloodmoon Pack doesn't want me here despite being their alpha's fated mate.

It's hard to wrap my mind around the fact that I'm not a Marked Crest shifter. It's fair to think it's as equally hard for them to still see me as a wolf shifter from a rival pack.

"You're thinking way too hard when the sun hasn't even crested the horizon yet," Kane comments. With his arm draped over my lower half, he slides his hand underneath me, wrapping his fingers around my hip. He squeezes the meaty flesh while pulling me firmly against his front, securing me to him like he's afraid I'll bolt.

"I'm not going anywhere." A breath I hadn't realized he was holding leaves his lips, warm air coating my chest and hardening my nipples. "Not unless—"

Kane moves fast, jumping from his lying position to being over me, his legs straddling my hips and his arms braced against my shoulders.

As if that would hold me in place if I didn't want to be under him.

"Unless what?" he demands, growling over me. The fright in his eyes from hours ago returns, or maybe it never left during his slumber.

"I killed someone. A pack member no less, or does last night not ring a bell?"

"You doled out the only fitting punishment for betrayal. That was your right as alpha." He says *alpha* through clenched teeth, his canines elongating like he wishes he could do the same.

"I'm no one's alpha, Kane. That's you, not me." I blow out a tired breath.

"Have you not been hearing me, or do you not know?" Kane's brows furrow, the line between them deepening.

"The Luna thing?" I ask, almost rolling my eyes, reminded of the memory when Kane's father commented on the subject.

It doesn't work like that, Kane.

That was close to the point in which I ducked out when all eyes were on Kane and my father.

Kane nods his head.

"Jagger mentioned it, but I never got a chance to ask him

more, and yes, I heard you say it to..." I pause, my voice cracking. I can call him my father in my head, but I can't bring myself to say it out loud. "Elijah. But Luna wolves were called stupid myths in the Marked Crest pack. I don't know if I can buy it. It's all just too—"

"Trez told me you believe you're an alpha," he says like an admission, cutting me off, but I don't get the impression it's to speak over me. The feelings inside him are flowing steadily into me, leading me to think he's trying to stop my doubt from mounting. Kane continues when I remain silent. "All a Luna is, is a female alpha wolf shifter. It's not a stretch. Forget whatever those motherfuckers filled your head with. According to Storm, Richard isn't even a real alpha. Another dark witch gave him the power to control others, not fate."

Tension takes root between my shoulder blades, but it isn't my own. It's his. He wants Richard dead as much as I do, but with Kane, I feel his guilt as well as his almost broken restraint, telling me that if I want my pound of flesh, it's mine, not his.

I do want it, but I'm also still holding out hope that Salem handled it.

I won't chance going after him right now. Not when I have my baby to think about. I won't risk not coming home. But... if Salem doesn't end him and he comes after us, I will fight for my life, my child's life, Kane's, and everyone else I love and care about. If I'm honest, that's the entire pack... because this place feels like home. It feels like *my* home, and if it comes down to it, I'll defend it and everyone that lives here.

"What's the point of a special name then if they're just the same as normal alphas?"

"I never said a Luna was a normal alpha, Kate. Because you aren't. A Luna is special and rare and a fucking endangered supernatural. Alpha females are more powerful than regular alphas. You are more powerful than me."

"You almost had me until you oversold it." My lips purse, and then a scowl rolls across my features. I know because it's reflected in his annoyed eyes staring back at me. "Move. I'd like to get dressed now."

When he doesn't move, just hovers over me, looking at me like I need a spanking, I place one hand on his hip and the other on the back of his thigh and flip our positions, me now on top between his legs.

Kane's dick jumps at the contact, thumping my mound. I'd be lying if I said I didn't want him again, this time with more than just his fingers and tongue inside me.

"You are a Luna, *my Luna*," he grits through his teeth. "This pack's Luna wolf. You're their alpha too."

"So, we're equals now?" My question sounds filled with doubt, my sex drive forgotten.

Sure, I've heard him hint at that, but I've been shoving it out of my head as soon as it hits.

Where I come from, or... where I was stolen and taken, it isn't like that. We were ruled by one man with absolute power. Henrik was Richard's second, his beta, but everyone, including him, knew he didn't have any more say than the rest of us.

"In case you weren't listening when Jagger said it to my father, or when I told you..." He pauses and stares at me while taking a breath. "You're above me, Kate. A Luna wolf shifter holds the most power, more than I do. This is ultimately your pack, and we will follow your lead. But I also know you better than you think I do, and the thought of dictatorship boils your blood. I may have been the sole alpha for the last three years, but I've never made decisions that affect the pack without consulting Jagger and, often-times, Ashleigh. The pack even. If you want me by your side, that's where I'll be. Jag, Trez, and Ash with us."

"What if the pack doesn't want a Luna? What if Dante and Elijah don't get on board with that idea?" I can't help but ask. "What if they aren't okay with what I did, who I killed? Elijah said it himself: I can't do what I did, attacking and slaughtering another pack member. Dante agreed."

"First, fuck Eli and my dad if they don't get on board with any of it. Second, and do not take this as me defending your dad, but he didn't know Ronnie helped Hale and the witch take you. He didn't know because I didn't tell him. And now, I'd wager my parents and yours are feeling angry, but not toward you, Kate."

"Elijah wasn't exactly happy about what I did, so…"

"You didn't stick around to hear V's confession, did you?" His chest rumbles with a held-in growl as his amber gaze flashes blood orange. Kane blinks and they're back to amber.

"I was covered in blood. I left once you started going on about me being a Luna wolf. Elijah's shock and disappoint-ment was a little much," I admit.

Kane reaches up, cupping my face in his warm hand, his heated anger diminishing into empathy.

"He isn't disappointed in you, baby. I may be mad at our fathers, but I can tell you they're both torn up inside. It's up to Eli to make things right with you, so I won't get in the middle, but he is feeling a lot of self-hatred and failure."

"V… Veronica, right?" I ask for clarification, not wanting to dwell on letting my real father down any longer, knowing if I do, I won't be able to contain the emotions smothered inside me.

"Yeah. Ronnie's sister." Kane scoots himself up the bed until his back is against the headboard, me straddling his lap. "I don't know all the details, but V traded your life and Trez's to save herself and Laney. Her brother helped her. That was as far as I'd gotten when I realized you were gone. I couldn't feel where you were since our mate bond wasn't complete. I panicked. Then I ended up here."

Dots dance down my spine as if to tell me something.

But what?

"Is there something more? Something you haven't shared?"

"Yeah, Kate, there is." He breathes long and slow. "Hope you weren't thinking about killing her too."

"Why is that?"

"My mom already did."

Both of my eyebrows lift in surprise.

"Minutes after I left, Jagger told me she sliced V's throat with her claws and ripped her head from her shoulders with her other hand."

My eyes round, remembering who all had been present before I left. "In front of her daughter?"

"Don't think mom was taking that into consideration after hearing that two shifters from her own pack were responsible for her son and you being taken from right under her nose. In her fucking home."

"Wow." I sit back—or fall back rather—onto the top of Kane's thighs.

"I don't know if Laney knew any of what her mom or uncle did, but I'll deal with it. Just be vigilant and don't trust her right now until we know. V wore a talisman around her neck. It concealed her deceit."

I cock my head and arch a brow. "That girl is the last person I trust, Kane." I deadpan.

"Care to elaborate?" he says with an edge of annoyance in his tone, and I almost choose not to answer him. He isn't that dumb, but instead, I purse my lips and spell it out for him.

"She wants you, and she never cares to hide it."

"You wanted me and never hid it either." The smirk on his lips makes me want to reach between us and twist his balls in the palm of my hand with my claws out.

But he'd probably like it, so I cluck my tongue instead.

"In all seriousness, stay the fuck away from Laney. I don't know how unhinged she is after what happened."

"I thought this was an equal partnership between us."

I'm about to cross my arms over my chest when he bolts upward and over me. His hand wraps around my throat as my back melts into the soft mattress, my head almost hanging off the end. Kane leans down, his claws just breaking skin.

"It is, and it's not. Ultimately, I'll defer to you more than I don't. But if you think I'm going to allow anyone near who could potentially harm you or him..." Kane's free hand rubs the length of my pregnant belly, and I swear a dam breaks between my legs as he bares his teeth. "I will maim. I. Will. Kill. Anyone. That hurts or tries to take what's mine."

"Ahh." A moan slash whimper exhales past my lips.

Fucking hell, he knows how to make a girl all needy and shit with his possessiveness. It hits differently when you can feel the promise in your bones, not just hear a declaration.

The ache between my legs intensifies until I'm panting.

"Fuck me. Fuck me now, Kane."

He rears up and back. The next thing I know, I'm on all fours.

"Fuck me hard," I say, out of breath despite Kane not being inside me yet. "I need you inside me. Fill me up. Please."

His long, thick cock slips inside, and his hips slam forward, shoving me. If his hands weren't holding my hips in place, I would have fallen off the bed I'm so close to the edge.

His fingers dive between the strands of my hair at the nape of my neck. Kane's claws scrape against my scalp when he curls his fingers. I'm yanked upright, my back to his chest. His mouth touches the shell of my ear. "Begging is going to make me come." He growls, feeling the vibration down to my core. "If I come before you do, I'm going to punish you, mate."

His hips buck forward, the tip of his dick hitting hard and grazing that sweet spot inside, making my eyes roll to the back of my head. His lips move down my neck slowly, stopping over his mark bite.

My hands find my tits, and I squeeze them, then rub my nipples between the pads of my thumbs and index fingers.

The hand in my hair releases me only to wrap around my front, holding the opposite side along my ribcage while his fingers, on his other hand, locate my clit.

He pulls back and slams into me again.

"Harder. Please fuck me harder," I beg again, needing more. "Fuck me like I'm your enemy, please."

"You're going to fucking kill me here, Kate." His breath warms my skin. "But I need you to come first. Outside, in front of the pack, I'll gladly do anything you say, obey any order you give, but when I'm inside you, and I tell you to fucking come, you come, goddammit."

I pinch my nipples, twisting them at the same time. Kane's index and middle fingers press against me harder while circling my clit so fast I can't keep up. He fucks me raw. Hard and fast. His cock rocking in deep. My pussy walls contract as unintelligible words roll off my tongue loudly.

He grunts but doesn't stop rutting inside me.

It feels so good I don't want it to stop.

Kane follows me over the cliff, coming with me and spilling inside me. Nothing could make me happier than this moment right now with him.

My always... my forever.

Kane and me.

39
KANE

If I hadn't needed to piss so badly, I would have happily passed out after pulling out of Kate's heat. I wouldn't have minded staying nestled inside her either, but the way my dick shriveled up after unloading everything I had, it was in its own state of comatose.

The fatigue is getting to me. My eyelids feel as if there are weights tugging them down. I'm sure not eating last night didn't help, but it's not like I haven't gone a day without a meal before. *Fuck me.* All I want is to crawl back in bed with my pregnant girl and sleep for a year, or at least until next month when the baby comes, but I have too much shit pressing down on my back to allow myself more than a few more hours of rest.

Ronnie and his sister are dead, and I'm not sad over their loss. Their betrayal cuts deep, but their deception fuels my anger. If V was hiding her emotions from me, then I have to believe her brother was too. For Laney's sake, I hope she was left in the dark and didn't know the things her family was responsible for.

Then there is Richard himself—the false alpha of The Marked Crest pack. Do I go after him, with or without Kate, for what he's done to all of us, what he's likely still plotting against us? Or do I wait for the day he brings another war to my pack?

There's no doubt in my mind that I have Caleb Drake and his pack's help if I want it. He wants Everhart's territory bad enough that he'd help us take him out. I won't, however, take the choice of Kate seeking her own revenge away from her if that's what she needs or wants. It's her call, but I also don't want to wait too long to end this rivalry once and for all.

As long as Richard Everhart breathes, my family isn't safe. That's an unsettling feeling that needs to be eliminated. But without the presence of my beast, I wouldn't stand a chance against another supernatural creature. He already has magic on his side, not that I don't in ways, but I'd never use Storm or her sister the way he uses Salem.

It's a lonely fate-forsaken place inside my chest having my mate, finally, after all this time while missing a whole other part of myself. I never thought I'd be pining for the wolf that lives within me. But that's exactly what's happening, and every second of his absence is another second closer to death.

I scrub my hand down my face and over my beard. It needs a trim, but I'll handle that after the sun comes up.

I figured Kate would have followed me to shower and clean my cum off her, but after washing my hands and honing my ears toward the open bathroom door, all was quiet, too quiet. I can't even hear her breathing.

Shucking the used, damp hand towel toward the back of

the counter below the mirror, I walk my naked ass back into the bedroom. My mate is nowhere in sight.

"Kate," I call out, my feet moving to the door and down the hallway.

It's dark, the lights are off, but I hear the faucet in the kitchen running. Before I reach the opening that leads into the living room with the kitchen to my left, the water shuts off.

When she comes into view, the moon shining on her sexy frame, she pulls the glass away from her lips and places it into the rectangular drop-in sink, then turns to face me.

From here, my keen eyesight can see the corner of her lips dipped upward. Her head jerks, and she says, "Come on," while walking to the door.

"Where the fuck are you going with my cum running down your legs?"

I cross my arms when she pulls open the door. Kate doesn't respond, just motions me to follow her, so my arms drop and my legs move toward her.

"It's three in the morning," I say when I step over the threshold. "We just marathon fucked. Can we go to sleep before we have to deal with people in a few hours?"

Kate's entire demeanor changes. I feel it before she flips around to face me, her knowing eyes landing on mine. "When was the last time you shifted?"

"Kate," I draw out, scrubbing my palm down my tired face, my exhaustion showing in more than just my eyes. It's in the way I move, slower than usual, lethargic-like. But it's not like I fucked her as though I didn't have the strength of a beast inside me. That was basic instinct and adrenaline mixed with an abundance of need.

"When?" she asks again, not budging on the subject.

"That's a priority for another day. Other shit—"

"I asked you a question, Mate. I want the truth." Her hands go to her hips.

Fucking hell.

I don't have the strength or the willpower to argue with her. It's pointless, useless really, when she can feel what's going on with me. I should have known Kate would find out now that we're fully bonded. I just didn't figure it would've been this soon.

"The night I kicked you out of our pack."

Her eyes flick away from mine. There's a pregnant pause long enough that I hear a bird chirp nearby. Probably in one of the trees that surround the cabin. Waves break against jagged rock in the distance, where the ground drops hundreds of feet to the sand below, leading into the ocean.

"That was weeks ago." The concern in her voice wraps around me like thick wool. "Kane." She sucks in a deep breath through her mouth. "You can't go *that* long without letting your wolf free. Tell me you aren't punishing yourself, punishing your animal for biting me."

A band slips around the organ in my chest, tightening and knowing that Kate is recalling what I told her. *My wolf claimed you, not me.*

Fuck.

Is there anything I can't screw up?

I've regretted those words since the moment they jumped off my tongue.

No matter if it was the absolute wrong way to go about it, my wolf claiming my mate was the best thing to ever happen to me.

"He's punishing me for what I did to you."

I let out a sigh, and when I do, pain shoots through my

chest as if an arrow pierced it. My fists fold and clench so tightly that my short nails dig into my palms. Forget my wolf's abandonment, Kate's emotions are going to be the death of me.

"I deserve worse." She stalks toward me, stopping when both of her big toes touch mine. "I don't deserve you, and he knows it. Hell, even I know it."

"Shift." Her tone is hard. It's an order.

"Baby, if I could, I would have done it long before now. You know shifting is mutual consent between yourself and your animal. I won't be able to until he's ready."

Which may fucking be never. But I don't voice that fear to my mate.

"I. Said. Shift." Her jaw locks.

"Kate, I—"

Before I realize what she's done, I blink, and her hand is wrapped around the nape of my neck, holding me in place with her claws sunken beneath my skin. I'm on my knees, staring up at two eyes that resemble blood moons.

She triggered her alpha power. It's mesmerizing. Impossible not to become paralyzed. Any amount of fight I had left is zapped. I'm left in a state of raw vulnerability. She could do anything she wanted, and there would be nothing I could do to stop her.

Is this what it feels like when I use my alpha power on others?

I've never experienced it. My father never once used his on me, though I never gave him a reason to, I suppose. I only use it on others, pack members, when it's a last resort. When I used it on Kate all those weeks ago, it was by accident. It hadn't been my intention. It just happened, and back then, I hadn't believed that's what it was.

"Shift, Kane. Shift... now, Mate."

My bones break, changing from a man into a massive, blond, deadly predator within the time it takes to pull in a long breath of air. It's been so long that the change gives me vertigo momentarily. Had I been standing on solid ground instead of my mind being pulled into a dark space inside my being, I would have lost my balance.

The blurriness fades, and I can see Kate through my wolf's keen sight. Her eyes are back to that radiant shade of blue I want to paint onto my next restoration. An old Bronco that I'll give to my mate. She'll need more than a racing bike to drive. The pack has plenty of vehicles, but I know Kate, she likes her own shit. So, that's what she'll get if she wants it.

"Aren't you a pretty boy," Kate says, her fingers weaving through the fur on my wolf's head, her nails scratching as she combs them back toward her. I feel the same things he does, and it's nothing less than being in seventh heaven. "Are you done being a dick to Kane now?"

My wolf grumbles in reply, his ears flicking. Kate makes a tsk-tsk noise, and he huffs back as if to say he was making a point.

Kate's eyes flash, her sexy, powerful alpha eyes coming to the surface once more.

Pressure rains down my back at the same time my wolf's ears flatten, and his legs lower him to the ground. It's a slight amount of pain, but not in a terror or violent sort of way, more like she's saying, *I'm sorry, do you want to repeat that,* type of authoritative way without saying the words.

"No more refusing to shift on either of your parts. That better be clear, wolf *and mate.*" She releases her hold and steps back several feet. Once she blinks, her eyes are normal again.

My wolf pushes off his paws to stand, his thick, big head just above Kate's pussy. From here, I can smell her and me mixed together, so I know he does too, her scent being the potent of the two. She makes my mouth water, salivating to taste her again.

So, I do.

Just as my wolf can push through me if he so chooses, I can too.

And that's what I do.

His front leg lifts, and he steps his paw forward. His cold nose nudges between her legs, inhaling her and making me lightheaded at the same time. His tongue laps, her taste coating my tongue.

Fuuck. My eyes close, savoring my mate.

"Oh, my God, no! No. No. No, you dirty flea bag."

That was hurtful and uncalled for.

He exhales dramatically through his nose, agreeing with me.

"Don't do that again. Never, never again. You hear me?!" He raises a brow at her antics. "I can't believe you. And don't look at me like that. That better had been Kane's idea, not yours. Save your nastiness for my wolf."

Kate steps backward, then back again, and I can't help the laugh that leaps out of me.

She's so fucking cute.

"You know what, I'm done talking to you. My wolf is going to go for a run. I'd suggest you come. She's a little rest-less inside me, so handle that, would you?"

Kate turns on a dime, her long, black hair swinging out as she whips away from my wolf, transforming into the most goddamn beautiful fucking creature to ever walk the earth. If I'd blinked, I would have missed it.

Her black fur is so rich that streaks of metallic blue sparkle in the moonlight. Then she breaks into a run. My dick hardens again, painfully seeking another release.

Or maybe that's my wolf's animal instincts I'm feeling; his need for his mate. His desire for the twin being to his soul. His fated mate. Maybe we were created for Kate and her wolf, but fuck if they aren't so fucking perfectly made for us. *For me.*

It takes him longer than it should, but I gather he's savoring the experience of simply watching her—his mate.

After another two heartbeats, he pushes off his paws and lays chase. Adrenaline courses through me, through us. His speed increases, gaining on her, but Kate's wolf is fast, the fastest beast I've ever seen. But right now, my wolf is going off sheer determination and sexual drive. A need to claim.

He jumps over a downed tree, flying through the air and landing back on his paws. He chases his prey, his legs burning, but he doesn't slow down.

A growl, deep, wanton, and raw, leaves his chest. I feel it vibrate through me, down the length of my shaft.

She makes it two miles through pack land before he closes the distance so that only several feet separates us from them.

In a leap I hadn't anticipated yet, he springs off his back legs, propelling himself higher than I remember him ever cresting the air, then comes down over Kate's wolf. Closing his teeth over the nape of her neck, he bites hard and forcefully. A yelp mixed with pain and pleasure leaves the wolf's throat, and at the same time, he connects them as one.

It's beautiful being somewhat of a spectator, watching something so basic and natural.

I can't feel what his mate feels like I can with Kate and her with me. Our wolves' connection, their emotions between them, are private, the same as Kate's and mine are between us.

While he holds his mate in place and ruts her, he breathes her in like he can't get enough. We're alike in that way. If it were my choice, I'd inhale Kate every second of every day for the rest of my life like oxygen. Fuck the fresh scent of nature. Give me my mate. She's all I need, all I want. She is my always and my forever. I want to live and breathe only her.

When he's done, he nudges the side of her neck in affection, then he licks the area his teeth marked for a long time. So long that his slow laps start to lull me into slumber.

He whimpers, and she does the same.

My wolf is finally at peace.

40
KANE

Watching him with Kate's wolf has me yearning to hold Kate in my arms. To kiss and lick and mark every square inch of her soft, creamy flesh. For her to do the same to me.

It's something I hadn't fully grasped just how fucking badly I needed until she gave herself to me when she claimed me last night. The bite on my neck itches, my supernatural healing ability already kicking in to seal it. It's a constant reminder of her and the memory of her teeth sinking into me.

My wolf senses what I want without me asking. I can feel his resolve to give me back my human form before he even does it, knowing he wants to keep his mate beneath him a little longer.

Kate feels it too, and I'm not surprised when the wolf below us rolls onto her back, shifting as she does. Kate's pretty, blue eyes stare up at my wolf, a relaxed smile on her face.

"Don't you dare lick me down there again, wolf," she says in reprimand, her lips spread wide in amusement.

His head dips to Kate's throat. He sniffs, pulling her scent in again, memorizing it, savoring her human side like he did her wolf. His tongue lolls out, licking the permanent mate bite between her shoulder and the column of her neck. The one that's sealed as a permanent scar for all to see. She's mine.

"Okay, pretty boy, let me have Kane back, please." She grabs his big head in both hands, bringing his eyes to meet her gaze. "You fucked your mate. Now, it's time Kane does his like I'm the enemy he once thought I was."

He snorts, understanding my mate's playful demeanor, but he doesn't obey her right away. Instead of shifting like I know he's going to, he pulls his head from her grasp and dips his snout once more. His tongue flops out, swiping long and slow.

"Oh, my God. You did not just lick my tit. You're so dirty." Kate covers her face with her hands.

He snaps his jaw mere inches from her, but he'd never bite her in a violent manner. That was his goodbye. Finally, he shifts us while standing over Kate's naked form. When I blink, already laughing, I'm on my hands and knees, towering over my mate.

The first thing I take note of is how reinvigorated I am. I feel stronger, more solid. My breathing is steady and clear. The power that radiates inside me hums stronger.

All because of her.

Her Luna power aids my super strength, and the alpha power coursing through me feels like a live wire. It's strange but feels right at the same time, like I'm no longer missing something vital.

"I think your wolf likes my wolf." Her hands fall away from her face, dropping palms up above her head, her dark hair splayed across the ground with dirt and leaves tangled in the strands.

"Seems to me, he likes *my* mate a little too intimately."

"Don't ever bring that up again. Your wolf is a perv." I chuckle because, again, she is so fucking cute. "Why are you laughing at me?"

"I'm not." She swats at me while scowling. "It was me. I made him lick your delicious little cunt, baby. He enjoyed it, by the way."

"Oh, my god. We're done."

She rolls onto her stomach in an attempt to get away from me, but when she lifts her ass in the air, I snatch her by the hip and shove my hardened dick against her meaty backside.

Leaning in, my chest to her back, I lower my lips to the shell of her hair-covered ear. "You were never my enemy, but I'll fuck you any way you want me to for the rest of my life, Kate. Just be mine forever."

She turns her head into me, her gaze catching and holding onto mine. Her strength shines through those blue irises, and it's hard to remember they were once smothered in gray.

"I'm yours, Kane. I'm yours whether the pack accepts me or not. I don't want to do this life without you either. No matter where the future takes us, you're my always too."

Music to my fucking ears. I just wish she had more faith in how others feel about her.

"The pack will accept you, Kate. Most of them already love you, have loved you. If not since that first visit, then by the second year you and Trez came, they fell in love with you both. They got to know you like I did. They became your friends, and now they're your family."

"That remains to be seen." I'm about to tell her she *will* see it when she continues. "I'm not ready to deal with the consequences of yesterday or how the pack may or may not see me, or even false alphas that mean us harm. Give me another hour, another hour of you inside me, then I'll face it all head-on." She sighs. "Please."

I push off the ground, standing to my full height. Kate rises, her back off the ground with her elbows digging into the loose dirt.

"On your knees, mate," I growl out, my tone hitting her eardrums with the authority of the alpha I am. Her pussy creams, the scent so pleasurable to my senses that my dick thickens and pulses painfully, needing the closure only her throat can offer. I palm myself, squeezing my balls and tightening my fist around my shaft. I pull my hand to the tip. "Now."

Her palms flatten to the ground, eyeing my junk and licking her lips. She then pushes herself into a sitting position. I step back and then step back again, putting distance between us. Kate twists her legs and leaning forward, gets to her knees with her arms by her side, her back straight with her head tilted slightly up.

"If you want this dick, crawl to me, my Luna mate. Crawl to me and suck me off."

Her body falls forward, her hands catching herself and looking so goddamn sexy on all fours. She crawls the short distance, her pace slow and measured, her ass swaying in the air, making me harder. If the tiny pebbles in the dirt are digging into her knees, Kate doesn't show evidence of discomfort.

My dick aches to have her lips around it instead of my fingers jerking my shit in perfect rhythm with her pace.

"You look hungry, mate," I tell her, a smirk ghosting my lips.

"Famished." Her eyes remain locked on the meat in my hand.

The way she's turned on affects me more now that we're bonded. I can feel her desire stronger than my own, making the connection between us powerful.

Pre-cum beads at the tip of my cock as she stops in front of me. Her hands glide over the tops of my feet and slowly up my hairy legs while lifting her torso to kneel in front of me.

"You're so fucking beautiful," I tell her.

Her palms wrap around my hips as her eyes lock with mine. My free hand cups her cheek, nearly covering one side of her face, and the need mixed with sheer happiness I see in her stare creates warmth radiating through me.

Fuck, she's given me so much peace in the last few hours. Sure, there is a lot left to untangle with us and the pack, along with our enemy pack, but she's here, and we're together.

"Take it, baby. Take my dick and swallow it down that pretty little throat of yours."

She leans in, doing as I've instructed, my palm sliding through her hair. Kate sucks me inside her mouth, and I have to lock everything down just to hold my position still and not close my eyes, getting lost in the pleasure.

My fingers fold in, fisting her black hair and pulling the strands taut and her back so that her beautiful eyes connect with mine. "But my cum isn't going to fill your belly this go-round."

She whimpers, and the vibration is like heaven on earth. My dick moves slowly over her tongue, the tip not quite reaching the back of her throat.

"I want my cum dripping down your chest when I chase you after this. I want everyone to smell me on you. I want the whole fucking world to know you're mine. Now, suck."

And she does, taking me as far back as possible, her throat tight, hot, and wet.

Kate doesn't roll her lips over her teeth, so my shaft scrapes against the edges every time she sucks me down her throat and pulls away from the base of my dick. Jesus, that feels good. So... fucking... good.

"Hands on your pretty tits, Kate. Play with them and make yourself wet for me. I'm going to need it. Because when I catch you, baby, I'm fucking that sweet ass."

She mewls around my cock, her hands leaving me to knead her breasts.

Fuck, do I wish I could live inside her like this, only slipping out to shove myself into another one of her holes. She's chaos and peace and bliss. She's everything and more.

Motherfuck, this feels good, so amazingly good, and not just from my end. I can feel Kate's pleasure as she pleasures me, bringing me to the brink of sanity. She feels empowered. She feels treasured, safe, wanted, needed... and above all, she feels loved.

Fuuuck, I'm going to come like a two-pump chump, and right now, I don't even fucking care. Kate did this to me. She gave me mind-blowing bliss, but most importantly, she claimed me as hers for the rest of our lives.

I yank my dick from her mouth, nearly losing my load down her throat.

"No, Kane. I want your cum. I need it," she cries out, and it's too fucking much. My balls seize.

"Open your mouth," I order, my breath coming out in pants as I jerk my dick aggressively. "Tongue out. Now!" I bark through clenched teeth, my orgasm rapidly coming to the surface all because my hot little mate begged me for my cum.

The crown of my dick smacks down onto her tongue as creamy white ribbons spurt off the tip, coating the pinkish-red flat surface and dripping down the sides, landing on her chest just like I'd originally planned. I come and keep coming, jerking my dick until every drop seeps out of me and onto her, Kate greedily accepting it all.

My knees buckle, and I fall to the ground in front of her. My lips find hers, covered in my seed and her saliva. She's messy and so fucking perfect; too perfect for me, but that doesn't stop me from slamming my mouth to hers, needing her lips like she needed my cum, my hunger only being sated by devouring this beautiful woman, my mate.

And fuck if I don't want her again. Need her again. Even out of breath and eating her mouth, sucking her tongue, biting her lips, my dick begins to come alive for her.

For only her.

My hand finds her throat, and I wrap my long fingers around it and push my claws out at the same time. I squeeze the slender column of her neck, forcing my lips to pull away, regretting the loss of them immediately.

Kate whimpers, the noise inflaming my cock even more.

"I'd punish you for that little trick, but I didn't think shoving my big dick into your asshole would be punishment enough."

"Ah," she moans, her arousal making me feel high with every breath filling my lungs.

I catch her stare.

"Run, mate. Run, and when I catch you, I'm going to pound that ass so hard you'll get that enemy hate-fucking you wanted so badly."

I yank her flush with my chest and dip my mouth to her ear. Running my hand down her arm and then over her small pregnant bump, I snake my hand between her legs, finding her pussy.

She's dripping wet, and it stretches my lips wide. I slip two fingers inside her heat, finger fucking her with three pumps, coating my digits.

"Maybe even more than your virgin asshole can handle."

I pull back, shoving my fingers into my mouth. The flavor of her juices popping on my tongue is fucking delicious.

I slide them out of my mouth, tilt my head, and arch a brow.

"Run," I growl.

41
KATE

Holy... *fuck me.*

And boy, did he.

I ran until my legs burned, screaming at me to slow down, to stop.

I pushed on for several miles. I wasn't worried about falling or tripping over anything, I'm a wolf shifter. In the unlikely event that occurred, my wolf would have changed and come down on all four legs to protect me and the baby.

I'd almost made it back to the cabin when he caught me, snatching me by my long hair, and by the time I blinked the pain away, I was safely in his arms and breathing heavily, my body humming and hungry for more.

I'm still starved for more as Kane kicks the door shut with his heel, the slamming of wood against wood cracking loudly against my ear drums. His arm slips from beneath my legs and they drop to the hardwood floor.

"Bend over the arm of the couch, mate. Ass up." When I don't jump into action, his palm cracks against my butt cheek, eliciting a fire that burns while he squeezes my meaty flesh with the same hand. "Now."

My legs obey before the order catches up to my mind, my naked torso bending over and positioning my ass high in the air as the morning sun begins to filter through the curtain-less windows; the one in the kitchen over the sink and the other to my left, here in the living room.

Kane moves in behind me, his crotch pressing against the crack of my ass and grinding. My claws break through my nail bed, sinking through the couch cushion. I don't even care that I'm damaging furniture needlessly. His big dick bobs between my spread legs, thumping my pussy lips.

"Jesus, Kate, you just dripped on me," he says.

The feelings that are coursing through me—Kane's emotions and how he's being affected right now—have too much of a profound effect on me. It's so erotic, and looking between my legs, I see my arousal splash onto the crown of his cock. I swear, that shit has been coming out of me like a leaking faucet, dripping nonstop since his dick slid over my tongue earlier.

"But I'm going to need more than that if I'm going to fuck your tight ass."

He lines the tip up to my entrance with one hand, and with the other, he grips the top of my thigh, then rams inside me, jolting me. He pulls out and does it again, harder, coating himself while filling me up.

I moan.

"Yes. Fuck me. Make me come all over you."

"You're going to come on me, baby, then I'm going to come in your ass, just like I promised." He pounds into me, burying his dick as deep as he can go. Leaning over my back, he keeps going in and out, in and out. It's so good, this connection between us. "Put my finger in your mouth."

I open, and his thumb slides across my wet tongue.

"Slobber all over it," he instructs, so I do, sucking and gathering the spit in my mouth to twirl all around his finger. "Make it wet for me."

Yanking it out in haste, he keeps pistoning in and out of my pussy so fast I don't initially feel his thumb push into my ass until he's pulling his digit back to the exit hole, only to push back in slowly, then back out again, each thrust in sync with his cock fucking me until my legs begin to quake.

Shallow, moaning breaths leave my mouth. I'm panting uncontrollably as my orgasm attacks me, wrecking me from the inside out.

Kane pulls out from my convulsing pussy, out from my ass.

"Fuck. My dick is drenched, baby. So creamy and glistening. I can smell you on me. If I didn't want to fuck your ass so bad, I'd make you clean up this beautiful mess of yours."

His words send me over the edge, and I feel moisture leak from my center as he spreads my butt cheeks apart.

"I need you again. Please, Kane. Fill me back up."

I push back, my ass seeking a release only his dick can provide.

"Please," I whine, knowing I'm not above throwing a temper tantrum if that's what it takes to get him back inside me. I need him so badly.

"Fucking hell, Kate, I can feel your need like it's my own. You're going to fucking kill me, baby."

"No, it's me that's going to die if you don't stick your dick in my ass already." I'm almost on the verge of bursting into tears. The ache between my legs is too much.

Finally, the head of his dick meets my flesh. Kane pushes forward.

"Fuuuck," he draws out, growling so deep my core clenches against the vibration. "The room is spinning. Your neediness is fattening my dick too much. I'm going to pass the fuck out if you don't tamper that shit down."

"I can't," I whine again. Using my heels and the palms of my hands, I push myself down his shaft, the stretch burning and making me clamp my teeth over my bottom lip so I don't cry out.

I'm only successful by maybe an inch before his hands force me from advancing more.

"Shove it into me, Kane. Fuck me so hard. Please. I need it. I need you. Just you. Please."

"Stop egging me on, mate." His chest rumbles. "I'm trying not to hurt you, but Jesus, your begging makes me weak. So goddamn weak."

He drives achingly slow, but Kane gives me the object of my desire, his big cock pushing into my ass until his groin smashes into the cheeks of my butt, his dick as far inside as it'll reach. He stops moving, and a sob breaks free from my throat. Tears crest my lower eyelids, falling to the cushion of the couch.

Wrapping his fingers gently around the upper portion of my arm, Kane pulls me up and my back against his chest as he glides my hair to my other shoulder, uncovering my healed but scarred bite mark.

"Don't cry, baby. I'm going to fuck you good. I promise."

"Please." I hiccup and sniffle, my chest shuddering. "I need my mate to fuck me."

The space between my legs throb. I can hear my clit pulsing with too much need.

"I want to bite you, Kate. Mark you again, but… but this time, I want your consent. Consent I should have asked for the first time."

I understand his human side would naturally feel bad for marking me, claiming me without asking permission, but his animal side doesn't play by the same rules.

"Bite me. Bite me and prove that you can bite me harder than your wolf," I demand, remembering how it felt the first time and wanting to experience that again. There was pain, but bliss overpowered any discomfort I was feeling.

"Jesus, you don't ask for much, do you." He somewhat laughs, but it's followed by a grunt when I pull away and then push his length back into me.

"You're my world. I want everything with you. Bite me, please," I beg, unashamed and needy. So needy.

"No, baby, you're my whole fucking world and a dream come true; one that I'll never deserve, but I'm selfish when it comes to you. You're mine. I'm never letting you go. I'll give you anything and everything you ever want. Just say it, and it's yours."

"In that case, fuck me and make it hurt, but love me while doing it."

"I'm going to fuck you like I love you because I do. More than anything. But I'm going to do so slowly." He moves his hips, pulling away. "Your ass needs to adjust to my size. I'm going to take care of you, Kate." I open my mouth to argue, to tell him I can take care of myself when he beats me to it. "Don't you dare spew that bullshit, mate! You do need me to take care of you just like I need you to take care of me. We're going to take care of each other for the rest of our lives, baby. That's just how it's going to be. Better get used to it now rather than realize I'm right later on."

Before I can respond, Kane's lips seal over the scar between my shoulder and the column of my neck. His canines break the skin and sink through flesh and muscle. Kane flexes his hips, pushing his dick back into me.

"Ahhh," I pant and find the back of his neck, wrapping my hand around him as he bites and fucks, holding him to me.

One of Kane's hands goes around my throat, his fingers tight, his claws inserting just the way I love. With his other hand, he wraps it protectively around my pregnant belly.

"Mmm." My eyes roll into the back of my head, my ass burning more with each push and pull.

Kane promised to fuck me good, and that's exactly what he's doing.

He fucks me slow and deep, and I feel everything. Every single sensation, every bit of pain and zing of pleasure. His emotions spill over into me; he feels complete. Whole. The same as I do.

We're connected, and I feel what he feels. I never imagined it would be like this, but now that I have it, I never want to lose it. He's mine. I'm his. A war of hearts and fate binding us together.

With one hand holding onto Kane's neck, I reach between my legs with the other while he's moving in and out of me from behind. My ass feels like it's being stretched to its maximum capacity, but there is so much pleasure humming inside my core that the burning dissipates. I press two fingers to my clit and circle. It's so swollen that it doesn't take much to send me over the edge.

Kane grunts, his movements hiccuping, but he quickly finds his rhythm again. Sounds leave both our mouths. Screams come from my throat as another orgasm spins and cascades through my body. Then he explodes inside me, shooting his load into the channel of my ass. His teeth and lips release me. His claws and hand fall away from my neck.

"Fuuck, baby. Fuck, you're so fucking perfect. Perfect and mine," he growls. Then Kane's tongue snakes out, swiping over the puncture wounds, sealing and healing the wound he created with shifter powers.

I fall forward, my energy zapped, my forearms resting against the cushion as I pull in a lungful of air.

Kane spreads my ass cheeks apart, but I wasn't expecting it, and my butt clenches. My mate's quick intake of air is the only sound other than my own breathing.

"Your asshole is so pretty with my cum spilling out."

42
KATE

I somehow made it into the shower despite my legs feeling like jelly. Kane followed, and I almost asked him to go to the lodge to clean himself up. I needed a reprieve, but we were filthy from him and his wolf's need for primal play with their mates.

It's not like I didn't enjoy being chased. I did, and now, that might become a morning routine. I also didn't stop him when he got down on his knees in the shower, his tongue eliciting another release from my body. Kane ordered me to come, and boy, did my pussy obey like a submissive bitch.

At the rate we're fucking, I'm not wholly sure it'll remain possible to take the wolf pup growing inside of me to term. But what the hell do I know? It's not like I had a mother or anyone to explain this shit to me. Annalise wants to be that person. I know she does, but I'm not there yet. I can't even bring myself to call her *Mom,* even though I've seen her daily since waking up in Kane's bed following my return. She hangs out with me more so than Trez and Jagger. She keeps me company. She's trying hard without it coming off that way.

"I need you to put some clothes on before I stick my dick in you again."

I turn away from the bathroom mirror, seeing Kane standing in the doorway, mostly dressed, wearing dark jeans and worn work boots, looking relaxed. I can feel his renewed strength through our bond, and it calms me for whatever reason to know Kane is back to himself again.

I just finished brushing my teeth and drying my hair. Now that we're into July and Kane doesn't have air conditioning in the cabin, it's time I move into the lodge. It's only been daylight for an hour, but it's already stiflingly hot.

"My vagina, my ass, and my throat need a break from you, so that isn't happening," I say, my voice lacking any sort of authority.

And Kane wants me to believe I'm a Luna wolf.

Yeah, okay, *sure.* I can't even tell him no and actually mean it. I'm starting to second guess if it's even possible that alpha power runs through my veins. Maybe my eyes having the ability to glow the color of a blood moon is actually because I'm pulling on Kane's abilities through our fated mate bond.

Kane snorts a laugh, pulling me out of my thoughts as he steps toward me with purpose, a smirk firmly in place on his handsome face.

Rolling my hips, I turn fully around, my back facing the mirror with my lower back pressed against the edge of the vanity. Kane stops in front of me, his legs spread. Leaning into me, his arms cage around my sides when he places his hands on the edge of the counter next to my hips.

"I'll give you a reprieve if that's what you need, but I don't think your pussy would agree."

"I think I know my pussy better than you do. There's a closed sign hanging down there. Wanna check?"

He arches a brow, then Kane shakes his head, his amusement boring into my eyes a breath before his hands move with shifter speed, going under my armpits and lifting my feet off the floor. My bare ass is placed on top of the counter, toward the back.

"What do you think you're doing?"

I lean against the mirror, the glass cool on my feverish flesh.

"You told me to inspect," he quips as he wraps his fingers around my ankle and brings one foot atop the flat surface while spreading my legs at the same time.

"I-I can go get dressed now." I gasp, sucking in a lungful of air as Kane's amber stare flicks to my center. His tongue darts out, licking his lips. A low growl rumbles around me and the need to clench my thighs together is my undoing. "Ah," I moan out.

Kane's eyes travel slowly back to mine. "Me and your pussy are best friends. No one knows her like I do. In fact, your clit looks slightly swollen with need, baby. Should I handle that?"

"No," I say too breathy. "You should not, and no, it isn't." *It so is, and it throbs.* Then my claws elongate, giving me away. My hips flex, moving in his direction on their own.

"Come on, Kate," he says, remnants of a whine in his tone. "I brushed my teeth earlier, and now I don't have you on my tongue anymore. Come on, baby, just one more taste. One more release for my pretty little mate's pussy. Don't you want your scent all over me if someone comes into the shop?"

Fire shoots through my eyes, roaring to life, and I know they're flashing the color of the prettiest moon I've ever seen: a blood moon. The symbol of Kane's pack. My pack.

But... is he goading me? Trying to make me jealous?

I bare my teeth.

"There's my Luna." His lips spread into a sinister grin while he brings my other foot to the countertop. His hands roam up my inner thighs, stopping at the top and applying a bit of pressure, holding me in place. "We both know you need your pussy licked, so let me oblige, mate."

My agreement is on the tip of my tongue when I feel the wetness between my legs streaming out of me. Kane's nostrils flare, his eyes flashing brilliantly, then snap to my center.

"Already making a mess, baby. It's like ice melting in sheets you're so drenched, and I'm dying of fucking thirst. You can either be a good girl and let me clean up your needy mess for you, or you can be a bad girl and deny us both what we need." His eyes come back to mine as his palms massage my inner thighs, making me drip more just by touching me tenderly despite the threat I can already feel he's about to drop. "But if you choose the latter, then I'll have no choice but to yank you down from there and make you clean this mess up yourself." The corners of his lips tip upward. "And as much as I'd enjoy watching you lick yourself up from the counter, I'd much rather get you off."

"Uh-huh." It's all I can say as I swallow the whimper trying to escape my throat. My heels press against the counter, using it as leverage to rock my butt, my eyes begging him to give me what he's offering.

"Uh-huh, I can eat you out?" He pauses, his head tilting, but I'm already nodding when he continues. "Or uh-huh, you want me to manhandle you and make you lick the counter clean?"

My head doesn't stop saying yes to both options. *Why in the hell does he make the latter sound so hot?* I'm pretty sure I'm sitting in a puddle of my own need.

"Fucking hell, you're so perfect. Dirty and perfect." His hands glide agonizingly slow until his thumbs find my pussy lips, and he spreads them apart. "I'm going to tongue fuck this pretty perfect cunt, and then I'm going to try not to fuck that dirty mouth of yours. My dick is so hard it hurts. And when I tell you to come, I'd suggest obeying your alpha's orders. But while I'm licking"—his thumbs slide into me at the same time—"I need you to be quiet."

"Why?"

His short, thick digits rock in and out of me. Kane lowers himself, going to his knees and pulling me to the edge of the vanity.

God, that feels good, but I need his head between my legs like I need air to breathe. He makes me so needy for him, for this. For anything that he'll give me.

"Your dad is here. Eli and I are already on the brink of a fight. I don't want to have to put him in his place today." His breath fans my center, warm at first, but then the space turns cold. "At least not when I have his daughter's scent all over my face and inside my mouth."

Kane attacks my pussy before I can reply, just as someone knocks on the door.

It takes a lot of effort not to cry out.

He repositions his hands, but his thumbs remain going in and out at a steady pace as he laps at my clit. My back arches, the top of my head rocking against the mirror. My hands find his hair, the strands pulled up in a half bun where the ends of his dirty-blond hair sticks out the bottom of the ponytail.

The friction that Kane's beard provides against my over-heated wanton flesh is almost as satisfying as the pleasure his tongue and fingers are gifting me. *He's never shaving that thing off.*

A moan sneaks out of my mouth, so I clamp down on my bottom lip, ignoring thoughts of anyone else who may be standing outside as another orgasm shudders through me, wrecking me in the best way possible.

At some point, my eyelids shut, and they're still closed, enjoying the after-bliss as my mate gently pulls me off the bathroom counter, my feet softly landing on the cool tiled floor.

When I open my eyes, my head tilted back, Kane is watching me with an easy smile on his face.

"Thank you," I say, returning his grin.

"Your pleasure is my pleasure. You never have to thank me, but you are welcome, beautiful." He cradles my face and dips his, placing a soft kiss against my lips. "Now, I have to get out of here before I say, fuck it, and stop caring that we have an audience. Meet me at the body shop in one hour."

"What's happening in one hour?"

"I'm going to fuck you on the hood of a car."

"Sounds counterproductive. Won't it get bent and dented the way we fuck?"

He smirks at my remark.

"Good thing there's nothing I can't fix when it comes to automobiles. One hour, Kate. If I have to come find you, I'm fucking your ass without mercy this time instead of your tight, sweet cunt."

I roll my eyes, but Kane pulls my body to him, my rounded stomach feeling just how much he needs a release of his own.

"You're such a fucking temptation." Kane's head shakes. "Put some clothes on, and maybe, if you're feeling nice, listen to whatever Elijah wants to say but do not let him or anyone else tell you what happened yesterday was wrong or that it wasn't your right to take a life. It was, and if he or anyone has a problem with that, they can take it up with me —their alpha."

"Kane," I start to reason, but he shuts me up with one look.

"One hour. I'll have more than my dick ready to feed you, mate."

43
KATE

After Kane left ten minutes ago, I pulled on a pair of black maternity leggings and a loose, sleeveless top, then slipped into a pair of cute flip-flops with sparkles on the top. I almost forwent the footwear, wanting to remain barefoot. There's just something so grounding and natural when the earth is connected to the bottoms of my feet. But I'm good with my choice for today. The entire attire is my mother's style, not mine, yet it's comforting wearing the things she'd wear herself.

I piddled in the bathroom, fixing my hair even though all I did was brush it again and then capture my long strands into a ponytail. Kane has a drawer full of them in the vanity. I used the toilet despite not really needing to go. Now, I'm pulling the door open and taking a deep breath as I step outside.

Elijah is seated on the top step of the porch, his back to me. There's a side-by-side parked in front of him.

I stop next to him, stepping down to the next step, then I lower my butt to sit beside him, my left arm brushing against his. He's wearing a cream-colored T-shirt and dark jeans with worn boots. Despite this moment being strange and a bit awkward, I've never shied away from Elijah or felt intimidated by him. The same warmth I feel in Annalise's presence is the same I feel with him.

After a minute of silence, he stands, cracking his neck. Then he turns to face me, his arm outstretched, offering me his hand. "Want to go for a ride?"

"Sure?" I say slowly, wondering if sitting this close to me was a problem for him. It came out more like a question, even though I hadn't really meant it that way to him.

I place my hand in his, and Elijah pulls me to my feet.

Does he hate me after what I did yesterday?

I saw Elijah sitting next to Ronnie when I approached. I hadn't considered if they were friends. Other than a few times I've seen them have small talk, I didn't think they were close. But what do I know? In the past, I've only ever stayed here for up to five weeks at a time. Nothing compared to the rest of the days of the year. Maybe I don't know Elijah like I thought I did.

Does he wish he'd never discovered I was his missing daughter?

What if Kane is wrong, and the majority of his pack won't accept me?

I want to live here. I've wanted that since the first time we arrived in Moonwake. But I don't want anyone to fear me or hold what I did against me for the rest of my life. I don't want to be the most hated person in my pack anymore. That was the role I played as a Marked Crest shifter. It's tiring, and if I'm honest, it mentally hurts too much.

Now that I have Kane, I'm not willing to give him up

either, but I also don't want to come between him and his pack, him and his parents, or his friends.

"Whatever is going through your head right now, I can assure you it's wrong."

I nod so he knows I heard him. I can't chance opening my mouth right now. If I try to speak, the dam will break, and I'll burst into tears. I don't want to disappoint him. I don't want to disappoint anyone.

As if sensing my inner turmoil, and with my hand still gripped in his much bigger one, Elijah tugs me down the last step and pulls me straight into his arms. Wrapping one arm around my back and his other hand around the nape of my neck, he holds me against his chest, hugging me, comforting me like I'd imagine a father doing with his daughter.

And at that thought, I lose it. My vision blurs as the inside of my nose stings. Tears rise to the surface and spill over the bottom of my eyelids and onto his T-shirt. He squeezes me tighter while a sob forces its way up my throat and past my lips.

Kate? Kane growls inside my head within seconds, reminding me that he can feel everything I feel and experience my emotions as if they're his.

I'm fine, I reply back as my arms wrap around Elijah's middle.

Do you need me? Kane asks. Knowing my mate would come if I needed or wanted him to, his voice soothes and calms the emotions running wild inside me. More tears seep out, but my body stops shaking. Elijah continues embracing me.

No. I'll see you in a bit. I'm fine. I promise. Work. Don't worry about me, I say, communicating with him in my mind.

I'm leaving the lodge now. I left all the spare keys to the vehicles that belong to the pack in the kitchen for you. Pick whatever you want, but if you need me, just say the word, and I'll come find you.

Noted. Get out of my head now. Love you, I add.

Love you too.

"Kate," my dad calls out, and I swear I bury my face farther into his chest despite no space separating us. "Did you get upset because I stood after you sat down next to me?"

I nod, silently answering him, but now I feel stupid. I don't cry in front of other people, aside from that one time recently in front of Kane.

If Eli is responsible for you crying, I'm going to knock his fucking head off, Kane says.

He's fine. Go away, I tell him, to which Kane growls inside my head.

His protectiveness is more endearing than I ever imagined. It isn't suffocating like I'd thought an alpha male would end up being toward me, and that's why I feared being anyone's fated mate until I learned Kane was mine.

"Do you hate that I'm her?" I ask, biting the bullet and asking the question I've been fearing the answer to. "That it turned out Trez and I are the missing—"

"My daughter is alive, and you're here." He pulls back, and I feel his brown eyes on me, so I force mine to flick to his. "I've begged for that every day since you were taken. It was the first thing I did when my eyes opened and the last thing I did before closing them. I didn't care who I was speaking to in the beyond, fate or a god, or even the king of the underworld himself. I would have done anything to get you back." He pauses for breath, pulling in a lungful of air through his mouth. "Can we go? I have a lot to say, a lot I should have already said."

My brows furrow, not understanding his need to leave like it's urgent or he's going to puke if he stays here a minute longer.

"I'm not that old yet, kiddo. My shifter nose is still as keen as it's always been. Every time that door opens,"—he jerks his head, gesturing behind me—"what do you think I get a whiff of?"

All the sex I had with Kane, I'm guessing, but I don't say that out loud. Just the thought is awkward enough.

"I've known Kane was my daughter's mate, your mate, for a long time. It's never bothered me, but now it's real and feels too sudden."

"So, how about that ride?" I ask for a lack of knowing what else to say.

Kane and me happening doesn't feel sudden. It feels like we've been on the path of a head-on collision for years. And I guess we have because we were *always* meant to be together.

After sliding into the passenger side of the off-road vehicle, I don't bother with the seat belt. I hate restraints unless it's Kane's hands or body pinning me down.

Ten minutes go by, Elijah's side-by-side bumping along the dirt trail at a slow speed. Now it doesn't feel like he's in a hurry as I sit next to him, a foot between us, in silence, him driving with one hand on the steering wheel and the other on top of his leg.

It's a comfortable silence. It always has been when I'm in Elijah's company. This really isn't different from any other time, except now I feel like a child waiting to be punished for doing something wrong and unsure of what the consequences of my actions are going to be while fearing my parents won't love me anymore.

I never felt this way with Dick. One, I didn't care what he thought, and two, I already knew he didn't love me. He told me often enough that I was a disappointment. It stung when I was a little girl, but it never crushed me. The thought of Annalise or Elijah, or both of them, hating me, regretting they found me after all these years, could very well send me spiraling into a debilitating depression.

What they think matters to me, and I'm not sure I would handle it well if they didn't want me here.

When another five minutes go by, and the only noise around us is the birds chirping, I ask something I've had on my mind since I found out his mate wasn't sleeping in their bed.

"Why is Annalise staying at the lodge?"

"She's angry with me, and she has every right to feel the way she does, but she's also mad at herself even though she's not at fault for any of this."

I'm not sure what to unpack first with that statement, but wanting to know what happened between them, I ask, "Why is she so mad she left her house?"

"Partly because seeing me, smelling us all over our house, makes her want to forgive me, and she isn't ready. The other reason being that Jag is there, and she's holding out hope that you'll move into the lodge, and then she'll have both children under one roof again."

The latter makes sense. She's a mom who didn't get to watch both of her kids grow up together, but he failed to explain their issue.

I roll my head, and either he senses my stare on him, or

he sees me looking at him from his peripheral vision. I arch an eyebrow, hoping he'll elaborate.

"She knew, Kate. She knew you were our daughter. She felt it in her bones, but I dismissed it after I'd thought Dante and I had proved you and Trez weren't our missing kids."

I heard about the blood tests they did and wondered how they even took samples without Trez or me knowing. It took me a day of thinking back to that first summer to remember. Trez misfired an arrow from a bow because he'd been fucking around and taunting me with it. It sliced through my upper arm, and I bled like a stuck pig for all of two minutes before my shifter healing abilities kicked in and sealed the wound. I retaliated, of course, because back then, I was that much of a child. I stabbed him with the same arrow that cut me.

Kane, Jagger, Ash, and even Maddy were with us, taking part in training Maddy, Trez, and me. I ended up laughing about the whole thing until Dante and Elijah gave an hour-long lecture on never harming anyone from your own pack, meaning Trez and me. But that's what we've always done. We're siblings, or at least, we thought we were. We bicker, and we get into tizzies, but I have his back and he has mine —always.

"You didn't know a witch had spelled us. I don't fault you, Elijah."

"I fault me. Your mom faults me, and she should." He brakes, slowing the machine, and then takes a right turn. "Kate, I didn't just ignore a mother's intuition. I brushed off my mate's instinct, and to some of us, that's a very deep betrayal, right up there with cheating, you might say. Annalise told me time and time again that her gut was telling her you belonged here. That you were ours. I got tired of hearing it, so I pleaded with Becca to talk some sense into her."

"I think you're being too hard on yourself, and she's being too stubborn if she can't see you exhausted your efforts to find us."

Annalise is for sure stubborn, but why hold this against her mate? Seems a bit harsh.

"You're also still young, and the whole fated mate thing is brand new to you. Take my word for it: when you can feel how strongly your mate believes something, don't act like they're the crazy one. Because that's what I did. I even threatened to not allow you and Trez to come back if she kept it up. That's what made her stop."

"Oh," is all I can say to that. If I were in my mother's shoes, I'd probably feel resentful and bitter too.

Ultimatums never work.

You'll either drive the other person away, or they'll eventually come to hate you.

"We did so many things wrong—Dante and me. We knew the only person who had anything to gain by taking one of our kids was Everhart."

"You were trying to protect your pack from another war."

The last war between The Bloodmoon Pack and The Marked Crest Pack, the only war between them that I know of, sounded bad from the stories I've heard. Dick still boasts about it from time to time. Very few shifters were lost on Dick's side, while over half of Kane's pack lost their lives. It makes me wonder if magic was involved to ensure a victory for The Marked Crest.

"It was a war we should have raged. And I'm sorry we didn't. I'm sorry I let someone take you. I'm sorry I failed you." He breathes out a heavy breath. "Then my own daughter showed back up over fourteen years later and I didn't even recognize her, didn't scent that she was you. I'm sorry, Kate. I'm so goddamn sorry. I'm ashamed of a lot of things, and I don't have the first clue how to fix any of them."

"Maybe the first step is talking to Annalise. You'll never fix anything with your mate while you're sleeping apart and refusing to even acknowledge their presence." I did that with Kane for several weeks, and all that did was prolong us from being together.

"Just because she doesn't want to be in the same room as me doesn't mean she isn't talking to me. Annalise is the sweetest woman in the world, but she can hold a grudge like no other, only this time, it's with me, and it's been coming for a long time. She's saying a lot," he admits as he taps his temple, telling me she's talking to him in his head.

I get the feeling she may be screaming at him. He's tensed up a few times already while he's been driving us around the pack. I noticed once his eyes squinted and his brows drew tight. It makes me wonder if her talking is more yelling rather than a calm conversation.

"Do you want me to talk to her?"

"Yes, but not on my behalf. Annalise needs to get all her feelings out in the open. I'm not worried that we won't work our shit out, Kate. I'm terrified she'll bottle it back up again, and the resentment she's feeling will turn to hate. That would kill me."

His fingers flex and squeeze the steering wheel with his shifter strength, and for a split second, I contemplate if the thin metal around the ring of the wheel is going to snap off, but after taking a long breath, Elijah eases up on his hold.

"All I need you to do, kiddo, is settle in, focus on yourself, and enjoy your new mate bond. When your pup comes, you'll be a busy momma. Despite being a supernatural creature, a baby will wear you out. Try to enjoy the next few weeks and keep spending time with your mom. She needs it, Kate. I think you need it too."

His words bring all of my emotions to the surface, shock being one of them.

"So, you *do* want me to stay in Moonwake?" I ask, my eyes staring out the opening where a windshield would be if he had one.

His arm flies out first, then the brakes lock. My back lifts away from the cushioned backrest as his forearm halts me from falling forward. He wasn't driving at any significant rate of speed. I could've easily braced my hands against the dash to catch myself if I had needed to.

When I glance at Elijah, he looks horrified and more ashamed than before.

"Have I given you the impression I don't want you here? You're my daughter. It would destroy me if I lost you again. Why would you think that?"

"I killed a man yesterday. You weren't exactly thrilled with me."

"That wasn't my finest moment, Kate. I'm sorry that I overreacted. Really, I am. I freaked out when I saw what was about to happen, and I didn't know why you would attack him like that. No matter what, I shouldn't have put my hands on your wolf."

Emotions shine heavily in his eyes, but I don't think any of them are the disappointment I feared.

"You aren't mad at me?"

"I've never been mad at you, Kate. For anything. I was

caught off guard yesterday. That isn't an excuse, but it's the only one I have to offer. Do I wish my daughter hadn't had to kill the man responsible for her being kidnapped twice? Yes. But maybe if I hadn't been so afraid to come see you, I would have known."

"Doubtful. I didn't tell anyone he'd followed me. I hadn't known about the original kidnapping until Kane filled me in after, but..." I trail off, not wanting to admit that I'm glad it was me who killed him. I'm not proud of it. But if someone else had taken care of it, I wouldn't have gotten the closure I never knew I needed until I saw him lying lifeless on the ground.

It's weird because I'm not upset that Becca killed Veronica instead of me. Maybe that's because I hope it gave her some type of closure too. At the end of the day, Richard Everhart is still the one responsible for it all. Everyone else was a pawn.

"I hate myself for being a coward and not coming to see you like your mom did. I felt what she felt when she saw you for the first time. I wanted that too, but I couldn't bring myself to face you when I'm the one that failed you."

"Maybe ease up on yourself. I can't imagine what the four of you went through when you discovered we were missing."

My baby isn't even here, I haven't even felt him move, but I still feel an overwhelming sense of protection toward my little wolf pup.

"It was hell. Over twenty years of living in torment while having to remain strong for the rest of the pack when all I wanted to do was curl up and die. I thought I did everything to find you and Trez, but I didn't. And knowing that might be even worse." He takes another breath, this time pulling air in through his mouth and forcing it back out between his teeth. "And now, I get the feeling you showing up here each year was on purpose and not by chance."

A chill ripples down my spine at his spot-on assumption.

"It was," I admit, recalling everything Salem laid out—Dick's real plan.

"Care to fill me in?"

My head tilts toward him, my eyes flicking to his. I want to give him the answers he's likely been chasing for twenty years. He deserves to know. Everyone does, but I feel like I need to talk to my mate before divulging to others.

"Let me tell Kane first, and then I'll share the little I know. Annalise should hear it at the same time."

44

KANE

The moment I realized Kate was crying, I almost ditched work to go find them. I wanted to beat Elijah's ass, still do, for making my mate so emotional she had to let it all out.

Crying isn't a bad thing. It's not weak. If you overfill a glass, it's going to spill over the edge, but that doesn't mean I was okay with her father being the cause of her tears.

I refrained when she told me to back off. It wasn't easy, but I trust Kate knows what's best for herself. I want her to have a good relationship with her parents. I may be at odds with mine and Elijah currently, but that doesn't mean I've stopped loving them.

Of course, if anyone even thinks about telling Kate she doesn't belong here I will lose my shit on them, no matter who it is. My suggestion, they better think long and hard before they go down that road. There is no going back. I'll banish everyone from the whole fucking pack before I let Kate leave, and if that day ever comes, I'm going with her.

Noise coming past the door that leads from the shop and

into the office area pulls my attention away from the car I'm standing in front of with the hood lifted. I've just finished prepping everything to yank the motor out. The owner dropped it off a few days ago. With everything she wants restored, it's going to take almost a year to complete.

The weather is stifling today, so hot that I didn't raise the bay door. Instead, I have the A/C running and my phone playing a playlist of musicians that were popular back in my teenage years.

The door coming into the shop opens, then slams. I arch an eyebrow at Kate, who looks downright murderous right now.

"You're late," I growl.

It's been well past an hour since I left her at the cabin with Elijah waiting outside for her. I saw the way he cringed when I opened the front door and walked out as I pulled on a black T-shirt. I knew what he was smelling because I was still smelling us too and enjoying the pleasant scent.

Out of pity for him and not wanting to bite his fucking head off for the way he reacted yesterday, I left with barely a nod in his direction. I keep several ATVs in a shed beside the cabin, so I didn't need to walk back to the lodge.

She marches in my direction on a mission, and I feel like the meat between my legs is going to be collateral damage with the vibes rolling off Kate.

"Why is *her* scent in every room up front and all over the place out here?" She demands, her arms crossing together under her chest.

By *her* I'm going to assume she means Laney. Ashleigh is here often enough that her scent permeates the shop too, but Kate's never acted this way toward my cousin.

"She works here. Or did, I should say. Laney is gone, Kate. I found that out when I stopped by the lodge."

"What do you mean she works here? Since when?"

"Not long after you and Trez went back to Rivermoon Mountain," I say, annoyed, hating the reminder of each and every time I had to watch her leave. "Why? Because I needed the help, and she asked for a job. You know how I am when it comes to helping out a pack member."

She grits her teeth and just stares at me, her breaths coming forcefully out of her cute little nose.

"Baby, if you want to leak all over my shop and mark your territory, by all means, go for it." I span my arms out. "I can't think of anything I'd enjoy more than smelling you all day, every day, while I work." I smirk, amused at her jealousy, but I'm not trying to pacify her either. Her scent covering every surface would be the best improvement to this place I can think of, but also torture. I'd want to fuck her instead of fixing broken-down pieces of shit and turning them back into prized possessions. "My Luna-girl is hot when she's worked up."

"Could you give that one a rest?" She purses her lips, then drops her arms to her sides.

"What's it going to take for you to believe you are, in fact, a Luna wolf shifter?"

"I don't know what to tell you." She steps away from me and then turns her head to look under the hood of the old 1971 automobile. "It's not that I don't believe you, but when something is shoved down your throat for years on end, it's difficult not to believe it yourself in ways." Her head tilts, her pretty eyes coming back to my stare. "I'll give Dick this, he was a masterful puppet master. Damn near everything out of his mouth felt like a lie, but he'd weave it in such a way I couldn't get past the self-doubt."

"I want that motherfucker to die a slow death," I seethe, my fists balling at my sides.

Kate goes silent, her eyes darting away from mine. A shiver runs down my spine like a bad omen.

"What?" My question seeps out through clenched teeth.

"There's something you need to know. Something Salem told me before she let me go. What Dick's truly after."

"Are we going to war?"

"No," she says so adamantly that I know she means it. But I also have a feeling that what she's about to share is going to make me rage. "I don't want that for our pack. I don't want lives to be lost senselessly. For all I know, he's already dead. He killed Salem's sister. It's why she helped me and why I'm here instead of who knows where. Salem went back to Rivermoon to kill Dick and anyone else that got in her way. I just don't know if she was successful or not."

"Storm hasn't been able to reach anyone from her coven. She's been trying for two weeks," I inform her.

"That can't be good." Kate's eyes widen.

"Probably not," I agree. "What's the rest? I can feel you have more to say."

"Did you know Dick used to be in the Bloodmoon pack?"

"That's news to me." Especially when we have records going back four generations, and he's not one of them.

"According to Salem, he was a long time ago. He had a fated mate from this pack, and she was an alpha female."

"She was a Luna," I reiterate, wanting my mate to be comfortable calling herself that.

"If you say so." She eyes me hard. "But not the point."

She continues after blowing out a breath. "He resented her for being stronger than him. He wanted to be an alpha more than he wanted anything else, including her. Salem said he traded his fated mate to someone in the underworld in exchange for being given alpha power and a longer than normal shifter life."

"From everything I know, demons aren't powerful beings. On Earth, they have to steal a host to be in physical form. There is only one that powerful, and like you have a hard time believing in a Luna, I've never seen evidence that the one touted as the devil even exists."

"Kane, you told me vampires exist. How is the darkest being imaginable a stretch for you?"

"I've met a vampire. Can't really say I want to do it again. Of course, I can't say I want to meet the devil either because I don't, but maybe. We exist. A lot of things that go bump in the night exist, whether supernatural or human. I suppose it's plausible."

"There's more," she says on a heavy exhale.

"She told me that Dick knew I was the next alpha's fated mate, your mate, and when he took us and had the dark witch spell us, she was also supposed to spell that when we conceived a child, he would be born an alpha."

"Our son isn't going to be an alpha, Kate." I stare at her, my brows furrowed, my anger on the brink of making my wolf shift, but also... I'm confused.

"Do I even want to know how you know that?"

"One of the many lessons my dad taught me over the years. It's a scent. One that isn't easy to pick out before birth. It took me years to master it. I'll teach you if you want."

"Maybe. But that feels weird and... intrusive."

She has a point. One I never considered before now.

"Why does he want our son to be an alpha?" I ask, hoping there are more details. I need to know everything so I can protect Kate, our son, and our pack.

"Salem laughed when she told me, but she said Dick thinks he can bargain for immortality this time around with an alpha's mate and an alpha child. The way she said it, it sounded like there was no chance in hell that would happen, but he didn't know that. But that bitch is also crazy—manic-like crazy. I took everything she told me with a grain of salt."

"So, what do you want to do, mate?" I shove my hands in the pockets of my jeans, almost afraid of what her answer is going to be. I don't want Kate to put herself in danger while pregnant. I don't want my mate to ever be in danger, but I'm also not the man who's going to stop her from doing something she feels is necessary. I do know the longer Richard's heart continues to beat, my mate, my son, my pack will never be safe.

"Does it make me a coward to want to do nothing right now, hoping Salem handled him like she planned to do?" Her brows furrow as she gnaws on her bottom lip.

I shake my head. "You aren't a coward because you're choosing not to start a war. I'll reach out to Caleb Drake to see what he knows. If Richard is dead, Caleb would have swooped in to claim his land and kill his pack. That's a plausible reason for Storm not being able to reach anyone from her old coven."

"Good idea."

She's nodding her head but looks like she's thinking about something else. After a beat, she turns to walk away from me but only gets two steps before she pivots to face me once again.

"What did you mean when you mentioned Laney was gone?" Kate's head tilts as her hands go to her hips.

"She ran off after Mom killed V. No one has seen her since. She isn't on pack land. Jagger thinks she took off in her wolf form. He said he didn't think anything was missing from her uncle's house, where she and her mother lived. V's car is still there, and so is Ronnie's truck."

"Do you think she's going to be a problem?"

"I don't know." I scrub my palm down my face, wondering when we'll be able to move on with our lives without shit in the background threatening to tear us and the pack apart. I don't like leaving anything unfinished or waiting for the next ball to drop. "I hope not, but if she becomes an issue, I'll handle it."

"We'll handle it," she clarifies.

Lifting my arm, I snag Kate around her elbow and pull her into an embrace.

"We'll handle it," I agree. "Just not today."

"Good." A smile inches slowly up her pretty face. "Because I seem to recall you promising to fuck me on the hood of this car"—Kate rolls her head, eyeing the raised hood with the cherry picker already in place in front of the car with the engine leveler and chains in place to remove the motor—"but it looks like that's going to be an issue."

"I also promised you food. Annalise cooked breakfast," I say, my dick already getting hard again. "I grabbed you a plate and stuck it in the fridge if you'd rather eat before I come inside your pretty little pussy."

Please don't be starving.

My crotch still fucking hurts from leaving with a

massive hard-on this morning after having my mouth and tongue on her.

"I want to be stuffed, but"—she shakes her head—"my preference isn't food." She pulls back and drops her eyes to the front of my jeans, then she bites her bottom lip and flicks her sexy stare up to my eyes.

Sliding my hands down her bare arms, I lace her fingers with mine in one hand, then step around her, pulling her behind me.

"Where are we going?" she pouts when she realizes I'm dragging her away. "You could at least do me inside the car if you can't do me on the car."

Grabbing the doorknob, I twist and yank it open and step inside the office space. The door closes on its own as I swing Kate in front of me and then hoist her into my arms.

"You wanted to rid all the scents of other women, so we're starting with the office, mate."

"Just how many women frequent here?" she huffs out, her jaw dropping.

Probably more than she wants to know about.

But I only have eyes for Kate.

My mate.

My always.

"None of them are relevant." I round the corner, stepping into the receptionist's area, where a counter runs the length of the space with the front door directly across from us. I sit Kate on the desk and step between her open thighs. "I only want to fuck you. In every room. On every surface. I wasn't kidding when I said you could drip all over the place, but that'll have to wait until I have time to play with you. Right now, I want you too damn much not to be selfish."

I go for the belt locked around my pants, snatching it

loose, and then unbutton my jeans.

"What if a customer walks in? The open sign is turned on, Kane, and I know the door is unlocked since I walked through it."

I shrug, not fazed in the least as I pull my zipper down.

"Guess they'll get an eyeful of my dick coming inside the most perfect pussy ever created. Pull your leggings down before I tear a hole in the crotch."

"Someone is impatient," she comments but complies without fuss as she leans from one hip to the other, dragging her pants down. Her flip-flops hit the floor first as she kicks her pants off.

"No, I need to come... so fucking bad right now, but we both know I'm not going to do that until you get off first." I grab her by the hips and pull her to the edge. "So, let's get you off, baby."

I align myself with her entrance, then push forward while pulling her onto my cock. My eyes close, allowing the feeling of her heat to wrap around me, coating me.

"Always so fucking wet for me."

Fuck.

I just want to spend the rest of my life making this woman happy, giving her everything she wants and needs. Spoiling her. Cherishing her. Because dammit, she gives me more than I deserve and everything I never knew I was missing, never knew I needed.

"Tell me you're mine," I demand, but she can feel the begging within my words, my desperate need to hear her say it despite feeling the truth between us.

"I'm yours. I'm your always, and you're mine, Kane Orion."

"Damn right, I am," I grit, straining to hold on as she

tightens around me, forcing my eyes to roll to the back of my head, the feel of her surrounding me pleasurable in the best and most torturous ways.

Forcing my eyes to open, I tip my head down to look my mate in her eyes. "And I'm going to keep you dripping for me... for the rest of our lives, baby."

I lean forward, capturing her lips, but it's my Luna that sears me with her kiss.

Thank you for coming back to me, Kate, I utter inside my head so as not to lose the connection of our lips. *For staying.*

Her arms wrap around my neck as my hips flex forward, her claws sinking deep into my muscles.

Fuuck, that's so good.

Kate's eyes change from blue to blood orange, my claws elongating at her alpha command, pushing through her soft skin. My dick pulses and thickens inside her, her walls squeezing me.

I forgive you, you know, right? Her words in my head a detonator.

I felt her forgiveness before now, but I needed to hear it.

I'll worship her for all of our days, making sure she knows how much I wholly regret how I treated her that night.

My submission is hers, only hers.

My alpha.

My Luna.

My always.

I gasp for breath, sucking the air from her lungs into mine. Kate comes around, and I explode inside her. Her screams and mine rocking the building like an earthquake.

After all these years, I finally have my fated mate.

Only, I didn't find her. She found me.

45

KATE

I t's been three weeks, and I swear, my belly has ballooned overnight. Everything is tight and uncomfortable, not to mention the sweltering heat makes it all worse. If every single wolf shifter in the pack didn't mosey in and out of the lodge all day, I'd lounge around naked. That's how miserable this is at times.

I'm starting to get the feeling I'm not cut out for doing this a second time. Annalise assures me that my emotions are normal and that I'll forget all about the misery once my son is born.

There's no doubt in my mind that I'll love the fur ball and protect him with my life, but the next time I go into heat, I'm latching a chastity belt around my hoo-ha and closing up shop until it passes. I'll have to have Maddy hide the key, or maybe Ivy will do it for me. They and Storm are the only ones Kane and I can't use our alpha powers on to demand it back when the heat cycle becomes unbearable.

Annalise is still sleeping at the lodge, but she doesn't spend all day here anymore like she used to. She comes and goes. Trez and Jagger are here daily, too. We all eat dinner together unless it's one of the nights during the week or on the weekend that the pack does a bonfire and cookout. They mostly sleep at Jagger's place not far from here. Though, I guess it's their place now like the lodge and cabin are Kane's and mine.

The front door opens, making my hand pause and my head snap up. Becca slips inside, closing the door behind her. She's dressed in dark-colored cargo pants and a loose white top. Her attire matches my style more than my mother's, but I've gotten so used to leggings that several pairs may be in my future once the baby is out of my tummy.

"You busy?" she asks, still standing by the door with her arms clasped behind her back, her heels tipping back like she's nervous. Not very Rebecca Orion-like at all.

"Not really. Annalise made a feast like she does every morning. I just finished cleaning up."

I swipe the used, dirty paper towel off the island and toss it in the trash. Turning my back to her, I quickly wash my hands and dry them using the dish towel that hangs left of the kitchen sink.

"You looking for Kane or Trez?" I ask when she continues to stand there, staring at me nervously.

"No. I'm here to see you. Figured it was high time to stop dodging you."

It did seem like she's been avoiding me. Last week I even speculated if it had anything to do with her not liking me being her son's mate, but then I started to recognize the emotions of others when they were close to me or while their eyes were on me. With Becca, I sensed sadness and regret and something else I couldn't put a finger on.

Those are the same vibes I'm getting from her now.

"Why were you dodging me?" I question while stepping in front of the refrigerator. Pulling the door open, I grab a bottle of water off the shelf. "Want anything?"

"No, thank you." She shakes her head and walks forward, nearing the island.

I close the door. Turning back to face her, I twist the plastic cap off and tip the bottle to my lips.

"It was my fault," she states, her words rushed. I arch an eyebrow, silently waiting for her to explain. "The night you and my son were taken. You were sleeping over at my house," she informs me. "Here, actually, back when Dante and I called the lodge home. You and Trez were having a normal sleepover like you did often. You two were inseparable. And…" Her hands go to her face, covering her mouth as a sob escapes her lips.

I slam the bottle onto the counter, not caring if I spill any. I skate to her quickly, wrapping my arms around her back and pulling Becca into a tight embrace. After several breaths, her arms drop between us and wrap around my wide waist, my belly pressing against her flat front.

"It's okay," I assure her.

"It's not. It's my fault that you and Trez didn't grow up here or have the life you were meant to have."

"We're here now. You can't change the past. It happened. We're back, and I don't blame you, Becca. It wasn't your fault. Bad people plotted against all of you. It's on them, not you."

"Dante, Eli, and the two older boys were on a camping trip," she continues like she didn't hear a word I said. "Annalise was enjoying a break she woke up to regret, and you were with me. It was my job to protect you and Trez. Don't you see I failed?"

I pull back to look her in the eyes but keep my hands cupped around her shoulders. Tears run down her cheeks, and everything in me wishes I could work the same alpha power Kane used on my mother when she was so upset weeks ago. Only I haven't learned how, but after today, Kane is going to stop everything he's doing to teach me.

"Stop blaming yourself. Magic was used. You know this, I know this, the pack knows it too. It wouldn't have mattered if we'd been at your house or somewhere else. They would have found a way. If you aren't going to stop feeling responsible, then you have to find a way to forgive yourself even though I don't believe you've done anything that warrants forgiveness, Becca."

"Maybe you don't, Kate, and"—she sniffles and breathes, her cheeks soaked—"I'm grateful you don't hate me for everything Everhart and his awful pack put you both through, but knowing all I know, it's hard to not feel partially responsible. If nothing else, I should have offered you and him a home that first year. We should have welcomed you as more than just guests. I'm sorry."

Over the years, I've shared a lot with Becca and Annalise. More than I would have if I'd known Annalise was my mother. It's not that I'm ashamed of what they know. But now I feel like I've placed a heavy burden on their shoulders.

I also know if she'd done that, we still would have ended up back in Rivermoon until Dick was ready to roll out his plan. He's cunning, and that still scares me. He would have used his witch to force us back. Becca wouldn't have been able to prevent that.

"Everything will be fine. We're home. We're back where we belong."

"I know."

"You good?"

"Yeah." She nods, her eyes red and full of emotions, her tears gone. "I just wanted to get that off my chest, and"—she pulls in a breath, then lets it flow back out of her mouth—"to see if you've seen your mo... I mean, Annalise."

"It's okay if you want to call her my mom. I know she is. I'm just not there yet, but I'll get there."

"Trez said those exact words to me a few weeks ago."

He told me when they found me, he returned to have his own heart-to-heart with his mother and that they've been building a relationship ever since. I'm happy for him. I'm happy for myself too. It feels like I get closer to Annalise with each passing day. Elijah and I have even gone on two other rides, me sitting in comfortable silence while he drives.

"She left the lodge an hour ago. Said she needed to grab some things from her house."

"Eli mentioned he was going to swing by their house too. That was about an hour ago," she tells me.

"Good. Maybe they're working their shit out."

"I hope so," she agrees. "She and I can make up tomorrow." She pulls in what feels like a cleansing breath as she closes her eyes. On a long exhale, they slowly open. "I'm going to go find my mate. That man knows how to soothe me better than I do myself. Thank you, Kate. Thank you for staying. Thank you for keeping Kane here. I was wrong when I said he shouldn't be alpha. He's good for the pack, and you're going to be great for all of us too."

"He is"—I nod—"and I hope so. I want to be."

She steps back and starts for the door when I say, "Why don't you and Dante come for dinner tonight?"

"We'd love to." She offers a smile then pulls the door open.

My eyes flick over her shoulder, seeing Maddy with Ashleigh standing behind her.

"Oh, hey, Aunt Becca."

She isn't Maddy's actual aunt. They aren't blood or even related by marriage, but I've never heard Maddy not refer to Becca and Annalise as her aunt.

"Hey, sweet girl," she says as she steps around them as they walk inside.

Once Ashleigh closes the door, Maddy purses her lips.

"Ash wouldn't let us come inside. Said you were consoling Aunt Becca."

"Eavesdropping?" I arch an eyebrow as I cock my head.

"It's part of my job." She shrugs, not bothered by being tattled on.

That makes a laugh bubble up my throat and past my lips. "That is so *not* your job."

I slide my stare to Maddy while she pulls out a stool, making herself comfortable.

"I thought you had class today?" I ask as the front door opens again, this time with Storm walking in, her long dress sweeping the floor as she swings around to push it closed.

Maddy is in college and mostly takes courses online during the fall and spring semesters, but she has one class she's been attending in person this summer.

"Her *professor* is out again today, so no class for our poor Maddy," Ash says in a mocking way that looks like she's trying to egg on her roommate.

They have a sister-like relationship, with Ashleigh being the overprotective big sister type. It doesn't help that Kane and Jagger view her similarly. With Maddy being human, they watch her like a hawk, which is another reason I was surprised Kane allowed Laney to work at his body shop when I've heard she's bullied Maddy since they were kids. I'm glad she's gone. Good riddance, I say.

"Why did you say it like that?" I ask, but with the way Maddy blushes, I'm confident I can guess.

"Because she wants to do him," Storm snickers. "Her much older, more experienced, and highly forbidden *professor*."

"You have the hots for your teacher?" I ask, laughing at Storm's comical dramatics.

"Mr. Ambrose is *not* that much older than me." She narrows her eyes at Storm, annoyed. When Maddy flicks her blue gaze back to mine, her long, wavy, sunny-blonde hair slips from, covering half of her face, making her tuck it back behind her ear. "He's thirty. And yes, I like him. He's hot. You'd understand if you saw him, Kate."

"She's in love with his accent," Ash adds.

"You guys are the worst friends ever," she tells them. "He's really sweet and smart and handsome and…"

"British." Storm laughs.

"And doesn't even know I exist, so it's a moot point. It'll never happen," she pouts.

"You're his student. He has to know who you are," I assure her, not liking that she is selling herself short. Maddy is beautiful. It's surprising she doesn't have a boyfriend. "Have you looked at yourself in a mirror lately? Girl, you're hot too."

"He calls me by the wrong name at least once a week. Trust me, Axton wouldn't recognize me if we bumped into each other outside of his classroom."

"I seriously doubt that," I reiterate. "Maybe he just doesn't want to get fired for fraternizing with a student."

"And he better keep it that way," Ashleigh growls. My stare slides to her hands resting on the island, her claws slowly extracting. "Or I'll shred his balls. Maddy needs to focus on her education, not some old man's dick."

"I have the highest grade in his class," Maddy defends herself. "Stop calling him old. He's only five years older than you."

"And not worth your time if he can't even remember his best student's name," Ash says in a scolding tone.

"Whatever." Maddy rolls her eyes as she pushes against the edge of the island, forcing the stool to scoot back. At the same time, a sound chirps, telling us someone received a text message. Maddy stands and pulls her phone out from her back pocket. When she eyes the screen, her facial expression turns to shock, then confusion, to lighting up like it's Christmas morning. "I'll catch you guys later."

She pivots and almost skips to the door.

"Who the fuck just texted you?" Ashleigh demands.

"Don't worry about it, *Mom*," she sasses, her tone deep like she's attempting her best guy voice. "I'm an adult." The door swings open, her phone still in her hands with her eyes glued to the screen as she walks out. "Later, Kate."

After hearing her feet stomp down the wooden patio steps, Storm rolls her head to Ash. "At least Maddy cares about school. Ivy wants nothing to do with it. She is such a pain in my ass."

"Why don't you let me talk to her," I offer. I overheard Kane telling Storm last week to register Ivy for high school.

"Yes, yes, and yes. Thank you, Kate." Storm sighs. "I love my sister, but she's at that age where she doesn't want to listen to reason and believes she knows what's best for herself."

"Know where she is?" I ask.

"Yeah. I was scrying her location before I came over. She was near yours and Kane's cabin fifteen minutes ago."

"Then that's where I'll start."

46
KATE

It's strange how easy it is to settle in the comfort of being surrounded by a pack that genuinely wants to be in my company. The Bloodmoon pack has been the found family I've desired to have for over five years. I just never imagined they'd become my actual family.

Kane is a generous mate, always making sure I'm satisfied rather than fulfilling his own needs first.

Our brothers bicker over who gets to go on runs with me at night. Kane and I have established a morning routine that I'm never giving up, but I also enjoy running in my wolf form with Trez and Jagger. I'd never admit this, but it's more fun with Jagger because he's as fast as me. Running with him is a challenge.

None of the male shifters in my life want me running alone since we haven't been successful in reaching anyone from Storm's old coven. It's like they've vanished or were cut off from outside contact. We don't know if Dick is alive or dead or if he's plotting something else against us.

The latter is the likelihood. He needs me and my son to

bargain for his own deepest desire: immortality. Can't say that I believe in that. Everything has an expiration date. But I'm not putting up a fight with Kane, our brothers, our fathers, or even Ashleigh. Sometimes, I see her wolf following me randomly between going from the lodge to the cabin.

I'm surprised she didn't follow me when I left the lodge in search of Ivy like she did yesterday. I searched all over for Ivy, but she evaded me. I also didn't try that hard to find her. I could have easily if I'd tracked her using her scent, but I figured she needed space if she was going out of her way to avoid me.

Your mate spends too much time with mine, Trez's thoughts rattle inside my head.

I don't know what happened or changed. Close to two weeks ago, I was bitching and had my brother on my mind when all of a sudden, he replied with, *well, hello to you too, sister.* We've been talking nonstop ever since.

Jagger is his beta and best friend. Get over yourself. My mate doesn't want yours, you crazy fucker.

I park the ATV in front of the cabin and then twist the key, turning off the machine.

It's interfering with me getting my dick sucked.

Pack responsibilities come before you getting off. Also, I didn't need that visual. You're an asshole.

I don't actually care. I can separate my closest friend's lover from my brother, that brother being Jagger and that friend being Trez, who I will forever consider my brother as well.

My asshole could also use attention right now.

I grumble both verbally and in my mind as I swing my leg over the seat and hop off, leaving the key in the ignition.

If I'm forced to hear about all the ways Kane's cock is satis-fying to you, then you're going to hear me bitch about not getting any from Jag.

He gets plenty of dick, and he gives plenty of his right back to his mate. His complaints are unfounded.

Yeah, well, it's expected as my best friend.

I'm also your brother. I feel his eyes rolling despite not seeing him.

True, but not by blood, so it's not weird anymore. Deal with it. Before he can come back with something else, I say, *I'm dealing with Ivy right now. Talk later, okay?*

He doesn't respond, but I know he got the message.

A storm is brewing in the Pacific. The wind kicked up an hour ago. With the temperature in the eighties, the breeze against my skin is welcomed.

I push the door open, seeing Ivy with her back to me and the volume on the television up higher than I'd like with my sensitive hearing.

"Do you often make yourself at home uninvited?" I cross my arms.

I hear her sigh, then she twists around from where her back was against the end of the couch.

"Like you care." She shrugs as she stands, a bowl of cereal in one hand, the television remote in her other. I can smell the sugary sweetness from here.

Ivy mutes the TV, then tosses the remote onto the couch.

She's right. I don't care if she hangs out here. She's welcome just like anyone else in the pack.

"I hate your mate," she says dramatically while walking to the kitchen. Once she's in front of the sink, she places the bowl down and runs water into the dish before turning the faucet off.

"Hate's a rather strong word, don't you think? You can dislike someone without feeling hatred. Is that negative energy really worth it?"

I step toward her, leaving the door open. It's stifling in here. The cabin could use fresh air since Kane and I have been at the lodge lately.

"Kane says I have to enroll in high school come September. It's bullshit. And even worse, Storm agrees with him."

"Did you consider they're only looking out for your best interests and that an education is important?" I reason.

"What would he know about an education? He's stupid and a big bully."

How childish sounding of the child, I think to myself.

"Kane doesn't bully, but he is the pack alpha. As long as you're here, what he and I say goes. News bulletin: I'm with him and Storm on this one."

"I'm not pack," she grits out.

"You are if you're going to stay here. Witch or shifter, you live here, you're pack."

"Then let me go home," she argues.

"Ivy," I breathe tiredly. "No one knows if you still have a home in Rivermoon," I say bluntly. "I can't in good conscience let you go back while the man that had your mother killed may still be alive. You wouldn't be safe there, whereas here, an entire pack of wolves plus your sister have your back."

"Kane won't let me use magic!" she yells while stomping her feet.

"That's isn't true, and you know it. He doesn't want you using dark magic. There is a difference."

"Not all dark magic is bad. I don't know why any of you

can't comprehend that. It's about how you use it. Your intention."

This is where I'm sort of on Ivy's side, but I haven't told her that. She makes a good argument, but after what Salem did, I don't trust it. I don't want to be near it. In fact, I don't want to be around any magic. I'm not comfortable with it being used on pack land, but I'm trying to keep an open mind. I don't want Storm or Ivy to feel suppressed. Magic is a part of who they are, the same as my wolf is a part of me.

"Ivy..." I begin, about to give in and tell her this, when a scent rich and smoky with traces of moss like Scotch wafts up my nose. The smell is old, ancient even, but I have no idea how I even know that fact.

I pivot, turning to face the door. Ivy sucks in a sharp breath.

A man stands just on the other side of the threshold. He's tall, not Kane or shifter height, but over six feet. He's lean too, dressed in an expensive tailored suit, wearing all black. It matches his midnight hair and eyes. A box is clutched between the inside of his upper arm and the side of his body.

The most unsettling thing about him is that I can't hear him breathing. He doesn't have a heartbeat. *How does he not have a fucking heartbeat?*

"Are you going to invite me in, Darling?" he muses, his accent heavy and British.

"Don't let him in, Kate. He's a bloodsucker," Ivy spits in disgust, her nose wrinkling, yet her trembling hands giving away her fear. She huddles against my back, shaking. Her admission causes my eyes to grow round.

"I'm sorry, a blood what?" I ask, flabbergasted.

I am pretty sure I understand what she means, but I need someone to clarify right the fuck now.

"I believe the term your rude little witchling *meant* was vampire," he bites out, his tone turning as dark as his eyes. His jaw locks.

My wolf growls from inside me, sensing the sinister vibe rolling off him in waves.

I go to step forward when he holds his hand up, his palm facing me like a stop sign.

"Stay where you are, Darling. You're close enough." He almost blanches, and that's saying something with how pale his skin is.

"Is your creepy ass afraid of *me*?"

He isn't creepy in a gross sort of way. Between the accent, his tall stature, the designer suit he's adorning, and the dark, tussled hair on the top of his head, it's all rather appealing in a gothic-like way. His creepiness is more bone-chilling. Demonic maybe. His skin lacks warmth like the sun hasn't touched it in centuries. And I get the feeling that if he wanted to harm me, kill me even, he could do so with a speed I'd never see it coming.

My wolf growls deep again: a warning. She doesn't like his presence. Her flight or fight instincts have kicked in, but mine haven't, which is strange but not something I'm about to ponder on.

"It's not you or your protective puppy dog that unsettles me, Love. It's your blood."

My brows turn inward, furrowing at his admission. *What's wrong with my blood?*

"Did your mate not warn you?" he inquires. "Luna blood is more addicting to us than heroin is to humans."

Did Kane put him up to this? Someone to convince me that Luna wolves really exist?

His head cocks to the side, studying me.

"You don't believe him," he muses, one side of his mouth tipping upward. "Interesting. I'd offer to sample you, Love, but I'm in a bit of a hurry, and I didn't come to drain a dog."

"Wolf," I bark.

"Tomato, to-mato." He shrugs. "You all smell the same. That wasn't a compliment, by the way."

"I understood the implied insult. Why are you here?" I demand.

"I brought you a peace offering." The box under his arm slips. He catches it with both hands, holding it out for me to see. "Something I think will wipe that murderous little look off your pretty face."

Kate, what the fuck is wrong? My beast is trying to tear from my skin. Are you okay?

How do you kill a vampire? I ask back, my eyes not leaving the creature in front of me—because this snobby motherfucker with his nose held high needs to go. I narrow my eyes on him.

"You're concentrating awfully hard, Darling. Did you tell your furry mate I'm here?"

"How could I? You failed to introduce yourself."

Excuse me? Kane wails.

"My apologies, Love. Axton Ambrose." He tilts his head respectfully, but the gesture just makes this situation more weirder.

Ambrose.

Why does that name sound familiar? I think to myself while shouting, *It's a simple question, Kane. How. Do. I. Kill—*

We're coming.

Of course, he is. Couldn't just tell me how to handle it myself. Knowing my mate, Jagger or Trez or both are running with him. Stupid men. I'll figure it out if need be. I'm not going to let this creature hurt Ivy or me.

"I'm going to sit this on the floor." He squats slowly, but when I blink, the box is already in front of my feet, and he's back to standing with his shoulder leaning against the doorjamb.

What the hell? How did he do that?

"You're going to open your present, Sweetheart. You're going to accept my fair trade, then I'm going to be on my way. There was really no need to call your mutt. If it's not already obvious, I'm not here to harm you."

The only way to kill a bloodsucker is to sever his or her head. Kane finally tells me.

"What's in the box?" I glance down and then back to Axton, his name tickling something in the back of my head.

"A souvenir," he offers. "My maker doesn't want you or the little thing in your belly. That's what you were told, right? By the angry, dark witch."

"Where's Aunt Salem?" Ivy juts from behind me, her fear overtaken by the mention of her aunt. "What did you do to her?"

"Darling, we need to wrap this up," he says, not acknowledging Ivy. "I suspect your overgrown dirty mutt is en route. He's no match for me," he touts in the most conceited aristocratic way I've ever heard. "I'd rather not have to put him down."

A growl, low and threatening, leaves my lips.

"You're adorable, Love. I can see the appeal. You'd make the cutest pet. Luckily for you, I desire another pet. Of the human variety," he clarifies when my brows furrow in concern. "And she's waiting for me to take her home. The longer this takes, the more likely she's going to damage her porcelain skin trying to get out of the chains I placed her in yesterday."

"Sounds like kidnapping," I snarl on behalf of someone I don't know.

"Sounds like fun." He gives me a pointed look. "What do my students say? Oh, yes, don't ick someone else's yum."

"So, she consented to being chained?"

"Darling, I haven't asked you about your love life, don't pry into mine. You won't find anything pretty or sweet." He turns up his nose, but then his dark stare goes pitch black. A chill races down my spine. "Open the box, Kate. I'm losing my patience, and I have better things to do than stand here at your door."

The fact that this man is a teacher is rather concerning after what he's admitted to.

I bend and grab it. It's not wrapped, nor is there much weight to it. It's hard plastic with an airtight lid that has a latch. I unlatch it with my eyes fixated on the vampire, not trusting his psycho ass.

The rotten dead smell of flesh hits before I pry the lid up. My eyes snap to the inside, seeing a severed, bloody hand with a metallic silver wolf tattoo blended into a full moon.

Dick. The hand of the man I once thought was my father, my alpha.

My wide eyes snap back to the vampire, a smirk now on his face.

"Is the gift to your liking, Darling."

Ivy peers into the box, a gasp leaving her mouth so loud it hurts my eardrum. A heartbeat later, she darts off behind me, running to the bathroom, I presume. My feet stay rooted to the floor as I recall Salem telling me that without his hand, his alpha power would be no more.

"Where is he?"

"Dead, Love. I killed him myself," he says like he's proud of himself, and well, maybe I'm feeling relieved. However, that doesn't tell me why he killed Dick. "My maker's wife apparently has a soft spot for you. His head was sent as a trophy to my maker, and I, out of the kindness of my cold, dead heart, brought his filthy paw to you. Now, your gratitude would be appreciated."

"You didn't do it for me, so why did you kill him?" My curiosity is too high not to ask.

"His usefulness to the king of the underworld was no more. I'm sure there is more to it than that, but that's all I know. If you'll say thank you, Axton, I'll be on my way. I can smell five wolves, dear. Trust me when I tell you it's in everyone's best interest for me to be gone when they arrive."

"I'm not buying that you brought me his hand and don't want something in return. So, let's hear it. Tell me what you want."

"Are you not going to thank me?" He sounds displeased at the thought.

"Thank you, Axton. Now, what the fuck do you want? My patience is waning, and trust me, I'll enjoy snatching your head clean off your shoulders."

"You're a crazy one, aren't you, Darling? I'd probably like you if I got to know you, and I don't like anyone." He chuckles. I cross my arms and press my teeth together. "I told you, Luna girl, my pet is waiting for me with a chain around her pretty little neck."

I suck in a breath, my eyes blinking, but when they open,

he's gone, and I'm standing there with my mouth hanging open.

Who the fuck did he take?

Before I can answer my own question, a blond wolf barrels through the door, shifting at the same time. Kane pulls me into his arms, his lips going to mine in panic, the box dropping to the floor with a thud.

"Kane—" I try, but he's mauling me like he thought he was going to lose me.

"Are you okay?" He pulls back, scanning me from head to toe. I barely see my father and brothers out of the corner of my eyes before my mate's lips are smashing against mine once again. Then he rips away from me. Turning his back to me, he looks in every direction, ready to neutralize any threat. "Where is he?"

"Gone," I assure him, thinking that'll settle Kane down. It doesn't. He starts for the door as an epiphany wraps around me. "Just wait." He turns back to face me. "Does the name Axton Ambrose mean anything to you?"

Kane stumbles back, his eyes wide, his emotions like a tsunami crashing into me.

"He's the first vampire ever created," my father answers. "Please tell me he wasn't here, Kate. Why the fuck would he be here?"

Because she wants to do him. Her much older, more experienced, and highly forbidden professor, Storm had said, to which Maddy replied, *yes, I like him. He's hot. You'd understand if you saw him, Kate.* Then her expression deflated when she said, *He doesn't even know I exist.*

But apparently, her assessment wasn't true.

"He wasn't here to harm me. He delivered that." I nod to the box that's been kicked several feet from me. Their eyes follow. "Dick is dead. That's one problem solved," I say, realizing it myself. Dick is dead, and a weight had been lifted. My son isn't in danger anymore, but...

"What is it?" Kane asks, feeling the way my thoughts are flickering from one emotion to the next.

"He took Maddy."

Growls and snarls come from all of them while the oddest realization festers. Maddy's biggest desire is to become a supernatural creature. No one here, including me, was willing to give her that.

What if...

What if Axton will give her everything she's ever wanted?

Thank you for reading A War of Hearts and Fate.
Does Maddy and Ax have a book planned? Yes.
*No date has been set for **A House of Blood and Lust**.*

ALSO BY N. E. HENDERSON

<u>SILENT SERIES</u>:

Nick and Shannon's Duet

SILENT NO MORE

SILENT GUILT

<u>MORE THAN SERIES</u>:

Can be read as standalone books but not recommended

MORE THAN LIES

MORE THAN MEMORIES

<u>THE NEW AMERICAN MAFIA</u>:

Must be read in order for the complete story

BAD PRINCESS

DARK PRINCE

DEVIANT KNIGHT

<u>STANDALONE BOOKS</u>:

HAVE MERCY

THE CONSEQUENCES OF LOVE AND VENGEANCE

A WAR OF HEARTS AND FATE

ABOUT THE AUTHOR

N. E. Henderson is an Amazon top 30 best-selling author who can't stand a long, drawn-out grovel by the hero in the book. If the heroine can't accept an apology and forgive the man she loves, does she even really love him?

When Nancy isn't reading books where the villain gets the girl or the latest supernatural epic romance, then she's likely creating the next badass heroine in her head. There are always scenes playing out, and she can't stand a weak heroine. Nancy can thank Jackie Collins for gifting Lucky Santangelo to the fiction world for that, and her mom who let a fourteen-year-old read Chances back in the late 90s.

Or she could be off playing in the dirt in her CanAm Maverick with her family. Characters create themselves when she's on vacation too. They never leave her alone.

Nancy lives in Central Mississippi with her husband, teenage son, and their bull terrier, Xena.

For more information:
https://linktr.ee/nehenderson
www.nehenderson.com

www.ingramcontent.com/pod-product-compliance
Lightning Source LLC
Chambersburg PA
CBHW071937210726
48293CB00001BA/134